FAMILY MATTERS

REBECCA WINTERS
Both of Them

A bride and groom...for the children's sake.

SHERRY LEWIS
Call Me Mom

*Being an instant mother was hard—
hiding it was even harder....*

Relive the romance...

Two complete novels
by two of your favorite authors!

Rebecca Winters loves a great many things: her children, her extended family and her friends. Besides teaching young people at her church, she travels to Laguna Beach, her favorite spot in California, and makes frequent visits to Denver, Colorado, to visit one of her married sons and his wife. An active genealogist, she's always busy tracing her family lines. Creating an ambience of French country in her home is an ongoing project. An avid fan of her hometown basketball team, the Utah Jazz, she has now discovered another sport—golf. At least when Tiger Woods is playing. Around 10:00 p.m. she turns on the TV to watch her favorite British comedies. When all is said and done, she leads a very rich, full life. But she does concede that writing novels adds the extra spice that makes every moment exciting.

Sherry Lewis enjoys traveling and always visualizes stories set in the places she visits. She's an inveterate reader—of course!—enjoys music of all kinds and loves long drives through the mountains. She says she thinks best when she's behind the wheel of her car and "that's usually where I get my inspiration." Most of all, she values her friends and family—a quality that shines through the pages of her prize-winning novel, *Call Me Mom*. Since writing this, her first Superromance book, Sherry has gone on to join the ranks of published mystery writers, as well.

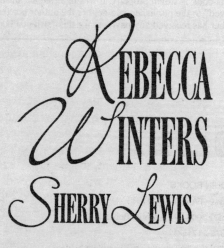

REBECCA WINTERS
SHERRY LEWIS

FAMILY MATTERS

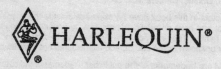

HARLEQUIN®

TORONTO • NEW YORK • LONDON
AMSTERDAM • PARIS • SYDNEY • HAMBURG
STOCKHOLM • ATHENS • TOKYO • MILAN • MADRID
PRAGUE • WARSAW • BUDAPEST • AUCKLAND

HARLEQUIN BOOKS

by Request—FAMILY MATTERS

Copyright © 2001 by Harlequin Books S.A.

ISBN 0-373-21715-3

The publisher acknowledges the copyright holders
of the individual works as follows:
BOTH OF THEM
Copyright © 1992 by Rebecca Winters
CALL ME MOM
Copyright © 1995 by Sherry Lewis
This edition published by arrangement with Harlequin Books S.A.

Visit us at www.eHarlequin.com

Printed in U.S.A.

CONTENTS

Both of Them
Rebecca Winters

Ramsey name would one be learned to place in life as one of the world's...

But the Ramsey have found, even quite without that fact,...
...baby girl... and they exchanged smiling... an... baby...
...her... need the... they... consternation... for a few...
...might appear in the...

Cassie... Miss... (something) never...
...to the time reserve time for... just down... answers... to...
...make the... first Cassie... since... between... to... know...

CHAPTER ONE

HE WAS THE BABY'S FATHER all right! The same olive complexion, the familiar obstinate chin, the identical hair, black as India ink. Even from the distance separating them, the resemblance seemed to shout at Cassie.

She leaned against the doorjamb in disbelief. Her sister's motherly intuition hadn't failed her, after all.

Cassie, from the first moment I held Jason in my arms, I thought there was something...different about him. If Ted was still alive, he'd say the same thing. Jason's not our son! I'm convinced of it!

Remember I told you how he was rushed to the intensive-care unit as soon as he was born? And remember my telling you about the disaster that brought all those victims to the hospital at the same time? There was so much commotion that morning, I honestly think a mix-up occurred and they brought me back the wrong baby from intensive care.

Jason belongs with his natural parents. Promise me you'll find my baby and take care of him for me, Cassie. Then I can die in peace.

Faced with the irrefutable proof of Jason's true paternity, Cassie went alternately hot and cold. Down to the smallest detail, like the shape of the long, square-tipped fingers, or the way one dark brow lowered with displeasure, nine-month-old Jason was a robust replica of Trace Ellingsworth Ramsey III, the autocratic male she could see through the doorway seated behind the desk. He was rapping out edicts over the phone to some no doubt terrified underling of the Greater Phoenix Banking Corporation.

Her eyes closed in reaction, because it meant Susan's natural son had left the hospital with this prominent, high-powered bank-executive and his wife. Susan's baby would now have the

Ramsey name, would now be assured his place in life as one of the Ramsey heirs.

Had the Ramseys, like Susan, ever wondered about that day nine months ago? Had they ever sensed anything about their baby that didn't seem right? Any physical characteristics, for instance that didn't appear in their families?

"Come in, Miss Arnold!" Trace Ramsey called out, not bothering to hide his impatience as he put down the receiver. Before entering the room Cassie darted a nervous glance at Jason, who was still asleep in his carryall next to the secretary's desk.

Though high heels added several inches to her five-foot-three inch frame, Cassie felt dwarfed by the dimensions of the walnut paneled office. To her disappointment there were no mementos or framed photographs of Ramsey's wife and son. Except for some paintings on the walls and a bonsai tree placed on a corner of his desk, the suite was immaculate, and blessedly cool.

She sat down in one of the chairs opposite his desk. "Thank you for taking time out of your busy schedule to see me this morning, Mr. Ramsey. I realize it was short notice."

His dark brows furrowed in undisguised irritation. "According to my secretary, Mrs. Blakesley, you have a highly confidential matter to discuss with me, which you refused to disclose to her."

"I couldn't say anything to her," Cassie said immediately, her guileless, leaf-green eyes pleading with him to believe her. "It's no one's business but ours. When I say ours, I'm including your wife, of course," she added in a soft voice.

He sat forward in the chair with his hands clasped on top of the desk, gazing directly at Cassie. She stared into his eyes, deep blue eyes set between impossibly black lashes. Like Jason's. The Ramsey eyes reminded Cassie of the intense blue in a match flame.

"My secretary never arranges appointments without first obtaining background information, Miss Arnold. She made an exception in your case. I hope for your sake you were telling the truth when you said this was a life-and-death situation. Lying to gain entry to my private office is the surest way to find yourself slapped with a lawsuit for harassment. As it is, I'm taking time from an important board meeting to accommodate you."

His arrogance took her breath away. If all this weren't for the ultimate happiness of everyone concerned, she would've relished

storming out of there and slamming the door in his good-looking
face.

"This concerns your son," she said quietly.

The menacing look that transformed his taut features made her
heart leap in apprehension. With dangerous agility, he got up
from his seat and placed both hands on his desk, leaning forward.
'If you're part of a kidnapping scheme, let me warn you I've
already activated the security alarm. When you walk out of here,
it'll be with an armed guard."

"Are you always this paranoid?" She was aghast; until now
it hadn't occurred to her that his wealth made him a target for
kidnappers. At the mere thought, a shudder ran through her body.

"You've got thirty seconds to explain yourself." The implicit
threat in his voice unnerved her.

"I-I think you'd better sit down," she said.

"Your time is running out."

In an attempt to feel less vulnerable, Cassie rose to her feet,
clutching her purse in front of her. "It's not easy for me to
explain when you're standing there like...like an avenging prince
ready to do battle."

He flicked a glance at his watch. "You're down to ten seconds.
Then you can explain all this to a judge." From the forbidding
expression on his face and the coldness of his voice, she knew
he meant what he said.

As worried and nervous as she was about confronting him with
the truth, she had to remember that this man and his wife were
her only passport to Susan's son. That knowledge gave her the
courage to follow through with her plan.

Taking a deep breath, she said, "I happen to know that you
and your wife have a nine-month-old baby boy who was born to
you on February twenty-fourth at the Palms Oasis Health Center.
My sister, Susan Arnold Fisher, also delivered a baby boy there
the same day.

"Until the moment she died, she believed that there was an
upset in routine because of the catastrophe—the chemical plant
explosion. It brought a flood of injured people to the hospital,
and somehow the wrong name tags were put on the babies' wrists
in the intensive-care unit. The result was that my sister was presented with your baby, and you and your wife went home with
hers."

The silence following her pronouncement stretched endlessly. His face looked impassive, hard and cold as stone. "All right," he finally muttered. "I've listened to your tale. Now I hope you have a good attorney, because you're going to need one."

"Wait!" she cried when he pressed the intercom button. She had expected this encounter to disturb him, but she'd never dreamed he would call in the authorities before she had convinced him of the truth!

"It's too late to backtrack, Miss Arnold."

A knock on the door brought Cassie's head around and she saw an armed security guard and a police officer enter the room with their hands on their unsnapped holsters. Behind them stood an anxious Mrs. Blakesley. She held a wriggling, squirming Jason, who was bellowing at the top of his lungs.

"What in the—?" Trace Ramsey stopped midsentence and raked a hand through his black hair, shooting Cassie a venomous glance. But she was too concerned to be intimidated; dropping her purse, she made a beeline for Jason.

Since Susan's death two months earlier, Cassie and Jason had become inseparable. She might not have been his biological mother, but she loved him every bit as fiercely. She felt guilt for leaving him in Mrs. Blakesley's care, even for such a brief time. He must have awakened after his morning bottle and been frightened by the unfamiliar face hovering over him.

"What's the trouble, Mr. Ramsey?" asked the guard. But Cassie didn't hear his answer, because Jason had caught sight of her. Immediately his lusty cries intensified, resounding through the suite of offices. "Ma-ma, Ma-ma," he repeated, holding out his hands.

Despite the gravity of the situation, Cassie couldn't repress a tiny smile, because it was Trace Ramsey's own noisy son creating all this chaos.

"Mommy's here, darling." With a murmured thank-you, she plucked him from the older woman's arms and cuddled him against her chest, kissing his damp black curls, rubbing his strong sturdy little back with her free hand.

Jason had made it clear that he wanted Cassie and no one else. He clung tightly to her and calmed down at once. Cassie felt a wave of maternal pride so intense she was staggered, and at the moment she knew she could never give him up. She knew she'd made a mistake in coming here.

With the best of intentions, Cassie had walked into Trace Ramsey's office and upset his comfortable, well-ordered life. If his reaction to a possible kidnapping attempt was anything to go by, his love for the son he'd brought home from the hospital was as great as hers for Jason. She wanted to honor her sister's dying wish, but she *couldn't*. She realized that now. It was wrong, unfair—to all of them.

"Mr. Ramsey?" she started to say, but the second she caught sight of his ashen face, the name died on her lips. In her preoccupation with Jason's needs, she hadn't noticed that everyone except his father had left the room. He stood motionless in its center.

Swallowing hard, she loosened Jason's fist, which was clutching her hair, before turning him around to face his father. Only seconds later, she heard his shaken whisper. "Dear Lord, the likeness is unbelievable."

Cassie's compassionate heart went out to him. She couldn't imagine what it would feel like to learn that she'd been nurturing the wrong child since his birth, let alone to see her own baby for the first time.

"That was my reaction as soon as I saw you," she said quietly. He looked away from the child then, and gazed at her, his eyes dark with emotion.

"He's called Jason," Cassie added. The sound of his name brought the baby's dark head around and he clamored to be held in his favorite position, with his face buried in her neck, his hand gripping the top of her dress for dear life.

"May I hold him?" Trace's voice sounded strained. He lifted his hands instinctively to take Jason from her.

"Yes, of course. But don't be surprised if he starts crying again. He's going through that stage where he won't let anyone near him but me."

Jason immediately protested the abrupt departure from Cassie's arms. His strong little body squirmed and struggled, and he kicked out his legs, screaming loudly enough to alert the entire building. But not for anything in the world would Cassie have intruded on this private moment between father and son.

They looked so right together, so perfect, it brought a lump to her throat.

Trace's gaze swerved to hers as he bounced his unhappy son against his broad shoulder, apparently unconcerned about his elegant, stone-gray silk suit. "Do you have a bottle I can give him? Maybe it'll quiet him down."

She should have thought of that. She began to rummage in the bag Mrs. Blakesley had brought in. "Here."

Gently but firmly he settled Jason in his arm and inserted the nipple in his mouth. He performed the maneuver with an expertise that would have surprised her if she hadn't known he'd been fathering Susan's son for the past nine months.

But Jason wasn't cooperating. He just cried harder, fighting the bottle and his father with all his considerable might. Cassie could tell that Trace was beginning to feel at a loss.

"Why don't you let me change him?" she suggested softly. "It might do the trick."

He slanted her a look she couldn't decipher and with obvious reluctance put a screaming Jason back in her arms. While Jason snuggled against her once more, his father reached for the baby quilt lining the carryall and spread it on top of his desk, pushing the telephone aside. Never had she imagined she'd be changing Jason's diaper there!

"Come on, sweetheart. Mommy's going to make you comfortable." Though Jason continued to protest vociferously and eye his father as if he were the enemy, she managed to make him lie still long enough to unfasten his sleeper and peel it off along with his damp diaper.

As she put on a clean disposable diaper, Trace murmured something unintelligible beneath his breath, and almost as if he couldn't help himself took Jason's right foot in his hands. For some reason the baby didn't seem to mind and actually relaxed a little, no doubt because he was receiving so much attention. His extremities had become of paramount importance in his young life.

Cassie had always been intrigued by Jason's right foot. The third and fourth toes were webbed, a characteristic never seen in either Susan's or Ted's families. His father seemed to find it inordinate interest, as well.

"He's my son!" Trace proclaimed solemnly, then let out a
y of pure delight. Fierce pride gleamed in his blue eyes.

"We probably ought to take the babies to the hospital and
ve their blood types checked against the records."

"We will," he muttered, "but the truth is sitting right here."
e grasped Jason's fingers and pulled experimentally to test the
by's strength. Jason caught hold with a firm grip and lifted his
ad and shoulders from the desk to sit up without help, pro-
cing a satisfied chuckle from his father. Jason had become
ually curious about the black-haired stranger who seemed to
ke such pleasure in playing with him.

Because it was cool in the room, Cassie searched for a clean
eper in the diaper bag. No sooner had she found one than it
as taken from her hands.

"I'll dress him," Trace stated. There was an unmistakable ring
possession in his tone as he proceeded to fit Jason's compact
dy into the arms and feet of the little white suit.

After snapping the front fasteners, he picked up his son, who
d by now stopped fussing, and held him against his shoulder,
nning his fingers through Jason's wild black curls. Cassie noted
at even their hair seemed to part naturally on the same side.

Needless to say, she'd been forgotten as Trace carried Jason
er to the window where the great city of Phoenix lay sprawled
fore them. Whatever he said was for his son's ears alone. She
ew that Trace Ramsey had already taken Jason to his heart.

Now there were two people in the world who loved Jason
tensely. And as soon as his wife was informed, there would be
ree. Everything had suddenly become much more complicated.
assie understood instinctively that Jason's father wouldn't give
anything that was his. But in this case they would have to
ork out vacation schedules, because she wasn't prepared to lose
son. She had come to love him too much.

"Mr. Ramsey? I have a plane to catch later today. Do you
ink we could meet with your wife this morning and tell her
hat's happened? I can hardly wait to see my nephew, and I'd
ke some time with him before I go back to San Francisco with
son."

"*San Francisco?*" He wheeled around, a grimace marring his
atures.

"We live there, Jason and I."

Her voice must have attracted Jason's attention because
cried out and reached for her again. When Trace continued
hold him, Jason wailed piteously and tried to wriggle out of
father's grasp. He had been a determined, headstrong child fro
birth. Now she knew why.

"It's time for his lunch, but a bottle will have to do." T
gentle reminder forced Trace to close the distance between the
and deposit Jason in her arms. But with every step he took, s
could tell he rebelled against the idea of relinquishing his new
discovered son even for a moment.

Cassie couldn't blame him. The situation was so emotional
charged she was afraid she would burst into tears any secon
Comforted by the familiar feel of Jason's warm little body, s
sat down in a leather wing chair Trace positioned for her. Jas
grabbed the bottle with both hands and started gulping down
milk.

Actually he'd been attempting to drink from a cup for the pa
week. But her pediatrician had said to use a bottle while th
were traveling because it would give him a greater sense of s
curity. Jason was such a noisy drinker, Cassie couldn't help sm
ing and felt Trace's eyes on both of them.

"My wife and I divorced soon after the baby was born,"
said abruptly. He paused, then went on, speaking quickly. "S
gave me custody and went back to her law practice in Los A
geles. I have my housekeeper, Nattie, to help raise my son. S
and her husband, Mike—who looks after the grounds—ha
worked for me for years. Nattie's wonderful with children, a
Justin adores her."

"*Justin!*" As she said his name, her mind grappled with t
unexpected revelation that Mrs. Ramsey was no longer a part
this family's life. She lifted her head and fixed imploring gre
eyes on Trace. "Tell me about Susan's son—your son," s
amended self-consciously. "What does he look like? I-I ca
wait to see him."

Without hesitation he strode swiftly to his desk and buzzed
secretary. "Mrs. Blakesley? Cancel all my appointments for t
day. I'm going home and won't be back. Tell Robert to have m
car waiting in the rear. We'll be down shortly. If there are a
urgent phone messages, give them to me now."

While he dealt with last-minute business, she felt his ga

linger on her slender legs beneath the cream cotton suit she was wearing. Cassie's heart did a funny little kick, and she forced herself to look away, studying the paintings hung on the walls of his office. Until now, Trace Ramsey had been the focal point of her attention.

If the decor was a reflection of his personal taste, he tended to enjoy the watercolors of an artist unknown to her. The paintings depicted a variety of enchanting desert scenes, in a style that was at once vibrant and restrained. She would have liked one for herself.

A loud burp from Jason brought her back to the present. Trace's spontaneous laugh made him look, for a moment, more carefree, and Cassie chuckled, too. Obviously Jason had finished his bottle without stopping for breath.

"Shall we?" Trace stood at the door holding a briefcase and the carryall, indicating she should join him.

"That's a beautiful boy you have there," Mrs. Blakesley commented to Cassie as they passed her desk on their way out.

"Mrs. Blakesley," Trace said to the older woman, his eyes still glowing in wonder, "I'd like you to be the first person to meet my son, Jason. When I'm in possession of all the facts, I'll explain how this came about, but for the time being I must ask you to keep it to yourself."

"I knew it!" The matronly woman jumped to her feet. Hurrying around her desk she shaped Jason's face with her hands. "Even before she said it was a matter of life and death, I knew it. He bears an amazing resemblance to you, Trace. I never saw anything like it in my life!"

A satisfied smile lifted the corners of Trace's mouth as he gazed down on his son.

Cassie could imagine all too easily what his secretary was thinking—that at one time Cassie and Trace had had an affair and Jason was the result. She wanted to set the matter straight, but Trace was already whisking her out of his office and around the corner to a private elevator.

When he'd ushered her inside and the doors were closed, he asked, "How did you get to my office?"

"A taxi."

"How long have you been in Phoenix?"

Jason's curious eyes darted back and forth as they spoke.

"Only two days this time."

"This time?" His black brow lifted in query. The elevator arrived at the ground floor and they stepped out, but Trace remained standing in the hallway as he waited for Cassie's answer.

"I've made several rushed trips to Phoenix in the past two months trying to find out if Susan was right about the switch. There were five couples who'd had a son at that hospital the same day Susan gave birth to Jason. I mean Justin."

Trace blinked. "I didn't realize there were that many. Palms Oasis is a small hospital."

"I know. I was surprised, too. Anyway, I visited each family in turn but came to a dead end each time. I began to think Jason was one of those rare accidents of nature, after all—the odd gene producing a throwback in the family. That is, until I saw you." She ventured a look into his eyes and wondered why she'd ever thought them glacial. "When your secretary told me you wouldn't see me without knowing the reason for my visit, I almost turned around and walked out."

His eyes turned an inky blue color and he sucked in his breath. "Thank God you didn't."

She gave a quick half smile. "You're not exactly an easy man to reach, Mr. Ramsey. No home phone. Security guards. I didn't have a choice except to meet you without an appointment. You'll never know how close I came to giving up. You were the last person on my list and it seemed like an unnecessary gesture, another exercise in futility."

"What made you so persistent?" he asked soberly.

"I have to admit that since I started looking after Jason, I've entertained some doubts about his parentage, too. I made up my mind to be as thorough as possible, so there'd be no lingering shadows when I returned to San Francisco to raise Jason as my son."

On impulse she lowered her head to kiss the child's smooth cheek. "And something told me that if I left without seeing you, I would always have these doubts...."

Just as she spoke, Trace moved closer. He cupped her elbow and guided her through the hall to a back door. A BMW sedan stood waiting in the drive. "Come here, Tiger," he said to Jason, lifting him from Cassie's arms and strapping him in the baby seat.

Jason took one look at the unfamiliar surroundings and began to scream.

"I think I'd better stay with him or you won't be able to concentrate on your driving." She climbed in back, then handed Jason one of his favorite toys, a hard plastic doughnut in bright orange. That calmed him and he soon grew absorbed in chewing it.

Trace leaned inside to fasten her seat belt. His action brought their faces within an inch of each other, and she was painfully conscious of his dark glossy hair, his clean-shaven jaw and his fresh scent—the soap he used? To mask her awareness of him, she pretended to adjust Jason's seat belt. Trace backed away from her and closed the door. In seconds he had gone around to the driver's seat.

"Thanks, Robert," he called to the garage attendant, and they were off. If the older man found the situation somewhat unusual, he didn't let on. But she could tell he was curious about Trace's little black-haired look-alike sitting in Justin's usual spot.

Despite the way he had treated her earlier, Cassie found herself warming to Trace. She liked the fact that he took his fatherhood role so seriously. And she liked the way he accepted a child's presence in his life, not worrying about his costly suit or his expensive car. She knew a lot of men who never allowed children inside their luxury cars.

They left the busy downtown center and drove north toward the foothills, where she could see Camelback Mountain in the distance. What impressed Cassie most about Phoenix was the cleanliness of its streets and the beauty of the residential lawns and gardens. The vivid flowers and shrubs, the sparkling blue of swimming pools...

This was the first time in months that she'd been able to appreciate her surroundings. The pain of her broken engagement, plus the trauma of trying to cope with Susan's death and Jason's needs—on top of running her home handicrafts business—had drained her. She couldn't remember when she'd been able to relax like this.

But her pleasure was short-lived. When she turned her head to find another toy in her bag, she discovered a pair of narrowed eyes watching her through the rearview mirror. If their guarded expression and his taut facial features were any indication, something unpleasant was going through Trace Ramsey's mind. She couldn't understand it, because only moments before everything had been so amicable.

Inexplicably hurt by his oddly hostile look, she closed her eyes and rested her head against the leather upholstery.

In fairness to him, she supposed, it wasn't every day a man kissed the child he thought was his son goodbye, only to be confronted with his *real* son a few hours later.

Again Cassie tried to imagine his feelings and couldn't. Only once in her twenty-five years had she heard of a case involving a switched baby. That instance, too, had been a mischance, sending two families home with each other's babies. Cassie didn't know the statistics, but figured such an accident had to be in the one-in-a-billion category.

Until now, most of Cassie's thoughts and concerns had been for Jason. But the closer they drew to Trace's home, the more excitedly she began to anticipate her first look at Justin. She found herself speculating on why the Ramsey marriage had fallen apart so soon after the baby was born. How could his wife have left her child and gone to another state to pursue a career? Didn't her heart ache for her son?

Cassie couldn't fathom any of it. She was so deep in thought she didn't realize the car had left the highway and turned onto a private road. It wound through a natural desert setting, dotted with saguaros and other cacti, to a breathtaking Southwestern house—a house that looked as if it had sprung from the very landscape.

The house appeared to be built on two levels, with a white-washed stone exterior and pale wood trim.

The architect who had designed Trace Ramsey's home had not only succeeded in reflecting the environment but had caught the essence of the man. The clean yet dramatic lines, the soaring windows, the quiet beauty of the wood, created a uniquely satisfying effect.

He continued driving around the house to a side entrance where Cassie caught sight of a rectangular swimming pool. Immaculate, velvety green lawns flanked the water, which was as blue as a deep-sea grotto.

Cassie gasped at the sheer size and beauty of Trace Ramsey's retreat, tucked only minutes away from the center of his banking empire. Cassie had never seen anything quite like this place. She'd spent the whole of her life in San Francisco, living with her widowed mother and sister in the bottom apartment of a flat-fronted Victorian house on Telegraph Hill. Cassie couldn't remember her father, who'd died when she was very young.

While she lifted Jason from his car seat, Trace came around and opened the door to assist them. The air smelled of tantalizing desert scents and was fresher than in downtown Phoenix. Cassie thrived in cooler temperatures; she estimated that it couldn't be much warmer than seventy-five degrees. Perfect weather for early December, just the way she liked it.

"Shall we go in?" He didn't seem to expect an answer as he gripped her elbow and helped her up the stairs to the entry hall, carrying the baby bag in his other hand. He didn't attempt to take his son from her, probably because he didn't relish a repeat of Jason's tears. But she could sense Trace's impatience to hold him.

Jason was fascinated by the click of her high heels on the Mexican-tile floors and kept turning his head in an attempt to discover the source. It was a fight to keep him from flipping out of her arms, especially since Cassie found herself so distracted by the beauty around her. Every few steps, she had to stop and stare at the dramatically cut-out white interior walls and bleached wood ceilings.

They walked along a gallery filled with lushly green trees and local Indian art. It looked out on the swimming pool, part of which was protected by the overhanging roof.

"Nattie? I'm home, and I've brought someone with me for lunch. Where are you?" Trace called out as they went down a half flight of stairs toward the indoor portion of the patio.

"Justin's been helping me water the plants. I didn't know you'd be back to eat. I'll get something on the table right away."

They entered a charming courtyard reminiscent of old Mexico, with a profusion of plants and colorful flowers. But Cassie hardly noticed the wrought-iron lounge furniture or the retreating back of the auburn-haired housekeeper. Her eyes fastened helplessly on the child in the playpen who had heard his father's voice and was squealing in delight.

The slender lanky child, dressed in a sleeveless yellow romper suit, was standing, a feat Jason hadn't yet mastered, as he clung to the playpen webbing, rocking in and out as he watched his father's approach.

Round hazel eyes shone from a fringe of fine, straight, pale-gold hair that encircled his head like a halo. His total attention was fixed rapturously on Trace.

Cassie came to a standstill. It was an astonishing sensation—a little like putting the final pieces in a jigsaw puzzle. The frame of this child's body was Ted's, but his complexion was Susan's. The shape of his eyes was Ted's, but the color was Susan's. The texture of the hair was Ted's, but again, the coloring was Susan's. The straight nose and cheekbones were Ted's, but the smile...

Cassie's eyes filled with tears. Her adored sister, who only eight weeks before had lost a valiantly fought battle with pneumonia, lived in her son's glorious smile.

"Oh, Susan!" She sobbed her sister's name aloud and buried her face in Jason's chest. She was overcome with emotion, with feelings still so close to the surface that she couldn't contain them any longer.

Jason fretted, patting her head agitatedly. Cassie fought for control and after a few minutes lifted her tear-drenched face to discover a pair of angry blue eyes staring at her, not only in silent accusation but contempt.

"What's wrong?" she whispered, attempting to wipe the tears from her cheeks. "First in the car, and now here. Why are you looking at me like that?"

CHAPTER TWO

IN THE SILENCE that followed, he reached for Justin and hugged him protectively, rubbing his chin against the fine silk of the child's hair. "I was counting on that reaction and you didn't disappoint me," he said bitterly.

They faced each other like adversaries. Cassie shifted Jason to her other arm. *"What reaction?"* She couldn't imagine what had caused such hostility.

"It's too late for pretense. Justin needs people around who see him for the wonderful person he is."

She shook her head in total bewilderment. "He *is* wonderful!"

"But—"

"But what?" she demanded angrily, feeling a wave of heat wash over her neck and cheeks. Jason could sense the charged atmosphere and started to whimper.

"You're no different from my ex-wife! She was so repulsed by Justin's deformity, mild though it is, that she wouldn't even hold him."

Deformity? "I don't know what you're talking about! Two months ago I watched my sister's body laid to rest and I thought her lost to me for the rest of my life." Her voice shook, but she hardly noticed.

Without conscious thought she lowered Jason into the playpen and reached for her tote bag. Oblivious to his sudden outburst, she pulled one of Susan's wedding pictures from the side pocket and held it up for Trace's scrutiny. It was her favorite picture of Susan and Ted, smiling into the camera just before they left on their honeymoon.

"When Justin's face lighted up just now, it was as if God had given Susan back to me. Take a good look at the picture, Mr. Ramsey. See for yourself!"

Grim-faced, he set Justin in the other corner of the playpen and took the photograph. Immediately Justin, too, began to cry. In an effort to distract the howling infants, Cassie knelt beside the playpen and started to sing "Teensy Weensy Spider," one of Jason's favorite songs. Within seconds, both babies grew quiet. Jason crawled toward her, while Justin clambered to his feet.

It was when he put out his left hand to grasp the playpen's webbing that she noticed the depression—like a band around the middle of his upper arm. Below the depression, his arm and hand were correctly shaped, but hadn't grown in proportion to the rest of his body. The deformity was slight, but it was noticeable if you were aware of it.

"You dear little thing." Unable to resist, she stood up and leaned over to take Justin in her arms. "You precious little boy," she crooned against his soft cheek, rocking him gently back and forth.

"Your mother and daddy would have given anything in the world to hold you like this. Do you know that?" she asked as he stared quietly at her. The seriousness of his gaze reminded her of the way Ted used to look when he was concentrating. "Susan made me promise to find you. I'm so thankful I did. I love you, Justin. I love you," she whispered, but the words came out a muffled sob.

She wanted to believe the baby understood when she felt his muscles relax and his blond head rest on her shoulder. For a few minutes Cassie was conscious of nothing but the warmth of her nephew's body cuddled against her own.

"I owe you an apology."

Cassie opened her eyes and discovered Trace standing not two feet from her, with Jason riding his shoulders. His sturdy little fingers were fastened in his father's black hair, a look of fear mingled with intense concentration on his expressive face.

She smiled through the tears. "He's never seen the world from that altitude before."

Miraculously Trace smiled back, their enmity apparently forgotten. Cassie's heartbeat accelerated as she found herself examining the laugh lines around his mouth and his beautiful, straight white teeth. She raised her eyes to his, and the pounding of her heart actually became painful.

"Trace?" the housekeeper called out just then, jerking Cassie back to reality. "Do you want lunch served on the patio or in the dining room?"

"The patio will be fine, Nattie." To Cassie he said, "I'll get the high chair. The boys can take turns having lunch."

The boys. Those words fell so naturally from his lips. Anyone listening would have assumed this was an everyday occurrence.

"Since Jason and I will have to leave for the airport pretty soon, I'd like to spend this time with Justin. Do you mind if I hold him on my lap to feed him?"

A scowl marred his features. "When's your flight?" he demanded, not answering her question.

"Ten after four."

"I'll get you to the airport on time," was the terse response. "Right now the only matter of importance is getting better acquainted." He grasped Jason's hands more tightly. "Come on, Tiger. We'll go get Justin's chair and surprise Nattie."

Jason forgot to cry because he was concentrating all his energy on holding on to his father. The two of them disappeared from the patio, leaving Cassie alone with Justin, who seemed content to stay in her arms. Compared to the sturdy Jason, Justin felt surprisingly light.

She sat down on one of the chairs at the poolside table and settled him on the glass top in front of her. Though taller and more dexterous than Jason, he hadn't started talking as well yet. Probably because he was too busy analyzing everything with that mathematical brain inherited from Ted.

Jason, on the other hand, never stopped making sounds and noises. He liked to hear his own voice and adored music of any kind, which was a good thing since Cassie played the piano and listened for hours to tapes of her favorite piano concertos while she designed and appliquéd her original quilts, pillows and stuffed animals.

"I know a silly song your grandma Arnold would sing to you if she were here." She kissed his pink cheek and took his hands, touching each finger as she sang. "'Hinty, minty, cutie, corn, apple seed and apple thorn, Riar, briar, limber lock, six geese in a flock, Sit and sing, at the spring, o-u-t out again!'" She made his arms fly wide and he began to laugh, a real belly laugh that surprised and delighted her. They did this several times before

Cassie heard a woman's call from another part of the house. Not long afterward, the trim sixtyish housekeeper appeared on the patio carrying two heaped plates of taco salad. Trace followed with the high chair in one arm and Jason in the other.

"I've got to meet the brave young woman who made it past Mrs. Blakesley and presented you with your son!"

She beamed at Cassie, who rose to her feet and balanced Justin against her hip while the older woman put the plates on the table. After wiping her fingers on her apron, she held out a hand, which Cassie shook. "I'm Nattie Parker and I have to tell you this is probably the most exciting day of my life! Talk about the spitting image!"

Cassie's eyes filled with tears as she looked at Jason. "He is, isn't he? And Justin is so much like my sister and her husband, I'm still in a daze. In fact, none of this seems real." She couldn't resist kissing Justin's silky blond head.

Nattie nodded in agreement. "That was a switch for the books. And to think you've been looking for Jason's daddy all this time, and Trace almost sent you away with the police. Shame on you, Trace," she said in a stern voice, but love for her employer shone through.

The woman's raisin-dark eyes fastened on Jason. "I can't wait another second to get my hands on him. He has the kind of solid little body you just want to squeeze, d'you know what I mean?"

"I know exactly," Cassie said, loving Nattie on the spot. She let her gaze wander to Trace, who was tenderly eyeing both his sons. One day Jason would grow into the same kind of vital, handsome, dynamic man....

At the moment, though, Jason was struggling with Nattie. He stopped when she handed him a cracker from her pocket; she gave another one to Justin with a quick kiss. "Come on, young man," she told Jason. "You can go with me to get the baby food. What would you like today? Beans and lamb? That's what your brother's having."

As she walked away chatting, Trace motioned Cassie to a chair. "Are you sure you want to feed Justin?"

"Positive," she asserted, placing him on her lap. Despite the cracker halfway in his mouth, he reached for the salad, which she pushed out of his way.

Turning her attention to Trace, who'd gone to the bar behind them, she said quietly, "Do you know what thrills me? He uses both hands in all his movements. That means he has the full use of his arm. He'll be able to do any sport or activity Jason can do." She paused to remove her fork from Justin's eager clutches. "Tell me what the doctors say about him."

Trace supplied napkins and iced fruit drinks before taking his seat. Their eyes met. "It's called an amniotic band. It tightened around his arm in the womb, cutting off some of the blood supply. The specialist says physical therapy to build up his muscles can begin when he turns three. By the time he's an adult, the defect will hardly be noticeable."

She leaned down and kissed Justin's smooth shoulder. "Well, aren't you the luckiest little boy in town. I wonder if you'll turn out to be as great a tennis player as your father. You're built just like him."

Trace looked pensive as he ate a forkful of salad. "Genes don't lie, do they?"

"No." She ate a mouthful of cheese and guacamole, then let Justin try a little of her pineapple drink.

"When did your sister first suspect Jason wasn't her son?"

"Her baby was rushed to the infant intensive-care unit as soon as he was born. A little later, the pediatrician told her he'd had trouble breathing on his own. She didn't actually hold him for about eight hours.

"When he was finally brought to her, his black hair and olive skin were so different from what she'd expected, she couldn't believe Jason was hers and told me as much over the phone. But since Susan's and my baby pictures show us with dark hair, I assumed Jason's hair would turn blond after a few months and didn't take her seriously. Until I saw him for the first time, that is."

Trace let out an audible sigh. "Unfortunately, I wasn't there for the delivery. The baby came sooner than we expected, and by the time I arrived at the hospital, Gloria was in her room and the baby was in the intensive-care unit. About a half hour later the pediatrician came to tell us about Justin. I went down to the nursery with the doctor and saw Justin for the first time lying in one of those cribs. The switch must have occurred in the unit."

She nodded. "Susan said the baby was born at 9:05 a.m."

Trace put down his fork and looked at her solemnly. "Our son was born at 9:04. And your sister was right. There were ambulances all over the place when I arrived. The chemical plant outside Phoenix blew up, killing a dozen people and sending dozens more to various hospitals. The place was swarming with hospital personnel, relatives, reporters. Because of all the confusion, I was delayed getting to Gloria's room."

She closed her eyes. "It sounds so impossible, so incredible, and yet that must explain why there was a mix-up. Do you think we should demand an investigation and lodge a formal complaint to prevent this from happening to anyone else?"

He was quiet so long she didn't know if he'd heard her. "Part of me says yes. Another part says accidents do happen, even when the greatest precautions are taken. Probably the chances of such a thing occurring again are something like a billion to one."

"I've thought that myself. We know it wasn't intentional."

After a pause he said, "In principle, I'm opposed to unnecessary litigation. This has become a sue-happy society. So, on balance, I'm against suing."

Cassie didn't realize she'd been holding her breath. "I'm glad you said that. I don't think I could handle an official investigation after everything I've been through in the last year with Ted's death—he was killed in an accident—and then Susan getting sick and...and dying." Not to mention Rolfe's recent engagement to a woman overseas, which had come as a painful shock to Cassie. She and Rolfe—her lifelong neighbor—had always been close, although she'd put off making a decision about marriage. But she'd assumed that when his studies were over, he would come home and they'd work things out.

"The newspapers would get hold of it and the publicity would be horrible," she said, shuddering at the prospect. "In the end all it would do is damage the hospital's reputation and ruin people's lives. I don't want this to affect the boys."

"I agree," Trace concurred in a sober tone. "However, we will get those blood tests and I'm going to write the hospital board a letter informing them what happened. I'll let them know that, though we're not pressing charges, we are requesting an unofficial inquiry to satisfy our questions. Indirectly it might prevent another mistake like this in the future."

"I think that's best, and I know Susan and Ted would hav

felt the same way. Mr. Ramsey, did you or your wife ever have any suspicions that Justin wasn't your son?"

He cocked one dark eyebrow. "I think at this stage we should dispense with the formalities. My name is Trace, and the answer to your question is a definite no. Gloria is a tall willowy blond with hazel eyes. Everyone assumed Justin inherited her coloring and slender build. But after looking at your sister and brother-in-law's photograph, I can see the resemblance to Gloria is superficial at best. Justin bears an unmistakable likeness to both his parents."

Cassie nodded in agreement. She wanted to ask him more questions about his wife, but Nattie's entry with Jason and the baby food prevented her. Jason now sported a bib, which he was trying to pull off.

While Trace relieved her of his son and slipped him into the high chair, Nattie put the food on the table. "Here's a bib for my golden boy." She tied it around Justin's neck. "Now all of you have a good lunch. I'll hold any phone calls to give you a chance to talk."

Trace didn't let Nattie escape until he had pressed her hand in a gesture that spoke volumes about their relationship. Justin was surrounded by people who loved him, and that knowledge brought the first modicum of peace to Cassie's heart.

For the next while Cassie told Trace about Ted's fatal car accident en route to summer camp with the army reserve and Susan's subsequent depression, which led to one of her chronic bouts of pneumonia after a troubled pregnancy. Without Ted, she couldn't seem to endure.

Justin behaved perfectly while they talked. Half the time he managed the spoon by himself without making any mess. Cassie wished she could say the same for Jason. Though he loved the lamb, every time Trace gave him a spoonful of beans he'd keep them in his mouth for a minute, then let them fall back out. And worse, he smeared the top of his high chair so it resembled a finger painting.

Trace surprised her by being highly amused rather than irritated. She could hardly equate this patient caring man with the forbidding bank official who would have sent her from his office in handcuffs without a qualm.

Halfway through his peaches, Justin showed signs of being

tired and his eyelids drooped. Jason was exhausted, as well. Unfortunately he tended to become even more restless and noisy before falling asleep.

She looked over at Trace who was chuckling at the funny sounds Jason made as he practically inhaled his fruit. "May I put Justin to bed?" she asked.

Trace flicked her a searching glance, then gently tousled Justin's hair. "Has too much excitement made my little guy sleepy? Why don't we take both of them upstairs? While you deal with Justin, I'll put Jason in the tub."

Cassie tried to smother a smile but failed. "I wish I could tell you Jason isn't usually this impossible at meals, but it wouldn't be the truth."

His lips twitched. "I'm afraid when my mother finds out about this, she'll tell you I was much worse. Like father, like son."

Carefully lifting Justin, she rose to her feet. "Does your mother live here in Phoenix?"

"Not only Mother but the entire Ramsey clan."

"You're a large family, then?"

"I have two brothers and a sister, all of whom are older with children," he informed her as she followed him to a hallway on the other side of the patio.

By now Jason's bib had been removed and Trace held his food-smeared son firmly around the waist. "Ma-ma, Ma-ma," Jason cried when he realized he was being swept away from their cozy domestic scene by this dynamic stranger.

"Da-da's got you, Tiger," Trace said, mimicking his son. Cassie's heart leapt in her chest. No man had ever had this physical effect on her, not even Rolfe. She'd loved him from childhood; he was the man she'd planned her future around. But the grief Cassie had suffered over her mother's death, followed by Ted's fatal accident and Susan's illness, had taken its toll. She wasn't ready to set a wedding date. Rolfe, hurt and disillusioned, had accused her of not being in love with him and had broken their engagement. The next thing she knew, he had gone abroad to study music. He was a gifted musician who'd been offered more than one prestigious scholarship.

Before Susan died, she'd said that a separation was exactly what Cassie and Rolfe needed. They'd never spent more than a week or two away from each other, and a year's separation would clarify their feelings. When they came together again, there'd be no hesitation on either side if a marriage between the two of them was meant to be.

Susan's remarks made a lot of sense to Cassie. But she hadn't considered the possibility that Rolfe would fall in love with someone else in the interim, nor that it would hurt so much. Now Susan was gone and Cassie would never again be able to confide in the sister who'd always been her best friend and confidante.

"Cassie?" Trace called over his shoulder with a puzzled expression on his face. "Are you all right?"

"Yes. Of course." She smiled. "I had to stop for a minute and look at all these watercolors. They're fabulous, just like the ones in your office."

"My sister, Lena, is one of the most talented artists I know, but she's so critical of her own work, she refuses to display any of her paintings in public."

"So you do it for her," Cassie murmured. She couldn't help but be touched by his loyalty to his sister. It was ironic, and somehow pleasing, that while she'd been reliving bittersweet memories of her own sister, she'd been gazing at *his* sister's work—a sister he obviously adored. There were many surprising and wonderful facets to Trace Ramsey's personality, as she was beginning to learn. "How many of Lena's paintings have you sold?"

"None," he said as they reached the second floor. "She made me promise. In fact, she hasn't signed them. But if she ever changes her mind, my walls will be bare."

Cassie could believe it. In fact, there were several paintings here that gave her ideas for wall hangings and rugs, but they were fleeting images and she couldn't do anything about them now.

Justin's suite of rooms had the Southwest flavor of the rest of the house, but concessions had been made to practicality, creating more traditional child's decor. Chocolate-brown shag carpeting covered the floors, and baby furniture filled the spacious room. A huge hand-painted mural took up one whole wall.

It was an enchanted-forest scene, with each little animal and insect possessing a distinct personality. Cassie was completely charmed by it and easily recognized the artist's hand. "Your sister painted this."

"Yes. That was Lena's gift to Justin," he called out from the bathroom. The minute the water started filling the tub, she could hear Jason's protests turn to squeals of delight. He always enjoyed his bath.

Cassie wondered if Justin liked the water, but she'd have to find out another time, because he was sound asleep, lying limp against her shoulder.

She gently placed him on his stomach in the crib and covered him with the cotton blanket. Automatically his thumb went to his mouth. He looked so blissfully content she didn't have the heart to pull it out again and risk waking him.

After leaning over to bestow one last kiss, she headed for the immaculate white bathroom accented, like the downstairs rooms, in natural wood. It was difficult to tell who was having a better time, Jason or his father.

Trace's white shirt-sleeves were rolled up above the elbows to display tanned forearms with a sprinkling of dark hair. His smile made him look years younger as he urged Jason to float on his back and kick his sturdy little legs. "That's it, Tiger. Make a big splash."

When water hit him in the face, he burst into deep-throated laughter. He sounded so happy that Cassie hated to disturb them. However, Jason had already caught sight of her standing there holding a fluffy tangerine-colored towel. He immediately tried to sit up, plaintively crying, "Ma-ma," and stretching out his arms.

"I'm afraid we've got to get going," she said apologetically to Trace who looked distinctly disappointed by the interruption. With undisguised reluctance, he wrapped Jason in the towel and started to dry him. "My luggage is being held at a motel in West Phoenix," Cassie went on. "We'll have to stop there on our way to the airport."

Trace frowned and she knew why. But he didn't understand what it was like to live on a budget. Even when her mother was alive and Susan was at home, they had all worked hard to make ends meet. And now that a future with Rolfe had slipped away and with little Jason to support, she had to be more careful than ever how she spent her money.

In the short year and a half Susan and Ted had been married, they had acquired some insurance and savings. But before her sister's death, Cassie and Susan had agreed that any money would be invested for Jason's education. Cassie wouldn't have dreamed of touching it.

When she started to gather up Jason's soiled outfit, Trace told her to leave it for Nattie to wash. "He can wear something of his brother's for the flight back, can't you, Tiger?"

After diapering him on the bathroom counter, he reached into the drawer for a pale green stretchy suit with feet and put Jason into it. Then he playfully lowered his head to Jason's tummy and made a noise against it, producing a gale of infectious laughter from his dark-haired son.

In a very short time, Jason seemed to have overcome his fear of Trace. Much more of his father's attention and he wouldn't want to leave, a thought that troubled Cassie more than a little. This was his first experience with a man and he appeared to be enjoying it.

Cassie couldn't help wondering if her letter telling Rolfe about her plan to raise Jason as her own son had something to do with his recent engagement. His fiancée was another violinist, a woman he'd met in Brussels. Cassie was tempted to phone him long-distance, despite the cost; that way, they could really talk. Maybe expecting him to take on Jason if he married her was asking too much.

Then again, maybe he was truly in love with this other woman. Cassie was so confused she didn't know what to think. They'd been childhood sweethearts and had turned to each other whenever problems arose. She'd never stopped loving him and didn't think he'd stopped loving her, either.

Peeking in on Justin one more time, Cassie had to resist the impulse to kiss him, for fear of waking him. He looked like Susan while he slept, a fair-haired angel with flushed pink cheeks. Once again she felt that tug of emotion and hoped, somehow, that Justin's parents knew their little son was happy and well in Trace's home and heart.

In no time at all, Cassie had thanked Nattie and was following Trace outside to the BMW. Without giving her a choice, he ensconced her in the front seat. As he strapped his son in the back, she could tell he had some serious concern on his mind.

Once again he wore that look of determination. It made her uncomfortable, and she wished Jason was fussing so she'd have a reason to hold him in her arms as a buffer against Trace. But

Jason's eyelids were fluttering, which meant he was ready to fall asleep any second.

When they had driven away from the house and were headed for the motel, Trace darted her a swift glance. "I want Jason close to me, Cassie," he said, using her name for the first time. "I've already missed his first nine months, and I refuse to lose out on any more time. I can tell you want to be with Justin just as badly. Let's be honest and admit the odd weekend here, the three-day holiday there, will never be enough for either of us."

Cassie had been thinking hard about that, too. Already the wrench of having to leave Justin hurt unbearably. But how soon would she be able to break away from her work to fly here again? With Christmas only three weeks away, this was her busiest time.

The money made from holiday sales would support her and Jason for at least five or six months. She didn't dare lose out on her most lucrative time of year. And her other job, playing piano for ballet classes four mornings a week, made it impossible to get away for more than a couple of days at a time.

"I agree with you, Trace, but I don't have any solutions, because I'm swamped with work and I know you are, too. I was going to suggest we trade the children from time to time."

The angry sound that came out of him made her shiver and immediately told her she'd said the wrong thing.

"Out of the question. As far as I'm concerned, six months with one parent, then six with the other is no alternative."

"I don't see that we have a choice."

"There's always a choice," he muttered in what she imagined was his banker's voice. "You could move to Phoenix with Jason."

She jerked her head around and stared at him in astonishment. "That would be impossible. I may not own a banking corporation, but my business is just as important to me. It relies on a clientele that's been built up over two generations of sewing for people. My mother taught Susan and me the business. Now I've branched into handicrafts. I wouldn't even know where to start if I had to relocate to a different city."

At this point they arrived at the motel. Without responding to her remarks, he got out of the car and went into the office to get her luggage. Within minutes he'd stashed it into the trunk and was back in the driver's seat. Before starting the car, he pulled a little black book from his pocket and asked for her address and phone number in San Francisco. Grudgingly she gave him the information; then they drove in painful silence to the airport, where he found a vacant space in the short-term parking lot.

He didn't immediately get out of the car. Instead he turned to her with a dangerous glint in his eye. "I'm warning you now that if we can't work this out, I'll take you to court and sue for custody of Jason."

"You don't mean that!" she burst out angrily, but the grim set of his jaw told her he did. Her heart was pounding so fiercely she was sure he could hear it.

"I'm his natural father and I'll be able to provide for his financial well-being in a way you never could. There isn't a judge in the state who would allow you to keep him. Bear in mind that the hospital will be called in to prove paternity and it could get messy."

"You told me you didn't approve of people who sued other people," she said, her voice shaking in fear and fury.

His eyes narrowed menacingly. "If you recall, I said, 'in principle.' But we're talking about Jason here, and what's best for him. You've already told me you're not married or even engaged." *But only because she'd put off Rolfe one too many times. Maybe it still wasn't too late.* "In fact," he continued, "I gathered from our conversation at lunch that you're not even dating anyone special who could help you raise him. You've only taken care of him for two months. You're not his parent. You're not even related."

"Now you listen to me!" Cassie whispered hoarsely, trying not to wake Jason by shouting. "I love that child with every fiber of my being. You're not related to Justin, either!"

"Justin's been my son since birth, and no judge will take him away from me. As his aunt, the most you can expect will be liberal visitation rights and a bill for exorbitant court costs and attorney's fees. Think about it, and give me your answer tomorrow night. I'll phone you at ten."

"Give you *what* answer?" she lashed out. "Do you know what you're asking? That I leave my whole life behind and move to a strange city with no friends, no support system, just so you can have your cake and eat it, too?"

"Naturally I'll provide for you and make sure you're comfortably settled until you can get your business going here. With my contacts, you would have no problem. Would that be such a penance when it means we would both have daily contact with the boys for the rest of our lives?''

Cassie didn't want to hear another word. ''Aside from the fact that the idea is ludicrous, has it occurred to you what people would say? People who don't know the true situation? I noticed you didn't bother to explain anything to Mrs. Blakesley. She probably thinks I'm one of your mistresses who suddenly showed up to ask for money.''

''I'm not particularly worried about what Mrs. Blakesley thinks,'' he countered smoothly.

''Maybe you're not concerned about your reputation, but I value my good name more than that!''

''More than you value a life with Jason and Justin?'' His question was calculated to reduce her arguments to the trivial. But by now she was on to his tactics.

''You can phone me all day and all night, but it won't do you any good. I guess I'll have to take my chances and let the judge decide when I can spend time with Jason and my nephew. See you in court!''

She didn't, couldn't, hide the disgust and anger in her eyes or her voice. Jumping from the car, she yanked the back door and reached for Jason, who was still sleeping soundly. Trace finally got out of the car to collect her bags from the trunk.

Unable to bear his presence another second, she walked toward the terminal with the baby in one arm, her tote bag in the other. Right now she wanted to put as many miles as possible between them. All the way back to San Francisco, she regretted her trip to Phoenix and wished she'd never heard of Trace Ramsey.

CHAPTER THREE

CASSIE TAPPED on her neighbor's door and let herself in. "Beulah? I'm back."

After climbing all those steep streets from the ballet studio in the bitter cold, the apartment felt toasty and inviting. San Francisco had been locked in fog since the night she'd flown in from Phoenix more than a week ago. It seemed to penetrate everything, including the ski sweater she wore over her sweatshirt.

"I'm in the studio," Beulah Timpson called out. The older woman had been like a favorite aunt to Cassie and Susan, and had come close to being Cassie's mother-in-law. For as long as Cassie could remember, Beulah, a talented ceramist, had lived with her three children in the apartment above the Arnolds'.

Cassie and Susan had been best friends with Beulah's two daughters and her son, Rolfe. It was in her late teens that the close friendship Cassie shared with him gradually changed into something else. When Susan's and Cassie's mother fell ill with cancer, Rolfe became a source of strength. Cassie turned to him more and more, and learned she could always depend on him to offer help and compassion.

Soon after her mother's death, he told her he loved her and wanted to marry her. Cassie happily accepted his modest engagement ring; by that time they were both seniors at the university, studying music theory. He played the cello and she the piano.

Rolfe wanted to get married immediately after graduation, but Cassie couldn't see any reason for urgency, since they were constantly together, anyway, and had no money. She encouraged him to get his master's degree in music while she worked on expanding her home sewing business. A year down the road as a Ph.D student, he'd be able to earn extra money teaching under-

graduates. By that time, she would have saved enough money
for a small wedding and a honeymoon. They'd live in her apartment, since Susan had already married and moved to Arizona.

Unlike Susan, who married Ted within eight weeks of meeting
him, Cassie wasn't in any hurry. She needed time to regain her
emotional equilibrium first. The loss of their mother had been
bad enough. But when she received the horrifying news of Ted's
untimely death, Cassie went into a severe depression. At that
point, her constant worry about her pregnant sister, whose history
of chronic pneumonia put her at risk, made it impossible for
Cassie to think about her own needs, or Rolfe's.

Then came a night when everything changed. For the first time
since she'd known him, Rolfe didn't seem to understand. In fact,
he refused to hear any more excuses and demanded that she set
a wedding date—the sooner the better. Since they'd already been
over that ground more than once, Cassie was surprised by his
demands. She'd never seen him so insistent and unyielding. She
asked him to leave the apartment, saying they'd talk again in the
morning, when their nerves weren't so frayed.

But he stayed where he was. In a voice that shocked her with
its anger, he accused her of using him. Cassie shook her head in
denial, but he was obviously too hurt to listen to reason and asked
for his ring back. When she begged him to be patient a little
longer, the bitterness in his eyes revealed his hurt and disillu-
sionment. He retorted that he hadn't pressured her to live with
him because she didn't approve of premarital sex. And since she
couldn't set a date for the wedding, he had to conclude she
wasn't in love with him.

Cassie hadn't been prepared for that, nor for his declaration
that he'd been offered a fellowship to study in Belgium and had
decided to accept it. He held out his hand and Cassie wordlessly
returned the ring.

He left at spring break, plunging her into a different kind of
despair, one of profound loneliness. But by then Jason had been
born and Susan was seriously ill. Looking back on that dreadful
period, Cassie wondered how she'd survived at all. If Jason
hadn't needed a mother's love and attention even before Susan
died, Cassie might have died of grief herself. And still Rolfe
stayed away.

Through it all, Beulah never pried or made judgments. As a

result, the two of them were able to remain firm friends. Now that her children lived in other parts of the state, Beulah seemed to encourage Cassie's friendship, even volunteering to tend Jason in the mornings.

Walking through the apartment to the workroom, Cassie found the older woman at her potter's wheel. She stopped short when she didn't see the playpen. "Where's Jason?"

Beulah was throwing clay and didn't pause in her movements. "He's downstairs in your apartment with his daddy."

"Beulah! You didn't!"

"I did." She concentrated on her work for a moment. "First of all, he's not here to kidnap Jason. He assured me of that and I believe him." Her voice was calm and matter-of-fact. She glanced up at Cassie, smiling. "The two of them are carbon copies of each other, just like you said. Since Jason seemed perfectly happy to go with him, I couldn't see that it would hurt. I never saw a man so crazy about a child in my life. Watching them together made my Christmas."

All the while she was talking, Cassie held on to the nearest counter for support. *She should have known he would come.* Hanging up on him every time he called had probably infuriated him. But she had none of the answers he wanted to hear.

After agonizing over the situation for endless hours, Cassie had decided a judge would have to sort it out. Though she ached to know and love Justin, it was clear that her nephew's world was complete and revolved around Trace. If she was patient, the law would eventually dictate visitation rights so she could get close to Susan's son.

As for Jason, she'd hang on to him as long as possible. There was no doubt in her mind that she'd lose him in the custody battle Trace was planning. In fact, he'd probably come to San Francisco to make sure she'd given him the right address before he had her served with papers. His presence meant she couldn't prolong the inevitable confrontation.

"Well? Aren't you going to go find the man and say hello? He flew all the way from Phoenix early this morning to see you. What are you afraid of?"

"I'm going to lose Jason."

"Nonsense. From everything you've told me about him, he isn't the kind of man who'd cut you out of Jason's life. Especially once he knows the personal sacrifice you went through trying to find him in the first place. Cassandra Arnold, it's because of you that he's been united with a son he didn't know existed. Do you think he's going to forget a thing like that? Or the fact that Justin is Susan's child?''

"You weren't there when he threatened me with a custody suit." She shuddered at the memory.

"No, I wasn't. But that was a week ago, and he's had time to think since then. So have you. The least you can do is hear what he has to say. You owe him that much after refusing to take his phone calls.''

Since there was no help from that quarter, the only thing left to do was go downstairs and see him, get it over with.

A feeling of dread formed a knot in her stomach as she thanked Beulah and headed for the ground-floor apartment, which was the only home she'd ever known.

After their mother's death, Cassie and Susan had taken over her business and pooled all their resources so they could continue to live there. When Susan and Ted moved to Arizona because of his job, Cassie stayed in the apartment. Although half the contents went off to Phoenix in the moving van, the place was still crowded to overflowing with furniture and mementos accrued over a lifetime. Cassie took the opportunity to clean house and quickly turned her home into a crafts shop of sorts. Right now, it was filled with Christmas orders—quilts, afghans, wall hangings, pillows, rag dolls, hand puppets, stuffed animals... The list went on and on.

Every nook and cranny of the small living and dining room contained evidence of her handiwork. Trace wouldn't be able to find a place to sit down. Even the top of the upright piano and bench were covered with stuffed Santas, reindeer and gingerbread men.

The two bedrooms were even worse. She kept her sewing machine and all the patterns and materials in her room, which hardly left enough space for her to crawl into bed at night.

Jason's room had become the depository for the larger stuffed animals and figures. They stood side by side, lined up against all four walls.

By Christmas Eve she should be able to find her furniture again. She'd had to put their two-foot Christmas tree with its homemade ornaments in the middle of the kitchen table. Jason loved the miniature lights and stared at them in fascination while he played with his food.

Taking a deep breath, Cassie entered the kitchen through the back door. She could hear Jason's shrieks of delight coming from the vicinity of his room. He was obviously thrilled to have his father there, and Cassie had to admit that fatherhood seemed to come naturally to Trace. It was possible that he'd already been given a court date; in that case, it wouldn't be long before Jason went to live with him and Justin.

She felt a pain in her heart as real as if she'd been jabbed with a knife. Maybe it was best he had come, after all. She couldn't live with the anxiety any longer.

Pushing the bedroom door open a little wider, she peeked inside. Jason was sitting in front of Trace, who was dressed in cords and a crew-neck black sweater, lying full-length on the carpet with his back toward her. His dark head rested on the five-foot-long green alligator Cassie had made for Susan. She'd added yellow yarn, to represent Susan's blond hair, and sewn the word "mommy" on the tail.

In Trace's hand was the eighteen-inch baby alligator with a green-and-yellow body and black yarn for hair; it bore Jason's name on the tail. He continued to tease Jason, tickling him gently and making him laugh so hard he was thrashing his arms and legs.

Suddenly Jason saw Cassie. He pointed a finger and tried to say, "Ma-ma," but couldn't get the words out and laugh at the same time. Alert to his every movement, Trace turned over on his back, resting his hand on the alligator's head.

His blue eyes searched hers for a long breathless moment. At least they didn't freeze her out as they'd done at the airport. "Hello, Cassie." Slowly his gaze traveled from her sweater-clad figure to her windblown hair and cheeks turned pink from the cold outside. "Your neighbor let us in. She seemed to think it would be all right."

Strangely affected by the intimacy of his look, Cassie smoothed the curls from her forehead in a nervous gesture. "I'm sorry you couldn't find a place to sit."

A smile lurked at the corner of his mouth. "Since Justin came into my life, I've discovered the floor is a wonderful place to be.

You meet all kinds of fascinating creatures." He rubbed his thumb over the alligator's glassy eyes. "Do you know I'm feeling deprived? There's no daddy alligator. I'm putting in an order for one right now. About six feet long with wild black hair and a scary grin, just like Jason's."

It sounded very much as if he was extending the olive branch. How could he be talking this way when they had resolved nothing? She was still reeling from the bitterness of their last encounter.

"Come on, Jason. It's time for a nap." She stepped over Trace and scooped the baby up from the floor. Trace stayed where he was while she changed Jason's diaper and put him in his crib with a bottle. It was actually time for his lunch, but she'd feed him later, after his father had left.

Right now she needed to know what Trace had on his mind, and she didn't want Jason upset if the conversation turned into another angry battle. "Let's go into the kitchen. Jason will settle down in a little while."

By tacit agreement they left him crying. She knew he was wailing out his disappointment and fury; he'd been having such a wonderful time, and then she'd come along and spoiled everything. It didn't make Cassie feel any better. But this talk with Trace was crucial—and there was no sense in postponing it.

When they reached the kitchen, she offered him a seat and began to fix cocoa for both of them. Nobody was going to say she was uncivilized on the way to her execution!

Because of the fog, the room was darker than usual, and the lights on the tree twinkled all the more cheerfully. Suddenly she felt too warm, with Trace so close and vital and alive. She pulled off her ski sweater and hung it over a chair back.

When she'd prepared the hot chocolate, she placed their mugs on the table and sat down opposite him. Briskly pushing the sleeves of her navy sweatshirt up to the elbows, she began, "I shouldn't have hung up on you—" she paused for a deep breath "—even though I was angrier than I've ever been in my life."

"I wasn't exactly on my best behavior last week," he admitted gravely. "Court isn't where I want to settle our problems."

Cassie had been expecting to hear anything but that. "I—know how much you love Jason. He's your flesh and blood. The problem is I love him, too." Her voice had that awful quiver again. "And I love Justin because he's part of my flesh and blood."

"I know." He sounded totally sincere.

She raised tortured eyes to him. "No matter how I try to come up with a satisfying compromise, it sounds horrible becau—"

"Because that's precisely what it is. A compromise," he finished for her. "The only way I see out of our dilemma is to get married. That's why I'm here. To ask you to consider the idea seriously."

"Married?" She felt the blood drain from her face. In the interim that followed, Jason's cries sounded louder than ever.

Trace took a long swallow of cocoa. "Surely I don't have to point out the advantages to you. With everything legal, your reputation won't suffer, Justin and Jason will have a mother *and* a father, and we'll have the joy of raising the children together in our own home."

"But we don't love each other!"

He gazed steadily into her eyes. "Our marriage will be a business arrangement. Separate bedrooms. You'll be able to start up your crafts shop in Phoenix without the worry of having to meet the monthly bills. And I'll have the satisfaction of going to work every day knowing the boys are with the only person who could ever love them as much as I do."

Her hands tightened around the mug. "But you're still young, Trace. One day you'll meet someone you truly want to marry. Just because your first marriage didn't work out doesn't mean there isn't someone else in your future."

"That works both ways, Cassie," he said in a deceptively soft voice. "You're a very attractive woman. I'm surprised you didn't get married years ago." *Rolfe tried,* a niggling voice reminded Cassie. "But the fact remains, I've been married once in the full sense of the word and have no particular desire to repeat the experience. As far as I'm concerned, the only issue of importance here is the children. They need *us,* you and me. And they need *us now!* Some experts say that the first three years of a child's life form his character forever. If that's true, I would prefer if you and I were the ones guiding and shaping the boys' lives."

She couldn't sustain his penetrating glance and pushed herself away from the table. In two steps she'd reached the window, but even if the mist hadn't been so thick, she wouldn't have seen anything.

What Trace Ramsey had proposed was a marriage in name only. A marriage of convenience, her mother would have called it. Cassie had heard the term, but she'd never known anyone who had entered into such an arrangement. It sounded so cold-blooded. No expectations of physical or romantic love. Just a convenient solution to a problem that concerned them both. The children needed parents, and she and Trace Ramsey could honorably fill that need and still stay emotionally uninvolved.

She heard the scrape of Trace's chair against the linoleum as he stood up and came to stand next to her. "I know what you're thinking, Cassie. You're considerably younger than I am, and you have a right to a life of your own. But as long as we're discreet, we could see other people on the side, no questions asked. If some time down the road either of us wanted out of our contract to marry someone else, well...we'd face that when it happened."

She gripped the edges of the sink so hard her knuckles turned white. "I think you're forgetting your ex-wife. Maybe she never bonded with Justin because, like Susan, she sensed he wasn't her baby. If she was to see Jason, isn't it possible she'd fall in love with him? I could certainly understand if she wanted another chance at marriage with you under those circumstances."

Cassie wheeled around so she could read his honest reaction but that was a mistake. Her kitchen was minuscule even with no one in it; now, with Trace blocking her path and the faint scent of his soap filling her nostrils, she felt almost claustrophobic.

"I'm way ahead of you, Cassie," he replied evenly, his hands on his hips. "I phoned her the evening you left Phoenix, but she was still in chambers so I sent her an overnight letter."

"And?" She held her breath, unsure what she wanted Trace to tell her.

"She never responded."

"Maybe she hasn't had time, or hasn't even seen the letter."

"You're very generous to make excuses for her, but no." He shook his head. "I talked with Sabie, her housekeeper. Glori read the letter."

"And she didn't want to see Jason immediately?" Cassie cried, incredulous.

"I knew she wouldn't. But on the off chance that she'd gone through a complete character change, I told her to let me know and I would make it possible for her to spend time with Jason. Otherwise, if I didn't hear from her, I would assume it made no difference to her."

"But Jason is her own baby!"

Something flickered in his eyes. "Not all women have motherly feelings, Cassie. She never pretended to be anything but what she is, a remarkable attorney who is now a city-court judge and hopes to one day sit on the Supreme Court."

Cassie couldn't comprehend it. Talk about opposites attracting! She might search the earth and not come up with a more caring, devoted father than Trace. "Did you know she felt this way before you married her?" she asked in a quiet voice.

"If I hadn't made her pregnant, we would never have married."

She swallowed hard as she tried to take in what he was saying. "Didn't you love her?"

"We cared for each other. We also understood each other. Marriage was never in our plans, and I knew she'd give up the baby for adoption. I found I couldn't let her do that, so I struck a bargain with her. We would stay married long enough to satisfy protocol, then divorce with the understanding that I received custody of the child."

She blinked. "How often does she visit Justin?"

"She doesn't. She never has."

"Not once?" Her eyes grew huge.

He reached out and smoothed a stray curl from her forehead. At his touch her body trembled. The same gesture from Rolfe had never affected her this way. "That's why her lack of response to my letter doesn't surprise me. Is there anything else I can clear up for you?"

Needing to put distance between them, she slid past him and gathered the mugs from the table. "What would your family think?"

His wry smile seemed to mock her. "Whatever we want them to think. We can tell them that the moment we met, it was love at first sight. Or we can say nothing and let them draw their own conclusions. I'm a big boy now. I don't need my family's approval for what I do."

Her mouth had gone so dry she could hardly swallow. "I don't like lies."

"Then we'll tell them the truth. That we've decided to get married to provide a home for Justin and Jason. Period."

When he put it like that, so bluntly, she didn't know what to say. "E-Excuse me a minute, I have to check on the baby."

To her surprise he shifted his position, preventing her from leaving the kitchen. "I have a better idea. I'll leave—to give you time to think over my proposal. I'm at the Fairmont. Call me there when you've made your decision."

Her heart started to hammer. "How long will you be in San Francisco?"

"As long as it takes to get an answer from you."

She averted her eyes. "If the answer's no, what will you do?"

The muscles of his face went taut. "You're going to say yes. The boys need you too much. In your heart, you know it's the only solution. What was it your sister said before she died—*Find my son and take care of him for me?* Now you can honor her request and be Jason's mother at the same time."

On that note he disappeared from the kitchen and out the front door of the apartment.

So many thoughts and emotions converged at once that Cassie couldn't stand still. As if on automatic pilot, she tiptoed to Jason's room and discovered him sound asleep in a corner of his crib, with his cheek lying on his bottle.

The poor darling had finally worn himself out. Gently she pulled the bottle away and covered him with a light blanket. She thought of seeing him only on holidays, of missing his first steps and not being able to take him to kindergarten on his first day of school....

If she married Trace, she would have the luxury of being a mother to Justin, as well. The four of them would be a real family, in almost all the ways that mattered. Many things about Trace still remained a mystery, but the one thing she knew beyond any doubt was his devotion to the boys.

Not every man would have married his lover to obtain custody of his unborn child. And a small voice told her not every man would have wanted Jason on sight—no matter that Jason was the son of his body, no matter how precious he was. In that regard Trace Ramsey was a remarkable man.

Was it enough? Would it be enough for her? Could she marry him knowing the most important ingredient in the marriage was missing? Knowing that because of their loveless arrangement, she would never have a baby of her own?

Maybe Trace could conduct an affair on the side; in all probability he was seeing someone right now. But Cassie wasn't made that way and knew herself far too well. Perhaps her ideas were old-fashioned and out of date, but if she took marriage vows, she would hold them sacred until she died. Or until Trace asked her for a divorce....

Was that what worried her most? That one day he would fall deeply in love and want a real marriage with the woman who had captured his heart? The thought left Cassie feeling strangely out of sorts and depressed, which made no sense at all.

She'd wondered more and more about the things Rolfe had said to her the night he'd walked out. With hindsight, she could see how much she'd hurt him by putting him off. But during that long dark period, she hadn't been capable of making a decision, hadn't been ready to make a commitment. Instead of clinging to him as his wife, she'd left him hanging while she dealt with her grief.

And her refusal to go to bed with him had probably planted more seeds of doubt. But Cassie's mother had raised her girls to value their virginity, to reserve physical passion for their husbands. That was why Susan was so eager to get married. In fact, Susan's intense feelings for Ted were so different from Cassie's easygoing, comfortable relationship with Rolfe they weren't even in the same league.

Susan and Ted couldn't stay away from each other, couldn't keep their hands off each other. Cassie had never been able to relate to those feelings. She loved Rolfe and always would, but she could wait until their honeymoon to express her love.

If she married Trace, there would be no problems in that area because he wouldn't be making physical demands on her. He'd be seeing other women. She was sure he'd be the soul of discretion. The little she knew about Trace told her he'd go to great lengths to keep his private life private, so no gossip could hurt the boys. They meant everything to him.

So why was she hesitating? Was she hoping against hope that Rolfe would break his engagement and come back to San Fran-

cisco to take up where they'd left off? How had Rolfe been able
to fall in love with another woman so fast? Was it because his
fiancée was willing to sleep with him? Cassie tried not to think
about him sharing intimacies with anyone else, because it hurt.
And, she supposed, because it was humiliating.

If they *were* sleeping together, that meant Rolfe wasn't really
missing Cassie. And if that was true, then he'd gotten over the
pain of Cassie's rejection and was making plans for a future that
didn't include her. But it hadn't been a rejection, only a plea for
more time.

So where did that leave Cassie? She had no guarantee that a
man would ever come along to love her, body and soul. At least
if she married Trace, she'd be able to indulge her longing to be
a mother. Otherwise she would remain on the fringes of Jason
and Justin's lives, never really involved. She couldn't bear that.

For the rest of the day she kept busy playing with Jason and
putting the finishing touches on an order for a pear tree with
partridges. After six o'clock, the doorbell rang continuously with
customers placing and picking up orders.

Not until she'd tucked Jason into bed and cleaned the kitchen
did Cassie work up enough nerve to reach for the phone. It was
almost eleven and she'd run out of reasons not to call. She'd
made her decision.

Her heart pounded in her ears as she asked to be put through
to Trace Ramsey's room, but after ten rings and no answer she
hung up. Maybe he was out, or had gone to bed. Whatever the
case, she'd have to wait until morning.

Perhaps it was just as well. If she awakened tomorrow still
feeling she was doing the right thing, then she'd try to call him
again.

Feeling oddly deflated despite her tension, she unplugged the
Christmas-tree lights and took a long hot shower. She checked
on Jason one final time, then hurried into her own bedroom, eager
for sleep. As she turned down the covers, she thought she heard
a knock at the door.

Beulah was the only person who ever bothered her this late at
night, and she always phoned first. Cassie had never had trouble
before, but there could always be a first time. With the stealth of
a cat she tiptoed to the living room and listened to see if she'd
been mistaken.

After a minute she heard another rap. "Cassie?" a voice called out in hushed tones. "It's Trace. Are you still up? I didn't want to wake Jason if I could help it."

Trace?

A kind of sick excitement welled up inside her. She braced her hand against the door for support.

"Just a minute," she whispered and rushed to the bedroom for a robe. After opening the door she belatedly remembered that her hair was still damp from the shower. Her natural curls had tightened into a mop of ringlets that only a good brushing could tame.

He stared down at her, the hint of a smile lurking in his startling blue eyes. The moist night wind off the bay had tousled his hair, and he wore a fashionable bomber-style jacket made of a dark brown suede. Cassie had no idea he could look so...so...

"The answer's yes, isn't it?" he said matter-of-factly. "Otherwise you'd have called me hours ago and told me to go back to Phoenix and start court proceedings. Because one thing you're not, Cassie, is a coward."

CHAPTER FOUR

"MISS ARNOLD?" Nattie's voice carried to Justin's bedroom, which now contained a second bed for Jason.

Cassie turned as Trace's housekeeper entered the nursery. "Can't you and Mike bring yourselves to call me Cassie? I realize Trace only brought me and Jason to Phoenix twenty-four hours ago, but you and your husband have been so wonderful helping us to settle in, I feel like we're good friends already."

The older woman's eyes lit up. "If you're sure."

"I am. So, what is it?" She returned to the job of fastening an uncooperative Jason into his new outfit.

"Trace asked me to take over in here so you can finish getting dressed. He's one man who likes to be on time—particularly for his own wedding. I'll finish doing those buttons and take Jason downstairs to Justin and his daddy."

"I appreciate the offer, but he's dressed now," Cassie murmured as she slipped on his little white shoes and tied them with a double knot so he wouldn't kick them off. She gave him a kiss on the cheek and handed him to Nattie, who promptly carried him out of the room.

Cassie followed her more slowly and then headed to her own room. There were three guest bedrooms on the upstairs floor of the house, with the nursery at one end and Trace's private suite of rooms at the other. Since he'd told Cassie to choose a bedroom for herself, she'd picked the one closest to the children. That way she'd be able to hear them if they cried during the night.

Though the smallest of the three, her room had its own ensuite bathroom, and the wicker furniture plus the charming window seat created a cozy feeling that immediately made her feel at home. She'd already spent several hours gazing out over the fascinating desert landscape, with the mountains in the distance.

Off-white walls and soft yellow trim blended beautifully to give the room a timeless dreamy feeling. Large green plants stood grouped in one corner; they were reflected in the sheen of flawless hardwood floors stained a warm honey tone.

Cassie couldn't wait to design an area rug that would incorporate the room's colors in all their subtlety. But her thoughts were far removed from that particular project as she finished dressing for her wedding.

If the image in the mirror didn't lie, she *looked* like a bride. She wore the trappings of a bride—large, marquise-shaped emerald ring on the third finger of her left hand, matching emeralds on her ears, which were a wedding present from Trace, a cascade of orange blossoms on the shoulder of her simple white Thai silk dress with its scooped neck.

Five weeks ago she'd been living with Jason in San Francisco, heartbroken over her sister's death and Rolfe's engagement, working furiously at two jobs in order to build a business that kept her busy all hours of the day and night.

Right now, that Cassie seemed a different person. Trace had pampered her so thoroughly she hardly recognized herself anymore. Once she'd agreed to marry him, he had taken time off from his banking affairs to stay in San Francisco both before and after Christmas. He'd helped her with Jason and made all the preparations for the marriage and her move to Phoenix. Meanwhile she'd wound up her business and called her old friends with the news—friends she'd hardly seen in the past three years. Her responsibilities had made a social life impossible.

Not since Rolfe's tenderness at the time of her mother's death had she experienced anything approaching this extraordinary feeling of being looked after, taken care of. In fact, Beulah—who to Cassie's surprise approved of their forthcoming marriage—commented that all Cassie had to do was mention something and Trace had it done before she turned around.

When Cassie asked if they could be married before she met his family, with only the babies and Nattie and Mike for witnesses, Trace agreed to her wishes and arranged a private ceremony at the county clerk's office.

In certain ways, Trace was the equivalent of a fairy godfather, and even if their marriage wasn't a normal one, she knew she was a very lucky woman. She told herself not to dwell on the past or reminisce about what might have been. But it was impossible to forget that for most of her life she had imagined walking down the aisle with Rolfe.

Without conscious thought she pulled his framed picture from a box of mementos she hadn't yet put away. She sank down on the bed to study his lean, ascetic face one more time. She couldn't help wondering what he'd thought when he received her letter. She'd informed Rolfe that she was planning to be married after Christmas. She'd told him the truth—that she'd accepted Trace's proposal in order to be a legitimate mother to both boys. She also admitted that she still loved him, that she would always love him and hoped he'd forgive her for ever hurting him.

When there was no return letter from Belgium, Cassie had to accept the fact that he was truly lost to her, but it still hurt. "Oh, Rolfe..." She wept quietly for the many memories and the dream that was gone.

"*Cassie?* Are you ready yet?"

At the sound of footsteps she panicked and thrust the picture beneath one of the pillows on her bed. But she was too late. Trace had seen the betraying gesture and in a few swift strides crossed the room and reached for the frame.

After studying the photo for several seconds, he raised his head and stared at the moisture beading her eyelashes. "I've seen this man's picture before. In Beulah Timpson's place."

His face hardened and a dull red tinged his smooth-shaven cheek and jaw. She was immediately reminded of the implacable man she'd originally met, the one who had accused her of being part of a kidnapping scheme. "What's going on, Cassie? When I brought you here to see Justin that first day, you told me you were unattached. I assumed you were telling the truth." His voice barely concealed his anger.

Cassie slid off the bed, furious with herself for having inadvertently caused this friction when he'd gone out of his way to make everything so wonderful. From the beginning Trace had been completely honest with her; he deserved the same consideration.

"I grew up with Rolfe," she began in a low voice. "We were once engaged, but things didn't work out. He asked for his ring back, and now he's engaged to someone else, someone he met

in Europe. I was saying goodbye to past memories. That's all.''
She gazed straight at him as she spoke.

Trace searched her eyes, as if looking for some little piece of
truth she might have withheld. "The ceremony takes place at
eleven. We still have forty-five minutes. It's not too late to back
out."

"No!" she cried instantly, surprising even herself with her
vehemence.

He pondered her outburst for an uncomfortably long moment.
"Be very sure, Cassie—and not just for the boys' sake."

For some reason his comment sent her pulses racing. "I am,"
she answered without hesitation, realizing she meant it.

He squared his shoulders and the tautness of his facial muscles
seemed to relax. He tossed the picture onto a stack of photos
piled in a cardboard box beside her bed. "Let's go, shall we?"

The next hour flew by as Mike took pictures of Cassie and
Trace holding the children, both before and after they arrived at
the courthouse. Justin fussed because he'd come down with a
cold. When the justice of the peace appeared and announced that
it was time, Justin didn't want to let go of Trace, and that started
Jason crying, too. Poor Nattie and Mike had to hold the children
and try to pacify them while Trace grasped Cassie's hand and
led her to the center of the room.

Despite the noise and impersonal surroundings, Cassie felt the
solemnity of the occasion and wished more than ever that her
mother and Susan were alive to share this moment with her. They
would have loved Trace on sight. Not even Beulah was immune.

Out of the corner of her eye she darted a glance at her hus-
band-to-be, who stood erect and confident. His snowy white shirt
and midnight-blue suit not only enhanced his attractiveness but
underlined his power; the red carnation he wore in his lapel
added a note of festivity and joy. *I'm actually marrying this man,*
she mused in awe and felt her heart turn over.

The justice of the peace bestowed a warm smile on them.
"Cassandra Arnold and Trace Ellingsworth Ramsey, after this
ceremony, today will be the first day of your life as a married
couple. You've come together in the sight of God and these witnesses to pledge your troth. Do you know what that means?"
He eyed them soberly, capturing Cassie's whole attention.

"It means commitment and sacrifice. It means enduring to the end, long after the fires of passion are tempered with the earning of your daily bread. It means forgetting self and living to make the other person happy, no matter the season or circumstances. Will you do that, Cassandra? In front of these two witnesses, do you take this man, of your own free will, to be your lawfully wedded husband?''

Cassie felt Trace's heavy-lidded gaze upon her. "Yes.''

"And you, Trace? Of your own free will and in front of these two witnesses, are you willing to take Cassandra to be your lawfully wedded wife, to assume this solemn responsibility of caring for her all the days of your life? Are you willing to put her before all others, emotionally, mentally and physically?''

Cassie thought his hand tightened around hers. "Yes,'' came the grave reply.

"If you have rings to exchange, now is the time. You first, Cassandra.''

Cassie had been wearing the simple gold band she'd bought for Trace on her middle finger so she wouldn't lose it. She quickly removed it and slid it on Trace's ring finger. The fit was perfect, and he gave her a private smile that unaccountably stirred her senses.

"Now you, Trace.''

Cassie held out her left hand so Trace could nestle the white-gold wedding band next to the beautiful emerald engagement ring he'd given her on the plane as they'd flown to Phoenix. His movements were sure and steady.

"That's fine.'' The officiant smiled once more. "Now, by the power invested in me by the state of Arizona, I pronounce you husband and wife. It's not part of the official ceremony to kiss the bride, but...''

Before the man had even finished speaking, Trace's head descended and his mouth swiftly covered Cassie's as he pulled her close, sending a voluptuous warmth through her body. Cassie hadn't expected more than a chaste kiss on the lips. She wasn't prepared for the heady sensation that left her clinging to the lapels of his suit.

"Ma-Ma! Ma-ma!'' Jason's and Justin's cries slowly penetrated her consciousness. Cassie moaned in shock and embarrassment, and broke the kiss Trace seemed reluctant to end. In that split second before she turned her burning face away, she thought she saw a smoldering look in his eyes. But by the time he lifted his head, it was gone. She decided she'd imagined it.

Moving out of her husband's arms, she shook the officiant's outstretched hand and thanked him, then hurried over to Nattie. Still holding Jason, the older woman gave her an awkward hug and murmured her congratulations. She handed the uncontrollable child to Cassie with a wry smile of relief.

He calmed down at once and started pulling orange blossoms out of her corsage. Trace was equally busy trying to pacify Justin, while Mike continued to take pictures. Cassie took one look at the flush on Justin's fair skin and said, "Trace, I think we'd better leave for the hotel. Justin should be in bed. He needs something to bring down his fever."

Within a few minutes the children were strapped into their seats in the back of Trace's sedan. Cassie hugged Mike and Nattie and thanked them again for everything, then at Trace's urging got into the car and they drove off.

The resort hotel, a few miles away in Scottsdale, had sent a basket of fruit and a congratulatory bottle of champagne to their suite. There were also two cribs; amused, Cassie wondered what the management thought about that as she busied herself putting the boys to bed, while Trace dealt with all the baby bags and luggage.

The hotel offered baby-sitting services, but Cassie didn't feel comfortable about leaving Jason and Justin with a stranger just yet. She urged Trace to go for a swim in the pool and relax. But he insisted on staying to help her settle the children, after he'd ordered lunch to be served in the room where he'd put his bags.

By the time both boys had fallen into an uneasy—and, as it turned out, short-lived—sleep, their lunch was more or less ruined. The pasta with its cream sauce had grown cold, the salad was soggy, the chilled white wine room-temperature. Cassie was too tired and anxious to care. All her attention was focused not on her new husband but on the two miserable little boys. Trace seemed equally distracted.

What should have been a fun three-day holiday, a chance for the four of them to really get to know each other, lasted exactly one sleepless night. Justin couldn't keep anything in his stomach; he was content only when Cassie or Trace held him. And as soon as Jason saw that Cassie's attention was diverted from him, he

wailed loudly, and not even Trace could settle him down for
long.

At eight the next morning, they packed up the car and drove
home, frustrated and completely exhausted. It had become apparent that they would have to take Justin to his pediatrician as
soon as they got home; in fact, Trace had called ahead from the
hotel. Leaving Jason with Nattie, the three of them went to the
clinic. Cassie was anxious to meet the man who'd been taking
care of Justin, because he would automatically become Jason's
doctor, as well.

Although Justin didn't have anything seriously wrong, several
days went by before he was restored to his normal sweet dis-
position. Several weary, emotionally draining days, especially for
Cassie. She'd spent all her time with the children since Trace
had returned to his office to deal with some very delicate nego-
tiations in his planned buy-out of a small Southwest banking
chain.

Then, on Friday morning Trace shocked her by announcing
that he'd invited everyone in his family to an informal garden
party that evening to meet his new wife and son. Understandably
enough, they were consumed with curiosity about his unexpected
marriage. Gathering all the relatives under one roof, he told Cassie, would provide the perfect opportunity to reveal the switch
and to explain their subsequent decision to marry for the boys'
sake.

Intellectually, Cassie saw the wisdom in getting it over with
as soon as possible. Emotionally, she was numb.

Alone with Trace and the boys, she could relax as she performed the normal duties of a busy mother without worrying
about others' reactions to their platonic union. Tonight, however,
she would be on trial in front of a roomful of Trace's relatives—
people who would draw their own conclusions about her motives
for marrying a man who wasn't in love with her.

She couldn't blame them if they believed her to be a merce-
nary person attracted to his money and social prominence, someone willing to be bought in exchange for mothering his sons.

None of them would understand her bond with Jason or the
happiness it brought her to raise him as her own son. Only Trace
knew.

Cassie dressed in the same outfit she'd worn to her wedding

and put on a fresh spray of orange blossoms Trace had thought-fully sent her. Needing her husband's support as never before, she took a deep calming breath as she prepared to meet his fam-ily. She clutched Jason in her arms, hugging him tight, then mus-tered her courage and walked slowly downstairs.

From the landing she searched for Trace's dark hair among the group assembled on the patio. But she soon realized black hair dominated the family scene; there was only a sprinkling of sandy-brown and russet hair. She gazed down at the group, pan-icking just a little as she realized that the adults and children chatting with one another numbered at least forty.

Justin sat contentedly on his grandmother's lap, examining her pearl necklace—real pearls, Cassie was sure. His hair gleamed a pale gold in contrast to her coal-black tresses, swept back in an elegant chignon. His complexion was pale against her darker skin. Somewhere in her ancestry there must have been Indian blood. Even at seventy, Trace's mother was the most beautiful woman Cassie had ever seen. In fact, the whole family had more than its fair share of tall, good-looking people.

There was a sudden hush as Cassie walked out on the patio. Rolfe had often called her his "pocket Venus." And right now she was more aware than ever of her full curves and diminutive height. She felt even more conspicuous being the only person, aside from Justin, with a head of golden blond curls.

To her relief, Trace broke off his conversation with a man she guessed to be one of his brothers and strode toward her. In a light tan suit with an off-white Italian silk shirt open at the neck, he looked so incredibly handsome Cassie purposely glanced else-where to prevent herself from staring.

She thought he would reach for Jason. Instead, he slid a pos-sessive arm around her waist and held her tightly against him. In confusion she gazed up at him, only to discover his eyes wan-dering over her face with unmistakable admiration.

At breakfast he had told her she would have nothing to worry about at the party. All she had to do was behave naturally and follow his lead. The trouble was, his act was too convincing, and she was distressed to find herself wondering how it would feel to be truly loved by this man. This complex man who presented a formidable, dynamic front to the public, yet could reduce her to tears with his sweetness when he kissed his sons good-night.

He turned to his family. "I know it came as a shock to hear that Cassie and I were married over the weekend. But what was I to do? My charming bride burst into my office a couple of months ago with an astonishing story—that Justin was really her nephew and that this little tiger was my natural son."

He reached for Jason, who'd been trying to wriggle out of Cassie's arms to get to his father. "It seems the babies were switched at birth." He paused dramatically at the incredulous murmurs around him. "We have subsequently found out that because of a disaster that stretched hospital resources to the limit, the infant intensive-care unit ran out of wrist tape. One of the nurses sent an orderly for more. When he returned, the identification bracelets were inadvertently put on the wrong babies."

The family's stunned reaction proved to be even greater than Cassie had imagined. For five minutes pandemonium reigned. It took another five before everybody settled down enough so that Trace could continue with the details. He briefly described the background—Ted's accidental death and Susan's unsuccessful struggle to throw off pneumonia, Susan's belief that Jason wasn't her son and Cassie's taking on the responsibility not only of raising her nephew but of uncovering the truth.

He kissed the top of Jason's curly head and unexpectedly smoothed a wayward lock of hair from Cassie's brow. Then, with a smile lighting his eyes, he said, "To make a long story short, the four of us got along so famously, we didn't want the fun to stop. So we decided to become a family." The sudden tremor in his voice added the perfect touch, almost convincing Cassie it wasn't an act. "Cassie, please meet my mother, Olivia Ramsey."

He turned to face the older woman. "Mother, may I present my wife, Cassandra Arnold Ramsey, and my son, Jason?"

"Trace!" Her cry held the joy Cassie had hoped to hear, dispelling her anxiety that Trace's mother wouldn't accept her new grandson—or her daughter-in-law.

While one of the wives relieved the older woman of Justin, Trace helped her to her feet. Dressed in deep-rose silk, she walked toward Cassie with the dignity of a queen.

"Welcome to the family, darling." She embraced Cassie warmly, then stood back, holding her lightly by the upper arms. Her deep-set, clear gray eyes searched Cassie's as if she were gazing into her very soul.

"I can't tell you how happy, how thrilled, I am by this news. Trace is my baby and he's always been my greatest worry. To see him settled at last, with a beautiful wife and two lovely children, has given me a whole new lease on life."

"Thank you, Mrs. Ramsey." Cassie could hardly form the words after the older woman's loving reception. That Trace's mother adored her youngest son was obvious. Cassie felt a sudden surge of guilt; she hated deceiving anyone, particularly this welcoming and truly gracious woman.

"Cassie, please feel free to call me Olivia, like my other daughters-in-law. 'Mrs. Ramsey' is so formal, isn't it?"

Cassie nodded, not trusting herself to speak as she blinked back tears.

"Mother?" Trace gently interrupted. "How about saying hello to my son. Jason?" He turned the baby around. "This is Nana. Na-na."

"Oh, Trace!" she cried, reaching for Jason, who showed all the signs of bursting into tears at the sight of so many strangers. "I can't believe I'm not thirty-three years old and holding you in my arms again. He's identical to you. Look, everybody! Another heartbreaker!"

Heartbreaker is right, Cassie thought, allowing herself a covert glance at her husband. He had probably been attracting the attention of the opposite sex since he'd been old enough to crawl!

But before she could dwell on that curiously disheartening fact, she and the baby were suddenly besieged with hugs and kisses. Such spontaneous warmth and affection made Cassie feel worse than ever about the pretense. All the cheerful joking from James and Norman, who'd introduced themselves as Trace's brothers, told her the family assumed Trace was in love. And everything he said and did tended to verify their assumptions.

But the excitement proved to be too much for the babies. Once Jason started crying, Justin quickly followed suit. Cassie extricated herself from a group of nieces who were fighting over who got to hold Jason and hurried to retrieve Justin, who was clearly unhappy being tended by one of his aunts.

The second he saw Cassie his tears stopped and a smile appeared. It was clear that during his brief illness, a bonding had taken place between them. He reached eagerly for her and wrapped his arms around her neck. Together they wandered over

to the banquet table the caterers had laden with everything from
luscious fresh pineapple slices to salads and salvers of prime rib.
Catering staff brought flutes of champagne and glasses of sparkling juice for the children.

As she handed Justin a piece of banana, Cassie caught sight
of a group of latecomers walking out on the patio. She saw Trace,
still carrying Jason, break away from the others and move toward
a slender, auburn-haired woman.

Lena. Cassie could tell by the tender expression on her husband's face that he had a soft spot for his only sister. From what
he had told Cassie, Lena resembled their father, Grant Ramsey,
who had died of a stroke a few years earlier, leaving his children
to carry on and expand the family business.

From the distance, Cassie watched in fascination as Trace bent
his head and filled Lena in on the details. Eventually Lena held
out her arms to Jason, who refused to go anywhere and clung to
his father. While everyone chuckled, Trace looked around until
he spotted Cassie with Justin, then pointed her out to his sister.
Lena left the group and hurried toward them.

Her hair had been drawn into a braid and hung over one shoulder. In comparison to Cassie's curves, Lena's build was thin and
wiry. Except for the same proud chin, Cassie saw very little of
Trace in his sister, whose pert nose and dark gray eyes made her
face gamin rather than beautiful.

She leaned over to give Justin a kiss on the cheek, but he
began to cry and tightened his hold on Cassie. Lena shrugged
good-naturedly, then turned her attention to Cassie, eyeing her
the way she might size up a scene she wanted to paint. "I'm
Lena Haroldson, Trace's sister, and I have to tell you I'm speechless at the news. You have to be the reason Trace looks ten years
younger tonight. If you can keep him this happy, I'll love you
forever." She smiled warmly, then added, "Welcome to the family, Cassie."

Though the words were meant to be complimentary, Cassie's
heart plummeted to her feet. It was obvious that Lena adored
Trace and guarded his happiness jealously. And it was equally
obvious that she was the one Ramsey Cassie would never be able
to fool.

"Thank you, Lena. I—I'm going to try to make our home a
happy one." At least that was the truth.

A mischievous smile lifted the corner of Lena's mouth. "I'd say uniting Trace with Jason is a giant step in the right direction. I want to hear all about it from start to finish, but tonight's not the right time. I suspect Justin needs to go to bed. How about lunch next week when you're settled in? I'll take you to my favorite restaurant."

"I'd love it." Lena would never know how much her friendliness meant to Cassie. "In fact, I've wanted to meet you ever since I first saw your watercolors in Trace's office. They're good—very good."

Lena shook her head, but by the way her eyes lighted up, Cassie could tell she was pleased. "Trace told you to say that, didn't he?"

"No," Cassie declared baldly. "He was too busy trying to haul me off to jail on a kidnapping-extortion charge."

"What?" Lena gasped. "That doesn't sound like Trace. I know he's got a tough reputation when it comes to business, but he wouldn't dare do such a thing to you!"

"I'm afraid I would and almost did," a deep voice interjected. "But in the nick of time this little fellow saved his mother from the long arm of the law, didn't you, Tiger?"

Surprised, both women turned to Trace who had approached them unnoticed. Apparently Jason had had enough partying for one night. His pale blue outfit was crumpled and stained with what looked like fresh strawberry. In spite of Cassie's precautions in double-tying his shoes, he had managed to kick one off, which Trace held in his free hand.

"Mama!" Always vigorous, Jason practically propelled himself out of his father's arms to reach Cassie. If it hadn't been for Trace's lightning reflexes, he would have landed on the floor. By now, Justin was being just as impossible and refused to allow Trace to hold him.

"Well, well, little brother." Lena grinned at Trace. "It looks like you've got competition."

Trace sent Cassie an enigmatic look that for some reason gave her an uneasy feeling. "I don't mind, Lena," he muttered. "Now if you'll excuse us, we'll put the children to bed. Be a sweetheart and hold down the fort till we come back." He bussed his sister's cheek, then slid one arm along Cassie's shoulders.

As they made their way inside, everyone crowded around to

say good-night to the boys. Cassie smiled and laughed, though it all felt a bit forced. Trace was making her unaccountably nervous.

"You didn't have to help me," Cassie murmured as they entered the nursery together. "Please feel free to go downstairs. It isn't very nice for both of us to disappear."

"You sound like you're trying to get rid of me," he said softly, but there was no amusement in his tone. "If I leave you on your own, you'll probably stay up here the rest of the night."

Perhaps he hadn't meant to sound critical, but his remark stung, increasing the tension she could feel building between them. She put a fresh diaper on Justin and eased him into his sleeper while Trace did the same for Jason. "Your family's wonderful. I wouldn't dream of offending them."

"Be that as it may, you seem to have no qualms about offending me." He paused, not looking at her. "Do me a favor. When we go back downstairs, pretend to like me a little bit."

His words produced a wave of heat that scorched her neck and cheeks. "I—I had no idea I had done anything else. I'm sorry, Trace."

After a slight pause he said, "It's not conscious on your part. You always treat me as if I wasn't there. I've never felt invisible before and don't particularly like the sensation. I thought we could at least be friends."

"We are." Her voice quailed despite herself.

"You have an odd way of showing it. Friends normally look at each other and smile once in a while, enjoy a private joke. You, on the other hand, reserve your affection strictly for the children. But you can't use them as a shield all the time."

She wheeled around, baffled by the total change in him. "A shield?" she cried, forgetting for the moment that their voices would keep the babies awake.

The dangerous glint in his eye unnerved her. "I don't know what else you'd call it. There aren't very many newlyweds who'd take two babies on their honeymoon."

Honeymoon? Cassie was aghast and looked away quickly. "After the chaos of Christmas and the move from San Francisco, I thought we agreed a little vacation with the children was exactly what we needed...so all of us could get acquainted away from the pressures of work and other people."

"If you recall, you were the one who suggested the idea. I simply went along with it, because I assumed you'd allow the hotel baby-sitters to take over once in a while to give us some time alone."

"I was afraid to trust them, particularly when Justin was running a temperature."

His jaw hardened. "That particular hotel has an impeccable reputation, with licensed sitters, a full-time registered nurse and a doctor always on call. If Justin had shown the slightest sign of any complication, we would have had the best care available at a moment's notice."

Her hands tightened on the bars of the crib. "I had no idea you weren't agreeable to the idea. You should have told me."

"I did, repeatedly, but you chose to ignore my hints and continued to cling to the children. Justin has become impossible. He knows all he has to do is look at you and you're right there to cater to his every whim. There *is* such a thing as a surfeit of attention."

Had she been spoiling Justin? Was Trace afraid she'd supplanted *him* in Justin's affections?

"I—I'm sure you're right. I've probably gone overboard in an effort to make up for lost time."

Her words didn't seem to mollify him. "You may not be sleeping in my bed, but in all other ways you're my wife, and there are things I expect of you besides being a mother to the boys."

What things? She had no idea all this had been seething inside him. "I'm not sure I understand you."

"How could you? We haven't had a moment to ourselves since we met!" He paused. "As chairman of the board, I attend a variety of social functions, and I do a certain amount of entertaining myself. Now that I'm married, it would create unnecessary and possibly damaging speculation if you didn't accompany me and fulfill your role as hostess when we're dining at home with friends and business acquaintances. Naturally the children won't be invited to those events," he added sarcastically. "Did you think you were being hired as a nanny when you accepted my proposal?"

"Not in so many words," she admitted, so confused by his anger that she didn't know what to believe. "But when you came to San Francisco, I was caught up in my feelings and concerns for the children—to the point that I wasn't capable of looking beyond their needs.''

"That was almost two months ago, Cassie. It's time we talked about *our* needs.''

His remarks caught her completely off guard. "Trace," she whispered, "your family is waiting for us. I don't think this is the time for the kind of discussion you seem to have in mind.'' She rubbed her palms agitatedly against her hips, noting that his eyes followed her movements with disturbing intensity.

There was a beat of silence, then, "For once you're right.'' He kept his voice low. "But be aware that I intend to pursue this after we say good-night to the family. In the meantime I would appreciate it if you'd join me in creating a united front. Mother would never admit it to you, but she's not as well as she pretends.''

Unconsciously Cassie's hand went to her throat. "What's wrong with her?''

"She had a heart attack recently. The doctors have warned her to slow down and take life easier. Since our marriage seems to have brought her so much pleasure, the last thing I want to do is upset her. She happens to believe that the greatest happiness in life is achieved through a good marriage. My divorce, I'm sorry to say, hurt her deeply, and ever since the attack she's been worried she might die before she sees me settled with a wife and family of my own.''

Inexplicably Cassie felt a strange, searing pain. Was *that* his underlying motive for asking her to marry him? The marriage would guarantee his mother's peace of mind and explain her reaction when they were introduced earlier in the evening. It was yet another example of Trace's unswerving devotion and loyalty to those he loved.

She took a deep, shuddering breath. "You know I wouldn't deliberately do anything to hurt her.''

His hands curled into fists, then relaxed, as if he had come to the end of his patience. "All I'm asking is that you try to act more natural and comfortable with me—even when the children aren't around.'' He sighed. "I don't understand you, Cassie. I can't figure out if you're still in love with your ex-fiancé, or if he did something to put you off men for good.''

CHAPTER FIVE

TRACE GAVE HER no chance to respond. He grasped her hand and started for the hallway; she didn't try to resist. It shouldn't have come as any surprise that while they mingled with the family for the rest of the evening, he kept his arm firmly around her shoulders. It was a deceptively casual gesture, but Cassie knew that if she tried to pull away, she'd feel the bite of his fingers against her skin.

Shortly before the end of the party, as people were preparing to leave, he lowered his head to Cassie's ear. She couldn't tell if the caress of his mouth against her hot cheek was intentional or not, but his touch shot through her body like a spurt of adrenaline. "It's exceptionally warm tonight," he whispered. "Join me for a swim after everyone leaves...and we'll continue what we started upstairs."

She bit the soft underside of her lip. The thought of being alone with Trace in the swimming pool made her panic. Since the kiss he'd given her at their wedding, she'd become physically, sensually, aware of him—something that had never happened with Rolfe in all the years they'd spent together.

She found herself remembering things Susan used to say about Ted. "I never want to say good-night to him, Cassie. One kiss isn't enough. All he has to do is touch me and I go up in smoke. Everything about him fascinates me, even the way he chews his toast. If we don't get married soon, I don't think either of us can hold out any longer."

Frightened that he could feel her trembling, Cassie eased herself away from Trace's hold. "First I'll have to help Nattie clean up."

"Nattie's job is to supervise the caterers, who were hired for that express purpose, and Mike has a whole retinue of gardeners to put the grounds in order. In case you're about to offer any other excuses, you can forget them. Tonight I need to be with my wife. Is a midnight swim and a little honest conversation too much to ask?''

His question whirled around in her brain as she said good-night to Trace's family and escaped to her bedroom. Out of breath from an attack of nerves and a heart that was pounding out of rhythm, she leaned against the closed door. That was when she spied a gaily wrapped package sitting in the middle of her bed.

There had been so many gifts since her arrival in Phoenix, she certainly hadn't expected any more. Curious, she walked over to pick it up, wondering if someone in the family—Lena?—had thought to welcome her with something a little more personal. Quickly she unwrapped the box and lifted the lid. A handwritten card had been placed on the layers of tissue.

"It occurred to me," the card read, "that Justin's cold wasn't the only reason you wouldn't swim with me in Scottsdale. In case you didn't have a decent suit and hadn't found the time to shop for one, I took the liberty of picking something out for you. The green matches your eyes. I couldn't resist. Trace."

Carefully she moved aside the tissue paper and eased out a two-piece swimsuit. It was more modest than some of the bikinis she'd seen on the beach, but the fact remained that she'd never worn a two-piece before. Though slender, Cassie took after her mother in the full-bodied-figure department.

She'd always felt more comfortable in a one-piece outfit, but she wouldn't have been caught dead in the only suit she owned. It was so old and faded that she was planning to throw it out. Trace had probably guessed as much.

She flushed at the thought. It seemed he knew her better than she knew herself and refused to take the chance that she would use the lack of a proper swimsuit as an excuse for not meeting him at the pool.

Suddenly there was a rap on the door. "Cassie? I'm giving you five minutes. If you're not downstairs by then, I'll be back up to get you, and a locked door won't stop me. It would be a shame to ruin that lovely dress you're wearing, but I won't hes-itate to throw you in, emeralds and all."

His threat galvanized her into action. In three minutes, her clothes lay everywhere and she'd put on her new swimsuit. She ran for her terry-cloth bathrobe, then dashed barefoot down the stairs.

The caterers must have cleared the tables in record time. When Cassie arrived on the patio, everything was quiet and only the lights from the swimming pool had been left on. The warm night air, sweet with the scent of sage blowing off the desert floor, felt like velvet against her heated skin. She'd never seen a more romantic setting in her life.

When she and Susan were little girls, they'd often played house on long Saturday afternoons. They always pretended they were married with families, living in far-off exotic places. But never in Cassie's wildest dreams had she imagined a setting like this, with a husband who looked like Trace, and children as adorable as Justin and Jason. If Susan could see her now...

"How nice to find my bride waiting for me." His deep, mocking voice startled her.

His bride? She whirled around in time to see Trace dive into the water and swim to the opposite end of the pool in a fast-paced crawl. Halfway back he stopped, treading water, and shook his head. In the near darkness she could just make out his dazzling white smile.

"Come on in. The water's perfect."

Even though he was some distance away, Cassie felt self-conscious as she removed her robe. "I love to swim, but I'm not very good at it."

"I usually swim early in the morning and again at night before I go to bed. Now we're married, we can work out together." Shivers raced over her body, because something in his tone implied that he expected her to join him on a regular basis and wouldn't take no for an answer. She couldn't understand why it mattered to him, since they'd be alone and there'd be no need to keep up the pretense. "It helps me unwind more than any sport I can think of." He looked at her a moment. "Are you about ready to jump in?"

She had just put a cautious toe in the water, bracing herself for the shock. But the temperature was so different from the chilly Pacific Ocean at Carmel, where she'd occasionally swum with Rolfe, it was as though she'd stepped into a bathtub. "I

don't even have to get used to it!'' she cried out in delight.
"Gaugin was wrong. Paradise is right here!"

She heard Trace's deep-throated chuckle as she pushed off
from the bottom step and swam to the other side, making sure
she didn't get too close to him. On her third lap across, she felt
a pair of hands grasp her around the waist and flip her onto her
back.

"Trace!" she gasped, not only from the unexpected contact,
but because he had taken her beyond the patio overhang and she
found herself looking up into a blue-black sky dotted with brilliant stars.

"I'm not going to let you drown," he reassured her. "Lie there
and relax, kick your feet. You're more rigid than Justin at his
worst."

Only once did she venture a glance at his face. His skin was
beaded with moisture and his black hair lay sleek against his
head. She quickly closed her eyes again. She felt helpless and
exposed with his gaze free to wander over her semiclad body.

It took all her control not to examine his hard-muscled phy-
sique with the same concentrated thoroughness. If she tried to
move, her arm rubbed against his hair-roughened chest, remind-
ing her how utterly male he was. Everything about him excited
her. His size, his masculinity, his firmly carved mouth.

She came to the stunning realization that the bittersweet ache
that seemed to be part pain, part ecstasy, was *desire!*

Susan had once tried to explain the sensation to her and had
finally given up. But she'd insisted that Cassie would recognize
it the moment she experienced it. She hadn't—until now.

Was this the way Rolfe had felt throughout their long court-
ship? If so, she had to admire his self-control. No wonder he
grew more upset and moody each time she put off the wedding.

Without even trying, Trace had brought her alarmingly alive.
From the first, he had accomplished what Rolfe had never been
able to do. If she'd desired Rolfe like this, wouldn't she have
wanted to get married as soon as possible?

Right now, she quivered with anticipation. She could hear
every breath Trace took and feel the heat from his body sending
a languorous warmth through hers. The longing to mold her soft
curves against his solid strength was fast becoming a driving
need.

Terrified that he could sense her desire and see the pulse throbbing in the hollow of her throat, she challenged him to a race. Without waiting for a response she catapulted out of his arms.

Of course he won. He waited for her at the far end of the pool with a rakish smile on his face. She touched the edge at least ten seconds after he did and drank in gulps of fresh air before bursting into laughter at her inelegant performance.

He studied her mouth intently, a gentle yet ironic smile curving his own lips. "Do you know that's the first time you've laughed with me when we've been alone? I like it."

Oddly embarrassed, Cassie sank down against the side of the pool until the water reached her neck. "As you've witnessed, I've got a long way to go to keep up with you."

His expression sobered. "I don't see our marriage as a competition, Cassie. What I'm hoping is that we'll share each other's lives. The children will grow up happier and healthier emotionally if they sense our marriage is a stable one. No one has to know what goes on—or doesn't—behind our bedroom doors except the two of us. Is that too much to ask? You don't dislike being with me, do you?"

Cassie was beginning to feel slightly hysterical. If he had any idea how much she didn't dislike being with him, he would run as far as he could in the opposite direction! Striving for composure, she smoothed several wet tendrils out of her eyes.

She didn't doubt his sincerity where the children's welfare was concerned. But now Cassie understood that his mother's fragile health had prompted him to enlist her cooperation in presenting a normal picture of married life to the rest of his family.

Her greatest problem would be to carry on a friendship, day after day, without ever betraying the physical side of her attraction for him. She finally said, "I admit it would be better for the children if they see us relating to each other as friends and companions."

Maybe she was mistaken, but she thought some of the tension eased out of him. "I'm glad you agree, because in two weeks the family's going on our annual skiing vacation to Snowbird, Utah, and I wanted to give you plenty of time to prepare for it."

She had that suffocating feeling in her chest again. "What about the children?"

"Nattie will take care of them."

"I see. How long will we be gone?"

"A week."

A week with Trace? Alone in the same room? She swallowed hard.

"Snowbird isn't the end of the earth, you know," he said harshly, his brows drawing together in displeasure. "You can phone the house every day to assure yourself the children are all right. If anything of a serious nature developed, we could be home in a matter of hours."

Cassie decided to let him go on believing that the children were her only concern. "You may as well know I've only been on skis twice in my life. I'm afraid I'd embarrass you on the slopes. Why don't I stay home with the boys and you go with your family? In fact, it might be a good time for Nattie to have a vacation, as well. She—"

"Either we go together, or we don't go at all!" he broke in angrily. Like quicksilver, his mood had changed. He suddenly shoved off for the opposite end of the pool, moving with tremendous speed. He was out of the water before she could call him back.

"Wait!" she cried out and swam after him, afraid she'd really alienated him this time. Unfortunately, she couldn't make it to the other end of the pool without stopping several times to catch her breath. She was terrified he would disappear into his own rooms, leaving her with everything still unresolved. "Trace," she gasped as her hand gripped the edge, "I was only trying to spare you. I ski like I swim."

He was toweling himself dry and slanted her a hostile look. "Do you honestly think I give a damn *how* you ski? Or even *if* you ski? I don't care if you lie around in the hotel bed all day watching television! From what I gather, for the last five years your life hasn't exactly been easy.

"Between Susan's and Ted's deaths, not to mention your mother's, a broken engagement and caring for Jason, you've had more to deal with than most people I know. And at the same time, you've been working all hours to earn a living. You don't seem to understand that I'd like to give you a chance to relax and play for a change, away from your work and the constant demands of the babies."

Her legs almost buckled at his unexpected explanation. Whenever she thought she had him figured out, he said or did something that increased her respect and made her care for him that much more.

A new ache passed through her body. She didn't *want* to care about him. She didn't want to worry about him—or think about him all the time. Lately she'd started fantasizing about what it would be like if he made love to her. Much more of this, and she'd end up an emotional wreck.

Her green eyes, wide with urgency, beseeched him to listen. "If I sounded ungrateful, I'm sorry. I suppose it's a combination of worrying about being away from the children for the first time and fear that you'll regret taking me along."

The expression on his face altered slightly as he held out her robe in invitation, but his eyes were still wary. As fast as she could manage, she clambered out of the pool and slipped her arms into the sleeves. His hands remained on her shoulders while she cinched the belt around her waist.

"You're an independent little thing," he whispered, kneading the taut muscles in her shoulders and neck. "It's time someone took care of you for a change."

She could feel the heat of his hands through the damp fabric. If he continued this, she was afraid of what she might do, afraid she'd embarrass them both. "You've spoiled me and Jason, and you know it, Trace. But I worry you've taken off too much time from your responsibilities at the bank, helping us move here and settle in. I wish there was something I could do for you in return."

His hands stilled for a moment. "There is," he muttered before removing them completely. Part of her was relieved he had broken contact, but another part craved his touch. Not trusting herself, she walked to the nearest lounge chair and sat down, making sure the robe covered her knees. This far from the pool, he was almost a silhouette in the near darkness.

"Tell me what's on your mind," she urged him.

He stood there holding both ends of the towel he'd slung around his neck. "You may not be an expert swimmer or skier, but your genius with needle and thread is nothing short of phenomenal. When I walked into your apartment with Jason that morning, I was overwhelmed by your talent and creativity."

A compliment from Trace meant more to her than the adula-
tion of anyone else in the world. "Lots of women do what I do."

"Perhaps. But the finished product isn't always a masterpiece.
I hope you won't be angry when I tell you I went through your
apartment rather thoroughly, examining the goods, so to speak.
Nothing bought for Justin in any store, anywhere, compares to
the quality and originality I saw displayed in your apartment. I
stand in awe of your accomplishments, Cassie."

"Thank you," she murmured shakily.

"I also felt like a fool for the callous way I suggested you
move to Phoenix when I had no idea of the complexities involved
in earning your livelihood." There was a slight pause. "Tell me
something honestly. Is your work a labor of love?"

She couldn't help but wonder what he was getting at. "Long
before I made any money at it, I loved creating an idea and seeing
it through to completion. It's...something I have to do. When
they find me dead, I'll probably be buried in batting, slumped
over my sewing machine with a bunch of pins in my mouth."

"Somehow I knew you'd say that." He chuckled. "You and
Lena are kindred spirits."

"I liked her very much, even after only one meeting."

"Maybe you're the person who'll make the difference." The
cryptic remark intrigued her.

"What do you mean?"

"You're both artists. You live in that elite world reserved for
those who were born gifted."

Cassie made a noise of dissent. "You can't seriously compare
what *I* do to her talent!"

"I already have." His firm tone told her that to argue the point
would be futile. "You make a child's world the most exciting,
magical place on earth, just as it should be. Lena makes it possible for those of us who shove paper around to enjoy the breathtaking beauty of the desert without ever leaving our air-
conditioned offices."

"There's a certain genius in shoving paper around. Particularly
your paper," she quipped. "Give me three days in your office
and your entire family would find themselves without a business
and no roof over their heads."

The patio rang with his uninhibited laughter. "Well, since you

brought up the bank, I have a proposition for you." Cassie sat
forward, instantly alert.

"We lease properties, both residential and commercial. Right
now, there's a studio vacant in Crossroads Square, an area of
Phoenix that attracts tourists, as well as locals. By most standards
it's not large, but it has four separate rooms with a cottage kind
of feel, like you might see at a beach resort in Laguna or Balboa.
It would be the perfect place to display your handicrafts. You
need a showroom."

She had been concentrating on the sound of his voice, and it
took a minute before she actually heard his words. She jumped
immediately to her feet. "There's nothing I'd love more. It would
be a dream come true, but I could never afford the rent, because
I looked into the possibility in San Francisco and—"

"Don't jump to conclusions until you've heard me out," he
cautioned before she could say another word. "How much do
you have saved from your Christmas sales after taxes?"

"About eight thousand dollars."

"With that much money, you could sign a six-month lease."

"But six months wouldn't give me enough time to fill it with
inventory, and then I'd have no money to reinvest in materials
and—"

She heard him make a sound of exasperation. "Cassie, you
said you wouldn't interrupt until I'm finished. Sit down before
you wear out my patio with your pacing."

"I'm sorry." With so much nervous energy to expend, she
needed some form of movement. She found a spot at the edge
of the pool and dangled her feet in the water, splashing gently.
He wandered over to her and it was then that she noticed his
right foot. Without thinking, she bent closer and touched it with
her index finger. *"You have webbed toes, just like Jason!"* Her
astonished cry rang out and she clapped a hand over her mouth
at its loudness.

"A legacy from the Ellingsworth side of the family," he
drawled in amusement. "Both of Mother's feet are simi-
arly...afflicted."

"I wouldn't call it an affliction," Cassie argued. "When I first
saw Jason's foot, I thought it was rather sweet. Susan and I
investigated the medical records available in both Ted's and our

family, but we couldn't find any mention of webbed feet. I guess that's when I started to take Susan's suspicions seriously."

"And your odd little duck turned out to be mine," he said, causing both of them to chuckle.

"Is that what convinced you he was your son?" She could still picture the expression on his face when he reached for Jason's tiny foot that first day in his office.

"No. I took one look at the shape of his body and his complexion. He had to be my son. The Ellingsworth webbed toes were just the final proof."

"And all the time I thought he was a Ramsey."

"Oh, I'm sure a little Ramsey is in there somewhere. But what's most important, he has you for a mother. You're a natural, did you know that?"

"Except I've been spoiling Justin, as you pointed out yourself."

"True, but no more than I've spoiled Jason," he replied with surprising honesty. "I admit I was somewhat hasty in judging you, especially since I've been equally guilty. However, I imagine time will remedy the urgency we both feel to make up for those lost months. And returning to your crafts work will put a balance back in your life. You've been missing that since you agreed to marry me."

Again his perception and honesty surprised her. She'd been so preoccupied by her new responsibilities and her growing attraction to Trace, she hadn't yet found a moment to give serious thought to her business. "Maybe a few years down the road I'll have enough money to look into the idea of opening a shop."

"But that might be too late for Lena."

Lena again.

"She needs someone outside the family who believes in her work and will encourage her to see it as a viable career. Someone who has validity in her eyes. I think you could be that person. You could infect her with your own interest. Your joy in what you're doing."

What was he getting at? "You mean like going into business with her? Opening a gallery with her art and my crafts?"

He nodded. "Maybe you could call it something like The Mix and Match Gallery—in honor of the unusual way we met and became a family." There was a perceptible pause, then he asked,

"Does the idea appeal to you?" She noticed the tiniest hint of anxiety in his question, as if her answer was important to him.

"Appeal?" She jumped to her feet and gazed into his face, giving him a full, unguarded smile. "It's a fantastic idea! In fact, why don't we call it Mix and Match Southwest, since we'll be mixing and matching her art and my crafts and everything will have a southwestern theme?" Her thoughts were tumbling excitedly over each other. "We could have a logo with a cactus and maybe a setting sun or a coyote, and...oh, it'll be wonderful!"

His eyes kindled. "You mean it? You wouldn't mind sharing space with her, provided she was willing? It would be predominantly your shop of course—at this stage, anyway. If necessary, I'll pay the rent for the second six months, only that would have to remain our secret. It seems to me that between the two of you, there should be enough profit to stay in business another year." He paused again. "Would it make *you* happy, Cassie?"

When they'd begun this conversation, she thought he'd brought up the idea of a gallery solely for Lena's benefit. But the concern in his voice just now led Cassie to believe he was trying to please her, too, and that belief filled her with an all-consuming warmth. "You know it would," she answered in an unsteady voice. "Do you recall that watercolor at the top of the stairs? The one with the little Hopi girl standing next to those rocks at sunrise?"

He nodded. "It's one of my favorites."

"Every time I pass it, I itch to get out my sketch pad and design dolls and wall hangings based on that lovely child. In fact, living in this house has inspired me with the flavor of the Arizona desert. I've already planned out an area rug for my room, and the watercolor of the flowering cactus hanging in your office would look perfect next to it. Trace, for the opening I could use a Southwest theme with Lena's watercolors as the focal point!"

Before she could say anything else, he lowered his head and pressed his lips to her forehead. "You have a generous nature, Cassie. I'm counting on you to win Lena over to the idea."

Her heart hammered in reaction to his touch—and yearned for more. "Maybe I could work up some items before we go to lunch next week and invite her back to the house. If she saw them arranged around the watercolors, it might excite her."

"I'm sure it will, but getting her to make a commitment is something else again." A troubled look entered his eyes. "In college she fell in love with her art teacher. They had an affair that ended when she walked into his apartment and found him in bed with another student."

Cassie cringed at the all-too-common scenario.

"Considering that she thought they were getting married, that alone would have been devastating enough. But not satisfied with betraying her, he attacked her art and told her she was wasting her time. His final insult pretty well destroyed her confidence. He told her she'd never be more than a mediocre painter at best."

"But anyone with eyes can see how brilliant her work is!" Cassie insisted. "When did this happen?"

"Twelve years ago. She hasn't done any painting since."

"You mean the watercolors in your office and here at the house were all done while she was still in college? She was that good, even back then?"

"That's right," he said, tight-lipped.

"Her teacher probably recognized her talent and couldn't bear the competition. No doubt her work surpassed his. I've seen the same situation in the music department at the university where I studied piano theory. To think she let his rejection prevent her from working at her art all these years. It's tragic."

He nodded gravely. "Her husband, Allen, knows she'll never be completely fulfilled unless she gets back to her painting. He's done everything possible to encourage her but she refuses to even talk about it."

"The hurt must have gone very deep."

"It did. And to complicate matters, she feels insignificant around the family, overpowered by us. She's not like you, Cassie. She would never have fought me for Jason the way you did. You live by the strength of your convictions and don't let anything defeat you. You're practical and resilient—a survivor. You'd stand alone if you had to. If some of your confidence could rub off on Lena, it might change her life."

"I'm glad you told me about her," she said in a small voice. "I'll do what I can. Now if you don't mind, I'm very tired and I need to go to bed. Good night, Trace."

His whispered good-night followed her across the patio and up the stairs.

Though he obviously meant his remarks as a compliment, her spirits plummeted. Apparently she and his ex-wife, Gloria, had something in common, after all. They were both the antithesis of the fragile, helpless woman who aroused a man's undying love and brought out his instinctive need to protect and cherish.

The Joan of Arcs of this world would always be admired, but they would remain on their pedestals *alone....*

CHAPTER SIX

EXCEPT FOR A VISIT to the vacant shop in Crossroads Square and the subsequent signing of a year's lease, Cassie saw Trace only in passing during the next week. He explained that he had a backlog of work; as a result, he stayed at the office through the dinner hour every night so he could catch up before they left on their ski trip.

Cassie told herself she was glad his banking responsibilities kept him away from the house. Without his disturbing presence, she could simply relax with the children and sew at her own pace. Trace had helped convert the middle guest bedroom into a workroom. The light was perfect. Best of all, she was close to the children and could hear them when they woke up from their naps.

But to her dismay, Trace was continually on her mind. His energy and vitality, his handsome face and powerful body, made it impossible for her to concentrate fully on anything else. And when he was home, even if he was locked in his study or playing with the children, she was aware of him. No matter the hour, her pulse raced when she heard his car in the driveway. But what alarmed her even more was the disappointment she felt when he drove off to work each morning.

After five whole weeks of his attention and companionship, she discovered life wasn't nearly as exciting without him around. Always before, she'd been able to immerse herself happily in her work, unconscious of time passing. Now while she bathed and fed the children or cut out patterns, she often glanced at the clock, estimating how many hours it would be before he came home.

Lena called early in the week to make a date for lunch. Cassie put her off until Friday so she'd have enough time to work up several pieces that drew their inspiration from three of Lena's paintings. Trace brought home one she'd requested from his office. She used another two from the group hanging on the wall along the staircase.

In order to make the impact as striking as possible, she enlisted Nattie's help in converting the dining room into a sort of gallery. The effect was even more stunning than Cassie had imagined, because the room, with its arboretum of exotic desert plants, lent itself perfectly to the Southwest theme.

Though she kept her thoughts to herself, Cassie felt that something out of the ordinary had been achieved. She could hardly sit still through lunch with Lena, waiting for the moment they would go home.

If Trace's sister sensed Cassie's suppressed excitement, she hid it well. She asked dozens of questions and insisted on knowing all the details of Cassie's life and the events that eventually led her to Trace's office. Several hours later, when Cassie invited Lena back to the house to see the children, Lena was still chuckling over Trace's initial plan to have Cassie arrested. But her laughter subsided when she caught sight of her own watercolors displayed with Cassie's creations in plain view of anyone standing in the living room.

Like a person walking through water, Lena moved into the dining room. Cassie followed a few steps behind, uncertain of Lena's reaction and almost afraid to breathe. Those paintings were associated with a painful time in Lena's life. At this early stage in their friendship, the last thing Cassie wanted to do was open old wounds or create a rift between them. It was because she had Trace's blessing that she dared to involve Lena at all.

Lena studied the arrangement in silence for a long time. "Do you mean to tell me you've made all these since you came to Phoenix?" she finally asked.

"Yes, except that they aren't completely finished."

"They're fabulous."

"Your paintings inspired them, Lena. I took one look at your little Hopi girl and I could visualize her adorable face on dolls and wall hangings and all sorts of things. Every one of your paintings has given me a dozen new ideas. I can't work fast enough to keep up with them."

"Trace told me you were a genius with fabric."

"And I told him that whoever painted those scenes in his

office has incredible talent. Your work excites me and makes me reach out for things I didn't know were in me. You know what I mean?''

Lena turned around and stared at Cassie. "You really meant what you said the other night, didn't you?"

Taking a deep breath, Cassie answered, "You already know the answer to that. Have I made you angry, using your paintings for inspiration without telling you?"

"Angry?" Lena's gray eyes widened in surprise. "I've never been so flattered in my life."

Cassie's body went limp with relief. "As you know, I've only ever sold out of my own home. At first I started making up dolls and stuffed figures from fairy tales and cartoons to help bring in a little more money. Pretty soon I was flooded with orders. I've sewn everything from frogs to princes. But I've never had a theme for my work or even considered it until I saw your paintings."

Lena fingered her long braid absently. "You obviously went to all this trouble—arranging everything so beautifully—for my benefit. Why?"

"Before I met Trace, I planned to open my own boutique in San Francisco as a showcase for my work. But everything changed when he asked me to marry him. Now that we're settled, I've used the profits from my Christmas sales to sign a lease on some space in Crossroads Square."

"Crossroads Square?" Lena mouthed the word wistfully, sounding very faraway. "That's a perfect place if you want to attract the tourist trade." She stared at Cassie in puzzlement. "Does Trace know about this? I-I thought you were going to stay home with the children."

"I do stay home. Every day. And I manage to enjoy the children and sew at the same time. How else do you think I could turn out so much work?" Cassie smiled mischievously. "But if I don't have a place to display and sell it, pretty soon Trace will have to build me a warehouse."

Lena burst into laughter. "You're a complete surprise, Cassie Ramsey."

"No." Cassie shook her head, liking the sound of her new name. "Just driven by a compulsion stronger than I am."

A shadow crossed Lena's face; she started to say something, then apparently changed her mind.

Cassie hesitated a moment, then decided to plunge ahead. "Lena, I have to admit I had ulterior motives in inviting you back to the house today. You see, I'm holding my grand opening in a month, and I need your permission to display the things I've already made. The fact is, I've copied your work and I really have no right to sell any of this." She gestured around the room. "Believe me, I'll understand if your answer is no. But as time is of the essence, I need to know how you feel...in case I have to get started on another theme entirely."

Picking up one of the dolls, Lena studied it carefully, then looked at Cassie, eyes brimming. "How could I possibly turn you down when you've done such exquisite work? It would be on my conscience forever."

Impulsively Cassie threw her arms around Lena in an exuberant hug. "I was praying you'd say that, because I can't think of another theme that could possibly work as well as this one. To be honest, I knew my opening would have to be unique in order to generate business. And when I saw your art, I was immediately drawn to it. I think other people would feel the same way."

In the heavy silence that followed her remarks, Cassie removed the paintings from the groupings of crafts, then leaned them against the far wall. Lena gazed at her uncomprehendingly, and Cassie had to bite hard on her lower lip to keep from smiling.

"Take a good look at everything without your paintings to show them off, Lena. The things I've made are nice in and of themselves, but the display falls flat, don't you think? Be honest now."

After another quiet interim, Lena nodded.

Crossing her fingers behind her back, Cassie ventured, "Would you allow me to use your paintings the way I've done here to open the show?" Without giving Lena a chance to respond, she rushed on. "I have to admit I've sketched out ideas for dozens of fabric crafts based on another ten of your paintings. If I work night and day, I can have everything ready for the opening. But without your art as a foil, I won't be able to achieve the same impact."

While Lena hesitated, Cassie quickly put the paintings back in place among the crafts for her sister-in-law's benefit. "You see? I'm right, aren't I?"

After a minute of studying the display, Lena nodded, looking slightly bemused. "Everything works perfectly together."

"Then you'll let me use them?"

"I'd be cruel if I said no."

"Thank you, Lena." Cassie couldn't help giving her another hug. "It's one thing to sell things out of your own home, and another to display them in a shop. I've been terrified at my own audacity. But with your paintings, I know the opening will be an eye-catcher."

Conscious of taking a calculated risk, Cassie added, "I noticed you haven't signed your paintings."

"No," came the quiet admission.

"I'm afraid you'll have to if I'm going to show them. Otherwise clients will assume I painted them."

Lena was examining the Hopi girl canvas, frowning in concentration. "I need to finish the detail on her dress if you're going to use this." She finally stood up and faced Cassie. "I'll tell you what. Ask Trace to bring home the paintings from the office you're planning to use. Next week I'll go to the art store for supplies and come over to sign them all."

"Don't you have materials at home?" Cassie asked, striving to remain unemotional when inside she was bursting with excitement.

"Heavens, no." She let out a bitter laugh. "I'm afraid my art career was very short-lived and I tossed everything out. In fact, I haven't touched a brush to canvas in years. When I worked on these paintings, I never dreamed anyone else would ever see them. I would have thrown them away, but Trace said he wanted them and offered me money to take them off my hands. Of course I wouldn't have let him pay me for junk." She sighed, shaking her head. "My brother..."

"He believes in your work."

Lena's gaze slid away. "Well, now that I've committed myself, I'd better look over everything you plan to use. I might find other details that were left undone."

"Lena, I can't thank you enough. To be frank, I've been frightened to tell you what I've been up to—particularly since I'm calling the shop Mix and Match Southwest. If you hadn't given your permission, I don't know where I would have turned for inspiration. Trace seems to believe in my work, as well. I—I want him to be proud of me.''

"In case you hadn't noticed, he already is," Lena said wryly. "Of all my brothers, I feel closest to him, and I can tell you honestly that when Allen and I arrived at the party, Trace's eyes had a glow I've never seen before. Only you could have put it there.''

"That's because he's so crazy about Jason." She fought to keep the tremor out of her voice.

Lena eyed her shrewdly. "Of course he is, but I saw the way Trace looked at you, the way he held on to you all evening. I've never seen him behave like that with any other woman.''

"Not even Gloria?"

"Especially not Gloria."

Cassie wanted to ask more questions about Trace's former wife, but restrained herself; this wasn't the right time. "Trace's attention to me was solely for your mother's benefit.''

"What does Mom have to do with how my brother treats you?" Lena asked in a perplexed voice.

"It's because of her heart condition. He wants her to believe our marriage is a love match."

"And it's not?" Lena burst out.

Cassie sucked in her breath. "Trace is grateful to me for uniting him with his son. But you might as well know he asked me to marry him and I accepted so neither of us would have to be separated from the children. I couldn't bear to lose them," she whispered.

"What?"

"Trace isn't in love with me, Lena. Ours is what people used to call a marriage of convenience. I can't go on pretending something that doesn't exist. At least not to you, because...because I want us to be friends."

"I do, too," Lena murmured, "but if you're telling me you're not in love with my brother, I don't believe you."

Lena's directness caught Cassie off guard and she felt heat rising to her cheeks. "None of it really matters, because Trace isn't interested in me that way. In fact, one of the conditions he set for our marriage was that both of us could see other people, as long as we were discreet."

"My brother said *that?*"

"Lena, we've never slept together. He's only ever kissed me once, the day we were married." Her voice trailed off as she recalled the thrill of it. Before Lena could respond, Cassie blurted out, "I can hear noises from upstairs. The boys must have awakened. I'll get them ready and bring them down."

Without waiting for a response Cassie raced from the living room and dashed up the stairs, thankful the babies had interrupted her painful conversation with Lena.

As Cassie changed their diapers, Nattie poked her head into the nursery. "Do you need help?"

"No. Jason seems to be a little off color, but I'm sure it's nothing. Since Trace won't be home for dinner, I can fix a simple meal for myself and the boys. So why don't you and Mike take the rest of the day off? You deserve a rest."

Nattie's face lit up. "You're sure?"

"I'm positive. Lena's going to stay a while and keep us company."

"All right. Thank you, Cassie. It's a joy to work in the same house with you."

"The feeling's mutual, Nattie. Go and have a good time."

When Nattie had left, Cassie dressed the boys and carried them downstairs to see their aunt. To her relief, Lena made no mention of their prior conversation and enjoyed getting to know Jason better while Cassie encouraged Justin to take a few steps. It wouldn't be long before he was walking on his own.

Jason, on the other hand, could crawl everywhere and went after anything he wanted with an unswerving certainty that reminded both women of Trace and sent them into gales of laughter. But, unusual for Jason, he soon tired and cried to be held.

Cassie and Lena spent the rest of the afternoon exchanging anecdotes about the children, but as the dinner hour approached, Lena declared that she had to go home and feed her starving horde. Cassie was reluctant to see her leave, but was growing concerned about Jason, who'd become irritable and weepy, despite his long nap. His forehead definitely felt warm to the touch.

She put Justin in the playpen, then walked Lena to the front door, carrying Jason in her arms. "I'll phone you as soon as Trace brings the paintings home from his office."

The other woman nodded. "Cassie, will you do me a favor and not mention this to anyone else in the family?"

"You mean about using your art for my opening?"

"Yes. I'd like this to be our secret, if you don't mind."

"Of course I don't. I'll tell Trace not to say anything, either."

"Good. It's just that I stopped painting years ago and, well, I just don't want to deal with everyone's speculations..."

Cassie put a hand on Lena's arm. "If that's how you feel, I understand. You have my promise."

"Thanks." Lena kissed Jason's cheek, then Cassie's. "We'll talk again soon. We'll be able to spend some time together during our trip to Snowbird, too."

Lena's unexpected warmth pleased Cassie. "Thank you for your help, Lena. It means more than you know."

Cassie had a feeling that her sister-in-law wanted to say something further—perhaps about her marriage to Trace. But Lena seemed to think better of it. As soon as she drove off, Cassie headed for the kitchen to get Jason a bottle of juice. Then she gave him a sponge bath to bring down his slight fever and put him back to bed.

But while she was taking care of him, her mind was on Lena. Though Cassie had obtained her permission to use the watercolors, it didn't mean she'd automatically begin painting again. Trace was right; Lena still sounded far too bitter over her ex-lover's rejection. She'd lost all her self-confidence and, even worse, belief in her own talent.

But she hadn't turned Cassie down, and that meant she'd taken the first, necessary step. Cassie couldn't wait to tell Trace. She listened for him all evening as she fed Justin and bathed him, then put him in his crib. Jason fell asleep almost immediately.

After turning out the nursery light, she went downstairs to put the crafts and paintings away and restore order to the dining room while she waited for Trace. Around eight she heard a car pull into the drive. Moments later, the sound of the back door opening told her he was home.

Cassie rushed to the patio to meet him, anxious to share her news about Lena. "I thought you'd never get here, and I have so much to tell you! Lena and I—"

His eyes looked warm and expectant, but the ringing of the telephone prevented further conversation. He reached for it, and

Cassie sat down at the small table, silently admiring the blackness of his hair, the laugh lines around his eyes and mouth, the deepness of his voice.

By his clipped response she could tell the call had to do with bank business; she hoped it wouldn't detain him for the rest of the evening. He pulled out his pocketbook and jotted down some notes, then finally hung up. She was bursting to tell him her good news, but swallowed her words when she saw his dark expression. One phone call had transformed him into a remote facsimile of himself. He turned his head to stare at her broodingly.

"What's wrong, Trace?" she asked in alarm.

"That was Western Union with a cablegram for you from a Mr. Rolfe Timpson in Brussels. I told the operator to go ahead and read it." He tore the page from his pocketbook and handed it to her.

The hostility emanating from him troubled Cassie a great deal more than the paper in her hand. Her gaze was drawn to Trace's crisp handwriting. "Dearest Cass," it read, "I got your letter and I strongly feel we have to talk. We've loved for a lifetime and I don't ever see that changing. I'm coming back to the States next month to see you. I'll call you as soon as I arrive in Phoenix. My deepest love, Rolfe."

After all this time, Rolfe was coming to see her. She would always love him in a special way. But her response to Trace in the pool had revealed a truth that changed everything where Rolfe was concerned.

What was it Susan had said? That Cassie and Rolfe had never been apart and needed the separation to make things clear, one way or the other....

They were clear, all right.

Her eyes shifted from the paper to the man who'd taken her heart by storm and brought her body to glorious life. *Oh, Trace, if you only knew...*

"He wants you back," he said in a harsh tone, "but that's just too damn bad because you're married to me now, Cassie, and that's the way it's going to stay."

If she didn't know why he'd asked her to marry him, his angry pronouncement would have led her to believe he was starting to care for her.

"Whatever Rolfe has to say, I'd never leave you and the children," she said honestly.

"Don't take me for a fool, Cassie. Do you think I don't know the bond that exists between the two of you? The years invested? The intimacy you shared?"

"We weren't intimate in the way you mean," she confessed in a quiet voice.

His eyes blazed. "If you're trying to tell me you never slept together in all those years, I don't believe you."

"Nevertheless it's true. Mother had very conservative beliefs and raised Susan and me to save ourselves for marriage. She challenged us to be the only girls in the neighborhood who didn't know all there was to know about what goes on between a man and a woman. She promised us it would be a lot more fun and exciting to learn along with our husbands."

He stared at her as if she was speaking a foreign language. "What went wrong between you and Rolfe?"

She wanted to blurt out that she wasn't in love with Rolfe. That was what had kept her from marrying him. But she hadn't known it, not until she met Trace. And fell in love with him.

"We were engaged a long time. When he pushed me to set a wedding date, I couldn't, because I was still grieving over my mother. After Ted was killed, he pressed me again, but I was so worried about Susan I couldn't even consider marriage just then, even though I loved him very much. I don't blame him for finally getting fed up and breaking our engagement."

"Is that when he left for Europe?"

"Yes. But none of it matters anymore. Trace," she began in an excited voice, "I wanted to tell you about Lena. She—"

"Not now, Cassie," he interrupted tersely. "I'm in the middle of a hellish merger and I'll be spending most of the night in my study."

Not since that first day in his office had he ever been intentionally rude to her. Here she'd done everything in her power to show him the past was dead for her and he treated her like this! Even if things had been different and she'd wanted to see Rolfe again, did Trace honestly believe she'd walk out on him and the children? He would have to divorce her before she'd leave!

He turned abruptly and took the patio stairs two at a time. Cassie felt like throwing something at him. After he'd disappeared from view, she stood there for a few minutes to get her temper under control, then went upstairs herself. When she heard Jason crying she made a detour to the nursery. The minute she picked him up she realized why he'd awakened in such distress. He was burning with fever. One look at the rash covering his chest and neck dispersed all thoughts of the tense scene on the patio.

She quickly undressed him and headed for the bathroom, knowing she had to get his temperature down as fast as possible. The rash covering his chest was a brilliant pink, and she could actually feel the heat radiating from his body. She filled the tub with cool water and lowered him in. He began to scream uncontrollably. All of a sudden she heard Justin, who'd been awakened from a sound sleep, bellowing at the top of his lungs, too.

"Cassie? What can I do to help?" came Trace's voice over all the commotion.

Relieved he was there, she turned to him eagerly. "Jason's fever is so high he has a rash. There's a new bottle of infant's pain reliever in the other bathroom. Would you mind getting it?"

"I'll be right back. And Cassie, don't worry too much. Justin once had the same thing. It looks like roseola to me. A virus— extremely uncomfortable for them but usually no serious effects."

Cassie nodded her relief but begged him to hurry. She was finding it difficult to calm Jason, who hated the cool water and fought her in earnest. Soon Trace returned, crouching beside her as he unsealed the brand-new bottle of pain reliever and removed the dropper.

He'd rolled his sleeves to the elbow, exposing his tanned hands and arms with their smattering of dark hair. "You continue to sponge him and I'll get this stuff down his throat. It should reduce his fever within half an hour and make him feel a lot better."

She couldn't figure out how Trace could remain so composed when she was practically falling apart with anxiety. After several attempts, Trace finally managed the impossible.

The sight of him bent over the tub ministering to Jason's needs filled her with an indescribable tenderness, and her earlier anger evaporated completely. But Jason seemed to be furious with her, and although it wasn't really rational, she couldn't help fearing that he'd never forgive her for this.

"Don't look so worried, Cassie," Trace said. "Jason's going to be fine, and in two days he'll have forgotten all about tonight. He already seems better, don't you think?"

Cassie reached out to touch Jason's cheeks and forehead. Trace was right. He wasn't as hot and had quieted down considerably.

"You're going to get better. Mommy and Daddy are right here. You poor little darling. You're freezing!"

"That's the idea," Trace murmured, continuing to scoop the cool water over Jason's blotchy red neck and chest.

"Mama. Dada." Jason called both their names clearly, and Trace flashed her a look of such sweetness, her breath caught in her throat.

With her upper arm she brushed the tears from her cheeks and grasped one of the child's hands. "Just a few more minutes and Daddy will take you out of the tub, darling. It'll be over soon."

Jason began to cry again and tried to sit up. It seemed like an eternity before his father finally said, "I think this little guy has had enough for now."

As soon as Trace lifted him from the water, Cassie had a towel ready and wrapped him in it. Jason clung to Trace as they left the bathroom. Cassie thought he'd take the baby to the nursery, but instead he headed down the hall for the master bedroom. Over his shoulder he asked, "Cassie, will you please bring me the juice I saw in his crib? If I hold him on my bed for a while, maybe I can get him to drink it."

Cassie hurried into the nursery for Jason's bottle, as well as a fresh diaper and a light cotton quilt. Justin was standing up in his crib, crying hoarsely. "Just a minute, Justin. Here, darling." She handed him a stuffed pig. "Mommy'll be right back."

The only time Cassie had been in Trace's bedroom was once with Nattie, when they'd put some clothes away in his drawers. She'd certainly never entered it when he was home. But right now she didn't think of that. She swept inside and dashed over to the side of the bed where he lay sprawled out full-length, his tie off and his shirt unbuttoned halfway down his chest. Jason lay in the crook of his arm staring up at his father, still whimpering a little but obviously content.

Trace took the bottle and offered it to Jason while Cassie

changed his diaper and replaced the damp towel with the quilt. She and Trace exchanged relieved glances, as Jason drank thirstily, even holding the bottle by himself.

Unfortunately, Justin was still howling mournfully. Trace sent Cassie a humorous smile, and something in his expression made her feel they really were husband and wife, in every sense of the words. She had to fight the impulse to lean down a little farther and kiss his mouth.

"I'm going," she whispered. "I'll be in the other room if you need me."

"Not yet," he said softly. He lifted his free hand to her face, shaping the palm to the contour of her cheek. "I was inexcusably rude to you earlier. Tell me what happened with Lena. Did you get anywhere with her?"

"Yes. She's willing to let me use her paintings for the opening."

There was a brief pause. "You made a better start than I'd hoped for," he said. "When we get to Snowbird, I intend to show you my appreciation. With no worries and no children, I'll be able to concentrate on you for a whole week."

Excitement coursed through her veins. For the first time since their wedding, they were going to be alone together, and Trace sounded as if he was really looking forward to it. Of course, she knew he was motivated by concern for his sister and by gratitude for Cassie's help, but she hoped he was beginning to be aware of her as a desirable woman.

"It sounds wonderful." She purposely kept her voice low and steady for fear she'd reveal too much. She left the room immediately afterward.

With her skin still tingling from Trace's touch, she quieted Justin by picking him up and carrying him downstairs for a snack. Happy to be cuddled, he ate a graham cracker and gulped down some warm milk. A half hour later he was ready for bed.

After she'd settled him for the night, she went directly to Trace's room and tiptoed inside. As she took in the sight of Jason lying on his father's chest, her eyes moistened. Father and son were sound asleep.

Careful not to disturb them, she felt Jason's forehead; his temperature had gone down, just as Trace had predicted.

Unable to help herself, she let her gaze wander back to her

husband, whose disheveled black hair made him look uncharac-
teristically boyish. For a few minutes she studied the lines of his
strong, straight nose and mobile mouth, the way his dark lashes
fanned out against bronzed cheeks. She stared at his arm, still
protectively circling his son.

I love him, she thought. *I love him so much I can hardly bear
it.*

Before she could do something foolish—like lie down next to
him—she crept out the door and flew to her bedroom, where she
could give way to her emotions in private. Trace would never
know how excited she was to be going on this trip with him,
how desperately she wanted to spend time with him alone. But
she'd have to be very careful never to let him know how much
she craved his touch. How much she craved not just gratitude
and respect, but love.

Unable to sleep, Cassie pulled on a nightgown and robe and
went to her workroom, where she could unleash her energy on
an idea that had been unfolding in her mind.

Going to her files, she found the pattern she wanted and began
cutting out fabric. Four hours later, a stuffed, six-foot alligator
with black hair and calculating blue eyes lay on the floor watching her with a wicked grin. Across the tail she had stitched the
word "Daddy."

When it was finished she opened the closet door and stood the
alligator on end in the far corner. To make sure it remained
hidden, she draped it with a swath of white canvas, then shut the
door.

If Trace ever saw it, he'd know the truth. He'd know she was
in love with him. Cassie couldn't imagine anything worse—because he wasn't in love with her. He'd feel only pity, and Cassie
didn't think she could stand that.

CHAPTER SEVEN

"I'VE NEVER SEEN so much snow," Cassie gasped as the large airport limousine carrying the Ramsey clan approached the lodge at Snowbird. She was pressed between Norman and Trace, who kept his arm constantly around her; her joy was diminished, since she realized it was a show of affection for his family's benefit.

"Actually Utah's had a mild winter this year," Trace said in a low voice near her ear. "I can remember coming up here several times when there were literally walls of ice. The state's in a drought cycle right now."

She surveyed the towering white mountain peaks knifing through the thin, freezing cold air. "You'd never know it." She tried desperately to appear unaffected by his nearness, but her heart was hammering out of control. She didn't know if her disorientation was due to the altitude or to the fact that she'd be sharing a bedroom with Trace in a few minutes.

"I can't wait to hit the powder!" James announced as the limo pulled to a stop. "Last one out brings the skis for everybody."

"Oh, brother!" This came from his wife, Dorothy, who sat across from Jane, Norman's wife. Lena and Allen shared the front seat with the chauffeur.

A great deal of good-natured bantering went on as they proceeded to find their bags and carry in their ski equipment.

The heat generated by a roaring blaze in the giant hearth off the lobby welcomed new arrivals. Cassie wandered over to it while Trace dealt with registration. A jaunty-looking Lena gravitated to the fire with Cassie, sporting an all-navy ski outfit that suited her trim figure perfectly. Cassie, on the other hand, felt conspicuous, dressed in brand-new fluorescent-green ski bib and white, green and blue matching parka.

Several days after Jason had fully recovered from his roseola,

Trace had purchased the outfit, along with skis and boots, and had brought everything home gift-wrapped. He made her open the packages the second he bounded in the house from work.

A card lying on top of the tissue had caught her eye. Gingerly Cassie picked it up and read: ''You have my undying gratitude for being such a wonderful, caring mother to our sons. I hope this gift will convey in some small measure my appreciation for the way you've turned this house into a haven I love to come home to. You've more than kept your side of our bargain, Cassie. I hope to show my appreciation when we go to Snowbird. We'll have a week to ourselves—a chance for Cassandra Ramsey to feel a little indulged for a change! Trace.''

The sincere sentiment had moved her. But his note didn't contain the words she wanted to read, to hear, above all others. The realization that Trace might never fall in love with her filled her with a sudden deep despair. She fought to keep a smile on her face as she thanked him for the presents. But knowing she couldn't keep up the pretense for long, she'd made an excuse to leave the room, claiming she wanted to phone Lena.

As she called her sister-in-law, she felt Trace's probing gaze and sensed a strange undercurrent that she found more than a little troubling. To her vast relief, Lena was home and Cassie launched into conversation about their ski trip with feigned enthusiasm.

Even when Trace left the room, she could still feel his strained reaction and wondered what had caused it. Maybe she hadn't sounded grateful enough. Or maybe he resented her talking on the phone the minute he came home from work.

Whatever the problem, for the next week Cassie had taken great pains to make their home the haven he'd mentioned in his note. In between her sewing activities, she went on a cooking spree and fixed delicious meals, preparing some of his favorite Southwestern dishes. But if anything, her actions seemed to increase the tension between them. The more she tried to please him, the more polite and remote he became. It reached the point that she'd actually dreaded their trip.

At least around the house, the children acted as a buffer. But now she'd be alone with a difficult husband for six whole days and nights. She wondered how she'd survive their vacation, or even *if* she'd survive.

"Well, well. Where did you come from?" a friendly male voice said directly behind her. Cassie turned around to confront what she considered the classic male ski enthusiast. He was athletically built, with light brown hair bleached by the sun and a tan that resembled leather. A confident smile revealed a splendid set of white teeth. The man simply exuded self-satisfaction.

"We're from Timbuktu," Lena unexpectedly blurted out in a brash tone meant to send him packing. But his confident smile didn't crack, and he continued to stare admiringly at Cassie.

"If you want some help with your technique, I'm your man. Name's Hank. You'll find me by the lift every morning. I give group and private lessons."

Cassie tried hard not to laugh out loud at the man's aggression, but she would never have responded as rudely as Lena had. She merely gave him a bland smile. "Thanks for the tip. If I decide I need instruction, I'll look you up."

"Great! In that terrific outfit, you'll be easy to spot."

"Our room is ready." Trace had found her and was looking every bit as disgusted as his sister with the other man's attention. Cassie hadn't heard that icy tone since the first day in his office, when he'd almost succeeded in having her carted off to jail.

An impish mischief made her green eyes sparkle as she said, "Trace, this is Hank, one of the ski instructors for the lodge. Hank, this is my husband, Trace, and his sister, Lena."

"How do you do?" Hank put out a hand, which Trace was forced to shake. "Your sister says you're from Timbuktu. As I understand it, you don't get a lot of snow in that part of Africa."

Hank had a sense of humor, she'd give him that. There was a protracted silence. "That's right," Trace finally muttered, stone-faced. He glared at Cassie. "Are you ready?"

Swallowing hard, she said, "Whenever you are."

"Then let's go."

In the uncomfortable silence that followed, she turned to Hank. "It was nice to meet you."

Hank grinned. "I always enjoy meeting people from foreign places. See you around."

Suddenly Trace was ushering her from the foyer, his grip on her arm firm. Lena found her husband, and the four of them rode the elevator together.

"Hey, why so serious?" Allen questioned his wife. "Can you

believe six whole days without the kids?'' He swooped down and kissed the end of her cold nose. "Brrr," he joked, causing Lena to laugh, bringing her out of herself. "It looks like you need warming up."

Cassie averted her eyes, envious of their easy relationship and their intimacy. When the doors opened to the fourth floor, she couldn't get out of the elevator fast enough and, apparently, neither could Trace.

"See you at dinner," they called out before the doors closed again.

Trace led the way to their room, which overlooked the snowy Wasatch Mountains where they'd be skiing. The afternoon sun glistened off the dazzling white peaks, making her eyes sting.

"I can't believe we're here. Only this morning I was looking out at the desert from the nursery window."

"And wishing you didn't have to come?" he asked grimly.

Cassie whirled around in surprise. "Why do you say that?"

"I'm not blind, Cassie. I saw the way you clung to the children this morning. Anyone would've thought I was dragging you off to—" he paused "—Timbuktu for a year, instead of a short holiday. Since I know you're dying to find out if they're still alive, I'll go downstairs and bring up the rest of our things while you phone home for a report."

He left the room before she could refute his words. But in all honesty, what was there to say? She *had* been dreading this trip, but not for the reasons he imagined. Snowbird had to be one of the most romantic places on earth—and it served as a painful reminder of the mockery of a marriage to a man who didn't love her.

Her gaze strayed to the two queen-size beds. She felt a wave of humiliation. Trace couldn't possibly feel any desire for her or he wouldn't have arranged for a room with two beds. Who in the family, except Lena, could guess that for the next week, Trace and his wife would be roommates, nothing more?

Hot tears spilled down her cheeks, but she quickly dashed them away with her hands. At home, when she grew frustrated over her futile love for Trace, she could escape to her sewing room or the nursery. But now that they'd arrived at the lodge, she had to make the best of an almost intolerable situation. She could think of only one thing to do. Ski!

Perhaps in six days she could learn the basics of a sport Trace loved. But she'd need lessons from one of the instructors—and judging by Trace's reaction, it had better not be Hank. Cassie disliked that type of obsessively flirtatious man, anyway. Perhaps there was another instructor available, one more interested in skiing than in the female skiers!

With an actual plan, Cassie felt a little better. She phoned the house in Phoenix, and Nattie put her mind at rest, assuring her the children were fine. She urged Cassie to forget everything and concentrate on Trace.

When she replaced the receiver, Cassie found herself wondering if Nattie's last comment was meant to be taken as a piece of womanly advice. The housekeeper knew Cassie and Trace slept in separate bedrooms. She probably found their relationship unnatural. *Well, so did Cassie!* But there didn't seem to be a thing she could do about it.

"Are they still breathing?"

Trace's biting sarcasm jolted her out of her reverie. She turned around, counting slowly to ten before answering. Somehow she had to salvage this trip; she had to get on better terms with her husband—who at the moment looked far too attractive for her peace of mind. The gray-and-black-striped ski sweater complimented his dark good looks and emphasized his trim, powerful build.

"The children are fine, and you're right. I've doted on them to the exclusion of too many other things. Maybe it's because I'm not their natural mother, so I've taken on a greater sense of responsibility than is warranted. Please believe me when I say I'm happy to be here."

At her words, the stiffness seemed to leave his taut frame and he moved closer. His eyes searched her face for endless minutes. "Cassie, I realize you led a completely different life until you married me, and I've expected far too much, too soon. Chalk it up to my boardroom tactics." With a slow smile that made her heart turn over, he put his hands on her upper arms. "For the rest of this week, could we pretend there's just the two of us and enjoy a vacation we both badly need?"

"I'd love it."

"Good," he whispered, then leaned forward to kiss the top of her head. Maybe it was her imagination, but she thought he buried his face in her hair an extra-long moment before lifting his head. Her body seemed to dissolve with desire. The slightest contact triggered a physical response she couldn't control, and she wondered if he could tell what his nearness did to her. ''Are you hungry?'' he asked as he stepped back, releasing her arms.

''Starving.

''Let's grab a hamburger. Then I'll take you out on the bunny hill and teach you a few fundamentals. In a day or two, you'll be ready to go up on the lift.''

Cassie would willingly have gone anywhere with him. And since he'd offered to give up his own skiing time to teach her, she could hardly refuse.

The rest of the day Cassie reveled in his company. She alternated between fits of laughter and spills in the snow—with the occasional success—as she tried to master the snowplow and the art of falling down safely. If Trace thought her a lost cause, he didn't say so. But she'd never seen him smile so much, which gave her more pleasure than she dared to admit, even to herself.

As the sun started to go down, he grew more playful and began tossing snowballs at her. She tried to escape, but her skis crossed and she fell headlong into the snow. When he saw her predicament, he took off his own skis and scooped up a fresh handful of snow. She struggled onto her side and giggled as he started toward her with a predatory gleam in his eye.

''No, Trace!'' she screamed through her laughter, trying to shield her face. With one gloved hand he easily caught her wrists and pinned them in the snow above her head, leaving the other free to begin his torture.

''Be kind,'' she pleaded on a shallow breath, her eyes half dancing, half fearful, as she met his gaze, which darkened in intensity the longer they stared at each other.

''My words exactly.''

A moan trembled on her lips at the passion in his husky voice. The blood surged through her veins as he lowered his head and found her mouth with his own, creating an aura of scorching heat despite the near-zero temperature of the air. Each kiss grew deeper, hungrier. Cassie could no longer contain her own frantic response. When he wrapped her in his arms and pulled her against him, she feverishly kissed him back, losing all sense of time and place.

"Good grief, Trace. You've got a perfectly good room at the lodge for that sort of thing. I think you'd better take a run with us and cool off, little brother."

Norman's teasing voice penetrated Cassie's rapture, and she pulled sharply away from her husband. Not only was she more embarrassed than she'd ever been in her life, but to be so rudely transported back to reality made her want to weep with frustration.

With enviable aplomb, Trace got to his feet, then helped her up and handed her the ski poles she'd dropped. Cassie couldn't recover her own composure as quickly. She had to support herself with her poles so she could stand upright while she faced Trace's two brothers, who stood there unashamedly grinning at her. She didn't dare look at Trace. At this point he could be in no doubt that his wife more than welcomed his lovemaking.

She heard him ask, "Hasn't the lift closed yet?" When James said there was time for one more run, Trace turned to her. "If you don't mind, Cassie, I'll go with James and Norman and meet you back at the lodge for dinner."

What was going on? He seemed to be relieved that his brothers had interrupted their lovemaking; he'd leapt at the chance to join them. Yet Cassie could have sworn he was as shaken as she was by the passion they'd just shared. She'd thought he would tell his brothers to ski without him, that he and Cassie had other plans.

What a fool she was!

Trace was a man of experience and he'd simply been having a little fun in the snow. He hadn't meant anything serious. Most likely he was already regretting their interlude, because he hadn't expected her to respond the way she had. Well, she'd make sure he wouldn't worry that she'd gotten the wrong idea!

Lifting her head, she smiled brightly at the three of them. "To be honest, I was hoping someone else would come along to entertain Trace. For the last while, I've been dying to take my poor aching body back to the room and have a long hot soak in the tub. The altitude has made me so tired, I think I'll have a quick sandwich and go to bed. By the time you return, I'll probably be out like a light until morning."

"You sound like Dorothy," Norman moaned.

Trace's expression became shuttered, as if her answer displeased him. She couldn't figure him out. "I'll see you later then," he murmured, turning abruptly to get his skis.

With an aching heart Cassie watched until the three of them disappeared over the crest of the beginners' hill. He didn't once look back or wave.

What did he want? Should she have begged him in front of his brothers? Begged him to stay, to keep up the pretense that they had a normal marriage? If he hadn't regretted those intimate moments in her arms, then why had he left her?

Cassie didn't know what to make of his erratic behavior. Vowing never to get into such a vulnerable situation again, she trudged back to the lodge, ate another hamburger and went up to their room. An hour later, she climbed out of the tub, almost overcome with lethargy. She searched for the red flannel nightgown she'd made especially for the trip and fell into bed, exhausted. Once under the covers, she let out a deep sigh and was aware of nothing more until she wakened early the next morning, suffering from hunger pangs and sore muscles.

She glanced at her watch, surprised she'd slept so long. Trace was in the other bed, still asleep. When had he come to bed? She could hear his deep even breathing and noticed a tanned arm and shoulder above the blankets.

Carefully she turned on her side to watch him. Everything about him enthralled her. If he only loved her and she could be sure of his welcome, she'd climb in beside him right now and kiss him awake. The longer she gazed at him, the deeper her yearning.

When she couldn't bear it any longer, she slipped out of bed and hurried into the bathroom to dress. Now was as good a time as any to start ski lessons. Maybe later in the day Trace would join her again and she'd be able to show some improvement.

As quietly as she could, Cassie left the room and went down to the lobby to eat breakfast and arrange for lessons. Fortunately there was a woman on the ski patrol who taught group lessons in the morning before the lift opened, and Cassie signed up with her.

The class contained both children and adults at various stages of proficiency. Cassie discovered that Trace had taught her well, because she could keep up with the best of them. When the lesson was over, she hurried back to the room to tell him, but he'd already gone.

The rest of the day brought little pleasure. The flirtatious instructor, Hank, saw her on the hill later in the morning and wanted to ski with her, but she refused. Then it was time for lunch. She joined Dorothy, Jane and Lena, who all declared they'd had enough skiing for one day. Apparently the men had gone off together, so the women decided to play cards in front of the fire. Trace didn't make an appearance until everyone gathered for dinner in the main dining room that evening.

He greeted Cassie with a kiss on the cheek as if nothing was wrong, and laughed and joked with the others. Everyone described the day's events; inevitably, one of the women brought up the fact that Cassie had had a ski lesson. Trace murmured something appropriate and said that when she felt ready, they would take a run together. On the surface his behavior appeared perfectly normal. But Cassie sensed his withdrawal.

As the evening wore on, the family stayed downstairs for the musical entertainment. Cassie couldn't enjoy it because, although Trace always acted the part of a polite, concerned husband, he had distanced himself from her. This, more than anything, convinced her he wanted to forget what had happened on their first day in the snow.

Pleading fatigue, one by one each couple headed up to bed until finally Cassie was left alone with Trace. "You seem tired," he said in that same polite voice. "Why don't you go up to bed? I'm going to have a drink in the bar."

Nothing could be plainer than that! Cassie murmured a good night and barely made it to the room before she broke down sobbing. She couldn't take it much longer.

The next day started out like a repeat of the previous one, with Trace still sleeping soundly in the other bed as she left for her lesson. She was still agonizing over Trace when she entered the lobby afterward. Lena was waiting for her and asked if she'd like to take a shuttle bus down to Salt Lake City to do some shopping. Allen's birthday was the next weekend and Lena wanted to get him something special. Cassie didn't have to think twice about accepting her invitation. She wasn't an enthusiastic shopper, but anything was better than spending the rest of the day on the slopes hoping she'd run into Trace, or worse, praying in vain that he'd come to find her.

Lena wanted to keep their expedition a secret, so Cassie left Trace a note saying only that she was going down the canyon. They left the lodge with a group of other people to do a full day's shopping and sight-seeing. The first thing Cassie bought was postcards, and while she and Lena ate Mexican food at Chef Trujillo's, she wrote short notes to some of her friends in San Francisco, including Beulah.

They spent the afternoon trailing in and out of shops. Cassie found hand-knit toques and mittens for the boys, some gourmet preserves for Nattie, and a small bottle of Canadian rye for Mike.

She managed to buy a gift for Trace, too. Quite by chance she'd seen a framed photograph of the mountains around Snowbird in a tourist shop, where Lena had already found another snow scene for Allen's gift. The shot was quite spectacular, with the early-morning rays tinting the snow-covered peaks. Luckily it didn't cost a great deal and was something she could buy with her own money, but she thought he'd like it.

By the time their bus pulled up to the lodge in the evening, the family had eaten and gone their separate ways. Cassie hurried upstairs with her packages, anxious to give Trace his present. But he wasn't in the room. If he'd gone to the bar, presumably he wanted to be alone, and she had no intention of disturbing him. If he was visiting with one of his brothers, she was equally unwilling to intrude. Dejected, she took a shower, put on her flannel nightgown and climbed into bed with a recent mystery novel she'd bought that afternoon.

Trace walked in half an hour later. Slowly Cassie's gaze lifted to his above the pages of the book. As always, she was achingly aware of him. He was dressed in sweats, with a deep tan that attested to a day's skiing—she noticed that instantly but she also noticed the tension in his posture and expression. "Hello," she said in an unsteady voice.

"So you're back." Grimacing, he tossed the room key on the table. "Did you have a good time?"

Cassie sat up straight, anxious to tell him about her day, to hear about his. "Yes. And I bought something for you. It's there on the bed."

He moved slowly to the bed and unwrapped the gift. "It's

beautiful, Cassie—but you don't have to bribe me into going home. I know you never wanted to come to Snowbird in the first place."

The book fell out of her hands. "I don't want to leave. I'm having a good time."

His expression grew bleak. "Well, I'm not. I brought you here to spend time with you. But every time I turn around, you're missing. The family is beginning to wonder what's going on."

Anger made her face feel hot. "I thought the purpose of this trip was to be by ourselves and do what we wanted. If you remember, *you're* the one who took off with your brothers the first night we were here." She could have bitten her tongue for referring to that evening, but it was too late now.

Trace's mouth hardened, as if he didn't like being reminded of the incident. "Did you go to Salt Lake City alone?"

Cassie averted her eyes. His unexpected question had conveniently changed the subject. "No."

"I didn't think so."

Throwing back the covers, she got out of bed to face him. To her dismay, his eyes traveled unhurriedly over her curves, which weren't hidden by the red fabric, then finally lifted to her flushed face. It was almost enough to make her forget what they were arguing about.

"In case you're thinking I was with that ski instructor," she said calmly, "then you couldn't be more wrong. For your information, I went to Salt Lake City with Lena—at her request. I thought you'd realize she and I were together. She wanted to buy something special for Allen's birthday and didn't want him to know about it."

"Be that as it may, your disappearances have pretty well let the family know that your interests lie outside your marriage."

"That's unfair!" she cried. "How can you say such a thing? Except for the first day, have you ever asked me to ski with you? Have you invited me out to dinner? Did you ask me to stay with you in the bar and dance?"

His expression was tight with fury. "After hearing you tell my brothers you were hoping someone else would come along to entertain me, I had doubts that any invitation of mine would be welcome."

Cassie's eyes closed tightly. "I only said that so you wouldn' feel obliged to stay with me. I know how much you love to ski with them.''

They stood facing each other in silence, like adversaries. Finally he said, "Whatever the reasons for our misunderstandings, this trip isn't working out. Be packed and ready to go in the morning.''

He placed the photograph and its crumpled wrappings on his night-table with a deliberate care that confused her. Then he disappeared out the door, leaving Cassie furious—and heartsick.

CHAPTER EIGHT

AFTER EATING a bit of the chicken salad a surprised Nattie had
left for her, Cassie started up the stairs to check on the children
whom she'd put to bed earlier. As she reached the first landing
she heard the phone ring. She fervently hoped it was Trace. He'd
left for the office after they'd returned from Snowbird that afternoon and hadn't bothered to come home for dinner. She dashed
into his study, picked up the receiver and said a nervous hello.

"Cassie? It's Lena!"

"Lena? What are you doing calling me from Snowbird?"

"More to the point, what are you and Trace doing back in
Phoenix? Allen and I decided to sleep in this morning. When we
got up, James told us you and Trace had left the lodge to go
home. Something about a problem with one of the boys. I think
everyone else believed it, but I don't. Can you talk, or is Trace
around?"

"He went to the bank to see if there was anything pressing. I
put the children to bed an hour ago and just had some supper."

"Then you can talk. What's wrong? You know I'd do anything
for you and Trace."

"You shouldn't have said that." Cassie swallowed back a sob.
"Trace and I have had one misunderstanding after another," she
said hopelessly.

"Which one of you called off the rest of your vacation, or am
I being too nosy?"

"Of course not. If you want the truth, I think he's tired of
having to pretend everything's perfect with us when we're
around the family. I never seem to be able to say the right thing.
We do much better alone at the house, with just the children.
Our marriage won't survive another vacation."

"I'm sorry, Cassie. This must be so hard for you. I was once in love with someone and I thought he loved me, until I learned the truth the hard way. It took me a long time to get over him, so I can just imagine what you're going through right now. I wish there was something I could do to help.''

"I appreciate your support and friendship. Unfortunately no one can make Trace fall in love with me," Cassie said in a voice that quavered despite her effort to sound matter-of-fact. "If it hasn't happened by now, it never will. That's the reality and I'm going to have to live with it. Don't forget, I went into this marriage for the children's sake."

"But the children will never be enough now."

"I hope you're wrong," she said softly, then broke off when she heard footsteps on the stairs. "Lena, I'll have to hang up. I think Trace is home."

"All right. I'll call you as soon as we get back."

"Thanks for everything." Cassie put down the receiver as the study door flew open and Trace stood there, silhouetted in the light from a hallway lamp. Cassie muttered a greeting, but something in his stance made her unaccountably nervous.

"You're upset. Did something go wrong with the merger while we were on our trip?" she asked.

"If you weren't so preoccupied with your phone call, you would have been able to hear the boys crying. Who has such a claim on your time you've been neglecting them?"

His unfair accusation stung Cassie to retaliation. "How dare you say that to me when you didn't bother to come home for dinner to be with them—or even call to let me know you'd be late!" she demanded, her chest heaving with indignation.

His hands curled into fists, and without volition, her eyes took in the strength of his body, the powerful thighs in tight-fitting jeans, the black knit shirt that clung to his chest like a second skin. They were close enough that she could feel the warmth of his body and smell the soap he'd used in the shower. Right now she couldn't think or move as desire for him engulfed her like a sudden burst of flame.

"I dare because I'm your husband." A hand shot out and grasped her wrist, bringing her closer and making her far too conscious of his body. "You still haven't answered my question."

She could have told him the truth—that it was Lena on the

phone—but she didn't. She was too angry, because he didn't seem to trust her. And at the same time she needed to put distance between them before she lost complete control.

"As I recall," she said coldly, "*you* were the one who said what we did with our private lives was our own affair, as long as it didn't hurt the children. I never question the unorthodox hours you keep, and I'm not doing anything you haven't done since the day we were married." She tried to pull away, but he held her fast.

"And just what is it you think I've been doing?" he whispered. "Making secret assignations behind your back? Why should I do that when I have a wife who seems perfectly capable of filling everyone's needs—but mine? I think it's time you took care of them."

In the next instant he drew her into his arms and found her mouth with a savagery that made nonsense of her efforts to resist. For so long she'd wanted him, but not like this, not angry and suspicious of her motives. Yet she wasn't prepared for the intimate caress of his hands against the skin of her back, where her blouse had separated from her jeans. His touch softened and Cassie melted against every line and angle of his hard body, helplessly yielding to the seductive pressure of his mouth, his hands.

Cassie hadn't ever known this kind of ecstasy before, and she didn't want Trace to stop. Her arms slid around his neck so she could get even closer. She wanted to give, and go on giving until he knew in every single cell of his body that she loved him. That she always would.

Perhaps it was her moan of pleasure that caused a shudder to pass through his body. The next thing she knew, he had thrust her away from him. She cried out in surprise and clung to his desk to prevent herself from falling.

The faint light made it impossible for her to see his expression clearly. But if his shallow breathing and the tautness of his body were any indication, he'd been equally disturbed by their passionate embrace.

Then she heard a muttered curse before he blurted out, "I had no right to lay a finger on you, Cassie, let alone demand an accounting. Whatever you do with your free time is none of my damn business. I'm the one who's broken the rules of our contract and I swear it won't happen again. Why don't you go on up to bed. I know you're under a lot of pressure, getting ready for your opening. I'll lock up and take a look at the boys before I turn in.''

She watched him leave the study and ached to call him back. But without knowing how he really felt about her, what he really wanted from her, she didn't dare. Living in the same house day after day had made them aware of each other to the point of physical need. She'd felt Trace's desire for her. But that didn't mean he was in love with her.

Drained from the explosive emotions, Cassie followed his suggestion and went to bed. But she was plagued with insomnia. Trace had set her on fire, exposing the primitive, womanly side of her nature, changing her preconceived notions about physical love for all time.

By two o'clock, her body was still reliving the taste and feel of his mouth and she couldn't fall asleep. Disgusted with herself, she went to her sewing room, where she immersed herself in work and didn't come out until seven in the morning.

When she went downstairs to start breakfast, she discovered that Trace's car wasn't in the driveway. He'd deliberately left the house early; when she realized this, her hurt intensified. She went through the motions of her morning routine, which included bathing and feeding the children. At noon Nattie took over so she could leave the house and drive to the gallery with as many things as she could load into the station wagon. This set the pattern for the next few days.

Besides all the new crafts she'd been making, she decided to sell all the stock items from her inventory, too. There was a second display room, which would be perfect. But even with Mike's help, it took several days to move everything from the house to the shop. During that time, she saw next to nothing of Trace, who came home too late to do more than kiss the boys good-night and disappear into his study.

On Friday, as Cassie was unpacking another set of freestanding shelves at the shop and trying not to think about the impossible state of affairs between her and Trace, Lena walked in, carrying some paintings.

Cassie stared at her sister-in-law. "I'm so glad you're back."

"I bet you thought I'd deserted you, staying so long at Snowbird, but Allen and I had to be alone. I've tried to make up for lost time today by signing the rest of the paintings. As you know, my car won't hold more than two at a time, so I'll have to make several trips."

Shaking her head, Cassie said, "We'll go back to the house in the station wagon and get the rest. Now that you've finished them, I'm going to stay here all evening and set up as much as I can to view the full effect." She glanced around. "I think I'm going to have to buy some more plants, though."

Lena scrutinized everything with her artist's eye. "I'll tell you what. I want to be home with the children for dinner. Then I'll come back here to help, but it'll have to remain our secret. Allen can think I've gone to a PTA meeting."

"Are you sure?" Cassie cried out excitedly. Trace would be overjoyed if he knew how involved Lena had become with Mix and Match.

"You're a remarkable woman, Cassie, but even I can see how much work still has to be done."

"The opening's coming up much too soon," Cassie agreed, "and there aren't enough hours in the day to accomplish everything. Now let's go home and get the rest of the paintings."

She didn't particularly relish the prospect of being at the shop alone at night and would be thankful for Lena's presence. Although she wasn't entirely comfortable with her sister-in-law's apparent penchant for secrecy, she could understand it, too. Lena was so terribly unsure of herself and of her talent.

As it turned out, Lena and Cassie worked side by side for the next two nights, attempting to set up the most appealing displays possible. And they shared more confidences. Cassie marveled at her sister-in-law's decorating sense and thanked her repeatedly before they parted company Saturday night.

"Don't forget Allen's surprise birthday dinner at seven tomorrow. I phoned Trace earlier and invited him, so he knows you're both expected."

And probably dreading another evening with me in front of his family, Cassie mused painfully. "Will everyone be there?"

"No. It's just going to be the four of us," Lena explained, lessening Cassie's anxiety somewhat.

The next morning didn't begin well. Nattie informed Cassie that Trace had left to keep a golf date with a business acquaintance. When he did come home, he spent some time with the children, and she didn't see him until they were ready to go to Lena's.

They behaved civilly to each other, but during dinner Trace couldn't have been more distant with Cassie, more removed from her emotionally—a fact Lena was quick to observe. While they cleared the table, she flashed Cassie a look of commiseration.

Cassie was grateful for Allen, whose conversation as he opened his presents provided the only comic relief. His eyes met his wife's as he unwrapped the framed photograph she'd bought him in Utah and he sent her a message of love so fervent that Cassie lowered her own eyes. She knew he must be remembering the private time he and Lena had spent at Snowbird. But the moment was brief and he quickly moved on to the other gifts, ending with Cassie's. Lena had told her that Allen loved to barbecue, so Cassie had made him a chef's apron embroidered with French cooking terms.

"So tell me, you lucky cuss." Allen poked Trace in the ribs. "How did you manage to end up with Cassie? She can cook, sew, she's a great mother and her skiing's coming along nicely. She's a looker, too."

Normally Cassie would have been amused by Allen's remarks. But she was too sensitive to Trace's mood just now. She found herself waiting uncomfortably for one of his carefully worded responses while she pretended interest in the birthday cake.

"You left out the part about her being a savvy business woman," Lena interjected on cue, saving Trace from having to utter a word.

"That's right," Allen murmured. "How's the shop coming?"

His question was directed at Cassie, but it was Trace who answered. "Judging by the nights she's stayed up sewing, I'd say she probably has more than enough things to fill several shops." Although his comment sounded innocent, Cassie wasn't deceived. She lowered her head, but not before Lena had sent her a sympathetic glance.

"When's the opening?" Allen asked, seemingly ignorant of the undercurrents. "Lena and I plan to be there."

"Next Saturday," Cassie said faintly. The tension emanating from Trace left her so nervous, she was finding it more and more difficult to speak.

Suddenly Lena cleared her throat and looked nervously at her husband. "Darling, I think it's time I made a confession." There was an air of expectancy after her announcement.

"We're not pregnant again, are we?" he teased, but Cassie could see the love shining in his eyes.

"No." Lena laughed. "When I told you I had meetings the last two nights, I was lying." Allen's smile slowly faded. "Actually, I've been helping Cassie at the gallery."

Allen blinked. "That's great. But why didn't you just say so?"

"Because...Cassie's using some of my old paintings as part of her display. At first I didn't want you to know about it because..."

He stopped eating his cake and gazed at his wife solemnly. "Does this mean what I think it means?"

She took a deep breath. "It means that I've been a fool to be so sensitive about the past."

"Honey..." Allen's hand grasped hers.

Something was going on here that Cassie didn't quite understand. Allen seemed overwhelmed with emotion. She automatically glanced at Trace and discovered his eyes focused on her, sending her a private message of gratitude. Even if the warmth in his regard had everything to do with her influence on Lena, Cassie basked in his approval. She had no pride anymore. She loved him too much.

In the background she could hear the phone ringing and then Becky, Lena's daughter, poked her head around the dining-room door. "Aunt Cassie? Uncle Trace? Nattie says you'd better come home. Jason woke up croupy."

The twelve hours following Lena's dinner party would have been a nightmare for Cassie if Trace hadn't been there to help nurse Jason through the night. First roseola, now a croupy cough that kept them all awake. By noon the next day, however, he seemed much better and Cassie finally relaxed.

She couldn't say the same for Trace. Fatigue lines etched his face from hour after hour of walking the floor with Jason. Cassie urged him to call Mrs. Blakesley and cancel any appointments for the day so he could go to bed. But Trace insisted he had to be at the bank for an important afternoon meeting and left the house at a run.

Once again she found herself marveling at the extraordinary strength of the man she'd married. Trace was unfailingly responsible, always dependable. The longer she lived with him, the more Cassie realized how much she, as well as others, particularly his family, relied on him. Though the youngest Ramsey, it was no accident that his brothers had made him chairman of the board. His confidence and his abilities made people put their trust in him.

Because he worked so hard, Cassie was concerned about his not getting enough rest, and she spent the remainder of the afternoon and evening worrying about her husband instead of Jason, who was starting to behave more like himself again.

Cassie had been asleep for some time when she heard a knock on her door. Alarmed, she glanced at the bedside clock, which said it was after midnight. The knock sounded again.

"Nattie?" she called anxiously and sat up in bed.

"It's Trace, Cassie. I need to talk to you. May I come in?"

"Yes. Of course." Her voice shook as she turned on the lamp and pulled the covers to her chin. "Is Jason bad again?" she asked as he entered her bedroom wearing his bathrobe. He must have come from the shower because the clean scent of soap wafted in the air.

Trace closed the door behind him and approached her bed. "No. I just checked on him. He's fine. So's Justin."

She swallowed hard. "When did you come home? I held dinner until nine, then put yours in the fridge."

"I'm sorry I was late again. I only just got home." The lines in his face were more pronounced than ever.

"You should have been in bed hours ago, Trace. You look exhausted. How did your meeting go?" Cassie had the hysterical urge to laugh because he'd never been in her bedroom this late at night before, and here were the two of them talking like a comfortably married couple.

"Very well, as a matter of fact, but I didn't waken you to talk about bank business. I have something much more serious on my mind."

"Is it about Lena and Allen?"

Her question seemed to baffle him. "No. Why would it be when things have never been better between them?"

"I meant to ask you about that. Why was Allen so overcome by what she said?"

"Because for all the years they've been married, Allen had a secret fear that Lena couldn't talk about her painting or even admit she was once an artist because she was still in love with her ex-lover. Allen hasn't always been the comedian he pretends to be. His jovial behavior has been a front for insecurity, even pain.''

"But that's crazy!" Cassie cried. "Lena adores Allen. She's confided everything to me, and I promise you, she got over that affair years ago. She asked Allen if they could stay on in Snowbird after everyone left because she wanted to have a second honeymoon with him."

The pulse at the corner of his mouth throbbed. "Every man should be so lucky. After her unprompted confession last night, I think he's beginning to believe she loves him wholeheartedly—thanks to you."

Cassie shook her head. "Not me, Trace. You. It was your suggestion that prompted me to talk to Lena in the first place. Somehow you have a gift for making everything right for everybody. The boys are very lucky to have a father like you," she said with a catch in her voice.

"I wonder if this gift you credit me with can fix something a little closer to home."

Her heart thudded painfully at his sober tone. "What is it? What's wrong?"

A grimace marred his handsome features. "When I asked you to marry me, we agreed that if there ever came a time when we didn't like the arrangement, we'd face that problem when it arose."

It was a good thing Cassie was already in bed or she might have fainted. "I remember," she whispered, hardly able to get the words out. "I've been aware for some time that you haven't been happy. Actually I've wanted to talk to you about it, but the opportunity never seemed to present itself."

After a long pause, he said, "That's my fault. I realize I've been impossible to live with. Cassie, I can't go on this way any longer."

A numbing sickness slowly crept through her body. "You don't need to say any more. I'll move out."

To her astonishment his head reared back. "What in the hell are you talking about? I came in here tonight to tell you I hate the rules of our marriage contract and I'm asking you to start sleeping with me in my bed.''

When his words sank in, Cassie felt herself go feverishly hot, then cold. She raised her eyes to him in disbelief. He muttered something unintelligible and shook his head when he saw her stunned expression.

"Living in the same house with you and not being able to make love to you has almost driven me out of my mind. Surely after the other night you can be in no doubt about how much I want you. I almost couldn't let you go.''

His admission opened a floodgate of emotions in Cassie. There was no mistaking the look of desire in his eyes as he sat down on the bed next to her and traced the outline of her flushed face with his fingers. "I'm aching to touch you and hold you all night long. You're in my blood, Cassie—and I know of only one way to solve that particular problem.''

In the next instant his mouth covered hers, forcing her head back against the pillow. For a little while Cassie refused to listen to her heart, which told her there was all the difference in the world between a man's desire for a woman and his love. The sensations his lips aroused against the tender skin of her neck and throat were so addictive she never wanted him to stop. She could no longer think coherently.

But when he lifted the covers to slide into bed beside her she couldn't help remembering that this was how his son's conception had begun. By Trace's own admission, he'd never have married Gloria if he hadn't made her pregnant. Their passion had resulted in a baby, but Jason wasn't the product of two people deeply in love who needed to express those feelings in the age-old way. They had divorced soon after the birth.

Cassie loved Trace with a fierceness he hadn't even guessed at. As for his feelings, she wasn't so naive that she didn't know this would be simply another night of physical passion for him. Sexual gratification, without the heart-deep commitment she desperately needed. Cassie had no way of determining how many times he'd experienced this same desire for the latest woman in his life. *Because that was all she was—and she happened to be available!* The word "love" hadn't even been mentioned. When he tired of her, they'd go back to being housemates again.

Unable to tolerate that possibility, she pushed herself away from him and got to her feet. When he stood up, they faced each other from opposite sides of the narrow bed. Trace ran a hand through his already disheveled black hair, a gesture so sensual she had to close her eyes against its appeal. He would never know what denying herself his lovemaking was costing her.

"The desire seems to be all on my part."

She swallowed hard. "When two people aren't in love, then it's wrong."

The silence seemed to stretch endlessly before he said, "It's inconceivable to me that a woman as warm and beautiful and desirable as you would be willing to go through her whole life without ever experiencing sexual intimacy. I was wrong in asking you to enter this farcical arrangement."

With those words Cassie lost every vestige of hope that he might come to love her. "So far, I—I've been...happy with it," she stammered. "I'm sorry if it hasn't worked out for you, since you've had ample opportunity to spend your free time with any-one you wanted, no questions asked."

His features could have been cast in stone. "You're right. I have," he retorted.

"I'll move out after the opening if that's what you want."

"It's not!" he fired back, sounding more intense than she'd ever heard him before. "The boys adore you and I have living proof that they're your whole raison d'être. Any problems we have are mine and mine alone." He strode from the room without a backward glance.

Since she couldn't imagine a life without him, she should have been overjoyed that he hadn't taken her up on her offer to leave. But once he'd gone, Cassie flung herself on the bed and buried her face in the pillow to stifle her sobs.

Contrary to her expectations, for the rest of the week Trace was surprisingly kind and considerate, and never once alluded to the ugly scene in her bedroom. He came home early every night to help with the children so Cassie would be free to prepare for the opening. It reminded her of the first few weeks of their mar-riage, when they'd enjoyed an easy camaraderie and shared the joys of caring for the children.

But in those early days she'd still retained the hope that Trace would fall in love with her and make their marriage a real one. All she could do now was shower her affection on the children

and concentrate on her business in an effort to ignore the aching
void only Trace could fill.

Late Friday afternoon, before the grand opening on Saturday,
Cassie was at the gallery finishing up some last-minute details
when she heard a familiar voice call her name.

She spun around to face the tall, rangy man with dark brown
hair and eyes who'd been watching her. "Rolfe!" Somehow in
the rush of things she'd completely forgotten about his coming
to Phoenix.

"You look wonderful, Cass." He held out his arms and she
ran into them, hugging him tightly. "I've missed you," he murmured into her hair.

"I've missed you, too." But the way he was holding her made
her realize he was about to kiss her and she quickly pulled out
of his arms. "I had no idea you were in town."

"I flew in an hour ago and phoned the number Mother gave
me. Your housekeeper said you were down here, so I thought
I'd come and surprise you."

"You certainly did that." She smiled, then asked deliberately,
"Did you bring your fiancée back with you?"

He frowned. "I thought you'd be able to tell from the telegram
that I'm no longer engaged."

"And you thought you'd come back into Cassie's life and pick
up where you left off?"

Cassie's eyes widened in astonishment to discover that Trace
had come into the shop and was strolling toward them, still
dressed in the suit he'd worn to work. He carried a sack of take-
out fried chicken. She was so surprised to see him and so thrilled
that he'd been thoughtful enough to bring dinner she wished
Rolfe a thousand miles away.

"Trace, this is Rolfe Timpson. Rolfe, I'd like you to meet my
husband, Trace Ramsey."

The two men took each other's measure, and Trace nodded,
but neither put out a hand.

"What is it you're after, Timpson? My wife is busy getting
ready for her opening. This isn't the best time to come calling."

Rolfe's gaze slid to Cassie's. "She knows why I'm here. Cassie and I have always belonged together. I made a mistake when
I broke our engagement. I was too impatient, but I've learned
my lesson and I want her back, no matter how long it takes."

"It's too late," Trace interjected before she could say anything. "Cassie's my wife now."

Undaunted, Rolfe continued to stare at her. "But I know how she really feels, and I have a letter to prove it. She married you to be close to Susan's baby, nothing more."

Dear Lord. The letter. Cassie had forgotten all about it. But that was before she'd married Trace and fallen in love with him.

Trace's body tautened. "That's right, Timpson. Now she's the mother of both my children, and that's the way it's going to stay. Have a good trip back to San Francisco." Trace put the food on the counter and darted her a mysterious glance. "I presume I'll be seeing you at home soon? Early enough to help put the boys to bed?"

"Yes," she called after him softly. "I was just closing up. Thank you for dinner." She would have kissed his cheek, but he'd already turned on his heel and walked out of the shop.

Rolfe studied her, and the silence stretched between them. "Did I misunderstand your letter, Cassie?"

She shook her head. "No. But I wrote it before I married Trace."

Again there was a long period of quiet. "You're in love with him, aren't you?"

"Yes."

He took a fortifying breath. "You were never in love with me, but I didn't want to believe it."

Cassie's eyes clouded over. "I'll always love you, Rolfe—like a brother. You're the most wonderful man I know, next to Trace."

"I threw it all away when I broke our engagement."

"No. Don't you see? If you'd really loved me the way I love Trace, you wouldn't have left. But you did because you sensed it wasn't right between us. And even if your engagement to the woman you met in Belgium didn't last, it proves you were ready for another relationship."

"I'll never forget you, Cass."

She smiled. "And I'll always remember you, because you were my first love."

CHAPTER NINE

CASSIE COULD HARDLY WAIT to get home to Trace. Maybe he wasn't in love with her, but he'd let Rolfe know in no uncertain terms that he wanted Cassie to remain his wife. It was a beginning, and she was determined that in time their marriage would become a proper one.

The minute Rolfe left the store, she closed up and sped home, snatching bites of the delicious chicken he'd brought her every time she stopped for a light.

The absence of his car in the drive sent her spirits plummeting as she pulled up to the house. And Nattie's explanation that he hadn't come home yet filled her with dread. She'd expected him to be here, playing with the children. Waiting for her.

When eleven o'clock arrived, he still hadn't come home. Cassie finally gave up her vigil and went to bed, needing sleep before her opening the next day. But it was fitful and she awakened restless and out of sorts.

The next morning after her shower, she put on a smart navy silk suit she'd purchased a few days earlier. The tailoring and sophistication bolstered her waning confidence.

Lena planned to meet her at Mix and Match at eight. Cassie went in to kiss the children goodbye before leaving for the gallery, skipping breakfast altogether. If Trace was up, she didn't see a sign of him, and she drove away from the house in tears.

"You look beautiful," Lena told her when Cassie arrived at the back entrance to the shop. "But you've been crying. What's wrong?"

"Let's go in and I'll tell you."

While they got the shop ready, Cassie explained what had happened the night before. "I don't understand him, Lena. He's like a wind that blows hot, then cold. I can't live the rest of my life this way."

"I don't like the sound of that. What are you planning to do?"

"I—I'm not sure. I have to get through today before I can make any serious decisions."

"Cassie, a word of advice. Don't act hastily. Give everything more time."

"Time seems to be making things worse."

She wasn't destined to hear Lena's response because a young man appeared at the door holding an enormous spray of the most exquisite yellow roses Cassie had ever seen. There had to be five or six dozen, at least. "I have a delivery for Cassie Ramsey."

"Oh, they're gorgeous!" Lena exclaimed. "And I have a pretty good idea who sent them."

Cassie signed for them, and when the delivery man had gone she hunted for the card tucked among the sprays of fern. "A woman like you makes her own luck, but you have all my best wishes just the same. Trace." The words reminded her forcefully of another time when he'd complimented her for being able to stand on her own two feet. *Alone.*

Crushing the card in her hand, she whispered to Lena, "Would you find a good spot for these so Trace will see them when he comes by later?"

Lena took the flowers from her. "Heavens, Cassie. You look so pale. What's wrong?"

"Nothing. Just more of Trace's...kindness. If you'll open the machine, I'll get busy putting out the rest of the door prizes in case we have an overflow. I'm being optimistic, aren't I?" She laughed nervously.

Lena slid a comforting arm around Cassie's waist before they both went to work. At five to ten, there were people milling around the store entrance. Her thoughts went back to a time in San Francisco when she hadn't a prayer of realizing her dream of opening a boutique. Again she had to remind herself how lucky she was. But at what price?

The next hour flew by in a blur of activity. Besides curious shoppers who lingered and raved over the displays, unable to make up their minds about what they wanted to buy, there must have been half a dozen more florist deliveries from every member of Trace's family, as well as the manager of Crossroads Square

At eleven o'clock, another flower arrangement arrived, from Beulah no less. And right after that, three men brought in an enormous flowering cactus. A banner that wished Cassie and Lena good luck was signed, "Compliments of the Greater Phoenix Banking Corporation."

The noon hour brought in more traffic, and suddenly everyone seemed ready to make purchases. At one point, Cassie looked up and noted to her astonishment that the shop was slowly being denuded of its inventory. She couldn't believe it.

"Mrs. Ramsey?" someone called to her.

She turned her head and thought she recognized the manager of a well-known restaurant down the street from Crossroads Square. "I know we've met, but I'm embarrassed to say I don't remember your name."

"Hal Sykes." He grinned. "Welcome to the block. I saw your ad in the paper and decided to drop in. I'm very glad I did. There are three paintings I'm interested in purchasing, but I don't see a price on any of them. Does that mean they've already sold?"

Cassie grinned widely as she looked at Lena, madly ringing up one sale after another. "I'll tell you what," she murmured. "You can talk to the artist, Mrs. Haroldson, and see what she says. Just a minute."

With her adrenaline pumping, Cassie worked her way through the crowd to the counter. "Lena, I'll take over here. There's a Mr. Sykes standing by the cactus who wants help. He's in the pink shirt."

Lena darted him a glance. "His face looks familiar."

"That's because we ate in his restaurant the other day."

"I remember. Okay. I'll be right back."

Cassie chuckled to herself in glee when yet another customer inquired about one of the paintings and left her card. Lena didn't return until a half hour later, looking positively dazed. "What did Mr. Sykes want?" Cassie asked between sales.

Lena blinked. "He offered me five thousand dollars for the three paintings over there. He's remodeling part of his restaurant and says they'd be perfect for the decor."

Keeping a poker face, Cassie said, "I hope you told him ten thousand or nothing."

"Cassie!"

"Well?"

"I—I told him they weren't for sale, but he wrote out a check anyway, and said he'd be back before we closed at seven, in case I changed my mind." She handed Cassie the check, made out to Mix and Match Southwest.

"I could use money like that to replenish my inventory," Cassie said matter-of-factly and put the check in the till. "Before you turn him down flat, why don't we talk about it? Say fifteen percent for every painting sold out of the store, and the rest for you?"

"Be serious," Lena said in a trembling voice.

"I am," Cassie came back. "A few minutes ago a woman told me she was interested in your sunset painting, the one with all the pinks and oranges. She's a New Yorker who wanted to take home a souvenir of Arizona. She's also an art dealer and offered four thousand for it. Here's her card. You're supposed to get in touch with her at that number next week."

"Hi, honey. How's it going?" a familiar voice broke in on their conversation.

Lena whirled around, her gray eyes luminous. "Allen!"

"I'm glad you're here." Cassie beamed at her brother-in-law. "Business is booming and we both need a break. Why don't you take your wife out for a quick lunch? When she returns, I'll grab a bite."

"Are you sure?" They both spoke at once.

"It's not quite as busy as it was earlier. But don't forget to come back. I can't run this place without you."

"A half hour," Lena promised. "No longer."

"Be sure and tell Allen about the nine thousand offered for your paintings already. And the day's only half over!"

In front of any number of interested customers, Allen let out a whoop of joy and swung Lena around before hustling her out of the shop.

Trace's clever scheme to help his sister looked as if it had succeeded, and Cassie couldn't help but take personal delight in the knowledge that she'd played a part. But with the steady stream of customers waiting to pay for their purchases, Cassie didn't have time to dwell on anything. Including the bleakness of her own future after she left Trace....

There had hardly been a lull since the doors opened. Naturally the opening would attract more shoppers than Cassie could expect on a regular business day. Still, she had to admit the large turnout was gratifying, and she prayed it augured well for future sales, since she wouldn't be depending on Trace's support any longer.

While she chatted with customers and took orders for items already sold out, she was making plans to search for a small apartment in Phoenix. She could live there and still have regular access to the children. She and Trace wouldn't have to see each other; Nattie and Mike could help make visitations smooth and pleasant.

Even if Cassie felt like the boys' mother, the fact remained that she was Justin's aunt and had no blood ties to Jason whatsoever. Under the circumstances, it would be wisest to move out of Trace's home now and establish herself in the community where she could earn her living. She'd see the boys whenever possible. As long as they wanted a relationship, she would be there for them in the capacity of aunt and friend.

No matter what Trace said, in time he'd fall in love and want to marry for all the right reasons, ultimately providing the boys with a stepmother. Painful as that would be to face, Cassie knew what she had to do for the welfare of all concerned.

"Look who I brought back with me." Lena's happy voice broke in on Cassie's thoughts as she was straightening the counter. She glanced up in time to see most of Trace's family enter the shop. The Ramseys' striking looks caused heads to turn. One by one they came over to give Cassie a hug while she thanked them for the flowers.

"I'm so proud of you, dear." Olivia patted Cassie's cheek. Then nodding toward Lena, who'd taken over at the cash register, the older woman whispered, "Bless you, Cassie."

"It's Trace's doing. You know that," Cassie whispered back.

"I know a lot more than you think."

Cassie barely had time to ponder her mother-in-law's mysterious reply, because there was a commotion at the door. As she turned her head, she caught sight of a tanned, relaxed-looking Trace, wheeling in the children seated in their two-seater stroller. Their entry caused delighted outbursts from his family, as well as other shoppers who crowded round.

Trace wore chinos and a navy sports shirt, open at the neck. The boys were dressed in identical navy sailor suits she'd made for them. On their feet were spanking white shoes and socks. They looked so marvelous Cassie forgot where she was and could do nothing more than lean against the glass countertop for support, feasting her eyes. There they were, not ten feet away. The three people in the world she loved more than life itself.

At that moment she experienced a pain so staggering she thought she might faint. Since the children hadn't yet seen her, she said, "Lena, excuse me for a minute." Without waiting to hear her sister-in-law's reply, Cassie hurried to the back room, which served as a supply area with an adjoining bathroom.

She waited until the wave of sickness had passed, then applied fresh lipstick before going back out. Trace was waiting for her on the other side of the door, his face alarmed. He put a hand to her forehead. "I saw you dash in here. You're white as parchment. Are you sick?"

Cassie took a deep breath. "No. It's probably a combination of nerves and the fact that we've been so busy all day I haven't had a chance to eat yet."

A pulse throbbed at his temple as he ushered her to a utility chair and forced her to sit down. "Then let's get you something right now. Lena said she'd be fine and Mother's watching the children."

"Actually, I don't feel like going anyplace, but a drink would be wonderful. There's a grocery farther down in the mall."

"Stay here and I'll get it." He was gone in a flash and returned not only with a carton of milk but an apple. Cassie thanked him and proceeded to enjoy both.

"The color's returned to your cheeks," he murmured after she'd finished the milk.

"I feel fine now, and a bit of a fool. Thank you for coming to my rescue. I should've packed a lunch and brought it with me, but I never dreamed there'd be so many customers."

He studied her face for a long moment. "I told the boys their mother's shop would be a raving success. They wanted to see for themselves, and so did I." He paused, still watching her closely. "I hope you don't mind."

Cassie jumped up from the chair and averted her eyes to hide the turmoil going on inside her. Did he mean what he was implying, or was this another ploy to convince the family they were a happily married couple?

"Of course I don't mind. I'm thrilled to see them. They look adorable in those outfits, don't they? Let's go find them."

Trace put a detaining hand on her arm. "Are you sure you're feeling all right?"

"Of course. I just needed a pick-me-up. Thank you."

Too affected by his nearness, Cassie hurried out front with Trace at her heels and discovered the boys being held by James and Norman. The minute the children saw Cassie they squealed in excitement and wriggled in their uncles' arms, trying to reach her.

With patrons in the store to wait on, she couldn't do more than kiss the children. They started crying when she left them to walk behind the counter.

"I'll get them out of here before we disrupt things any more," Trace offered.

"The flowers are beautiful. Thank you for making all this possible. And for coming."

She heard his quick intake of breath. "I'm your husband, for heaven's sake. Why wouldn't I be here?" he muttered angrily. She dared a brief glance at him and thought she detected a flash of pain in the blue eyes that bore into hers. He fairly bristled with emotion as he turned swiftly to gather the children. Cassie wanted to call him back, but now was not the time.

For the rest of the day she was haunted by the look in Trace's eyes, and she simply went through the motions as she greeted customers and rang up sales. By six-thirty the crowds had diminished; for the first time all day Cassie and Lena were able to straighten the remaining merchandise and start ringing out the cash register.

"All the Southwest pieces sold," Cassie commented in surprise. Automatically her eyes sought out the painting that had first inspired them, but it wasn't there. She frowned. "Lena? Where's your Hopi girl painting?"

Her sister-in-law blushed. "Would you believe Allen bought it and took it home with him? He left a check in the register."

"Good for him," she murmured. "Trace thinks it's your best painting and I agree with him. Lena, would you mind very much closing up for me tonight? I have something I need to do."

"I might as well start now, since I'm going to need the practice." Cassie's head lifted in query. "You might as well know.

I've been painting again and I've been having the time of my life. Allen and I talked about it over lunch. If your offer is still open, I'd like to be the other half of this business venture.''

Wordlessly Cassie flung her arms around Lena's slender shoulders and hugged her.

"Allen's coming any minute and we'll take care of everything. Go home to Trace," Lena urged.

"That's what I'm going to do. I love him and I'm going to tell him exactly how I feel. No matter what his response is, I can't hide my emotions any longer.''

But when she returned to the house, it was still and dark. The children were gone. Not even Nattie and Mike were around. In a state of panic, Cassie phoned the shop and cried out in relief when Lena answered.

"Lena, it's Cassie. There's no one home, not even the children. Do you have any idea where Trace might have gone with them?''

"I think I heard Mom offer to take the boys overnight.''

"Thanks. I'll call over there.'' Sure enough, Olivia Ramsey was baby-sitting and told Cassie that Trace had said something about working late at the office. Cassie thanked her and hung up the phone, a plan already forming in her mind.

She ran to her workroom closet and retrieved the six-foot alligator hidden behind the material. After stuffing it into the car, she sped along the highway toward the heart of Phoenix. Nighttime traffic was moderate, so she made it downtown within half an hour. Fortunately, the parking lot, almost empty now, stayed lighted all night long. As she drove in, she immediately saw Trace's black Mercedes, and she pulled up next to it, her heart hammering almost painfully.

The alligator made an awkward burden but she managed to half-carry, half-drag it to the security guard's cubicle. He had no idea who she was, since she'd been in the bank only once before. It seemed a century ago to Cassie.

He stared at the alligator, then at her, his eyes narrowing suspiciously. "Can I help you, ma'am?''

"My husband is here working late. I decided to surprise him.''

He looped his thumbs over his belt, drawing her attention to his hip holster. "The only person in the building is Mr. Ramsey.''

"I'm Mrs. Ramsey. We've never met." She put out her hand but he didn't shake it. Cassie's mood bordered on hysteria—why was she barred from seeing her own husband?

"I'll have to call and let him know you're down here."

"But that would spoil my surprise." She tried to appear friendly as she said it, hoping to win him over. But the man remained adamant.

"Sorry. I can't let you in without his okay."

She bit her lip in frustration and searched in her handbag for her wallet. "Here." She thrust her credit cards and driver's license at him.

He glanced at them, then shook his head.

She sighed angrily. "Then you leave me no choice. Will you please let him know Cassie would like to see him?"

The sandy-haired man nodded and picked up the phone. "Mr. Ramsey? There's a woman down here who claims to be your wife. She says her name's Cassie and she has ID to that effect—but you never know..."

Cassie tapped her foot impatiently as the guard gave her the once-over.

"She's about five two or three, blond, green-eyed. She's also good looking—and, uh, built, if you know what I mean," he murmured in a lowered voice, but Cassie heard him and felt heat rush to her face. "The thing is, she's carrying this stuffed animal around that's bigger than she is," he confided. "Yes, sir." He nodded, then turned to Cassie. "Can I see that thing, ma'am?" he asked unexpectedly.

"Be my guest," she muttered, wishing she could throw it at him.

Putting down the phone, he grabbed the alligator and looked it up and down, then examined it front and back, before picking up the receiver again. "It's a green 'gator about six feet in length with black hair, blue eyes and a wicked grin. It says 'Daddy' on the tail." He laughed as he spoke. After another moment, he said, "Yes, *sir!*" and hung up. All signs of mirth had vanished.

"*Now* do I have your permission to go up?" she asked in her iciest tone. Enough was enough!

"Sorry, ma'am. I can't let you do that." After propping the alligator against the glass, he reached for his belt, and before she knew what had happened, he had fastened something metal around her wrist. She was so astonished she'd actually stood there and let him handcuff her to his wrist.

"Now, wait just a minute!" she raged, trying to pull away from him, thinking it had to be a trick. But she might as well have saved her energy.

"It seems a woman bearing your description barged into his office a few months ago with some outrageous story. He said if you were the one, you could be dangerous. He told me to detain you until he comes down and checks you out. I'm only doing my job, ma'am."

"Which you do admirably, Lewis."

Furious, Cassie turned in the direction of her husband's voice. He stepped out of the elevator, his black hair attractively mussed, still wearing the casual navy outfit he'd had on earlier. Without giving her as much as a glance, he reached for the alligator and studied it thoroughly.

"She's the one, Lewis. Unlock the handcuffs and I'll take her upstairs. I want an unofficial statement from her before she goes anywhere."

"Yes, sir!"

Firmly gripping her elbow with one hand and clutching the alligator under his other arm, he guided her into the elevator. "By the way, Lewis," Trace offered before the doors closed, "she *is* my wife, but don't let anyone else know she's been running around loose on the premises carrying this monster."

The elevator began its ascent. "And now, Mrs. Ramsey..." Trace backed her into a corner, trapping her with his powerful body and the green felt alligator. "You have exactly ten seconds to explain yourself. I'm counting."

He looked and sounded every bit as forbidding as he had that first day in his office. But this time, she wasn't planning to reason with him. Nor was she going to bait him.

"I'm in love with you," she admitted simply.

"Since when?" he retorted with lips tantalizingly close to hers. The elevator doors opened and he urged her out, but she was barely aware of her surroundings.

"Since the moment you first accused me of being part of a kidnapping scheme, she whispered."

His left brow dipped in displeasure, just like Jason's always did. "Don't lie to me, Cassie."

"I'm not. I swear it!" she cried. "In spite of everything, I felt this overwhelming attraction to you and I knew from your re-action how much you adored Justin. I began to realize then that I'd met the man I wanted to live with for the rest of my life."

She felt his body tauten. "Why didn't you admit it when I took you to Snowbird, or the other night when I was begging you to sleep with me?"

"Because I didn't think you loved me! You never told me you did."

He groaned, shaking his head impatiently. "Because I didn't want to scare you off after that absurd marriage contract I'd made with you. Don't you know I fell in love with you the second you raced across the office to comfort my howling, black-haired son? I thought if I could ever get you to love *me* that fiercely, I'd be the happiest man alive."

"Trace..." She reached up to cover his mouth with her own, revealing the burning intensity of her need, realizing that this was what they'd both been hungering for from the very begin-ning. One day soon she'd tell him about her talk with Rolfe. But not right now.

Right now... She moaned in ecstasy at the way Trace was making her feel, the things he was doing to her with his hands and mouth.

"Do you have any idea the kind of hell I've been going through, waiting for Rolfe to show up, terrified you'd decide to go back to him?"

"I have an idea, yes," she said softly, pressing hot kisses against his eyes and lips. "All this time I've been afraid you wanted to make love to me because it was convenient, that even-tually you'd grow tired of me and I'd end up being ex-wife number two."

"Never!" He kissed her long and hard. "I should have told you how I felt when I came to your apartment in San Francisco. But I was afraid to admit the truth—it seemed too soon to be feeling like that. We barely knew each other. And after that fiery scene at the airport, I couldn't risk losing you, so I had to come up with a foolproof plan to make you fall in love with me."

She traced his mouth with her fingertips. "And you succeeded. To be your wife, even if it was in name only, brought me more happiness than you can possibly imagine. I knew then that my feelings for Rolfe weren't the kind a woman has to have for the man she marries. I love you, darling. Only you. Forever.''

"I've waited to hear those words for so long," he whispered against her lips. Then he started to kiss her with passionate urgency, bringing to life every nerve ending in her body. The world reeled away as Trace picked her up in his arms. Ignoring the alligator, he carried her into a room she hadn't seen before. It looked more like the interior of an elegant hotel.

"This isn't part of your office, is it?" she asked, trying to catch her breath when she saw the photograph she'd given him hanging on the wall.

Trace favored her with a voluptuous smile. "We're about to begin our honeymoon in my penthouse suite."

Cassie blinked. "I didn't even know you had one. Is this where you stayed on the nights you weren't at the house?"

"That's right." He carried her to the big picture window, which looked out over the city of Phoenix. "I've spent hours standing here, gazing in the direction of our house, wondering if you ever lay awake nights wanting me, aching for me the way I did you."

Cassie pulled his head down and moved her lips sensuously against his. "Let's go to bed and I'll show you what it's been like for me."

She blushed at his appreciative chuckle and hid her face in his shoulder. "To think Jason brought me here...to this..."

"Cassie!" He tightened his arms around her. "What if you'd given up your search too soon?"

"But I didn't." She bit delicately on his earlobe, producing a groan that vibrated through her body. "Susan wanted Jason to be united with his real father, and I wanted that, too."

He pressed her closer still. "I love your sister for that. I love our sons, but above all, I love you, Cassie. I need you in all the ways a man needs his wife. Don't ever stop loving me."

His vulnerability was a revelation to her. "Why do you think I agreed to your scheme to open a shop for Lena's sake? I planned to be so well and truly tied to you you'd never be able to get rid of me."

A deep, happy laugh came out of Trace as he moved them toward the bed. "My adorable wife, much as I love my sister, *you* were the real reason I thought up that scheme. I hoped it would fulfill you so much you'd never leave me. I threw in Lena's problems to win your sympathy, hoping but never dreaming she'd actually go along with it.''

Cassie had never known this kind of joy before. She sought his mouth again and again, craving the feel and taste of him. ''Then you got more than you bargained for, because tonight she informed me she wants half interest in the business. Apparently she's started painting again.''

She felt his fingers tighten in her curls. ''I know. Allen confided as much to me earlier today. He's anxious to talk to you and thank you for helping strengthen their marriage. But I told him he'd have a long wait because I had plans of my own where you were concerned.''

''I'm glad you said that,'' she murmured. ''You're right—Jason and Justin are entirely too spoiled. Another baby would be good for them—and for me. How about you?''

His smile slowly faded, to be replaced by a look of such burning sensuality she trembled in his arms. ''I'm prepared to indulge your desires indefinitely, Mrs. Ramsey.''

Call Me Mom
Sherry Lewis

CHAPTER ONE

"ROLL UP THE WINDOW, Michael." Abby Drake turned the steering wheel and brought the Toyota around a sharp curve in the unfamiliar road. Warm summer rain splattered through the open window, threatening to soak the children.

"Roll up the window, Michael," Erin echoed softly, as if Abby needed an interpreter.

"I like the feel of the rain," Michael protested. But at Abby's warning glance into the back seat, he reluctantly complied.

Sighing, Abby returned her attention to the road. Had she made a mistake agreeing to this? Things hadn't gone according to plan since they'd left Tempe, and were getting worse by the minute.

Lightning flashed, momentarily illuminating the road and the dense forest on one side. Though Abby knew the other side of the road dropped sharply away toward the Columbia River, she couldn't see it through the storm.

"How much longer till we get there?"

"I don't know, Michael. I'm doing the best I can."

"I'm tired of sitting here."

"Have a cookie," Erin suggested.

Good idea. Abby wished she'd remembered the cookies herself. But concentrating on the road for so long had obviously taken more out of her than she'd expected. At least Erin, at eleven, was old enough to help with her brother. And at almost nine, Michael didn't require the kind of care a younger child would.

"I want to sit in the front seat," Michael muttered.

If they didn't find Pine Cove soon, Abby knew she'd have

to pull off the road to rest. The unfamiliar highway and four long days of travel had taken their toll.

All that mattered was reaching Pine Cove and the house she'd rented for the summer. Then she'd get the kids into bed, take a hot bath and go to sleep. Everything else could wait until tomorrow.

Straining to keep her eyes focused, she negotiated the wet road slowly until Erin lunged upward in her seat, her hand pointing over Abby's shoulder. "There's a sign!"

"Thank God." Pine Cove, Washington. Population 800. Perfect. They should be safe here.

She found Water Street easily and followed it to number twelve, a weathered gray house facing the town square. Block lettering on the roadside mailbox read Z. HUTCHINGS. She'd made it to the right place.

Because it stayed light so late in the summer, Abby had expected to arrive before dark. But negotiating the narrow winding road had put them behind schedule, and the sun had gone down well over an hour ago. Since she'd never spoken directly with their landlady, Abby could only hope Mrs. Hutchings would still be awake.

She grabbed her sweater and looked back at the kids. "Are you ready?"

Erin frowned at the water streaming down her window. "I don't want to get wet. Can't we wait here?"

"I'll come." Michael flung his door open, letting in the rain.

"Please, Erin. You know I can't leave you here by yourself. Grab your sweater." Abby pushed open her door and stepped out into the storm.

With a sigh, Erin followed.

Light shone from the front window, leading them easily up the walk. Mrs. Hutchings must still be awake, Abby guessed, so this shouldn't take long. The last time Abby had spoken to her friend Ted, he'd assured her everything was arranged. All she had to do was pick up the keys and get directions to the house.

Searching in vain for a doorbell, she rapped her knuckles against the door and waited. And waited. With a sinking heart, she knocked again. If anything else went wrong, she didn't know what they'd do. She hadn't seen a motel in miles. The kids couldn't stay awake much longer, and neither could Abby. Mrs. Hutchings *had* to be awake.

Rain poured from the roof onto the unsheltered porch as Abby huddled deeper into her sweater in a futile attempt to stay dry. The kids looked as miserable as she felt, and Abby knew she had to get them settled—soon. At last, after what seemed an eternity, the door opened to reveal a round little woman, her wrinkled face beaming up at them from beneath a halo of wispy white hair, her hands clutching a walker.

"Mrs. Hutchings? I'm Abby Harris." She had to stop herself from saying Drake.

"Oh. My dear. Weren't you coming in tomorrow?"

Abby's heart plummeted. Disaster. Surely Ted had explained that they'd get there as soon as they could, and *no later* than tomorrow.

"Well, I can't let you stand there all night," Mrs. Hutchings said, backing away from the door.

Warmth wrapped itself around Abby's shivering shoulders as she and the children entered the house. Mrs. Hutchings turned in the narrow corridor with some effort and shuffled toward a large living room. "Come in here and sit down. You're probably wet through."

Michael and Erin dropped onto the sofa, but Abby faced the window and looked out at the storm. Since it was June, she'd imagined clear skies and hot sun; instead, she found gray cloudy skies and pouring rain. She hoped it wasn't an omen.

"Mrs. Hutchings—"

"Call me Zelda, my dear. We're not formal around here."

"Zelda," Abby started again. "If I can just get the key to the house and some directions, we'll get out of your way."

"But I'm afraid the house isn't quite ready. I wasn't expecting you until tomorrow."

After so long on the road, they needed the house—now. Abby had pushed herself harder than she should have to get here, and none of them could stand another minute in the car. They'd been on the road since six-thirty that morning. Her back hurt, her neck ached, and her eyes burned. She knew the children were just as miserable. They all needed the comfort of a warm bed and the quiet of a place of their own.

Mrs. Hutchings fluttered her hands. "I don't even know if the house is fit for you to stay in it tonight. No, I can't let you go over there by yourself. I'm going to call my nephew. You can wait here until he comes. He takes care of everything at the house for me—has done since my husband passed on. I'll have him go with you and help you get settled."

Abby bit back a protest and resigned herself to wait. She might not like the idea, but she had no alternative.

KURT BUTTONED himself into his heavy rain gear, muttering under his breath. All week he'd promised Brody they'd watch the NBA play-off game together. They'd gone to the FoodWay and stocked up on chips and soft drinks, popcorn and beef jerky. Everything Brody wanted. And though Kurt had seen the boy enthusiastic about very little since his mother had left nearly two years ago, this had come closer than anything else.

Then Aunt Zelda had called.

And now Brody sat in front of the television looking sullen.

"I'll hurry back," Kurt promised. "I won't stay long."

"It's all right."

"Look, I'm sorry about this," Kurt continued. "She said it was urgent and I need to make sure she isn't sick, but anything else can wait until morning. I'll be back before the first quarter's over."

"Right."

"Are you sure you don't want to come?"

Brody's eyes flashed up from the television screen for a second, filled with scorn. "To Aunt Zelda's? No thanks."

"I can always send Cindy home again," Kurt pressed. Their neighbor, a high school senior next year, stayed with Brody while Kurt worked and on the very rare nights he went out without his son.

Brody shook his head. "No, I'll stay here."

"Okay, but save me some popcorn."

With a noncommittal shrug, Brody turned back to the game,

and Kurt studied him for a long moment before yanking up his collar and heading out into the storm. Of all the nights for Aunt Zelda to decide she needed something, why did she have to pick this one? And why did she have to call *him?* Couldn't she call Jack—just this once?

Jamming his Jeep Cherokee into gear, Kurt pulled onto the highway as thunder rolled overhead. No, Zelda would never call Jack. The older of the two brothers, Jack had never had much patience with their aunt. He'd used his other obligations, including taking over as editor of the *Pine Cove Patriot* after their father's death five years ago, as an excuse to avoid Zelda's demands. So Kurt always got the call.

He didn't usually mind so much. His legal practice in Pine Cove couldn't exactly be described as demanding, and after Laura had left, he'd had too much empty time on his hands. He'd actually looked on Zelda's demands as a blessing in disguise for the first several months after the divorce.

But lately he'd grown more used to life as a single parent, and his practice had picked up. He didn't need Zelda—or anyone else—to fill his days anymore. He *did* need to spend time with Brody and help his son make the adjustments Kurt had finally managed to make himself.

He turned left onto Water Street and saw an unfamiliar car parked in front of Zelda's house. That must mean the summer renters had arrived. Kurt bit back an oath. He'd expected to have another day to get the place ready. So much for his promise to Brody. This would probably take longer than he'd thought.

He still couldn't understand why Zelda had decided to rent his grandparents' house at the last minute. She'd talked all spring about hiring a contractor to fix the place up, then out of nowhere she'd gotten this idea to rent it for the summer. And as usual, she'd asked Kurt to get everything ready.

Well, he wouldn't do it tonight. He'd hand the guy the key and give him directions. Anything more could wait until the morning.

He pounded up the walk and burst in without knocking. Water dripped from his coat onto the rug. He shook his head and

watched droplets of water fall from his hair onto the floor. In
the living room, he heard voices and the sound of Zelda's
walker.

"Here he is!" Zelda cried. "Take off your wet things and
come in here for a minute, Kurt. I want you to meet Abby
Harris and her children."

Zelda had always been headstrong, and she'd grown stubborn in her old age. Arguing with her tonight wouldn't get him
anywhere. She'd never agree to send the renters another twenty
miles to the Hi-Tide Inn, though it was exactly what she should
have done under the circumstances.

He hung his coat on a hook by the door and followed the
sound of voices into the living room. Two children sat on the
sofa drinking cocoa. The boy smiled. The girl didn't shift her
attention from the mug in her hand.

Across the room, Zelda hovered around a small blond
woman. She'd pulled out one of her blankets and had it tucked
around the woman's legs. As he watched, she stuffed a corner
of it into the space between the woman and the chair. The
woman looked up and met his gaze with clear blue eyes, but
agitation played across her face, as if Zelda's ministrations
weren't really welcome. Her face was pale and drawn, and the
children had that hollow-eyed look Brody always got when he
stayed up too late.

But Zelda didn't seem to notice. She sent him one of her
motherly smiles. "This is my nephew, Kurt Morgan. He lives
just up the highway from where you'll be. Kurt, this is Abby
Harris. I imagine you two will get to know each other pretty
well. This young man seems about the same age as Brody."

Abby Harris shifted in her seat, pulled the blanket away from
her legs and tossed her damp hair with her hand the way Laura
used to after a shower. She flashed him a glance loaded with
impatience. "How far away is the house?"

At least she didn't expect him to sit around while she
warmed up. "It's a couple of miles out of town," Kurt explained. "It'll take us about ten minutes to get there. You can
follow me. It's on my way—" He stopped and looked around

the room again, only now realizing that something wasn't right. "Did I misunderstand? Isn't your husband here with you?"

The girl finally looked at him, her eyes darting up in surprise, but Abby Harris smiled easily. "My husband is working in Europe this summer. The kids and I are here on our own."

Great. Now he'd have to get the house warmed up for her before he could go back home. From outside, sounds of the storm intruded, and rain poured in sheets from the darkened sky. It would take forever for that old mausoleum of a house to heat up. And common courtesy prevented him from leaving them alone to unpack their car in this storm. With a silent apology to Brody, Kurt knew he had no choice but to help them get settled.

Abby watched the emotions play across Kurt Morgan's face. He didn't want to be here; she could tell from the frown that drew his brows together. He probably blamed her for making him come out in this storm.

She struggled out of the heavily padded chair and faced him, though she had to crane her neck to do it. "Please don't feel you have to help us."

"The house is old and the heating system is pretty outdated. Unless you're familiar with old wood-burning stoves—"

"Of course she isn't," Zelda stated firmly. "You're not leaving them over there with no heat or hot water."

No hot water? Abby was startled. What kind of place had Ted found for them? She'd lived on her own for the past several years, but she'd always relied on her landlords to get the furnace working or the water heater going. As much as she wanted to be alone with the kids right now, she'd have to let Kurt Morgan come with them.

IT TOOK THEM nearly fifteen minutes to reach the sprawling old Victorian house. Abby stayed close behind Kurt Morgan's Jeep, until he finally turned off the road onto a gravel drive.

"It looks creepy," Erin whispered from the back seat.

Though she secretly agreed, Abby put on a brave face. "It'll look better in the daylight. Grab everything you can and let's make a run for it."

They didn't have far to go from the drive to the wide porch that wrapped around the house and provided shelter from the storm. But by now, Abby was thoroughly soaked and a chill had seeped into her bones. She knew the children must be just as uncomfortable.

Kurt unlocked the door and held open the screen for them. The house certainly was large. And old. And cold. Maybe having him there wasn't so bad, after all. Still, she hoped he wouldn't stay long. Exhaustion tugged at her eyelids, threatening to throw her off balance.

"Is your car locked?"

She struggled to focus on his face. An attractive enough face, even if he didn't know how to smile. Tiredly, she shook her head. "The trunk is."

"Tell me which bags you need first and I'll bring them in. Then you can change into some dry clothes while I start the fire and check on a few other things."

"My black garment bag, I guess. My overnight bag. Erin's suitcase is the blue one and Michael's is brown." She held out her keys to him.

Without another word, he ducked back into the storm and reappeared a few minutes later carrying the bags she'd requested.

"Your rooms are all upstairs." With a jerk of his head, he indicated they should follow him.

The climb was torture to Abby's weary limbs. Erin and Michael dragged themselves up the stairs behind her. Exhaustion had finally claimed Michael and stopped his complaints, but Erin's mood hadn't altered—she was as closed as ever.

At the top of the stairs, Kurt Morgan turned to the right. He placed Michael's bag on the floor in the first room. Sheets and blankets lay folded on top of the bed, and no doubt the other rooms were in the same condition. They couldn't even lie down until they'd made the beds.

Abby blinked her eyes against the fatigue. "Do you know how to make the beds yourselves?"

Kurt looked back at her and Abby realized her mistake.

Michael shrugged but Erin nudged his shoulder. "Yes, we do."

Kurt looked away as if he'd lost interest in their conversation, but Abby knew she'd have to watch herself more carefully. Especially when she was so tired.

Erin's suitcase went into the second room, then Kurt led Abby down the hall. Situated at the front of the house, her room overlooked the Columbia Gorge. Large French doors opened off one wall, and against the opposite wall, a wide bed with an elegantly carved headboard beckoned to her, promising rest.

"This was my grandmother's room," Kurt told her. "You'll enjoy it, I think." He lowered her bags to the floor and flicked on a light switch by the outside doors, illuminating a large deck. "It's not much to look at now, but in good weather it's a beautiful view."

"I'm sure it is."

"Well—" he turned to face her again "—I'd better go build that fire. Anything else you need?"

"Really, Mr. Morgan—" Abby started.

"Kurt. Nobody uses last names in Pine Cove."

"Kurt, then. I appreciate all your help, and I'll have to thank your wife for being so patient."

Something flashed in his eyes before he turned away. "I'm not married. My son's with the sitter and I'd like to get back to him, but it'll only take a few minutes to get the fire going."

Abby watched him cross to the stairway and felt herself smile. His obvious concern for his son and his willingness to help her in spite of it drew her to him. There was definitely something about Kurt Morgan she found appealing, and knowing he was divorced only reinforced it.

When he'd disappeared down the stairs, she closed her door and changed quickly from her wet clothes into a pair of gray sweats. She pulled her hair into a ponytail high on her head, then made the bed. Ignoring its invitation, she crossed the hall to Erin's room.

Abby pushed the door open, knocking softly. Erin had fallen asleep sprawled on the now made bed, her wet clothes still on.

She seemed so grown up when she was awake, but watching her sleep, Abby realized she was really little more than a child. A child who showed the signs of everything she'd been through the past few years.

Abby roused Erin enough to get her into clean dry pajamas and tucked her into bed before going to Michael's room. He'd been more successful, managing to strip out of his clothes and pull the covers over himself. Touching a kiss to her fingertips, Abby pressed them softly to his cheek before she tiptoed out of his room.

From far below, the sounds of tools clanging on metal floated up to the second floor. Mr. Morgan—Kurt. Obviously still working on the furnace.

Padding down the stairs in her stocking feet, Abby took in more of the house as she went. A large living room opened off to the left under her bedroom. On the right, a wide doorway led into another large room; probably a parlor a hundred years ago, it looked like a family room now.

Kurt had brought in the rest of their bags and stacked them inside the front door. Her camera equipment, another suitcase each, miscellaneous duffel bags. Enough stuff to last them through the summer. She hoped.

Behind the stairs she found the kitchen, a large white room with old-fashioned fixtures and a prehistoric range. Abby had certainly never seen anything like it before. No matter, she reassured herself, they wouldn't use it much. With the schedule she'd been keeping till now, she rarely cooked anymore, and she didn't plan to hone her skills this summer.

Walking toward the back door, Abby pulled aside a ruffled curtain and looked outside. Light from the windows spilled across a narrow yard and illuminated the trees at its edge.

Somewhere close by, another clang sounded, followed by a muffled oath. Despite herself, Abby's lips curved into a smile.

She looked through an open door and found him stretched out on the floor, his head nearly concealed beneath a monstrous black contraption. Thank goodness he'd stayed—she'd never have known what to do with that.

"Everything all right?" she asked.

Startled, Kurt brought his head up, ramming his forehead into the old stove. He fell back to the floor with a groan.

She'd knocked him out! Racing across the room, Abby knelt over him. What had she done? She touched his forehead and his eyes fluttered open.

Green eyes. Incredible eyes. Words froze in her throat. Something inside her melted, and her hand trembled as Kurt gazed at her for one long moment.

"Ouch," he whispered at last.

Jerking her hand away, Abby broke eye contact. "Are you all right?"

"Fine." He pulled himself to a sitting position.

Uncomfortably aware of him, Abby pulled away. "You're sure?"

"Yeah. You just surprised me. You shouldn't sneak up on a man like that."

As usual, when she became too tired, she grew emotional. Tears threatened to fill her eyes. "I'm sorry." She turned away, but she knew he'd seen the tears.

"Don't worry about it." He got to his feet and reached a hand toward her. Reluctantly she took it and allowed him to help her up. He touched his forehead and winced, then grinned, exposing disarmingly appealing dimples. "I got the fire going, but you'll probably have to wait until morning for a bath or shower. Did Zelda send over enough bedding?"

Abby didn't trust herself to look at him, but managed a nod.

"Well, then..." As he bent down for his jacket, Abby felt her eyes drawn to him again. What was she doing? He *was* attractive, but that didn't excuse her acting like a schoolgirl. She didn't even *like* the plaid-shirt-and-jeans, outdoorsy kind of man. Dragging her eyes away, she resolved to ignore her reaction to him. By morning this fatigue would be gone and she would be more rational.

Tomorrow she *had* to be rational. She'd need to think about the house and the kids; she'd have to worry about food. And she'd find a phone booth and make the first of the calls that would eventually let the folks in Tempe know they'd made it safely.

"Is there anything else you need?" Kurt asked her.

Like a healthy dose of common sense? "No. We'll be fine. Thank you for everything." Now, more than ever, she wanted Kurt Morgan to leave. Fatigued and overwhelmed by everything she had to deal with, she'd lost control of her emotions.

"Maybe I should leave my number for you." Kurt crossed the kitchen and rummaged through a drawer until he came up with a scrap of paper and the stub of a pencil. "I'll leave you the one at home and at my office," he said. "I'm usually at one or the other, but if you can't reach me, my secretary will know where to find me. You can call Zelda if you want, but it might be quicker to let me know if something needs to be fixed. She'll just call me, anyway."

Abby waited in silence as the pencil scratched against the paper. Kurt held it out and when she took it, she made certain their fingers didn't brush.

The silence stretched uncomfortably until, without warning, it was shattered by a scream. "Abby!" Michael's terrified voice carried through the house.

Dropping the paper on the counter, Abby turned. But before she could get through the kitchen door, Michael called out again. And by the time she reached the stairs, his terrified cries had roused Erin, who stumbled through her door onto the landing.

Abby felt Kurt behind her, matching her stride as she bounded up the stairs and burst into the boy's room. In the dim light from the hall, Abby could see Michael's tear-streaked face and quivering shoulders.

She sat on the edge of the bed and pulled him to her. Whispering soothing words, she tried to still his fears, all the while cursing herself silently for not expecting this. The nightmare had come every night of the last four.

"Is he all right?" Kurt stood in the doorway, silhouetted by the light behind him.

"He'll be fine," Abby answered.

"Is there anything I can do?"

"No!" Realizing how sharp she sounded, Abby struggled to soften it, to force a smile to her lips. "It's nothing—really."

After a slight hesitation, Kurt nodded. "Well, you have my number if you need anything."

"Yes. Thank you."

She held her breath until he turned away, and released the tension in her shoulders only after she heard the front door closing behind him.

For a long time after Kurt left, Abby held Michael against her, stroking his hair away from his forehead. Erin stood in the doorway.

"My dad was here, Abby," said Michael. "I saw him."

"No, Michael. It was just the dream again."

Erin tiptoed into the room and sat on the foot of the bed, her face heavy with worry. "Isn't Michael *ever* going to get better?"

"He'll be fine. Sometimes these things take time. We have to be patient—all of us, including Michael. It won't go away overnight." Holding Michael's shoulders, Abby moved him away from her slightly. "We have another problem, though. You know what you did?"

Michael shook his head solemnly.

"You called me Abby."

The little boy's face paled.

"You must both remember what we talked about. Even when the nightmare comes, even when you're afraid, you mustn't ever call me Abby, remember? Call me Mom."

CHAPTER TWO

KURT AWOKE EARLY to the pressure of Pride's cold wet nose on his arm. With a groan he rolled over and squinted through one eye. At least the sun had come out this morning.

Pride pushed at him again and whimpered, wanting to go outside.

"Hold on, boy. I'm coming." Kurt slid out of bed and stumbled into the bathroom still half-asleep. Throwing cold water on his face helped to wake him up a little. At least he wouldn't kill himself tripping over a rock or a branch on the shore. He reached for the towel and patted his face, wincing slightly when he touched his forehead, grimacing when he remembered why it hurt.

But the memory of Abby Harris's face as she'd leaned over him made him smile. With her long blond hair and clear blue eyes, she was a beautiful woman. She even looked good in those sweats she'd been wearing. Abby Harris was as unlike Laura, with her dark dramatic elegance, as any woman he'd ever met.

But she was married. *Mrs.* Harris. With a husband somewhere in Europe. The smile slid from his face. Never in his life had he allowed himself to find another man's wife attractive. And after experiencing the pain of losing his own wife to another man, he wouldn't let the same thing happen to Abby Harris's husband.

He dragged a Seattle Supersonics sweatshirt over his head, found his sweatpants at the bottom of the clean clothes in the laundry basket and shoved his feet into running shoes.

Brody's room showed no signs of life yet. Kurt had come home at the end of the third quarter of the game to find his son asleep on the floor. When he hadn't been able to rouse him, he'd carried him to bed, and Kurt's hopes for a chance to strengthen his bond with Brody had suffered a setback. He knew Brody resented his leaving last night, though he pretended not to care. And Kurt would have to find some way to mend this latest fissure in their relationship.

He left a hurried note on Brody's dresser. Unnecessary, really, but Brody still had some anxiety about being deserted after Laura had left them. If she'd ever bothered to call, Brody might have healed faster. But two of Brody's birthdays had passed, two Christmases, and Laura hadn't given any indication that she even remembered his existence. If she'd made any contact at all, Brody might have come through the divorce more easily. But Laura had never looked back, and Brody was the one who suffered.

Whistling softly for Pride, Kurt headed out the front door. Might as well get the ritual over with before the dog decided to prove just how badly he needed to go outside.

Out of respect for his aching head, he walked along the shore of the wide Columbia River, refusing to let the dog bait him into a game of tag. The black Labrador bounded away, wagging his behind furiously before lunging back at Kurt, nipping his legs and tugging on his sweatpants. But after several tries, Pride seemed to tire of the game and tried his luck chasing gulls, instead.

Kurt wasn't looking forward to facing Brody. But maybe this time there wouldn't be a problem, he thought hopefully. Maybe the game had held Brody's attention until he finally couldn't keep his eyes open any longer, and maybe he'd never really noticed how long Kurt was gone.

And maybe somebody would sight flying pigs over the river this morning.

The second he returned from the walk, Kurt knew he had trouble. Again. Brody sat at the kitchen table, his eyes glued to the back of a cereal box.

"Hey, sport." Kurt tried for a cheerful tone to set the mood.

"Hi." Brody's sullen response was as full of anger and resentment as Kurt had come to expect.

Crossing to the table, Kurt took a chair. He had no idea what to say or how to make this better. "Listen, I'm sorry about last night."

"It's okay."

But it wasn't okay, and Kurt knew it. "Zelda's summer renters got here a day early—a woman and two kids on their own. The heat wasn't even on in the house—"

"It's okay, Dad," Brody interrupted impatiently. "It was stupid, anyway."

"Brody—"

"Stupid!" The boy pushed himself away from the table. "I only said I'd watch the stupid game because I knew *you* wanted to. I didn't care about it."

"Brody, please."

"I said I don't care!" Pain stretched across the boy's face and Kurt's insides twisted. Tears filled Brody's eyes. He dashed them away angrily with the back of his hand, stomping from the house and slamming the door behind him.

Kurt tried to shore up his flagging spirits, but Brody's hostility hurt more than he ever would have imagined. In a way, it reminded him of his mother's aloofness after Kurt's father had died; she'd become fiercely independent, refusing to allow anyone too close. Within a year, she'd left Pine Cove and settled in Florida by herself. Brody had obviously inherited his grandmother's emotional makeup because he'd reacted to Kurt's divorce in a similar manner. And he'd been protecting himself ever since.

Kurt got up from the table and began stacking dishes. He wished he knew what to do. Brody had been wounded and he needed time to heal, and Kurt would do whatever it took to help him.

Frowning into the sink, he settled the stopper and ran hot soapy water over the dishes left from last night's dinner. Brody needed security. He needed to feel safe. And he needed to feel loved.

Kurt's sister-in-law, Theresa, insisted the boy needed a mother, but Kurt knew he wasn't ready to plunge into those waters again. He wanted no romantic entanglements. Brody's needs would be better met if Kurt didn't even consider getting involved with anyone for a long time. At least not until the boy had a chance to get over his mother's desertion.

Kurt looked out the window and watched a truck rumble past on the two-lane highway. He'd built this house only a couple of miles from town, but for a boy Brody's age, it might as well be the moon. Pine Cove didn't have a big population of nine-year-olds, and Brody's only close friend lived at least ten miles away. Too far for the boys to travel on their own.

But Michael Harris was here now. He was within walking distance and the boys were just about the same age. Maybe they'd become friends. Brody could have someone nearby, at least for the summer. An unexpected twinge of excitement crept up Kurt's spine at the thought of seeing Abby again, but he pushed it away.

Brody needed someone his own age to hang around with. Kurt didn't worry about him while Cindy was there, but three months without a close companion would make the summer drag by for the boy. And Kurt wanted to avoid that.

Feeling pleased with himself, Kurt began to whistle as he washed the dishes. He'd find a reason to visit the Harrises soon and take Brody with him. Finding Brody a friend might not solve everything, but it would be a start.

ABBY BROUGHT the car to a stop in the parking lot of the FoodWay. They'd already driven through the entire town looking for a restaurant and had eventually ended up at the grocery store. She'd counted on finding a place where they could have breakfast this morning, but she'd only found Jay's Drive-In and it didn't open until eleven o'clock. She couldn't make the kids wait that long to eat.

She'd chosen Pine Cove specifically for its off-the-beaten-track location, but she hadn't realized until now exactly what that meant. Obviously she'd have to spend time in the kitchen after all. Maybe she ought to buy a cookbook.

As soon as the car came to a stop, Michael jumped out, but Erin hesitated. "I don't think the store's open," she said cautiously.

"It *has* to be open," Abby replied. "It's the only place in town with any food, and if we don't find something to eat soon, Michael could get dangerous."

"But there aren't any cars in the parking lot and it looks dark in there."

Abby examined the parking lot and store again with a sinking heart. The place *did* look deserted.

Michael darted to the front of the store and jumped on the pad leading to the automatic door. Nothing. He pushed on the door. Locked.

Abby leaned out the window. "Is there a sign that says what time it opens?"

"Ten o'clock."

Two hours. She groaned, resting her head against the steering wheel. They hadn't eaten anything since an early dinner the night before. Except cookies.

Remembering that, Abby found new hope. They couldn't have eaten them all last night. "Where did you put those cookies, Michael?"

Scuffing his tennis shoes against the pavement on the way back to the car, Michael shrugged his shoulders. "We ate 'em."

"*All* of them?" Abby turned to Erin.

Erin nodded, keeping her eyes downcast.

Abby was amazed. There must have been three dozen cookies in that bag. How could two children devour so many? A few, she'd told them. Have a few. She'd never meant for them to eat them all.

Maybe she'd made a mistake in volunteering to do this. Two short weeks ago she'd been at home in Baltimore. Now she was three thousand miles away, with two kids, trying to grow accustomed to using a phony name. She'd chosen a shortened version of the kid's last name to make their adjustment easier, but answering to Harris didn't come naturally to her. On top of that, she was living in a town that didn't appear on the map and staying in a monstrous old house that didn't even have a microwave oven.

She hadn't expected any of this when she'd returned to

Tempe, Arizona, where she'd grown up, seeking her own sanctuary. After seven years on the Baltimore Police Department
as a crime-scene photographer, she'd finally burned out. She
could no longer handle the brutality she saw every day. She
couldn't photograph the results of one more act of violence.

Domestic violence affected her the most, probably because
it was so senseless. She'd transferred to the department three
years ago, and she'd expected to get over her initial shock. But
her job had become steadily more difficult, instead of less.
She'd never developed an immunity to the brutality she saw.
Her co-workers had assured her she'd toughen up, but she
never did.

Then, less than two weeks ago, she'd seen one set of victims
too many—a four-year-old girl savagely beaten to death by her
father. And the mother so emotionally and physically abused
she'd lost the strength to fight for her child.

Abby's stomach had revolted at the wounds inflicted on the
girl by her father, and instead of taking the photographs, she'd
run away. How could a parent do that to a child? Why did
people like that *have* children when others, like Abby, could
never have the children they longed for?

After a week of sick leave, Abby still couldn't force herself
to go back to work. So she'd taken a leave of absence and gone
home to Tempe, expecting to find a place to heal and time to
reach a decision about the rest of her life.

Instead, she'd found a new nightmare. Her older sister, Rachel, had recently been released from the hospital, a victim of
spousal abuse. And the niece and nephew Abby hardly knew
were being terrorized by their violent father.

For years, Rachel had kept the abuse a secret from everyone.
Abby hadn't been home in more than five years and she'd
spoken to Rachel infrequently on the telephone, but she
couldn't shake the feeling she should have recognized Rachel's
symptoms. Having seen so much of it in her career, why hadn't
she been able to sense it in Rachel's life?

Her husband, Vic, had been a hard worker and a handsome
charming man. At first. But within a year of the wedding, Rachel had begun to change and *that* should have alerted Abby

that something was wrong. Rachel's dwindling self-confidence and her uncharacteristic withdrawal at family get-togethers were clues Abby had ignored.

Rachel had stayed with Vic—at first because she believed the children needed their father. And after the abuse started to spread to Erin and Michael, fear had kept Rachel immobile. Without her, the children would have been completely at Vic's mercy, and Rachel knew he would have destroyed them eventually. But when she'd finally realized she couldn't protect Erin and Michael, Rachel took the children and left him, then filed for divorce.

After a lengthy custody battle, Vic was granted visitation, but only under supervision. Rather than pay child support for children he refused to see under those conditions, he'd asked the court to terminate his parental rights. And because of his history of abuse, the court had agreed. But even after the case was settled, Vic had continued his attacks and his threats to get the children back. Finally, when she was admitted to the hospital following a vicious beating, Rachel had been driven to hide her children from their father. And Abby had offered to take them.

Within twenty-four hours of her arrival in Tempe, Abby had contacted Ted Daniels, an old friend on the Baltimore Police Department. He'd talked often about his summers in Washington State, and since nobody in her family had ever been there before, it seemed like the perfect place to hide. Ted's mother knew Zelda and had given Abby a glowing recommendation, so Abby had been able to rent Zelda's old house immediately.

But now Abby was responsible for keeping the children safe, and she didn't know if she could handle the job. Rachel's children hardly knew her. And she didn't think she knew them well enough to convince anyone she was their mother. Using an unfamiliar name kept her constantly on edge, and having worked for the police didn't qualify her to prevent a kidnapping. She'd let her desire to help Rachel and her children cloud her judgment.

Michael pulled open the back door and flopped into the car. "I'm hungry."

"I know," Abby replied wearily. "We're all hungry."

"I know what we can do!" Michael said. "Let's call Mr. Morgan. He'll know where we can find something to eat."

Mr. Morgan. The thought of him hitting his head on the stove made Abby wince. And just as quickly, the memory of Michael calling out her name in terror brought the cold taste of fear to her mouth. They couldn't afford any more mistakes like that one.

Besides, Abby didn't know if she *wanted* to see Kurt Morgan again. It'd been a long time since she'd met a man who'd attracted her so completely on first sight. And she was much wiser now than she'd been then. Time, her divorce and too much pain had taught her lessons she wouldn't soon forget. She didn't need any more complications in her life.

"I don't think I ought to call Mr. Morgan," she said. "We can stand it for another couple of hours, can't we?"

Erin leaned back against the seat, looking almost relieved. "I can stand it. I'm okay."

Michael wailed, "I'm hungry, Mom!"

"Please, Michael."

"But I'm starving to death!"

"Don't, Michael," Erin said. "Abby's doing her best."

"*Mom.* And she's starving me to death."

"All right!" Abby gave up. "I'll find something for you to eat if you'll just be quiet. Keep your eyes peeled for a gas station or something where we can get a candy bar."

"A candy bar? For breakfast?" Michael looked doubtful.

"It's all we're likely to find in the next two hours."

"It's all right Ab—Mom," Erin said softly without facing Abby. "About the candy bars, I mean."

"It's really not," Abby said, watching the girl, "but we've got to have something, and I don't know what else to do. When the grocery store opens, we'll stock up on some real food."

"Okay."

Erin's calm acceptance, her almost obsessive need to make sure nobody took offense at anything she said, worried Abby. While evidence of the strain they'd been living under erupted in more obvious ways in Michael, Erin kept her feelings locked carefully away. She seemed serious—too serious for someone her age—and Abby wondered what it would take to break through her barriers. And whether *she* was capable of breaking through them.

Driving slowly along Front Street for the second time, she studied the town. Besides the FoodWay, it boasted a number of small stores, a barbershop, three charter fishing outfits, a bakery with a Closed sign in the window, a small fabric shop, a drugstore and a movie theater.

Several old houses had been converted into businesses—a law office, a beauty parlor and a bicycle shop. At the end of the block, a large sign rose into the air signaling a gas station.

"There's one!" Michael exclaimed, nearly jumping into the front seat with excitement.

Abby noticed that the station contained a small food mart. Relieved, she pulled into the lot and parked the car. Digging through her wallet, she handed each of the children three dollars. Michael and Erin ran from the car and into the station, and Abby grabbed her purse to follow. Surely they could find *something* to eat here, even if it wasn't particularly nourishing.

Suddenly Abby stopped, recognizing the Jeep Cherokee parked in front of the gas pumps. Kurt Morgan's—unless someone else in town had one exactly like it. And unless someone else in town stood over six feet tall and had wavy brown hair and dimples.

"Abby? Good morning!" Kurt lowered a paper bag onto the floor of the back seat and strode toward her.

He was the last person she wanted to see, but how could she avoid him? "Mr. Morgan," she said formally.

"Kurt. How's the house? Everything all right?"

"Yes, thank you." She took a step away, but he followed.

"Anything else you need this morning?"

"No. Everything's very nice." She scanned the parking lot, hoping to discourage further conversation.

"Not much fog today," he continued. "Were you able to look around outside?"

"The view of the river's spectacular."

"Best in town." He grinned, revealing straight white teeth and deepening his dimples.

Until that moment she'd hoped to convince herself that her attraction to him last night had been an aberration. But as the light danced across his hair and the gentle breeze lifted it from his brow, as his eyes narrowed in a squint against the morning sun and his lips curved in a smile, her heart skipped a beat.

And like a young girl, she couldn't do anything but smile at him foolishly, although every logical instinct screamed at her to get away from him as quickly as possible. She couldn't afford any involvement with other people right now—especially not with a man.

Kurt stuck his hands into the pockets of his faded jeans. "Actually, I'm glad I ran into you," he said. "I wondered whether Michael likes to play baseball. We're just starting our Little League season, and I know Brody would love to have another boy his own age on the team."

"Oh, I—" How on earth would she know the answer to that?

"My brother Jack's the coach and I'm the assistant this year, so we can get Michael signed up with no trouble."

As Michael's mother, she'd know the answer. "It's just that I don't think—"

"It'll be good for him. Fresh air and exercise..."

"I really couldn't—" Had Rachel ever mentioned anything about Michael and baseball?

"The games are one of the highlights of summer here," Kurt continued, oblivious to her discomfort. "Everybody gets involved. It'll be a great way for all of you to get acquainted with people in town."

"Michael doesn't really—" Frantic to stop babbling and give Kurt an answer, Abby drew in a deep breath and blurted, "You see, Michael isn't very athletic and it makes him feel funny—different from the other boys. It's been quite a problem the past few years and it's something my husband and I try to avoid whenever we can. I just don't think I should put Michael in that situation."

Kurt's brows knit as he took in her words. "Oh." The word

dropped between them and fell flat. "I'm sorry. But listen, if he wants to learn, there's no better place than right here. The boys are all in it for fun and most of the parents aren't terribly competitive. We make sure everybody plays, even the kids who aren't very good."

Abby shook her head and backed away. She couldn't let him talk her into it. After yesterday evening's disaster, she didn't intend to put Michael in a situation where he might inadvertently say the wrong thing.

Kurt opened his mouth to speak, but from behind them, Abby heard someone shouting.

"Hey, Mom!" It took her a minute to recognize Michael's voice and realize he meant *her*. "Look at this!" He held up two cellophane-wrapped packages of doughnuts and ducked back into the building.

A moment later Erin appeared carrying a small brown bag, and Michael bounded back outside, followed closely by a slim blond boy about his own age. He'd only been inside a few minutes and he'd already found a friend.

"Mom! Mom, guess what!" Michael said excitedly. "They have a Little League team here! Isn't that great?" He turned back toward the other boy who looked uncannily like Kurt. "I was starting pitcher last year on my team. Do you think I could pitch here?"

Even without looking at him, Abby felt Kurt's eyes on her and felt the heat of a flush creep up her face. She couldn't think of a thing to say that would explain her obvious lie.

With Michael and the other boy beaming at her, their eyes full of anticipation, and Kurt staring at her like he expected an explanation, she couldn't make matters worse by refusing to let Michael play. It would raise too many questions.

"That's fine, Michael," she said, forcing a smile.

Kurt put his hand on the other boy's shoulder. "Great. Brody and I will pick Michael up for practice late this afternoon if you'd like."

"Thank you, but I'll make sure he's there if you'll just let me know where and when."

"Sure." He took a piece of paper from his pocket, scribbled

the information on it and handed it to her. "Practice starts at five. We'll see you then, I guess."

Abby tried to muster a weak smile, but Kurt had already turned away. He and Brody settled into the front seat of the Jeep and he drove off without a backward glance.

Something inside her felt...odd as she watched them go. Disappointment? Embarrassment that she'd been caught in a lie? But why? Nothing mattered except keeping Erin and Michael safe, and if she had to lie to do it, she would.

So why did this odd feeling curl inside her as Kurt Morgan drove away? And why did she find herself caring very much what he thought of her?

AT TEN MINUTES to five, Abby pulled into the parking lot at River View Park. The park consisted of nothing more than a few swings, a lopsided teeter-totter, two picnic tables and three dusty baseball diamonds already alive with small children.

Michael strained eagerly against his seat belt. "I hope they'll let me pitch."

"I haven't decided whether or not I'm going to allow you to join," Abby warned. "I'm still not convinced it's a good idea."

"*Please?*"

"I'll think about it."

Michael's face fell and he looked close to tears.

"I didn't say no, did I?" Abby said, more kindly. "I told you I'll think about it. Now let's find out where you're supposed to be."

She'd hoped to fade into the background during the practice, but even before Michael got out of the car, Kurt was making his way through the tangle of children toward them.

He greeted Michael before looking inside the car. With a smile in Erin's direction, he turned to Abby. "Come and meet my brother, Jack. He can tell you what equipment Michael needs and you can fill out the registration forms. Then I'll introduce you to a few people."

Abby didn't want to meet people and she wanted to stay as far away from Kurt Morgan as possible. She wanted their pres-

ence in Pine Cove to remain relatively unnoticed. And she
wanted to minimize the risk of future slip-ups.

Erin's round eyes stared out of her pale face. The girl hadn't
made a sound, but if the prospect of meeting people bothered
Abby, she knew it terrified Erin. Abby knew she shouldn't have
let her embarrassment at getting caught in a lie force her to
compromise their safety like this. She should grab Michael and
leave immediately. And she should get Erin away from the
small crowd.

Turning to call to Michael, she saw the wide smile on his
face. She hadn't seen him smile like that once in five days. He
obviously needed interaction with children his own age. How
could she deny him that?

Unfortunately relenting meant staying here, at the ball park.
If Vic *did* manage to track them in spite of all her precautions,
he might not approach the children while they were with her,
but she didn't think he'd hesitate to act if he found either of
them alone, even with strangers around. She shared Rachel's
fear that Vic would kidnap the kids, and knowing how often
parental kidnappings happened, Abby didn't dare let them out
of her sight.

But staying here meant being near Kurt. And being near Kurt
meant dealing with this attraction, which hadn't lessened since
her first glimpse of him. And that meant trouble.

Kurt led them through the crowd to a narrow bench. "Have
a seat," he said. "I'll go find Jack. Michael, grab a glove and
start warming up with Brody. He's over by second base."

Without another word, Kurt disappeared, leaving Abby and
Erin alone and uncomfortable on the wooden bench. Abby
didn't want to do this. She *hated* baseball. It had to be the most
boring sport ever invented. Steven, her husband, had been an
absolute nut about the Orioles, and as their marriage splintered,
Abby had grown to hate every minute she spent at the games.

Dust rose from beneath the running feet of the players, but
a breeze from the Columbia River cooled the air and kept the
temperature pleasant. The chain-link screen pinged and rattled
as a high inside pitch escaped the catcher's mitt, and excited

shouts from children on the field punctuated the silence between Abby and Erin.

The girl's rigid back and downcast eyes told Abby more forcefully than words how Erin felt about being here. If Abby let Michael play, she had to expose Erin to crowds and strange people, and Abby had already sensed Erin's fear of both in the short time they'd been together.

A few minutes later Kurt reappeared, bringing another man with him. Though he bore a resemblance to Kurt, the features that made Kurt's appearance so intriguing failed to have that effect with the second man. His face was too lean, his nose too sharp, and the lines stretched over his cheeks too tightly for him to be considered handsome. But he had the same friendly smile and dimples, and Abby liked him immediately.

"Jack Morgan," he said, extending his hand. "Why don't you fill out the registration forms while you're watching the game? The Fee schedule is listed on the back of the green sheet. You can make the check out to me or to Jefferson County Recreation. I'll get it from you after practice." He leafed through a sheaf of papers and handed her a small packet.

If she decided to let Michael play, she'd pay cash. Everything she did or bought for the next three months would be paid for in cash. The only way to protect their anonymity was to avoid using checks, credit cards or anything else with her real name.

"Well, I..." Abby began, but Jack had already turned his attention to Kurt.

"I put the camera over by my gear. I need you to get a few pictures of the team this week, or the parents with scrapbook fetishes are going to have my head."

Kurt groaned.

"Look—" Jack held up his hands as if to ward off Kurt's protest "—I've got enough to tangle with right now and I really need your help. Just grab the camera."

With another grin in Abby's direction, Jack sprinted onto the diamond, shouting directions at the boys.

Kurt turned back to Abby and Erin. "We usually sit on the

bleachers back here.'' He indicated a shabby stand of seats behind them.

Surely he didn't intend to sit with them all afternoon, Abby mused. An assistant coach must have things to do. Keeping Erin here would be uncomfortable enough without the added worry that one of them might say something wrong in front of Kurt. But how could she refuse to join him without raising questions in his mind?

Resigned, Abby took Erin's hand and followed Kurt again through the crowd of children. The girl's hand remained stiff and unresponsive, and her eyes reflected her uneasiness.

The bleachers were nearly empty except for five or six women and two men, all of whom eyed them curiously. In the second row, a pretty brunette stood as they approached.

"Brody's looking good tonight," she said. "He should do better this year, don't you think?"

Kurt gazed out onto the field. "I hope so. Last year was pretty rough on him."

The woman kissed Kurt's cheek lightly and smiled at Abby. "I'm Theresa Morgan, Jack's wife. And you're Abby Harris? Kurt told us you'd be bringing your son to practice today. And this must be your daughter—Erin, isn't it?"

Erin managed a tiny smile and sat gingerly on the peeling bleachers. Abby perched uncomfortably beside her.

"I'm glad you're here," Theresa went on. "Brody's needed a friend close by. And quite frankly, having another woman around won't hurt him, either. So, how do you like the house? It's beautiful, isn't it? And the view! You couldn't find a place in town with a view like that."

Theresa's enthusiasm drew Abby in immediately. If she'd come to Pine Cove for any other reason, she'd enjoy Theresa's company.

"What position does your son play?" Theresa asked, pushing her sunglasses onto her head and squinting at the field.

Kurt's eyes flickered in Abby's direction, but this time she knew the answer. "He likes to pitch."

She held her breath, waiting for Kurt to ask her why she'd

lied before. But though he studied her for a long moment, he looked away without a word.

Theresa nodded. "We can always use another good pitcher." Seeming to tire of the action on the field, she looked at Erin. "How old are you, Erin?"

"Eleven," Erin said quietly.

"I remember being that age." Theresa met Abby's eyes with humor. "Nine and eleven? Those are fun ages."

Maybe. If the "parent" had some clue as to what she was supposed to do. Abby's lack of experience left her feeling lost.

Theresa gave Erin a playful nudge with her shoulder. "We've got some awfully cute eleven- and twelve-year-old boys around here. Maybe after practice, I'll introduce you to some of the kids your age."

Erin pulled away sharply and trained her eyes on her feet.

Hoping to distract Theresa from Erin's reaction, Abby smiled. "I don't think so, but thanks," she said. "We're all still pretty tired from our trip and we really should leave right after practice."

From down on the field, Jack signaled to Theresa with a raised hand. Rolling her eyes in mock exasperation, she shrugged. "I'll see you again later. I'm being summoned." With a big smile she hurried toward her husband.

Abby searched the field and found Michael and Brody still throwing a ball back and forth. Michael handled the ball easily. Even to Abby's eye he looked natural, almost graceful. Surely Kurt noticed how well Michael played—but so far he hadn't said a word about her lie. And though she suspected he'd raise the subject sometime, she was grateful for the respite. Maybe by the time he brought it up, she'd have thought of a believable excuse.

As the practice progressed, Kurt responded to Brody's obvious need for approval, raising his thumb in the air to signal a good catch, whistling and clapping whenever Brody hit the ball during his turn at bat. But though Brody glanced into the bleachers often to receive his father's praise, he never smiled back.

On the other hand, Michael seemed content without Abby's

attention. Too content. Too obviously disconnected from her. He ran, threw, hit and caught the ball with ease, scarcely noticing whether she was still there. And by the time practice ended, she was filled with a sense of fear that Kurt had noticed how separate Michael kept himself from her.

Other children ran to parents and received pats on the back and ruffled hair with pleasure. But Michael stood apart from Abby and scarcely looked at her until she told him how well he'd done.

"So are you going to let me play?" he asked.

"I guess."

"You guess yes? Or you guess no?"

The sight of his little face alight with such eagerness softened her heart. Ignoring the voice of caution, Abby relented. "All right, you can play."

Michael smiled. "Really?"

She nodded.

"Thanks." He hesitated for a moment, as if he thought he should make some physical contact with her, but he turned away, instead, and raced back onto the diamond to return his equipment.

Abby watched him go. She hoped letting him play wouldn't be a problem. It was only Little League, after all. In a town of eight hundred people.

Kurt observed Michael and Abby, and once again had the feeling that something wasn't right. He'd tried all day not to wonder about them, but their relationship bothered him. Why had Abby lied about Michael? The boy was a natural at the game.

He told himself that maybe she just didn't want to spend the summer watching Little League games. Maybe she felt he'd backed her into a corner—and resented it.

He shook himself mentally. He wanted Brody to have a friend. Period. Abby Harris and her opinion of *him* weren't at issue.

He'd already decided to ignore the magnetic pull she seemed to have on him. And he'd promised himself to remember, at all times, that she had a husband.

He wondered for a moment whether the absent Mr. Harris worried about her. Or did he know she loved him and so trusted her to remain faithful, no matter where he went or how long he spent away from her?

Kurt had once trusted Laura, and look where that had gotten him. He'd never suspected her of being unfaithful until the end. He'd been a fool to believe her reports of boredom when she came home from her business trips to New York, San Francisco and Los Angeles. He hadn't expected her to give up her career or curtail the travel it required, even after Brody came. But neither had he expected her to spend increasingly *more* time away from home—which she seemed to do even when her job didn't demand it.

By the time they'd moved back to Pine Cove from Seattle, he'd sensed it was over between them; by then the damage had been done. And less than six months after he'd finished the house, she was gone. She hadn't called or written to Brody once since the day she walked out. He'd heard just two months ago that she'd gotten married again, this time to some hotshot lawyer from L.A.

Brody tugged at his sleeve, drawing him back to the present. "Can Michael come over for ice cream?" he asked.

Kurt hesitated. Abby hadn't given him any reason to believe she'd be interested in any relationship with him. When he met her eyes, Kurt felt her shutting him out. Just as she should. But a tiny spark of disappointment ignited inside him.

He pulled himself together to answer his son. "Brody and I usually have ice cream after his practices. Would you like to join us?"

Abby reacted immediately, shaking her head and looking almost nervous. "No. Thank you."

"Maybe another time, then," he said pleasantly. Throwing an arm across Brody's shoulders, Kurt deliberately turned his attention away from her.

He couldn't deny that something about her drew him, but he'd just have to avoid her whenever possible. No sense taking unnecessary chances. He hadn't reached thirty-four without realizing physical attraction had very little to do with logic. The trick was to keep from acting on the feeling.

He found Abby attractive, yes, but in an abstract way, he told himself. Like a beautiful painting. Just because he found her looks appealing didn't mean that *she* attracted him. After all, she was another man's wife.

Kurt steered Brody toward the Jeep. But as he walked, he watched Abby's trim figure ahead of him. Dragging his eyes away from her, Kurt studied the clouds and tried to ignore the sudden pounding of his heart.

CHAPTER THREE

ABBY SPREAD peanut butter on a slice of bread and reached for the jar of strawberry jam. Across the table, Erin studied her fingers and Michael drummed his hands on his knees to the rhythm of a tune only he could hear. They'd been in town just over a week. Michael had fallen into a pattern easily, but Erin was still as remote as ever. And every day, Abby struggled to find something that would pull a positive response from the girl. "Do you two want to do anything special this afternoon?"

Erin shook her head, but Michael looked up. "I've got practice at five."

Abby smiled. "How could I forget? Erin?"

"What?"

"Isn't there anything special you'd like to do?"

Erin's head tilted and Abby held her breath. Maybe Erin would voice an opinion, express a preference, look Abby in the eye...

"No" was all she said.

Abby stifled the feeling of defeat and tried to keep her voice light. "How about taking a drive?"

Erin shrugged. "If you want to."

"Can Brody come?" Michael stopped playing the drums and leaned forward eagerly.

"I don't think so," Abby replied simply.

"Why?"

"Because I'd like it to be just us—our family. We need some time together."

"But—"

"Please, Michael."

Slumping back against his seat, Michael turned away, of-

fended. Would she never say the right thing? Abby wondered.
Would she always hurt one of them by trying to do the best
thing for the other? She'd been dragging Erin to Michael's
Little League practices, making her face the crowds and the
noise. Now, when she wanted to give Erin some quiet time,
Michael felt betrayed because she wouldn't invite his new
friend.

She jabbed the knife into the jam and spread a layer over
the peanut butter, settled the top slice of bread in place and
handed it to Michael. "Another time, okay?"

Michael accepted the sandwich, but shrugged unhappily.
"Okay. But he's not going to have anything to do."

"I'm sure he'll find something," Abby said firmly. "What
did he do before you came to town?"

"Nothing."

"Nothing? All summer long?" She tried to bite back a smile
at Michael's theatrical tone.

"Yeah. And he hates it. His dad's never home, you know."

"I don't think it's quite that bad. His dad has to work, but
he's home in the evenings, isn't he?"

"Yeah. He's home in the *evenings*." Michael gave her a
look full of meaning. But it didn't change her mind. Easing
Brody's summer boredom didn't fall in her list of top priorities.

Abby started on another sandwich and studied Erin. She
didn't even know whether Erin wanted or needed time with
Michael. But Brody had appeared at their back door every afternoon since they'd arrived, and Michael had raced off to play,
leaving Erin alone. Abby couldn't help thinking Erin needed
some time with her brother.

When Brody showed up today, Abby would send him home
with an invitation to come back tomorrow. Surely he'd be all
right for *one* day.

She handed Erin her lunch and reached for the lid to the
peanut-butter jar when a knock sounded at the back door.
Brody. Just like clockwork.

Michael leapt from his seat and opened the door before
Brody could knock again. "Hey! You brought your rocket

launcher! Cool! Bring it in and show my mom. I'm still eating. You want a sandwich?''

Abby reached for the bread again. Of course Brody would want a sandwich. She'd fed him lunch every day this week. And she didn't mind, but today she had other plans. Well, she'd let Brody finish his sandwich and a glass of milk and hope that it wouldn't make it harder to scoot him out the door when the time came.

"Hey, Mom," Michael continued, "look at this. This is the thing I was telling you about. That I saw on TV—remember?''

Out of the zillion things he'd pointed out? Of course she didn't remember. But she smiled and studied the long plastic tube and the spongy-looking rocket with interest, hoping she'd remember it when Christmas came around.

"My dad gave it to me for my birthday last month," Brody explained, taking the sandwich and pouring a glass of milk.

"Isn't it great?" Michael plopped back onto his chair.

"It's great." Abby stacked the pieces of the rocket launcher in the corner and started clearing away jars.

"What are we going to do today?" Brody asked.

Michael sent Abby a veiled glance. "Um..."

"Actually, Brody, we have plans to go somewhere as a family. But Michael can play all day tomorrow."

"Oh." Brody flushed a deep red. "Okay." He sounded all right, but Abby's conscience twinged.

"Is your dad at work?" she asked the boy.

Brody nodded and drank the rest of his milk.

"He's always at work," Michael chimed in.

"Not always." Brody wiped his mouth with the back of his sleeve and pushed away his plate.

"Yeah, but a lot," Michael muttered.

Abby closed the refrigerator door. If Kurt's work habits were a sore spot with Brody, the last thing he needed was Michael egging him on. "Michael, don't—"

Brody jumped up and gathered the pieces of his rocket launcher. "He doesn't work as much as my mom used to. But he's still gone a lot."

He sounded so sad Abby's resolve crumbled. She couldn't exclude him. "Then maybe you'd like to go with us."

"Really?" Brody dropped the rocket launcher and wheeled around to face her.

The eagerness in his expression convinced her as nothing else could have. "Really. I'll call your dad and make sure it's okay."

Michael bolted out of his chair and nearly tackled her in an enthusiastic hug. "Thanks. You're great."

Brody smiled shyly. "Yeah. Thanks."

The two boys sprinted out the back door, shouting as they raced across the lawn. At the table, Erin picked at the remains of her sandwich.

"I hope you don't mind that I invited Brody," Abby said.

Erin shook her head and almost met Abby's eyes. "I don't mind."

"You're sure?"

This time, Erin looked up. "I like Brody."

Abby smiled. "I'm glad." She glanced out the back door at the two boys. "They sure seem to get along well."

"I think Brody likes being around you."

"Me?"

"Because of his mom leaving and everything."

Erin surprised her. She seemed so quiet and withdrawn that Abby sometimes wondered if she paid attention to anything around her. Obviously she did.

"Really?"

Erin nodded. "He says we're lucky to have such a neat mom who takes us places and does things with us."

Brody didn't know their outings came about mostly because of her desperate attempts to keep the children occupied. But before Abby could respond, Erin darted out of the kitchen and ran upstairs. Abby cleared away the rest of the dishes, but Erin's words kept buzzing around in her head as she worked. She'd been curious about Kurt and Brody—whether Kurt's ex-wife lived nearby, whether Brody spent summers with Kurt and the rest of the year with his mother. But it sounded like Brody's mother was completely out of the picture.

She watched the boys race past the window and her heart went out to Brody—a father who worked too much, a mother who'd walked out on him. No wonder he enjoyed spending time with them.

Abby genuinely liked him. He was a good boy who needed love and understanding as much as Erin and Michael did. And he'd found something here that made him happy.

Wiping the table with a damp cloth, she settled the bouquet of daisies Brody had given her yesterday in its center and reached for the telephone. Now came the hard part.

Telling herself she didn't *want* to call Kurt, she excused her eagerness to hear his voice with the knowledge that she couldn't just disappear with his son for the afternoon. If Brody continued to spend so much time with them, she'd probably have to speak with Kurt more often.

She just hoped her heart wouldn't thud like this every time she had to call him.

KURT FLIPPED through the Baxter file for the second time. That deed of trust had to be in here somewhere. He just wasn't concentrating.

The look on Brody's face at breakfast this morning still haunted him. During the past month, Kurt's law practice had taken an upswing and now demanded more of his time. But every extra hour he spent away from home only widened the gap between him and his son. He could see it in Brody's face, and that look had been there again this morning. Brody equated working extra hours with his mother's desertion, and he was preparing himself for Kurt to follow her lead.

He picked up the telephone and punched in his home number. But when Cindy answered, she confirmed his suspicions that Brody had already finished his chores and gone to Abby's to play with Michael.

Kurt picked up the receiver again and punched in half of Abby's number, then hung up quickly. Why didn't he just call her and ask about Brody? Why did he imagine one phone call would be out of place? After all, he had every right to check on his son. It was the most natural thing in the world. Why did he think Abby would read something else into it?

Because he wouldn't only be calling to check on Brody. Because he *knew* that's where Brody was. And because he'd also be calling to hear Abby's voice.

Cursing under his breath, Kurt returned to the Baxter file and worked his way through each document, finally locating the deed of trust third from the top. Right where it should have been. He tabbed it for future reference and tossed the file onto the growing stack on the corner of his desk.

Maybe he should check with Abby to make sure she didn't mind Brody hanging around so much. If she wasn't married, he wouldn't hesitate. Or if her husband had come to town with her. Or if she wasn't so beautiful.

He reached for the telephone, dropping his hand guiltily when a knock sounded on the door. "Yes?"

Naomi pushed the door open and stuck her head inside. "I'm going to have to take a little extra time at lunch today. I hope that's okay."

"Sure. Everything all right?"

"Not really."

Naomi had married Bill Franklin, her high-school sweetheart, right after graduation. For a long time they'd been happy, but when Bill lost his job last year, he'd started drinking. Bill's unemployed status and his drinking made Naomi unhappy. And their relationship had gone steadily downhill. "Anything I can do?"

Naomi shook her head. "Not yet. But I'm getting closer."

Kurt tried not to frown. He hated to see Naomi and Bill break up, especially when he believed they could save their relationship if they worked at it. But Kurt's own marriage hadn't been a success, and he didn't have any right to give unsolicited advice. "What time are you going?"

"Now. I'll be back as soon as I can."

"Just leave the door to my office open so I can hear your phone and see anybody who might wander in."

Naomi pushed the door open wider. "I really appreciate this."

"It's no problem."

Naomi smiled at him and turned away. He and Naomi were cousins and had grown up together, as close as siblings. If she needed time away from the office, he wouldn't deny it to her. In fact, he wouldn't mind taking some extra time himself. For Brody... But there was work he needed to finish first.

He turned his attention to the Hailey file. An easy divorce. No mudslinging, no name-calling, no custody battle. He tabbed the pertinent pleadings, tossed it onto the stack and grabbed the Simpson bankruptcy file. The pending motion in this one was a little more complicated, and he still had to decide whether to drive up to Seattle for the hearing next week.

He'd found the motion and settled back to read it when Naomi's telephone rang, startling him. He punched in the code to pick up the call from his office. "Kurt Morgan."

"Kurt? It's Abby Harris."

Abby. He struggled to keep his voice calm. "Is everything all right?"

"Everything's fine. I'm calling because I was planning on taking Erin and Michael for a short drive up the coast this afternoon and I wondered if Brody could come with us." Her voice floated through the wire, warm and pleasant. An easy voice to listen to.

"That's fine."

"You don't mind?"

He chuckled. "Not at all. I appreciate your including him. You're sure he's no trouble?"

"He's no trouble at all."

He glanced at his watch. "What time should I pick him up?"

"What time will you be finished there?"

"I usually don't leave until five or a little later, but I can break away whenever."

"Why doesn't he just stay with us until you're finished? You can pick him up on the way home."

Kurt felt a smile stretch his face. "Fine. I shouldn't be too late."

"I'll see you then." Abby said softly, and broke the connection.

Kurt replaced the receiver gently and studied his schedule for the rest of the week. He appreciated Abby's interest in Brody. He appreciated her taking him along on this jaunt with her own kids. But he couldn't help feeling guilty that someone else had to provide Brody with the attention he should be getting from his father.

He noted with satisfaction that Naomi hadn't penciled in any appointments tomorrow. If he prepped all the files this afternoon, he could take the day off and spend some time with his son.

KURT CALLED to Brody for the third time and added a dash of salt to the scrambled eggs. Breakfast. A real breakfast like they hadn't enjoyed together since Kurt couldn't remember when. And a whole day to spend with each other.

Brody stumbled into the kitchen, his hair hanging in his eyes, his face puffy from sleep. "What are you cooking?"

"Scrambled eggs, toast, hash browns..."

Brody flashed him a confused look. "Why?"

"Why not?"

"You never have before."

Kurt struggled to keep a smile on his face. "Pour yourself a glass of milk while I dish up these eggs, okay?"

"I guess." With a shrug Brody turned away, but he still looked uncertain. He poured his milk in silence and took his place at the table.

Not for the first time, Kurt felt the width of the chasm that had opened between them since Laura left. But he was determined to keep it from growing. He filled their plates and took his own seat.

"What would you like to do today?"

Brody shrugged, "Probably just go to Michael's."

"You two seem to be getting along well."

"Michael's fun. Even his sister isn't a big pain like a lot of girls."

"I'm glad you've found somebody to hang around with while I'm at work." Kurt paused. "Mrs. Harris doesn't mind you being there, does she?"

"Nah." Brody shoved a heaping forkful of food into his mouth. He finished chewing, then continued. "She's pretty cool for a mom. She doesn't make Michael do a lot of junk before he can play or anything. And she likes having me around. She told me so."

The look of amazement on his face twisted Kurt's heart. "I'm glad," he said simply.

"She wants me to help Erin look for some clamshells and stuff. Since I've lived here so long, she thinks I know all the best places to find them."

"She's probably right."

For an instant Brody's startled eyes met Kurt's, but the boy glanced away so quickly Kurt wondered if he'd imagined it.

"Yeah, well. I don't know." Brody shoveled more food into his mouth and kicked his legs the way he did whenever he felt agitated.

Now what had he said wrong? Something had struck a nerve, but for the life of him, he couldn't imagine what. "Instead of going to Michael's today, how'd you like to go fishing with me?"

"Fishing?" This time confusion mixed with an equal part of doubt, but Brody's legs stopped swinging. "Since when do you like to fish?"

"Grandpa used to take Jack and me all the time when we were boys."

"Then how come you don't fish anymore?"

"Good question. That's why I took the day off. I thought I'd try it again. Are you game?"

Brody almost seemed interested. Almost. But he shook his head. "I can't."

"What do you mean?"

"Abby wants to take us on a picnic so we can start Erin's collection. I promised her I'd go."

Kurt's stomach knotted with unexpected jealousy. "Maybe Abby could make it another time. It's a good day for me—I don't have any appointments."

"You can still go fishing without me."

Without Brody, what would be the point? It was supposed

to be a bonding thing, something to bring father and son closer together. "Look, Brody—"

The telephone jangled, and as if anxious to escape the conversation, Brody jumped out of his chair to answer it. "Hello?"

His face brightened. "Hi. Yeah. Eating breakfast with my dad."

It must be Michael. At least Kurt had been right about one thing. Michael's friendship was good for Brody. It was just Brody's relationship with his dad that needed work.

Brody laughed.

Kurt had to reach the boy. Maybe it had taken him too long to see how much Brody had suffered after his mother left. He hadn't really started trying to help Brody with his grief and his fears until they'd already begun to ease, to mend on their own. But maybe Brody was mending the wrong way. The way broken limbs sometimes did....

"Dad?"

With a start Kurt realized Brody had been waiting for a response from him. "What?"

"It's for you." Brody handed him the receiver and slid into his seat. "It's Abby."

Kurt tried to still the sudden pounding of his heart. "Good morning."

"Good morning. I just wanted to make sure it would be all right with you if I take Brody on a picnic with us while you're at work."

He could say no and then Brody would go fishing with him. Once he got Brody alone, he was sure everything else would begin to fall into place.

But glancing at his son's rigid shoulders and the defiant tilt of his head, Kurt knew he couldn't do it. "It's fine, and thank you. He was just telling me about it. You're sure?"

"Brody's a lot of fun," Abby said lightly.

Obviously Brody didn't present the same sullen face to Abby that he did at home. But why would he? Brody's problem was with Kurt, and only Kurt could resolve it.

Refusing to let Brody go with Abby and her children would only cause Brody to pull away. He'd let him go now and organize something for the next time he had an open day. He'd keep on trying until he broke through. He would not—could not—turn his back on his son any longer.

"BRODY, CARRY THE ICE out to the cooler for me, okay? Michael, will you take this bag with the paper plates in it?" Abby ran back over the list in her head to be sure she had everything. She wanted this picnic to go well. For Erin's sake, she wanted to create a wonderful memory. And she didn't want to start off on the wrong foot by forgetting anything.

"What do you want me to do?" Erin stood just inside the door, wide-eyed and uncertain, almost as if she expected Abby to shout at her.

"Make sure the front door is locked. I'll lock the back door on the way out."

"We never lock our house." Brody hoisted the bag of ice onto his shoulder. "Nobody does in Pine Cove. Naomi—you know, my dad's secretary—says it's kind of weird that you even lock your car when you go to the store."

Abby knew people in small towns involved themselves in the affairs of their neighbors, but she certainly wasn't used to it. She didn't even know the names of most of her neighbors in Baltimore, and no one there paid the slightest attention to what she did.

But with Vic's threats haunting them, Abby would continue to practice security measures. She nodded at Erin, a signal to lock the door, anyway, and checked the last bag to make sure the plastic utensils had been included. "Looks like we have everything. Let's go."

Within minutes, they'd made their way out of town to the picnic area a few miles west. The boys, wrapped up in their enthusiasm for their new friendship, leapt from the car as soon as she drew to a stop, and scrambled over the boulders toward the fenced-in scenic overlook area. With the powerful river serene and blue and the sky only slightly overcast, it was the perfect place to help Erin unwind a little.

Watching the boys, Abby felt her spirits soar. They *all*

needed this—fresh air and exercise, and the water-cooled breezes in their hair.

She let the boys run for several minutes before calling them back to help unload the picnic gear. Defying local opinion, she locked the car and followed the kids to a stand of trees near an outcropping of granite boulders where several picnic tables overlooked the rocky shore. Michael and Brody chose the one closest to the water. Abby arranged the picnic on the table while the boys raced and climbed and Erin sat on a boulder watching ships on the river.

Abby approached the girl quietly and touched her hair. "What do you think? Beautiful, isn't it?"

Erin nodded, but she didn't say anything.

"I'm glad we came," Abby continued.

Erin's shoulders tightened and she dropped her head so her hair obscured her face.

Abby must have said the wrong thing—again. "Do you want to walk with me for a few minutes before lunch?"

Though Abby knew Erin wouldn't refuse—she carried too much fear inside to do that—she ached at the way the girl agreed to something she wasn't sure she wanted to do. In silence, they climbed down the rocks and strolled to the edge of the overlook. At the far end of the park, Michael and Brody squared off against each other for a race back to their picnic table, so Abby turned in the opposite direction.

Becoming friends with Brody had been wonderful for Michael. Though he still bore obvious emotional scars from his recent ordeal, for the past two nights he hadn't had the recurring nightmare in which his father came to snatch him.

But Erin remained distant. Impossible to reach.

Abby wanted to gather the girl in her arms and comfort her, but she feared that kind of contact would have the opposite effect. Instead, she stuffed her hands into her pockets and looked straight ahead. "We haven't talked about what you'd like to do this summer."

"Anything you want is okay with me."

Abby could have predicted that response. "But what do *you*

want to do? Michael's already found the Little League team, so I think he's set. Would you like to play, too?''

"I don't know."

"Erin, I want you to be happy."

"I'm all right. Really." But the girl refused to meet her eyes and no smile crossed her lips.

Abby wished she could ask someone about eleven-year-old girls and the way their minds worked. She longed for help in understanding the psyche of an abused child. But she was on her own, and she had no idea whether to push Erin for an answer or drop the subject.

After a moment of strained silence, she decided to drop it. For now. Especially since the increased volume of shouting behind them meant they were about to be overwhelmed by the boys.

Michael and Brody raced past them and ground to a halt several feet ahead. They looked happy and content, their faces red from exertion, their chests heaving under their shirts as they panted for air. Brody leaned over and grabbed his knees, struggling to catch his breath. But something in the distance claimed his attention. Following the direction of his gaze, Abby saw the small silhouette of a man with a fishing pole.

"Is that my dad?" Brody wondered aloud.

Abby's heart gave a surprising lurch. Why did she always feel that sense of anticipation at the thought of seeing Kurt again? Squinting, she studied the figure, but after a few seconds Brody shook his head.

"No. That's not him." He rolled his eyes at Michael. "He wanted to take the day off work and go fishing with me."

"Cool!" Michael exclaimed. "Why didn't you go?"

"Because I already said I'd come with you guys."

Why hadn't Kurt said something about his plans when she called to ask if Brody could come with them? He hadn't sounded overly warm on the phone, but she hadn't noticed any anger. "Maybe you should have gone with your dad," she said.

"I didn't want to. I wanted to come with you."

"It might have made him feel bad."

Shaking his head, Brody looked at her as if she was crazy. "No, it didn't. He didn't care."

She didn't contradict him, but doubt must have shown in her face because Brody stiffened.

"He *didn't*," the boy insisted.

"He probably cares more than you know."

"No, he doesn't. All he cared about was my mom, but she left. And now all he cares about is work."

Everywhere Abby went she ran into another casualty of the war being waged in the name of love. Rachel, Erin, Michael— and now Brody. Not to mention the hundreds of people she'd photographed, whose names she couldn't remember but whose faces she would never forget.

Seeing the pain on Brody's face, Abby longed to help him. She had no doubt he'd misunderstood his father's sentiments. After all, she'd seen how eager Kurt had been to get home to Brody the night they'd arrived and she'd seen him at Little League practices, giving Brody encouragement and support. Obviously Kurt was no better at reaching his son than she was at getting through to Erin.

But she believed Kurt could eventually reach Brody if he didn't give up. And though she might not reach Erin today, eventually she *would* break through. She had to. She couldn't allow anyone or anything, not even Kurt Morgan and his son, to distract her from her own priorities—the two children who'd been told to call her mom.

CHAPTER FOUR

KURT GLANCED at his watch when the telephone gave the double ring that signaled an inside call. Three o'clock, and he still had a full two hours of appointments to go. Kurt groaned. It had already been the day from hell.

In the week since Brody had turned down the fishing trip in favor of a picnic with Abby, Kurt hadn't had a minute's respite. With the work flow interrupted by another battle between Naomi and Bill, nothing at the office had gone smoothly for several days.

Switching off the cassette recorder he'd been using for dictation, Kurt snatched the receiver from the hook. "What is it?"

"It's Aunt Zelda." Naomi spoke in a tight whisper.

Kurt felt himself cringe. Not now. He'd talk to Zelda any time but now. "Tell her I'm not in."

"*You* tell her you're not in. *I'm* not lying to her."

"Thanks a lot." He should never have hired his cousin as his secretary—not if he hoped to avoid Zelda's calls.

"You're welcome." Naomi broke her connection and after a few clicks, Zelda's call came through.

"Are you busy?"

"A little." He'd learned long ago that claiming the pressures of the office carried no weight with his aunt. She had her own agenda and rarely let anyone sidetrack her, regardless of the other person's commitments.

"Have you gone out to fix Abby's porch yet?"

He'd seen Abby at Little League practice, but he'd managed not to get too close. In spite of his best intentions, he found himself more and more drawn to her. So he'd been trying to stay away. "I'll have to stop by after work, Aunt Zelda. I can't go right now."

"You're going to have to," his aunt said emphatically. "Now she's got a problem with the washer and she says there's water everywhere."

Looking at his desk, he bit back an oath of frustration. He couldn't very well leave Abby standing in water for another two hours.

"Naomi tells me she can cancel your afternoon appointments, so I don't see why you can't run over there now."

Considering that Zelda had already dismissed every conceivable obstacle, he couldn't, either. "I'll go."

"Right away?"

"Yes, Zelda. Right away."

After he'd hung up, Kurt cleared his desk quickly. Grabbing his jacket from the coat tree, he slung it over his shoulder.

The outer office stood empty. Naomi certainly knew how to disappear quickly after putting him on the spot. He needed a secretary with a little backbone. Somebody who could stand up to Aunt Zelda. Unfortunately he'd never met anyone—except Jack—who could do that.

He left a note on Naomi's desk telling her he wouldn't be back and placed a small cassette tape on top of it. Sweet revenge. Naomi hated to transcribe dictation.

Because he'd made a court appearance that morning, he'd worn a suit to the office. He'd have to stop at home to change. And on the off chance Brody hadn't already finished his chores and gone to Abby's, Kurt could pick him up and take him along. With Brody there to provide a distraction, maybe Kurt could avoid being alone with her.

Relieved to find an easy solution, he enjoyed the drive home. The sun peeked through a few clouds on the western horizon and the earth took on a golden glow as evening neared. He loved the drive along the Gorge and the sight of the Columbia River as it rolled toward the Pacific less than fifty miles away.

Along the highway, the forest grew to the edge of the river, and where the trees ended, the ground fell away sharply to the water. Kurt's house stood almost squarely in the center of a

five-mile stretch of highway with a clear view of Castle Island.
The combination of earth, water and sky never failed to inspire
awe in him.

Surprisingly Brody was still on the riverbank with Pride.
Kurt waved, then ducked inside to change into jeans and a shirt.
When he stepped back onto the deck, he shouted through
cupped hands, "Hey, sport! Want to run over to Michael's
house with me?"

Brody tossed the branch he'd been holding and raced toward
Kurt, his face bright with a smile Kurt knew wasn't meant for
him. "Sure, but can I take Pride? Michael hasn't been over to
see him and he's never had a dog."

Fighting to keep his tone light, Kurt returned the smile.
"Never had a dog? Poor guy!"

"I know. He told me his mom hates dogs. She's allergic or
something."

So Abby did have one or two flaws. "Shocking."

"I'm serious, Dad."

"So am I."

"Dad—"

"Sorry."

"You're weird." A tentative grin appeared on Brody's face.

Kurt matched it. "I wondered when you'd notice." He put
an arm around Brody's shoulders and headed toward the driveway, more confident than he'd been in a long time that things
were looking up.

ABBY PACED the length of the living room, peered through the
front window and retraced her steps. She'd called Zelda over
an hour ago asking for the name of a plumber. But Zelda had
insisted on sending Kurt.

Abby had managed to lessen the flow of water, but she
hadn't been able to close the rusted valve completely, and a
slow stream still swirled from the laundry room into the
kitchen. She needed help, but she didn't want it to come from
Kurt. Every time she ran into him, his appeal grew stronger.
The air became almost electric whenever he was near, and the
sound of his voice on the telephone made her weak.

Michael's friendship with Brody only complicated the situation. If the boys hadn't become such good friends, Abby might have been able to avoid Kurt, but with the boys spending so much time together, she and Kurt were inevitably thrown together, too.

She saw Kurt at Little League practice, and every time she went to town she seemed to pass him somewhere. She did have to call him if she wanted to invite Brody along with them, but she refused to call him about every little thing that went wrong with the house.

She'd avoided reporting the broken screen door on the back porch, and they'd ignored the leak under the kitchen sink for more than a week. She'd never mentioned the loose board on the porch, though Zelda had somehow found out about it. And she'd even tried to handle today's plumbing crisis on her own. But unfortunately she needed help with this one. She just didn't want it to be Kurt's help....

The sound of a car in the driveway caught her attention. Racing to the window, she peeked through the lace curtains at the white Jeep Cherokee. Her heart leapt.

She heard a dog bark and then a door slam. She pulled back from the window and waited until the sound of hurried footsteps reached the porch.

As she opened the door, the dog barked again, closer this time, and a huge black head poked through the opening. The animal pushed the door open the rest of the way and nudged Abby with its nose.

Abby smiled and scratched behind one ear, and the dog looked up at her with huge brown eyes, leaning its head against her thigh.

Brody followed, dismayed. "Pride, stop that! Sit! I'm sorry, Abby. He just got away from me."

Pride nudged Abby's hand again and she ran her fingers across his short coarse hair. "He's just fine. He's not hurting a thing."

Brody seemed confused. "I didn't think you'd like him."

"Are you kidding? I love dogs." She scratched the soft spot

beneath the dog's chin and laughed at the adoring look in his
eyes. "Especially great big beasts like this one."

Brody turned his head and spoke over his shoulder. "Look,
Dad. She likes him."

Kurt rounded the corner of the house carrying a toolbox, and
Abby's heart raced the way it did every time she saw him.

He took a step forward, but his eyes narrowed. "Looks like
you've made a friend for life."

"I've had worse friends."

"So have I." He glanced down at his toolbox. "I'll go
around to the back. I just...I thought maybe you were having
trouble with the dog, so I came..." His voice trailed away and
he fixed her with his steely eyes again.

What was wrong with him? "This sweet thing wouldn't give
anybody trouble, would you?" Pride wagged his tail and
nudged her hand again. "Unless he didn't think he was getting
his share of attention."

Brody wound his fingers through Pride's collar and tugged
him away. "I thought Michael said you were allergic to dogs."

Abby froze. Now she knew why Kurt was looking at her
that way. He'd caught her again. Somehow, in innocent conversation, Michael must have said his mother was allergic—
and Rachel was. But Abby wasn't. What else had he told
Brody?

Oblivious to the tension in the air, Brody tugged at Pride's
collar. "Can I show him to Michael?"

"Sure. He's around back with Erin."

Brody bounded down the steps and raced the dog across the
yard. Abby watched them go, aware that Kurt did, too. When
they'd disappeared, she turned back, nearly sick to her stomach
with anxiety.

Her mouth felt too dry to form words. She thought of a
dozen things she could say and discarded them all because she
couldn't think of any reasonable explanation to offer.

Kurt shifted the toolbox to his other hand and avoided meeting her eyes. "I'll just check on that problem you're having."

"Right. I'll show you." As if he didn't know his way
around.

Kurt's lips formed a thin smile as he waited for her to lead him to the kitchen.

She'd mopped up the worst of the water, but the floor was still wet and slippery. Walking cautiously, she was concentrating so much on her feet that when he took her arm to steady her, she wasn't prepared. She stiffened as the skin on her arm burned from his touch.

She didn't dare look up, fearing the telltale blush that must be coloring her cheeks. She couldn't speak, not trusting her voice. After she'd crossed the worst of the floor he released her; anxious to get away from him before she revealed too much, Abby increased her pace the last several feet into the utility room.

"Here it is," she said stupidly.

Kurt looked around with a grimace, setting the toolbox on the washer. "Did you unplug it or is it still connected to the electricity?"

"I couldn't move it enough to reach the plug."

He nodded, pulled the machine easily away from the wall and disconnected its power. Studying the pipes and hoses, he finally located the broken one and smiled with satisfaction. "It could be worse. This shouldn't take long at all."

She told herself she'd been waiting to be sure he didn't need her help. And now that he knew what was involved, she could leave him to the job. But knowing what he must think of her after catching her in another obvious lie burned her heart, and it took all her willpower to turn away.

Kurt hammered at the pipe fitting with the wrench, releasing a little of his frustration. Something was wrong here, and he couldn't ignore it any longer. He twisted the joint and banged again. Abby and her kids were hiding something.

Using the pipe wrench, he loosened the fitting and caught the dripping water with a rag. There were too many unanswered questions. Take the night they'd arrived, for example. Sure they'd been tired, but who had Michael seen in his nightmare? Why had Abby said Michael couldn't play baseball? Why did Michael claim his mother was allergic to dogs when she obviously wasn't? And why was Erin so quiet and with-drawn, reserved beyond mere shyness?

He cursed under his breath and checked the next joint. He liked having Michael close enough for Brody to play with, but if something strange was going on here, maybe it wasn't a good idea to let them get any closer. He slid his hands up the pipe and hammered at the fitting again.

Though he couldn't deny the strange pull Abby exerted on him, she *had* to be hiding something. But what? Why? He'd interviewed witnesses in court many times over the years, and he'd heard too many lies and half-truths to ignore the signals Abby sent out. His heart tried to tell him not to worry, but his internal warning system was sounding an alarm.

He should see what he could find out about her—at least find out what Zelda knew about her and where she came from. Surely Zelda had asked for references before she'd rented the house. It would be easy enough to check them out.

Despite his questions, Kurt couldn't get her image out of his mind. When he'd followed Abby through the house into the kitchen, he hadn't been able to tear his eyes away from her trim figure, from the way her jeans hugged her bottom, the way her ponytail exposed the nape of her neck. And when he'd taken her arm to help her across the wet floor, the heat of her skin had shocked him.

But how could he feel that way about her? She was married. *Married.* Why did he want to forget that? Why did his thoughts keep straying to this woman's face, her sapphire eyes and the citrus scent of her hair?

Throwing himself into his work, Kurt tried to beat Abby's image away, as if by sheer physical labor he could exorcise the power she held over him. But the job wasn't hard enough or long enough to do the trick.

When he'd finished the washer and had nailed down the loose board on the porch, he went in search of her, telling himself he couldn't leave without letting her know he'd fin-ished. He searched the living room and family room without success and was just turning around to go back for his tools when she appeared at the top of the stairs.

With the late-afternoon sun streaming through the windows and glowing around her, she was a vision. He blinked slowly, trying to ignore his sudden desire. "The washer's fixed."

"Great." She came down a few steps, waited as if she expected him to speak, then asked, "Would you like a glass of iced tea before you leave?"

He should say no. He should just grab his toolbox and get out before he said or did something he shouldn't. Instead, he mumbled, "Sure. Thanks."

Following her into the kitchen, Kurt tried to still his too-rapid pulse. Watching her reach for glasses and pour the tea, he tried to drag his eyes away. But by the time she sat across from him, he couldn't do it any longer. His senses whirled as he watched her drink, watched her throat move and the moisture on her lips when she lowered the glass.

Fighting his impulses, Kurt reminded himself that somewhere halfway around the world, there was a man who had the right to gaze at her like this. And suddenly he felt an urgent need to know more about her husband. The mysterious Mr. Harris.

He was nothing more than a remote concept, an unreality. Maybe if Kurt knew more about the guy, he'd have an easier time putting Abby out of his mind. And it might even answer some of his other questions.

He gulped his own drink and felt a little control return. Grasping at his one coherent thought, he said, "So...your husband's working in Europe this summer?"

Abby felt her eyes widen with surprise and belatedly managed to make herself nod. First the incident with the dog and now questions about her husband.

"What does he do?" Kurt looked at her expectantly.

"He's a consultant." A *consultant?* That was it? The minute Kurt turned his incredible green eyes in her direction, she started babbling like a fool. Why on earth had she asked him to stay?

She knew he was waiting for her to say more, but she lifted the glass to her lips again to buy some time.

"In what field?"

"Field?" *Don't sound like an idiot. Take a breath. Now another.* "Computers. He's helping American firms set up new systems in Europe."

She tried in vain to remember the details of the story she'd worked out so carefully, but she somehow knew Kurt wouldn't believe it, and she couldn't force the words from between her frozen lips.

"The kids must miss him."

"Yes." *Dear God, he was going to ask the kids about this.* But surely they'd remember all the details of the story the family had worked out in Arizona—wouldn't they?

"Do they look like him?"

Shaking her head, she spoke softly. "They both look more like my side of the family. Michael looks a lot like my dad and Erin looks just like...like my sister, Rachel." She couldn't believe it—she'd almost slipped again. Steeling herself, she met his gaze with a determined one of her own. "I can sure see the resemblance between you and Brody."

Kurt grinned. "Yeah, poor guy. Is this the first time your kids have been away from their father for so long?"

"Yes." Gnawing at her lower lip, she looked away. She had to get him to change the subject.

"I wondered, because they seem to be making the adjustment pretty well."

Pretty well? When Erin scarcely spoke to anyone and Michael still had nightmares three nights out of five? "Erin's having trouble. She misses things at home, I guess—friends and her routine. But it's been great for Michael to have Brody so close."

"It's been great for Brody, too. He's had some difficulty adjusting to his mother's leaving."

At last. A subject she could talk about without feeling nauseated. "I've noticed some things..."

"He has other friends whose parents are divorced, but he's the only one we know whose mother walked out. We had real trouble the first couple of months after Laura left, but things are a little better now."

But not entirely better, Abby knew. Still, Kurt gave Brody

lots of attention and encouragement, and his heart seemed to be in the right place where his son was concerned. "Maybe he just needs more time."

Kurt hesitated, then shook his head. "I don't think so. He needs stability. I think back to summers when I was a kid—the things Jack and I did together. We had a great childhood. Brody's alone. And he's old enough now that, should I get around to giving him a brother, they'll never be really close." He smiled thinly. "But you're here this summer, and at least he's got Michael...."

Uncertainty lingered behind his words. "But...?" Abby prompted.

"I'm a little worried that he'll get *too* close to Michael."

"You want him to spend less time with us?"

Kurt looked disconcerted at her question. "I thought so. Now I'm not so sure what I want. He likes being over here so much I hate to tell him not to come. But—"

"You want me to promise not to hurt him."

Kurt smiled. "Yes."

"I'd never intentionally hurt him."

"I already know that."

Abby studied a scratch on the table. "I won't let him get too attached—is that what you want to hear?"

"Yes. And no." Kurt grinned and lifted his glass.

His smile made her pulse race, but his words stung. She tried to smile back. At least she admired his honesty. "Brody said you're an attorney. That surprises me."

He looked confused. "Why?"

"You just don't seem the type, I guess."

"Yeah, well, that's what my ex-wife thought, too." His voice took on a steely tone.

"Oh." She felt the flush of embarrassment creep up her face. She hadn't intended to touch on a painful subject. "But do you enjoy it?"

"Yes, I do now. The thing is, I've always wanted to help people. To make a difference. For a while I thought the only way to do that was to work my way up the ladder in a big firm, put in ninety billable hours a week and schmooze with the boss like crazy. But I hated every minute of it, so I came back here. That's when I realized I can make more of a difference here than I ever would have in Seattle.''

She liked the way his eyes seemed to glitter when he got excited. "How?"

"Help one person and you indirectly touch the lives of everyone they know. It's a great feeling—but there's not a lot of money in it.''

This time she laughed, and when Kurt joined her, she realized she'd never heard him laugh before. It was a warm friendly sound, and she felt it in every nerve of her body. She suddenly knew she wanted to hear him laugh again. Often.

As if echoing them, childish laughter sounded close to the house, followed by Pride's enthusiastic barking. Footsteps pounded up the steps to the porch, and Abby heard the back door open. Swiveling in her chair, she saw the door hanging from the frame, and her eyes flew to meet the question in Kurt's.

"When did that door break?" he asked.

Erin let it close with a bang and lowered her eyes before she spoke. "It's been like that as long as we've been here. And the sink, too.''

"The sink?"

"It leaks."

"You should have called me." The moment they'd shared was over. He stood and picked up his tools. "It'll only take me a minute to deal with them right now.''

He worked quickly, and in less than an hour he'd fixed the sink and reattached the screen door to its frame. He dusted his hands on his pants and gathered his tools again. "That door really needs to have the screen replaced, but I'll come back for that later.''

Abby could only nod. How could she explain why she hadn't called him to fix these things? That she'd been avoiding him? That she'd discovered this overwhelming attraction to him and she'd been trying to keep him away?

Between the lies about baseball, the dog and now this, he'd surely wonder why she was acting so strangely. And to make matters worse, this time together hadn't done anything to cure her. She wanted to be with him now more than ever.

She watched him pick up his toolbox and walk with Brody back to the car. As the Cherokee sped down the highway, she drew in a deep breath and cursed herself for a fool.

Just looking at him made every coherent thought disappear. And when he looked at her, she lost her power to concentrate on anything except the width of his shoulders, the firm set of his jaw and, of course, those eyes. She could lose herself in those eyes.

The strain of keeping the children occupied must be getting to her. Not to mention her constant worry—whether she'd managed to keep their whereabouts secret and whether Rachel was safe.

She longed to hear from Rachel. The children needed to speak with their mother, but Abby couldn't allow that to happen yet. Only when Rachel believed they were safe from Vic would she send a signal through prearranged channels. Then Abby would be free to let her know where they were.

But until that time, Abby couldn't do anything. And the children grew more restless and discontented every day. On their afternoon drives, they'd already explored almost every side road in the vicinity, and she'd taken more picnics in the past two weeks than in her previous thirty-two years.

At least Michael was busy with Little League and Brody, but his sister had nothing to distract her. And Abby hadn't yet found a way to break through Erin's barriers.

And *she* had nothing, except this attraction for Kurt Morgan. She'd thought once about planting a vegetable garden in the wide backyard, but abandoned the idea when she realized they'd have to leave before they could harvest anything. Housework kept her busy several hours a day, but left her mind free to wander. She had to find a distraction soon.

Behind her a floorboard creaked in the hallway. Abby turned quickly, startled by the noise.

Framed in the open door, Erin looked like a small child. "Abby?" She took a hesitant step forward. "Do you think Mom's all right?"

Though the reason for the girl's concern saddened her, the fact that she'd come to her about it gave Abby hope. She tried to smile but feared the effort was wasted. "Yes, I do."

"But we haven't heard anything."

Abby gathered Erin to her. "That's a good sign. As long as my friend Ted doesn't contact us, everything's all right."

"Nobody even knows where we are."

"Our family doesn't, but they know who to contact if they need to reach us. And if anything had happened to your mother, Grandpa and Grandma would have let us know."

Erin stared up at Abby in silence, her eyes huge with fear. Finally her face puckered and tears slid down her cheeks. "He...he said he'd kill her. He said no matter what she did, he'd kill her if she took us away from him."

Though Rachel had been married to Vic for more than fifteen years, Abby had never known him well, as she'd moved away shortly after Michael's birth. But she'd seen enough men like him over the years to know Erin's concerns were valid. Though he no longer had any legal claim on the children, Abby absolutely believed he'd try to carry out his threats to take Erin and Michael from Rachel.

The family had pooled their resources, raising funds to keep Abby and the children in hiding for three months. They all hoped Vic would calm down enough by then to make it safe for the kids to go home. Or else Rachel would have to leave Tempe and take them somewhere safer.

She smoothed Erin's hair from her forehead. "I know how worried you are, but we have to believe that your mom's going to be all right. She's a strong woman. It wasn't easy for her to send you two away."

Erin's chin quivered. "It's her birthday next week and we're not even there. Can we call her?"

"I wish we could, but it's not safe," Abby explained. "Besides, it would make your mom worry more, wondering whether your dad would figure out where you were from the phone call. *She* doesn't even want to know where you are so she can't slip up and say the wrong thing."

Erin turned away. "I wish she was here."

So did Abby, but she wouldn't make Erin feel worse by admitting it.

She watched Erin walk away, then she sank into a chair and buried her face in her hands. She had no idea what to do for Erin. She didn't even know what she wanted to do with her own life, once this was all over.

She worried constantly about the effect her inexperienced care would have on Erin and Michael at this vulnerable stage of their lives. She'd seen too many bad parents over the years and the damage they wreaked on their children. After observing so much violence perpetrated in the name of love, and after losing Steven because she couldn't give him children, Abby's focus had shifted from home and family. Having made her life in other areas, she sometimes felt overwhelmed by the demands placed on her by Rachel's children, their needs and fears.

Pushing herself away from the table, Abby gathered the glasses she and Kurt had used. On top of everything else, she'd met a man whose very existence complicated everything. She knew Kurt didn't accept her story at face value, but she hoped he wouldn't do anything to jeopardize their safety.

She was drawn to him, and she knew she'd seen a similar interest in his eyes. But she couldn't give in to it. In fact, the only positive thing about the situation was that Kurt thought she had a husband. And that would keep him from pursuing her. At least it had so far.

She couldn't allow herself to want anything more than friendship from Kurt. Casual affairs didn't interest her, and anything else was out of the question. He wanted a wife and more children—he'd made that clear. But Abby's life ran on a completely different track.

After they'd tried for three years to have a baby, Steven had insisted on subjecting her to a series of fertility tests that had left her feeling dehumanized. And when the doctor had handed down the proof that Abby would never bear a child, Steven had been bitterly disappointed.

In the end, her inability to give him what he wanted most had driven him away. After the pain of losing him had dulled, she was realistic enough to recognize that most men wanted children. And those who didn't were too focused on their careers to attract her. So she'd given up her hopes of a family, and she'd put any serious involvements far behind her. She wouldn't go through that kind of humiliation again for *any* man.

And that included Kurt Morgan.

CHAPTER FIVE

BRODY REACHED for the volume control and turned up the music. Kurt winced inwardly, but struggled to keep his face impassive and his mind on the road. The last thing he wanted
right now was to antagonize his son.

Well, his visit with Abby hadn't been a *total* disaster. Not
if you didn't count that he hadn't learned enough about the
mysterious Mr. Harris to drive *Mrs.* Harris out of his mind.
And if you didn't count that he'd come away even more attracted to Abby than ever.

Meeting her had been good for Brody in one way, but in
another it had driven the wedge between Kurt and Brody even
deeper. All the boy could talk about was Michael and Erin—
and Abby.

Kurt shook his head and ran his fingers through his hair. He
knew beyond a shadow of a doubt that listening to stories about
Abby, even hearing her name, made him want to spend time
with her. And that was dangerous.

If he spent a little more time remembering Laura—and the
pain she'd caused—he'd probably put Abby out of his mind
soon enough, Kurt told himself grimly. He didn't need a
woman in his life right now. And he definitely didn't need a
married woman, no matter how she made him feel.

But what frightened him the most was the fact that she felt
something for him, too. He could see it in her eyes. And if
Abby ever looked at him the way she did in his dreams, he
didn't know what he'd do.

Besides, Kurt had a son who needed his time and attention.
Abby connected well with the boys because she was home all
day. When the boys wanted to do something, she was there;

when they wanted a picnic, she could provide one. And she took them both.

That was the answer. He had to find something he could do with the boys together. He let up on the accelerator and met Brody's curious gaze with a smile.

"I've got an idea, sport. What do you think about asking Abby if Michael can come for a sleep over?"

That earned him a wide grin. "When?"

"This weekend if she'll agree to it. Okay?"

Brody settled back into his seat and nodded. He didn't speak again, but Kurt felt a difference in his attitude. And for the first time in days, Kurt knew he'd finally found something that would help him connect with his son.

ABBY ADJUSTED the shutter speed on her Nikon, focused on the sun peeping up over the tops of the pine trees to the east and waited. Holding her breath, she watched the sun climb a little higher, then she snapped the frame and got off another shot before the light changed.

Silence surrounded her, broken only by the gentle sound of the river far below and the occasional cry of a gull. The air, fresh from the water, carried a chill over the rocks.

She focused on a tree, lifeless and barren, silhouetted against the sunrise, and snapped three more frames. The camera rested easily in her hands, as naturally as if she'd shot her last crime scene the night before.

She hadn't used her cameras in over a month. The thought of picking them up, changing lenses, focusing and adjusting F-stops frightened her. She doubted she'd ever be able to return to her career. Even now, putting her eye to the viewfinder brought snatches of scenes—tragic, violent, horrible scenes—to mind.

Watching the sky lighten after a sleepless night, Abby had suddenly thought she could do this. Something from outside had seemed to draw her. With the children still asleep, she'd felt free to venture onto the riverbank as long as she kept the house in sight.

She'd grabbed her camera and a roll of film, leaving her

lenses and extra equipment behind. She didn't want to do anything elaborate this morning—but she just hoped the cool clean air would help her work through some of the problems that had driven her from Baltimore in the first place.

So much had happened since then. Even after more than two weeks in Pine Cove she had no idea if they were safe here, and she didn't know how much longer she'd have to wait.

Lately she'd done nothing *but* wait. She waited to hear from Rachel or her parents. Waited to hear from Ted. Waited for Vic to find them. Waited for the nightmarish crime scenes that haunted her to fade. Waited for disaster to strike.

And she waited to see Kurt again.

She couldn't do anything to change the situation, and that was what made it so frustrating. She didn't like not being in control, and everything about her sojourn in Pine Cove reminded her how little control she had.

She'd told herself a thousand times that if Vic knew where they were, he'd have made a move by now. But she couldn't shake the almost overwhelming sense of apprehension.

Rocks shifted underfoot as she sought a new position, scanning the horizon through the camera. She might not return to a career with the police force, but she could never give up photography completely.

In the distance, she picked up a figure—actually, two. A man and his dog walking on the shore. Her heart fluttered. She liked the picture they made: the man long, lean and relaxed while the dog frisked at his side.

She focused and shot, advanced the film and waited until they got close enough for the camera to pick up what she now recognized as Kurt's face. She'd been wondering whether she'd ever be able to photograph a human being again, but she captured this picture of him and his dog with ease.

She saw the moment he spotted her. She caught the slight hesitation in his step before he raised his arm in greeting, and her heart raced.

Lowering the camera, she returned his wave. Half of her longed to rush back to the safety of the house. The other half felt overjoyed at seeing him here alone. She hesitated, uncertain, and then Pride recognized her and bounded across the shore.

The dog nudged her enthusiastically, wriggling against her before turning back to Kurt as if to say, "Look who I found!" Kurt arrived, breathless, a minute or two later.

"Hi." He wiped his forehead with the back of his hand. Even in the morning chill he'd worked up a slight sweat.

The air seemed almost magnetic, and Abby had to struggle to keep her face impassive. She replaced the lens cap and let the camera hang from the strap around her neck. "Are you taking the dog for a walk? Or is he walking you?"

Kurt laughed, that warm rumbling sound that started deep in his chest. "Sometimes I wonder. Doesn't it say somewhere that man is supposed to be the superior beast?"

"I'll bet whoever said that never checked with his dog."

He smiled and Abby's breath caught in her throat. She'd been deeply in love with Steven, but even he had never affected her like this.

Kurt ran his fingers through his hair and nodded toward her camera. "I noticed your equipment the night you arrived, but I haven't seen you out here before."

"I haven't taken any pictures since we got here."

"Our scenery finally got to you, huh?" He turned to look at the sun over the trees. "Morning is my favorite time of day. I miss it if I don't get out here first thing. Even if I do have to bring a friend."

As though he knew they were talking about him, Pride tugged at Kurt's pants, wagging his tail furiously.

Abby laughed, then moved away from him. "It's quiet here in Pine Cove."

"Don't let it fool you. We get started early in the morning— at least the fishing boats do. The rest of the town is a little more laid back, I guess. It isn't like— Wherever are you from?"

"Baltimore," she said automatically, and then caught herself.

Why had she said that? She'd gone to such lengths to work out a believable story, but every time she got around Kurt she said the wrong thing. She was supposed to stick as closely to their history as possible so they didn't get confused. She was supposed to say they were from Phoenix.

"Baltimore." His brows knit in confusion. "What brought you clear across the country for the summer?"

Abby struggled to maintain a calm exterior. She had to keep her guard up better than this. "My husband spent some time in the area years ago. He thought we'd enjoy it."

"And do you? Enjoy it?"

"Very much."

"Good." He looked toward the river, hesitating before he spoke again. "I wondered whether Michael would like to come for a sleep over with Brody. If it's okay with you, how about Saturday night?"

She knew she should say no, though every instinct told her Michael was safe with this man. But could she trust her instincts? Since the minute she'd agreed to hide the children from their father, she'd realized how easy it would be for Vic to grab one of them if they got separated from her. Would this be placing Michael in potential jeopardy?

Fleetingly she wondered about telling Kurt the truth, but she discarded the idea immediately. She barely knew him, and the stakes were too high for that kind of gamble. Besides, she'd trusted a man before—Steven—and look where that had gotten her. No, she was on her own.

But knowing that didn't make her choice more clear. She had to protect the children—but she also had to help them heal. She didn't want to make them prisoners of their fears.

Hoping she was making a wise decision, she said, "This Saturday would be fine. And maybe next Saturday, Brody could sleep over with us."

"It's a deal. I'll call you about it later in the week." He smiled again, the dimples tucking into his cheeks.

Too soon, he turned to go, and with regret she watched him walk away. He strode across the sand and rocks, his shoulders swaying beneath his light jacket, the breeze lifting his hair into the sunlight. A pleasant warmth curled through her, spreading with careless abandon. Every time she saw Kurt, the feeling grew. All her stern admonitions to herself to keep things in check did no good. All her resolutions to be careful around him were useless.

Kurt Morgan made her blood race, her head light and her skin tingle. But she didn't dare get involved with him. If she couldn't avoid him, at least she could discourage the interest she saw in his eyes; it shouldn't be too difficult if she played the part of a married woman the way she was supposed to. She'd just have to ignore the disappointment that filled her at the thought of discouraging Kurt's attention.

ABBY FOLDED her sweater under her on the bleachers and savored the rare sun on her shoulders. She pulled the baseball cap lower on her head to shield her eyes and squinted at the sea of children on the field. So far she hadn't seen Kurt, but since this was the Jets' first game, she knew he'd be here.

Beside her, Erin propped her feet on the row of bleachers in front of them and stared straight ahead.

Abby touched Erin's back lightly. "Can you see Michael out there?"

Erin shook her head and looked away from the field.

"Do you want a soda?"

Erin shook her head again.

"Would you mind handing me one?"

Erin opened the cooler and dug through the top layer of ice. "Do you want me to open it for you?"

"I can do it. Thanks." Abby turned back to the diamond, but her attention remained firmly focused on the girl. Erin still reacted to the abuse so differently from Michael, closing herself off and burying her emotions. And she was pathetically eager to please Abby—or to avoid *dis*pleasing her. As each day passed and Erin remained untouchable, Abby despaired of ever reaching her. She didn't know the best things to say, the right things to do or the proper way to react, and Erin kept pulling farther into her shell.

Erin shifted position and stared at the field again. There had to be something Abby could do to reach her, something that would help her recover in the same way Brody and Little League had helped Michael. But what?

On the field, a boy in a Jets uniform swung at a high, outside pitch. A strike. Behind them, a man swore at the coach, the batter and the umpire.

Men still frightened Erin, and she shuddered and looked down. Abby groaned inwardly, praying the man would keep quiet. But when the boy took another swing at a pitch even Abby could see was impossible, the man swore again and shot to his feet.

"I'm going down there to see what the hell's going on." His words slurred slightly and the unmistakable odor of alcohol floated on the air.

"You're not going anywhere," a woman said in a harsh whisper. "Sit down and quit making a fool of yourself."

"Hey! Jason ought to be on the starting lineup. I don't want anybody making him look bad."

"Nobody's doing anything to him. Sit down."

Without glancing up, Erin sought Abby's knee and clenched it. Putting her arm around Erin's shoulders, Abby held her close.

The boy stepped up to the plate again, determination on his face. From his position on the edge of the field, Kurt called out something and the boy smiled grimly.

"Don't screw this one up, Jason," the man behind them shouted. "Keep your eye on the damn ball."

Several heads in the front rows turned to look at him.

"You've had too much to drink and you're embarrassing him," the woman hissed.

The man swore. "Jason doesn't care if I have a beer now and then. *You're* the one with the problem."

Erin tensed and Abby held her breath. Jason let the next pitch go by, and the umpire called it a ball.

"Don't look up," the man shouted.

"For Pete's sake, Bill—"

"Just back off, Naomi."

"You're doing it again," she warned.

"Doing what?"

"This. We can't go *anywhere* without you making a scene."

"Oh, shut up." His words carried a threat, but his voice had lost some of its conviction. "I only had a few beers. Why do you always have to make such a big deal out of it?"

Jason swung at the next pitch and connected weakly. The ball skittered across the grass and was picked up by the shortstop, but Jason tore down the baseline and made it in time.

With his son safe on first base and the crisis apparently averted, the man settled his weight back on the bleachers.

Beside Abby, Erin relaxed slowly, but tears filled her eyes. "I thought he was going to hit her."

"Oh, sweetheart." Abby pulled her closer.

"My dad gets mean when he drinks," Erin said softly.

Keeping her arm around the girl's shoulders, Abby tried to focus on the game, but she was too conscious of Erin's fears to enjoy it even a little.

If coming to the games meant exposing Erin to the things she feared most, Abby couldn't let Michael finish the season. She'd thought Michael's involvement with Little League was wonderful. She'd even wanted to find something similar for Erin. But Erin wasn't ready for this. It wasn't fair to subject her to situations so painful for her, but Abby couldn't let Michael come to Little League by himself, any more than she could let Erin stay home alone. So which child's needs did she meet?

Two interminable innings passed before Abby saw Kurt on the edge of the field as he made his way toward the bleachers. He wore shorts that exposed his trim legs and a short-sleeved shirt, stretched across his chest and back, tucked firmly into the waistband.

Even the sight of him at this distance sent her pulse into overdrive, but today's incident only reinforced what she already knew. She had no business falling for this guy when she was in the middle of a family crisis.

Spotting them, Kurt waved and started up the bleachers, stepping gingerly through the crowd and tossing greetings to the people he passed. People liked him, that much was obvious. *She* liked him. But even if her present situation was different, she knew they'd never make it together. She'd watched Kurt with his son and listened to him that day in her kitchen talk about giving Brody a brother at some future time—and Abby simply couldn't give him what he needed. She refused to let herself get caught up in something that could only end in pain.

Kurt greeted her with a lopsided grin and wedged himself into the narrow space beside her. Where his thigh brushed hers, her flesh tingled.

He pointed toward his sister-in-law on the coach's bench by the field. "Theresa wanted me to invite you to the potluck dinner next Wednesday. Everybody—parents, kids, families—gets together every year. It's not a big deal, really, but she thought you might like to come."

"I don't think so." Not after Erin's reaction to the incident with the man behind them. And not when sitting this close to Kurt drove Abby to distraction.

"It's informal," Kurt continued. "All you have to do is bring a salad or a dessert or something. Glen Bybee always provides the soda, and the coaches usually bring burgers and hot dogs."

Michael would love it, but Erin would hate it. "I really don't think so, but thank you." Abby turned away and let her eyes roam the field as if Kurt held no more interest for her than anyone else in Pine Cove.

"Brody will be awfully disappointed if he has to go alone. At least let me pick up Michael and take him with us."

She'd already given in to the sleep over, but she couldn't let Michael go to a party without her. She opened her mouth to refuse again when the man behind them shouted an obscenity and leapt to his feet. Erin's shoulders hunched defensively and Abby felt her inch closer. Michael might be flourishing on a diet of picnics and Little League, but Erin's immediate need for security had to take priority.

She stiffened and tried to force steel into her voice. "I really don't think that would be a good idea."

Kurt looked away, surveying the field. After a moment, he shrugged. "Whatever you want to do is fine. Theresa just asked me to mention it."

His voice sounded hard, knife-edged. She knew she'd offended him. But she didn't dare risk exposing Erin to situations she couldn't handle. Still, she wasn't prepared for the knot of pain that formed in her stomach when he turned away from her.

She said his name softly, willing him to understand what she couldn't explain. But if Kurt heard her, he didn't acknowledge it. Rising, he cast an almost impersonal glance at her and nodded coolly. "Then I'll see you later."

Before she could think of a way to stop him—or even an excuse for doing it—he'd reached the bottom row of the bleachers, jumped lightly to the ground and walked to the bench where Jack and Theresa sat. He never looked back.

Tears pricked at her eyes and a lump formed in her throat. Dammit! If she'd met him at any other time, they might at least have been friends. Why did she have to meet him now, at the one time in her life she couldn't afford even his friendship?

WELL, SHE'D CERTAINLY put him in his place. Kurt couldn't believe he'd set himself up for a fall again after everything Laura had put him through. He couldn't believe he'd allowed himself to think he and Abby could be friends. And he couldn't believe how cold she'd looked.

He walked slowly back to the coach's bench, trying to maintain his dignity. Dropping onto the seat, Kurt felt Theresa staring at him, but he refused to meet her eyes. Why had he let Theresa talk him into being her messenger? Now she'd want to know what Abby had said, and what could he tell her? That he'd fallen for a married woman who wanted nothing to do with him? And that because of him, Abby refused to come to the dinner?

What would Theresa say to that? She'd been the one who'd listened to him endlessly after Laura left. She'd provided the voice of reason when he'd despaired of ever feeling whole again. She'd seen his pain, and she knew only too well what Brody still struggled with.

So, how could he dream about another man's wife? How could he even *think* of doing something that would inflict the

same pain he'd experienced on some other guy? It was insanity.
For the life of him, he couldn't understand why Abby affected
him this way—why late at night, just before he drifted off to
sleep, Abby's face shimmered before him. Even Laura had
never made his blood race like this, made him weak with desire. No woman had ever brought him to the brink of abandoning all his principles just to be with her.

The touch of cool fingers on his knee made him jump. Theresa leaned toward him. "So, is she coming?"

"No."

"Why not?"

"I don't know. She doesn't want to."

"I should never have let you talk to her," Theresa said impatiently. "You're as bad as Jack at arranging things. I guess
I'll have to do it myself. Tell Jack I'll be back in a minute."

Knowing that Abby would refuse Theresa as summarily as
she'd rejected him didn't completely salve Kurt's bruised ego,
but it helped a little. In fact, he actually managed to focus on
the game for long enough to see Brody get on first base and
Michael hit a double.

But when Theresa didn't return by the bottom of the fourth
inning, Kurt began to wonder. And when she rejoined him at
the top of the fifth wearing a Cheshire-cat grin he lost every
ounce of good humor he possessed.

She wormed her way into the space beside him and slapped
him on the back. "We're picking her up at six-thirty on
Wednesday."

KURT LOWERED the cover on the barbecue and looked over the
railing of the deck to where Brody and Michael were tossing
sticks for Pride to retrieve. After the way Abby had acted at
the game on Thursday, he'd been afraid she might change her
mind about letting Michael sleep over. But she'd kept her word
to the boys, no matter how she might feel about him.

"Burgers will be done in five minutes," he called.

Brody waved to him and tossed another stick. Pride raced
after it, and when he appeared a few seconds later, he ran to
Brody, depositing the stick like a prize at the boy's feet. Boys

and dogs belonged together. Both Pride and Brody had long ago forgotten that Pride was actually Kurt's dog—except when it came time for a walk in the middle of the night.

Kurt opened a bag of chips and poured a few into a bowl. He placed plates and cups around the table and fished a pickle from the jar with a fork. "Hey, guys," he called. "Time to wash up."

By the time the boys got to the table, Kurt had the burgers on a plate. "This is a make-your-own dinner," he told Michael. "Fix yours however you want."

Michael grinned and slathered mayonnaise on his bun. "I love hamburgers."

"Me, too," Brody agreed, reaching for the catsup.

"We used to have 'em every week at home." Michael said. "But not anymore."

Brody's face reflected deep sympathy. "Why?" Considering how often Kurt fixed burgers, Brody probably couldn't imagine a week without them.

"Because my...my mom doesn't like 'em."

"So why'd you have 'em before if your mom doesn't like 'em?"

Michael shrugged. "I don't know. We just did." He reached for the chips. "You know what I want to do?" he asked, changing the subject. "I want to go in the ocean."

"Can you swim?" Kurt asked.

"Yeah. Pretty good, anyway. In a swimming pool. I've never been in the ocean before."

"Never?" Brody echoed.

"Nope. It's too far away. I'd never even seen this much water until I came here." Michael stuffed his mouth and chewed happily.

Kurt put a few chips on his own plate. "I thought Baltimore was close to the ocean."

"I don't know. I've never been to Baltimore, either. Can I have another Pepsi?"

Kurt felt himself pull back as if he'd been slapped. Never been to Baltimore? But just three days ago, Abby had told him they lived there. With his appetite fading rapidly, he dropped his unfinished hamburger onto his plate.

Another lie. And since Michael had no reason to lie about playing baseball, seeing the ocean, his mother liking dogs or being in Baltimore, *Abby* must be lying. But why?

The rest of the meal passed slowly. Each extra serving of potato chips, the extra burger for both boys, the endless refills of soda nearly drove Kurt out of his mind. He couldn't think now, not with the boys needing his attention, but giving it to them undivided was impossible.

At last dinner was over and Michael and Brody rushed away, oblivious to Kurt's mood. He rinsed and stacked the dishes quickly, but he couldn't get his mind off Abby, and he couldn't come up with one acceptable excuse for her lying to him.

By the time he'd finished the dishes, the boys had spread sleeping bags on the living room floor and were engrossed in a ninja movie. Since Kurt knew he wouldn't be able to concentrate, anyway, he decided not to join them.

Sitting on the deck to watch the sunset, he was close enough to hear them and far enough away to tune out the movie. And in the silence, with only the sound of the river for company, he could start to sort out his tangled thoughts.

He might have been able to believe that Abby was just uncomfortable around him, except that he knew he hadn't done anything to make her feel that way. He told himself she was just cautious, a lone woman in a strange town, but that made no sense. She'd been as relaxed and unguarded when she'd talked about Baltimore as Michael was when he'd said he'd never been there.

He'd thought briefly about it before, but now he seriously considered investigating her background. If he was half the father he wanted to be, he couldn't allow Brody to continue his friendship with Michael without clearing things up. The mysteries surrounding Abby Harris and her children raised too many red flags for him to ignore any longer.

If he thought she'd tell him the truth, he'd go straight to her. But she had something to hide and he didn't expect her to willingly answer his questions. Besides, if there *was* a problem, confronting Abby would only make her defensive.

Well, he still had friends in Seattle. And first thing tomorrow he'd make a few calls.

Kurt propped his feet on the wooden railing. He'd been sitting in that position for several minutes when a small noise behind him caught his attention.

From the gathering shadows, Michael appeared with Brody in his wake. "Kurt?"

"What is it, guys?"

"Can we talk to you for a minute?"

"Sure." He lowered his feet to the ground and leaned his elbows on his knees. "What's up?"

Michael drew in a deep breath and darted a glance at Brody. "My mom is going to take me off the team, but I don't want her to." Tears glistened in the boy's eyes, but he dashed them away with the back of his hand.

Battling his sudden anger, Kurt struggled to keep his voice steady. "Why is she going to do that?"

"Because...I don't know. She didn't tell me."

"I don't understand."

"She didn't tell me why. She just said I had to get off the team."

"I'm sorry. I know you must be disappointed and we'll miss having you. You're a great pitcher."

"Can't you talk to her and ask her to let me keep playing?"

Not in a thousand years. Kurt would never interfere in an argument between a parent and child, unless the child were obviously being abused or mistreated in some way. "I don't think that would be such a good idea," he said evenly. "This is between you and your mom."

The expectation died from Michael's eyes and he stared at his feet. "She won't listen to me."

"She might."

Though he'd remained silent so far, Brody stepped forward, his eyes bright. "You have to talk to her, Dad. Make her let him stay on the team."

"Brody—"

"I told him you would, Dad. He just *has* to stay on the team."

He shouldn't get involved. He couldn't. "Look, guys, it's just not a good idea to get in the middle of somebody else's family disagreement."

Michael turned away, his shoulders slumped and his head bowed. "I knew it was stupid to ask you."

"Michael—" Kurt began.

"So you're not going to do anything?" Brody's voice sounded sharp in the silence of the night.

"I can't."

Michael turned halfway back and pierced Brody with a stare. "I *told* you he wouldn't do anything."

Brody's eyes flickered to Kurt's face, and in them Kurt saw bitter disappointment and anger. Asking him to help had been Brody's idea, and Kurt had refused. Now what would happen to Brody's trust in him?

He shouldn't allow himself to get involved in a dispute between Abby and her son. But he couldn't destroy his own son's faith in his willingness and ability to help.

He closed his eyes against the sudden pounding in his head and, knowing he might regret it, nodded slowly. "All right, guys, I'll see what I can do."

"Really?" Michael sounded ecstatic.

Kurt opened his eyes and met Brody's gaze. At least the anger had faded.

"Thanks." Brody's lips curved in a smile.

The boys started toward the house together, but at the back door Michael stopped, spoke briefly to Brody, then ran back. "Could you do me another favor?"

Resigned to his involvement, Kurt tried to muster a smile. "What kind of favor?"

Michael pulled an envelope from under his shirt and thrust it at him. "Will you mail this for me?"

Kurt took the envelope and turned it over in his hand. It was addressed to Rachel Harrison at an address in Tempe, Arizona. The name struck a chord deep in his memory, but not close enough to the surface to connect with anything.

"That's it? Mail a letter? I think I can handle that."

Michael seemed to sag, as if a weight had been removed from his shoulders. "It's just a note to a friend of mine. It's her birthday."

"Okay." Kurt tucked the envelope in his pocket. "I'll mail it for you tomorrow. Is that all right?"

Michael's face split in a grin. "Perfect. Thanks a lot." Turning, he ran back to the house and slammed the screen door behind him.

A few minutes later, Kurt remembered tomorrow was Sunday. And even if he made a special trip into town, the post office wouldn't do anything with the letter until Monday. Fingering the envelope in his pocket, he told himself it could wait. If he mailed it from the office on Monday, he wouldn't be breaking his promise.

CHAPTER SIX

ABBY PULLED the brush through Erin's hair and tried to capture the curls in her other hand. Though she was concerned about Michael's spending the night apart from her, she couldn't help being glad to have a little time alone with Erin. Since the game, Erin had been even more withdrawn. But every time Abby tried to talk about the incident at the ballpark, Erin managed to dodge the conversation, and now Abby had no idea how to get her to discuss it.

But avoiding the issue only helped Erin suppress her fear and anger. And that didn't help her heal.

Pulling a stubborn strand of hair into line, Abby put down the brush and used her fingers to smooth Erin's bangs back. "Are you glad to have a night without Michael?"

Erin shrugged, but didn't say a word.

"Did you get much time on your own in Tempe?"

After a slight hesitation, Erin shook her head.

"Tell me about things there—you know, your friends and other girl stuff."

"I didn't have very many friends."

"Really? That's hard to believe." Though her heart twisted at the Erin's tone, Abby was determined to keep her own manner light.

"Why?" Erin asked tentatively.

"Because you're so smart and pretty."

Erin snorted in disbelief and stared at her feet.

"I'm serious," Abby persisted.

"No, I'm not."

Abby shrugged. "I felt the same way at your age. I guess it's natural."

Erin's eyes darted up. "You did?"

"Absolutely. I hated my hair, I thought my eyes were too small, I hated my nose—"

"But you're beautiful."

"So are you."

"I'm funny-looking. My hair's too frizzy—like Medusa."

"Medusa? Erin, you have beautiful hair. Where on earth did you get the idea that these gorgeous curls look bad?"

When Erin turned away and didn't speak, Abby had her answer. Vic.

Swallowing her anger, Abby kept her voice steady. "Sweetheart, you're going to be an absolute knockout in a couple of years, and all your life women are going to be wildly jealous of this hair. Believe me."

Erin looked up hesitantly, a tiny smile on her lips. "Do you think so?"

"I *know* so. What do you say we put a little of my makeup on you for fun? We can try some things out and maybe you can help me come up with some new ideas." Abby returned the smile, but when Erin's gaze shifted away, Abby's nerves pricked. "What's wrong?"

"Nothing."

Abby released Erin's hair and took the girl's hands in her own. "Tell me about it."

"Nothing. It's okay."

Pulling Erin into her arms, Abby kissed her forehead and whispered, "Oh, Erin, can't you see it's not all right to never talk about it?"

Erin didn't respond immediately, but trembled slightly. Abby forced herself to wait for an answer, content to just hold her niece. After a few minutes she felt Erin relax slightly.

When she spoke at last, the girl's voice was so quiet Abby could barely hear it, even in the silent house. "I put on some of my mom's makeup once and my dad...my dad hit me."

Abby had expected it, but hearing Erin admit it hurt more than she'd anticipated. She couldn't frame a response, only held Erin tighter.

In the early years when she'd gone home to Arizona, Abby

had battled her own pain and envy watching Rachel and Vic with their children. Had she ever suspected the truth, even a little?

If Erin and Michael had been *her* children, she would never have allowed anyone to hurt them. For one moment, as she held Erin, Abby imagined the girl as her child; and for the first time, anger at Rachel for allowing Vic to abuse the children rose to the surface of her consciousness. But as quickly as it came she pushed it aside, and guilt took its place.

She knew how difficult it was for women to stand up to an abusive partner. She'd seen the damage that resulted from any show of independence too many times over the years to have preconceived notions about what women should do in abusive relationships. But she couldn't shake the tiny seed of anger that had sprouted, and she couldn't ignore the feeling that curled around her heart when she looked at Erin.

She'd always loved children, but after learning she'd never have any of her own and then losing Steven, she'd started protecting herself from caring too deeply about other people. But in just a short time with Erin and Michael all her efforts at self-protection had come undone. As though Erin and Michael had each tugged at a stray piece of string and unraveled the cocoon in which she'd wrapped her heart, she felt raw and exposed and more vulnerable than she had in years.

Worst of all, she knew that when the time came to give them back to Rachel, she'd have to deal with a whole new heartache. Maybe it would've been better to keep her heart locked away. She didn't know how she'd handle the pain of letting them go when this was over.

She stroked Erin's hair back from her forehead and smiled what she hoped was a reassuring sort of smile, praying the tears that stung her eyes weren't visible. They'd made a little progress tonight and Abby's hopes brightened.

Pushing away a surge of longing to have Michael at her side, she told herself again that he needed this time with Kurt and Brody. Michael needed—so did Erin—a positive male figure in his life, someone who could help negate Vic's mark on him. And Kurt Morgan could do it.

Maybe she should explain their situation to Kurt and ask him to help Erin and Michael. Instinctively she knew he'd never do anything to hurt them. Giving herself a mental shake, she pulled back. She must *never* tell Kurt the truth. No matter how much she might want to. And letting the children grow too close to him would be a big mistake. The more comfortable they all got around him, the more likely they'd be to let things slip.

Though she knew Kurt wouldn't intentionally jeopardize their security, she worried that if anyone else started asking questions or probing into their history, the kids might make a mistake. *She* might make a mistake. And if they became the objects of scrutiny, they could be at risk.

She'd seen too many instances over the years where one seemingly insignificant detail had led to fatal disaster for someone. It was a chance she simply couldn't take.

STANDING IN THE MORNING sunlight as it streamed through her window, Abby folded the last towel and placed it on the foot of her bed. She stepped back to survey the stacks of clean laundry with pride. The longer she stayed in Pine Cove and the longer she lived this fantasy, the more she liked it.

She glanced down the hall through the open door and smiled at the sight of Erin on her bed, an open book in her lap. If only she could find something that combined the best elements of her life in Baltimore and this one.

But the best elements of this life included children, and she would never have any. Angry with herself for dwelling on the impossible, Abby scooped up the stacks of clean towels and headed for the linen closet. When a car slowed on the highway and turned into the drive, she shoved the towels inside and ran to the window. It was Kurt bringing Michael home.

She hoped Michael had enjoyed himself at Brody's last night, but even the comforting light of morning hadn't weakened her resolve to keep him from forming a deep attachment to Kurt. She knew how easy it was to be drawn to Kurt. She'd already made more than enough mistakes around him, and she couldn't take the chance of any of them making more.

Michael leapt from the Cherokee and raced to the front porch. An instant later, Kurt's door opened and her heart began to hammer. Why was Kurt coming in?

She sprinted to the bathroom and quickly checked her appearance. Jeans and a T-shirt, white tennis shoes and a pathetic-looking French braid. Not a speck of makeup. She tucked a few loose strands of hair into place and tried to rub some color into her cheeks as she heard the front door open.

"Mom?"

She took a deep breath. "Up here."

Footsteps pounded up the stairs and a second later Michael burst into her room. "Kurt's here. He wants to talk to you."

Her heart beat a staccato rhythm. "Tell him I'll be right down." Was she imagining it, or did Michael look guilty? "What does he want?"

Michael studied his feet. "I... I'm not sure."

There it was again, that guilty look. Only this time, Abby *knew* she'd seen it. Something was wrong. Why else would Kurt want to talk with her? Had Michael told him something he shouldn't?

She descended the stairs slowly, dreading what Kurt had to say. When she found him in the living room, his face confirmed her worst fears. This was no social visit.

With his features schooled into a mask, he seemed reluctant to look into her eyes. "Sorry to barge in on you when you weren't expecting company." His voice sounded flat, almost wary.

He knew. "Michael didn't give you any trouble last night, did he?"

An expression flickered across his face too quickly for Abby to read. "No. Nothing like that."

Abby sat on one end of the sofa and tried to steady her shaking knees. Michael must have really slipped up. She'd have to explain somehow. Would Kurt understand? Could she expect him to participate in her cover-up?

"Would you like to sit down?" she said. With trembling fingers she indicated a chair, but he moved to the other end of the sofa and lowered himself onto it.

"I don't know quite how to start, so I'll just say it," he began uncomfortably. "Michael told me last night that you're taking him off the team. He asked me to talk to you about letting him play."

Afraid she hadn't heard right, Abby stared at him in silence. The team?

"He's really disappointed, Abby."

The team. Relief threatened to escape as a laugh, but she clamped her mouth shut and contained it. Kurt would never understand that reaction.

With the threat of exposure gone, she felt a slow warmth begin to curl within her as their eyes held. "I see" was all she said.

He looked away, breaking the spell, and took a deep breath. "I'm sorry for sticking my nose in where it obviously doesn't belong, but the boys caught me in a weak moment and I promised I'd talk to you. Michael likes playing—you know that." He moistened his lips and tried to smile before rushing on. "I know you had some reason for not wanting him to play this summer, but you let him join the team, anyway. And I think it'd be a big mistake to change your mind now."

He obviously hated doing this, and the mere fact that he'd let the boys convince him to approach her against his better judgment endeared him to her. She battled the urge to put her hand on his.

She couldn't sit this close to him or she'd touch him. And the desire to do so confused her. She'd never met a man who brought to life such a need for physical contact.

She got to her feet and walked to the front window, keeping her back to him. She had to lie to him again, but she couldn't look him in the eye when she did it. "One of the reasons we decided to spend the summer away from home was because we had trouble with Michael in school last year—bad grades, that sort of thing. Nothing terribly serious, but my husband and I decided that Michael needed to spend the summer in more serious pursuits. Michael caught me in a weak moment and I agreed to let him play, but Bob isn't happy about my decision and I can't go against his wishes. I know how unfair this seems to you, but Michael understood how strongly his father felt…'' She let her voice trail away, hoping Kurt would accept the story and let the matter drop.

Heavy silence fell like a curtain between them. After several seconds, she heard the sofa creak lightly as he stood. "I'm sorry I interfered. Of course you have to do what you think is right."

She didn't move until the sound of his footsteps had died away and the front door clicked shut behind him. Only then did she acknowledge her disappointment that he hadn't followed her to the window, that he hadn't felt the same need to touch her. Though she'd promised to keep their identity secret when she left Rachel in Tempe, though she knew the very real threat Vic posed to Erin and Michael, some part of her wanted Kurt to demand more acceptable answers than the ones she gave.

He'd noticed the discrepancies in their stories—he'd be a fool not to. And Kurt was no fool. But his ready acceptance of her explanations bothered her. If their situations had been reversed, she would have wanted to know more. Her personal interest in him would have demanded it.

But Kurt obviously didn't share that interest. It had been easy for him to walk away.

KURT FLIPPED through his appointment calendar and noted with satisfaction that he didn't have any hearings or appointments penciled in. It looked like he'd finally found a free day. And he could use one.

Client billing demanded his immediate attention, payday was at the end of the week, quarterly taxes were due soon, and he'd let his correspondence go begging for too long.

And he wanted to make a few phone calls about Abby Harris.

Rifling through a filing cabinet in Naomi's office, he pulled out a stack of billing forms and an armful of files, took them into his office and grabbed his coffee cup. Near the coffeepot in the second-floor file room, he found Naomi.

She looked up as he approached, her face a study in misery. "Hi. How was your weekend?" she asked.

"Fine. Better than yours, I'd guess."

"I don't know how much longer I can stand it. Bill spent the entire weekend in front of the TV with a case of beer. He won't even look for jobs in the paper anymore, and now he's talking about moving—as if he'll magically find a job if we leave here."

"Maybe if you went to a big city..."

"Kurt, I'm the only one bringing a dime into the house. If I lose this job, what are we going to do? How am I supposed to support Jason on nothing?"

Kurt poured his coffee and let silence hang in the air for a minute. When Naomi started thumbing through the stack of filing again, he took the hint and changed the subject. "I thought we could spend the day catching up on some things we've gotten behind on in the last few weeks."

She closed her eyes and rolled her head back. "Not today," she groaned.

"I'm afraid so. I'll have some billing slips ready for you in a little while, so come into my office after you've finished up here."

"Billing? Ugh."

"Pays our salaries," he reminded her with a smile as he filled his cup. "Give me half an hour."

He went back to his office and closed the door. He pulled his Rolodex toward him and looked up the number of an old law-school friend who'd left his practice to become a private investigator in Seattle. He'd ask Tony to make a couple of discreet inquiries just to be sure Abby wasn't hiding from the law or masking a criminal record. He dialed half the number, hesitated, then slammed the receiver back on the hook.

Did he really want to do this? He had to consider Brody's safety. And he had to consider his own heart.

He picked up a file and tried to complete his billing slips from the pleadings inside, but concentration eluded him. Instead of briefs, petitions and affidavits, he saw Abby. He heard her voice, saw her smile, smelled her perfume. Instead of weakening, his attraction for her seemed to be growing.

Kurt knew Abby was hiding something, and ignoring the discrepancies in her stories was no longer an option. So he could either run a quick check and set his mind at ease, or he could forget about her. But he could no more forget about her than he could ignore the lies.

This time when he picked up the phone, he dialed Zelda's number. After he'd inquired about her health, answered her questions about Brody and the house, and promised to drive her to Seattle sometime next week, he posed the question he'd been dying to ask.

"Did Abby give you a home address when she called to rent the old house?"

"Why on earth would you want to know that?"

"It's not important, really. I can ask her later, but she wanted me to ship some things of Michael's back home for her, and I can't find where I put the note with her address on it."

"Well, you're just going to have to get it from her, because I never talked to her. It all came up so suddenly...."

Internal warning bells sounded and Kurt's pulse raced. "Who did you talk to?"

"My cousin Edith's daughter, Lorna."

"Lorna? In Portland?"

"Yes, that's the one." Zelda confirmed. "Oh, Kurt, my program's coming on. Why don't you just get the address from Abby? It would be so much easier than trying to pretend you hadn't lost it. I don't know why men have to be so silly about admitting they've made a mistake—"

The connection severed suddenly, leaving Kurt staring at the receiver and battling a raging headache. Without giving himself another chance to back down, he punched in Tony Graham's number in Seattle and left a message on his friend's answering machine.

"BUT THAT'S NOT *fair*." Michael backed away from Abby, his eyes wide and glistening with tears. "Why did you even let me play in the first place if you're going to take me off the team now? Didn't Kurt talk to you?''

"Yes, but I still have to do what I think is right."

"What did I do wrong?"

"You didn't do anything wrong, Michael." Abby tried to explain. "It's because of Erin."

"You're going to take me off the team because Erin got scared of some guy? Just don't bring her to the games anymore."

"You know I can't let you go by yourself."

"I wouldn't be by myself. I could go with Brody and Kurt."

"No."

"Why?"

"You know why. If your dad finds us here, he won't hesitate to try and take you, especially if he finds you alone. Nobody else understands the situation, and nobody else can protect you. We have to stick together, Michael. We have to watch out for each other."

"But you let me sleep over at Kurt's and you weren't there."

"That was a little different. You were at Kurt's house—safe, not out in public."

Michael backed away another three steps and sent her a look full of venom. "I wish we never came here. I wish we were back home with my mom."

"I know," Abby said wearily.

"I wish I was with my *dad!*" Michael bolted from the room and ran upstairs.

He didn't mean it, Abby told herself. In his frustration he'd said the one thing he could think of that would upset her. She was right, wasn't she? Even though Michael loved to play, she couldn't jeopardize Erin's progress by forcing her to go to the games.

On the other hand, what would taking Michael off the team do to him? Maybe Kurt was right. Michael had been doing so well, and now she'd probably sent him into a tailspin.

How was she supposed to know what to do? Maybe she *had* been wrong. Maybe she'd overreacted to the incident at the ballpark and Erin's response to it. But the memory of Rachel's

injuries and Vic's threats terrified her; knowing she'd just begun to tap the well of Erin's fears worried her, and having
Michael's needs so different from Erin's confused her. She
didn't know what was best for them. She wasn't their mother.

How did Rachel do it? How did *any* mother do it? Abby had
to be a different parent for each child, and she struggled constantly to avoid putting the needs of one over the other. She
knew she didn't have the skills Rachel did. You couldn't just
take over a pair of kids and expect to know exactly how to
react to every crisis.

Suddenly exhausted, she followed Michael up the stairs. He
was sitting on his bed, his back to her, his shoulders slumped
in dejection.

"Michael?"

"What?"

"Can we talk about this?"

"What for? You've already made up your mind."

Abby sat down beside him and touched his arm. "Not completely."

"You mean you're not going to take me off the team?"

"I mean if it's that important to you, maybe we ought to
talk about it some more."

Michael's eyes flickered toward her uncertainly.

"But since Erin's involved, maybe we ought to include her.
What do you think?"

Nodding, Michael met her gaze more steadily.

"Do you want to go get her?"

"Okay." He jumped off the bed and took two steps away
before turning back. "I don't want her to be scared at the
games."

"I know, sweetheart."

"But she's afraid of everybody."

"That's why I'm concerned. But maybe we can help her."

"I didn't mean it—what I said downstairs."

"Oh, Michael, I know." Abby pulled him to her. "I know
you didn't."

He leaned against her briefly, warm and smelling of fresh
air and sunshine. Abby clasped him close for a heartbeat, then

released him and sent him scampering from the room in search of his sister.

When he returned a few minutes later, Erin trailed him hesitantly. Abby motioned them to sit beside her.

"We've got a problem," she began, and was startled to see the frightened look creep into Erin's eyes. "Michael wants to keep playing Little League ball. He's pretty determined about this and it's important to him. But on the other hand, Erin doesn't like the games and she doesn't like the crowds."

"I don't mind," Erin said quickly.

"You were scared at the last game, and I don't like to see that happen to you."

"But I don't mind. Michael can still play."

Though Erin's words carried conviction, Abby saw no signs of it in her face. "Why do I think you're just saying that so Michael won't be upset?"

Erin looked away. "I'm not."

Abby tipped the girl's face toward hers and looked deep into her eyes. "It's all right to admit you were frightened the other day."

Erin jerked away. "I wasn't frightened."

"Sweetheart, you give in on an awful lot of things just to keep people from getting upset with you. I understand why you've done it in the past, but it's not like that anymore. It's okay to disagree with me on things. It's okay to disagree with Michael. We're not going to hurt you. If you don't want to go to the games, say so. We'll work out a compromise that can make us all happy, but you have the right to say how you feel."

"I don't mind the games, I guess, as long as people leave me alone. I don't want to talk to a lot of people."

"Fair enough. We'll try it again and if it gets too bad you let me know, okay?"

Erin nodded.

"Promise?"

"Promise," Erin said softly.

"Well, kiddo—" Abby turned to Michael "—it looks like you get to stay on the team for a while. But you owe Erin for this one—big time."

Michael grinned and jumped up. "Thanks, sis." He bounded out the door and down the stairs.

Erin followed more slowly, turning at the door and smiling shyly. Abby forced an answering smile. Erin should have been bright and eager, surrounded by friends and developing an interest in boys. Instead, she looked like a whipped puppy most of the time.

Well, they'd made their decision and Michael would stay on the team. But how would she ever explain her change of heart to Kurt? Since she'd blamed her initial decision on her husband, the sensible way out was to give him the change of heart.

She crossed to Michael's window and looked out onto the highway. Less than a mile through the trees, Kurt's house stood above the Gorge. If not for the dense forest, she might have been able to catch a glimpse of it, maybe even catch sight of him on the shore from time to time.

But that would only make things worse. She thought of him too much already. Her days were too empty. They'd settled in, the house was running smoothly, and for the first time in her life, Abby had time on her hands.

She'd been so worried about taking care of the kids, she hadn't really considered how she'd spend her days. Laundry and dusting and meals could only occupy her for so long. She had to find something else to do—quickly. Before she drove herself crazy with these unrelenting thoughts of Kurt.

ABBY STARED at the office door, hesitant to enter now that she'd arrived. She could have called. She could have gone to Jack to get Michael back on the team. But she'd come to Kurt's office, instead.

She could still leave. But if he'd seen her approaching through one of the windows, what would he think when she didn't come in?

Sucking in a deep breath, she pushed open the door and stepped into a small reception area. A dark-haired woman Abby recognized as the one whose husband had frightened Erin looked up and smiled. "Can I help you?"

"Is Mr. Morgan available?"

"I'm sorry. He's in court this afternoon." She paused. "You're Abby Harris, aren't you?"

Abby nodded, wary of the woman's friendliness.

"I'm Naomi Franklin. Kurt's cousin, as well as his secretary. And I'm glad to finally meet you. I've heard a lot about you." She held up a hand and gave a little laugh. "All good, of course."

Abby smiled. "It's nice to meet you."

"We don't get a lot of summer people in Pine Cove. Most of our tourist dollars come from fishing expeditions on the river, but there aren't many places for rent in town. Not like some of the towns on up the coast."

"That's probably what makes it so nice here." Abby tried to sound relaxed, but this kind of casual curiosity was exactly what she worried about.

Nodding, Naomi leaned back in her chair. "I was surprised when I heard Aunt Zelda had decided to rent Grandma and Grandpa's old place. How on earth did you get her to agree to do it?"

"Through a friend."

Naomi looked confused. "Oh. I thought your husband made the arrangements."

"No, my husband spent a few summers in the area as a boy. A friend of the family found the house for us." She turned to go.

But Naomi stopped her. "Kurt should be back in a few minutes. Do you want to wait?"

"Maybe you could just give him a message for me."

"I'd be glad to, but you're welcome to wait if you'd like."

What would be most natural—to wait or leave? She didn't want to field any more questions, but she didn't want to do anything that would further spark Naomi's curiosity.

Before she could answer, the telephone at Naomi's elbow rang, buying her some time.

"Good afternoon, law office." Naomi sent her an apologetic smile over the receiver. "No, I'm sorry, he's not in. May I take a message?" She paused to listen, then lifted her eyebrows as if the caller had said something out of the ordinary. "What was your name again? Graham? And you're a private investigator in Seattle? No, I don't know what he wanted. He never mentioned it to me.'' She sent Abby a conspiratorial glance, then bent over the yellow message pad.

Private investigator? Abby's heart thudded in her ears. Why did Kurt want a private investigator? For a case? Naomi obviously didn't know the person, so it wasn't someone Kurt interacted with on a regular basis.

Abby tried to keep her hands steady as she clasped them together on her lap. He couldn't be investigating her. Why should he? She drew a deep breath and closed her eyes, letting the air escape slowly. She must be paranoid—a side effect of hiding out.

"I'll give him your message.'' Naomi replaced the receiver and tore the message from the pad, stabbing it onto a spindle in the middle of her desk. "If you want to wait, you can sit in Kurt's office, It's more comfortable, and I'm sure he won't mind. Can I get you something to drink? Coffee? A soda?''

If Kurt was due back soon, it might be better to wait. And his office would protect her from Naomi's questions. "Do you have a Diet Pepsi?''

Naomi nodded and pushed herself away from the desk. "Just go through that door. I'll be right back.''

Abby walked slowly into Kurt's office. It was a spacious room with two huge bay windows overlooking the street and a heavy wooden desk centered between them. The blinds had been raised to let in daylight, and though the sun hadn't actually come out from behind the clouds, light filled the room. She had no trouble picturing Kurt here.

One wall held a large framed seascape done in oils; the other had smaller frames and wooden plaques scattered across its surface. Abby moved to that wall and studied the diplomas and the plaques engraved with his name from various organizations to which he'd donated his time and talents: legal services for the poor, a battered-women's shelter and a center for underprivileged children. She liked this image of Kurt and it matched the way he talked about his dream of using his profession to help people.

At the sound of heels on the wooden floor in the reception area, Abby turned back just as Naomi entered, a glass in one hand and a can of Diet Pepsi in the other.

"Just make yourself comfortable here. Kurt should be back any minute."

Abby accepted the drink and moved toward one of the chairs opposite Kurt's desk. "You're sure he won't mind my waiting in here?"

"Not at all." Naomi ducked back into the outer office and returned waving the message slip before she dropped it onto Kurt's desk. "I can't wait to find out what *this* is all about." She turned and headed toward the door. "I've got to pull some files. I'll be just upstairs if you need anything."

Abby sipped her drink and let her eyes wander to the slip of paper. She felt another chill at the thought of Kurt's contacting a private investigator. And once again she pushed it away. It meant nothing. Nothing.

She waited several minutes, battling the uncomfortable feeling, but in the end, discomfort won. Grabbing her purse, she slipped out of Kurt's office. Naomi's office was empty, so Abby paused and jotted a message on a piece of paper. "Kurt—Bob changed his mind. Michael can stay on the team." Signing her name, she returned to his office just long enough to leave the note on his desk.

He might not have hired somebody to check up on her this time, but she couldn't afford to be careless around him in the future. And since she didn't trust herself when she was around him, she needed to stay away.

Remembering the potluck dinner tomorrow night, she cursed herself for giving in to Theresa's persuasion. Kurt would be there, and she couldn't ignore him without causing speculation. Damn.

Sighing, she stepped outside and headed for her car. She never should have agreed to go.

CHAPTER SEVEN

KURT GLANCED at his watch and noted the time with dismay. Nearly four-thirty already. He'd promised Theresa he'd bring chili to the potluck tonight and he'd planned to leave work early, but time had gotten away from him.

Reluctantly he cleared his desk, stacked the files on his credenza and retrieved his jacket. As he patted the pockets for his keys, the rustling of paper brought him up short. He'd forgotten to mail Michael's letter—again.

He pulled the envelope from his pocket and studied the child's writing. Rachel Harrison. Again he had the feeling he'd heard that name before, but he didn't know where or when, or even in what context. Maybe he should call Tony Graham back and give him that name, too.

Flipping off the lights, he left his office and looked around for Naomi. But she'd either taken the mail for the five-o'clock collection, or she was in the filing room. He thought about dropping Michael's letter on her desk, then decided against it. He'd already held on to it for two extra days. He owed it to Michael to put it in the mail himself.

Getting into his car, he tossed his jacket across the front seat and placed the letter on the dash, intending to mail it after he stopped at the FoodWay.

Making a mental list of the items he needed, he drove quickly to make up time. It wouldn't take long to throw the chili together, but with less than two hours until dinner he'd be lucky to make it.

After a brief stop at the FoodWay, he pulled into the driveway a few minutes after five. Juggling his keys, two grocery sacks and his jacket, he was just opening the front door when the telephone started to ring.

He shouted for Brody, hoping for some help with either the groceries or the phone, but got neither. Staggering into the kitchen, he dropped the groceries on the counter and reached for the phone.

"I'm so glad you're there!" Theresa cried. "We've got a problem. Amber twisted her knee this afternoon playing tennis."

"Is she all right?"

"She's fine. We're at the clinic now, but it looks like we'll be late and Jack's supposed to be in charge of the barbecue. Can you go over to Doug's a little early and take charge until we get there?"

Kurt glanced at the groceries scattered across the counter. "How early?"

"Glen Bybee's supposed to be there at six-fifteen with the drinks. Can you be there by then?"

He'd never make it. But after everything Theresa and Jack had done for him the past couple of years, he had to try. "Sure, no problem."

"And could you do me another favor? Would you pick up Abby and her kids for me?"

Anything but that. After hiring a private investigator to check her out, how could he spend the evening with her? "I don't think—"

"She has no idea where the Pierces live, and I told her we'd pick her up so she won't feel funny about coming. I don't want her to think we've forgotten her, and you're the only other person in town she'll feel comfortable with. Would you mind? Please?"

Oh, yes, he'd mind. He'd have to start the evening bewitched by Abby's smile, her laugh, her face. He'd have to smell her hair and try to make conversation, hoping he didn't let his feelings show. And all the time he'd be on the lookout for more of her lies. Hell.

He heard himself say, "All right. I'll do it." But he knew when he said it he was making a mistake.

"Wonderful. Thanks loads. We'll see you later." Low-pitched mumbling sounded at the other end. "Oh, and can you stop by and pick up my casserole for me? It's warming in the oven."

"Sure."

"Tell the kids everything's all right." More mumbling near the phone. "And take the shiny garbage can for Glen to put the drinks in. It's in the garage with the barbecue things." Her voice was muffled for a minute, as if she'd placed her hand over the receiver. "Listen, we've got to go. We'll be there as soon as we can." The line went dead.

Kurt replaced the receiver in a daze. Focusing on the one thing he could do something about, he browned chilies, garlic and onions, added leftover pork roast and thickened the gravy. Leaving it simmering on the stove, he showered and shaved, nicking himself twice in the process.

With Brody's help, he loaded the food into boxes in the back of the Cherokee to prevent spills and pulled onto the highway a few minutes ahead of schedule.

The sun reflected on Michael's letter on the dashboard. He'd have to drop it in the mailbox on the way into town after he picked up Abby and the kids. Feeling a little guilty at not keeping his promise, he retrieved the envelope and stuffed it into his shirt pocket. With luck, Michael wouldn't realize it was his letter when Kurt mailed it.

THOUGH SHE STILL DOUBTED the wisdom of going to this party, Abby couldn't deny she was looking forward to spending time in a social setting with other adults. As long as she stayed away from Kurt, she'd be all right. If she didn't let herself talk with him alone and if she didn't look into his eyes, she could maintain her equilibrium. Otherwise, she'd be lost.

Why did she feel this way about him? She thought she'd put all this girlish stuff behind her. That wasn't to say she'd never thought about trying marriage again, but she hadn't let herself dream since she'd pulled her head out of the clouds and faced life realistically.

Knowing that her attraction to Kurt couldn't be anything

more than a physical one didn't help. If she'd been another kind of woman, she might be tempted to let it run its course, just to get it out of her system. But she'd never been one to indulge in indiscriminate sex, and besides, she had the children and her supposed marriage to consider. Indulging in a physical relationship now would be totally irresponsible.

Through the open French doors of her bedroom, she heard a car slow and turn into the drive. It must be Theresa already. But crossing to close the doors, she caught a glimpse of Kurt getting out of his Cherokee and Michael racing across the lawn toward him.

"Mom! Kurt's here."

As usual, her heart hammered, sending a steady beat through her veins and thrumming in her ears. She caught herself checking her reflection in the mirror and turned away. If jeans and a cotton blouse weren't attractive enough, it was too late to do anything about it now. Besides, she reminded herself, she didn't *want* to be attractive for him.

"Come on, Mom!" Michael shouted again.

On the lawn below, Erin crossed slowly, almost reluctantly. Michael might be excited to see Kurt, but Erin wouldn't be comfortable with him. And neither would Abby.

She closed all the open windows, went down to the kitchen for the pasta salad and made sure the doors were locked before she joined the others at Kurt's Cherokee. Erin and Michael climbed into the back with Brody, leaving the seat beside Kurt for her.

Erin huddled against the door, Michael bounced enthusiastically, Brody talked a mile a minute, and Kurt scarcely spared Abby a glance as she climbed into the front seat.

"Theresa asked me to pick you up on my way," he explained. "One of her kids pulled her knee and they had to take her to the doctor."

"Is she all right?"

"It's nothing serious. Theresa said they'd be home soon, but I need to get there a few minutes early. I hope you don't mind."

Abby minded everything about this situation: the intimate

smell of his soap, the way his slightly damp hair intrigued her and the way his jaw, where he'd nicked himself shaving, invited her fingers to touch. But she shook her head. "Of course not."

Kurt's hands gripped the steering wheel and a muscle worked in his jaw, but his eyes didn't stray from the road. He relaxed only when Michael asked him a question.

After a few minutes of baseball chatter, Abby tuned them all out and stared out her window at the forest. Trees crowded together and thick undergrowth colored the forest every shade of green imaginable. The sun, kinder here than in Arizona and weaker than in Baltimore, had gone behind a cloud.

After leaving Arizona the first time, she'd been amazed by any climate that produced vegetation naturally. After all the years in the East, she now delighted in the more moderate climate of the Pacific Northwest. If she'd been thinking of changing locations, she might consider this one. She wouldn't want to live in a place the size of Pine Cove, of course, but maybe Seattle or Portland.

"...so is it okay, Mom?" Michael leaned forward and broke into her thoughts. "Can Brody still sleep over on Friday?"

For the first time that evening, Kurt met Abby's eyes, questioning her. Why? What did he think she was? An ogre? She'd invited Brody to sleep over, and she wouldn't change her mind at the last minute.

"Of course he can," she answered.

"Great." Michael fell back against his seat, contented.

Kurt tightened his hold on the steering wheel.

"We're looking forward to having Brody stay over," she said.

His jaw clenched and his eyes narrowed. What on earth was wrong with him? Didn't he want Brody to sleep over? It'd been his idea to have Michael over. Now that it was her turn to reciprocate, he seemed unwilling.

"He *can* come over on Friday, can't he?" She shouldn't press him, but she couldn't help herself.

His eyes flicked over her for an instant, as if he was taking her measure. Slowly his lips curved in a smile, but his dimples refused to appear. "Yeah. Of course he can."

When he turned his attention back to the road, Abby studied his profile. Something was definitely bothering him, but she couldn't imagine what.

He pulled into the driveway of an old white house, and Abby's thoughts ceased abruptly. The house was immaculate, the garden thriving. Flowers and ground cover grew with abandon in bright, seemingly unplanned splotches of color in front of the house and up both sides of the walk. But where were they? He hadn't said anything about stopping, and Theresa had told her the Pierces lived on the north side of town.

Maybe they had to pick up someone else. The thought brought relief tinged with regret. She didn't want to be alone with Kurt, even with the children in the car, but she didn't want to share him, either.

Kurt must have sensed her confusion. "Jack and Theresa's place. I'm supposed to pick up a few things for them."

She nodded and looked again at the house. Now that she knew, she had no trouble picturing Theresa on the wide front porch or cutting flowers from the garden. The place radiated Theresa's warmth.

"Can I help?"

Kurt hesitated, then gave a slight nod. "Sure." He turned to the kids. "You three wait here. We'll be right back."

They approached the front door in silence, uneasiness hanging heavily between them. At last Abby could stand the silence no longer. "They have a nice place."

Kurt looked around, as if seeing the house for the first time. "It's the house I was raised in."

"It's very nice," she repeated. She sounded like a fool. Better not to talk at all.

The front door swung open and a young girl of about thirteen launched herself at Kurt with a cry of glee. Laughing, he hugged her close, swinging her off her feet. "My niece, Sara," he told Abby when he'd lowered the girl to the ground. "Sara, this is Abby Harris."

Sara grinned happily up at Abby, then tugged at Kurt's hand. "You've got to come and see my new mountain bike."

"Hold on a minute. We're running late. We have to get your mom's casserole and some stuff from the garage, and then we're out of here. How about if I see the bike tomorrow?"

Pouting a little, Sara let go of Kurt's hand and shrugged. "I guess."

Kurt turned to Abby. "Why don't you go with Sara and get the casserole while I head out to the garage?"

Without the slightest hesitation, Sara grabbed Abby's hand and pulled her through the front door into the cool house. "The kitchen's back here. Come on and I'll show you where everything is. I didn't know you were coming with Uncle Kurt. I wish I could go with you, but my mom says I have to stay here and take care of the kids until she gets back."

Abby followed Sara through the darkened hallway into the kitchen, listening with half an ear. Like the outside, the kitchen felt homey and warm. Everything gleamed from recent cleaning, but the house retained its lived-in feel. Cozy.

Sara searched a drawer full of kitchen towels. "Don't you think Uncle Kurt's great?" She found an oven mitt and held it out to Abby.

"Yes, I do," Abby answered truthfully, taking the mitt.

Sara boosted herself onto the counter and kicked her legs. "I like being around him now more than before."

Abby opened the oven door and tried to pull out the casserole dish with only one mitt. "Before?"

"Before Aunt Laura left. He was sad all the time then. But he's a lot more fun now."

Abby tried to picture Kurt sad, but had no success. He'd never said much about his ex-wife. All she knew was what Brody had told her—which wasn't a lot. But suddenly she wanted to know everything about her.

Abby could understand a failed marriage—they happened all the time. But she couldn't understand how Laura could walk out on Brody, even if her love for Kurt had died. Abby constantly battled the ache over her inability to have children, and to willingly give up a child was something she couldn't comprehend. But pumping a thirteen-year-old for information wasn't an acceptable way to get answers.

She dragged her attention back to the oven. "Do you have another mitt or a hot pad?"

Sara jumped down and searched until she came up with one. Abby drew the casserole from the oven as Sara swung herself back onto the counter.

"Your daughter could stay here with me if she wants," Sara offered, "and go to the party with us when my mom and dad get home."

It sounded like the most natural thing in the world, and any typical young girl would probably jump at the chance. But Erin wouldn't consider it—even if Abby would. "Maybe another time. She's kind of shy."

"Oh. Okay." Sara looked confused for half a second, but let it pass. "Maybe Kurt could call my mom and talk her into letting us go with you."

"Do you think we should bother your mom at the doctor's office?"

Sara shrugged, her disappointment evident. "No, I guess not. But I'd rather go with you than wait here."

Sara's easy affection for Kurt amazed Abby. Her own relationships with Erin and Michael paled in comparison. Kurt had a natural way with children and an open, honest affection for them that drew them to him. He was a good father. He needed more children.

With that dampening thought, Abby took the casserole back outside where Kurt and the children waited. He took the hot dish and placed it with the other food in the back of the Cherokee before climbing behind the wheel again.

Abby took her seat beside him and studied his face. He had a nice face, so handsome he took her breath away. Funny, but he seemed even better looking now than when they first met. She forced her gaze away and looked out the window, but her determination didn't last long and she stole another glance.

His profile, his strong jawline, the intensity of his gaze on the road, only made him more attractive. She pictured him laughing, his mouth wide, dimples dipping into his cheeks, eyes dancing at something he found amusing, and her senses jumped. No matter what he did, he was attractive. Too attractive. Again, she tried to picture him sad, stuck in an unhappy marriage, but failed.

He took his eyes from the road for an instant and caught her staring at him. She looked away, embarrassed, and wished with all her heart he didn't attract her so.

Mumbling something Abby couldn't make out, Kurt slowed the Cherokee in front of a mailbox as they entered town. Rolling down the window, he leaned out and dropped a letter into the box. As soon as the letter disappeared, he looked into the back seat and smiled. "Who's ready for the party?"

"AREN'T THERE SUPPOSED to be people in these pictures?" Jack groaned and shoved the stack of photos back at Kurt.

Kurt stuffed the pictures back in their envelope and then into his pocket. He picked up the barbecue tongs and pushed a hot dog closer to the flame. "I didn't want to do the job in the first place."

"I haven't had a decent picture in the *Patriot* since Kenny left town. People are getting tired of it."

"Then hire somebody. I'm not a photographer."

Jack rolled his eyes at the suggestion. "Who am I going to get in Pine Cove?"

"Don't ask me. It's not my problem." Kurt flipped a couple of burgers. He didn't mind helping out from time to time, but not if Jack was going to complain about it. He already handled almost every demand Zelda made, and now Jack expected him to spend the summer taking photographs for the local paper.

Jack poked a potato chip into his mouth. "Look, it's no big deal. All I need is a couple of decent pictures every week." He waved at Bill and Naomi as they came through the patio door, narrowing his eyes in disapproval when he saw the beer can in Bill's hand.

Kurt looked out across the patio and caught a glimpse of Abby and Erin sitting with Theresa and Merilee Pierce. He nodded toward her. "That's who you ought to talk to—Abby Harris."

"You think so?"

"I've seen her taking pictures on the beach, and she seems to know her way around a camera. She might enjoy doing a bit of professional photography."

Jack appeared interested for half a minute. "I might go for it if she wasn't only here for the summer."

Kurt looked at Abby again, steeling himself for the now familiar jolt of electricity he always got when he saw her. "I thought it would get me off the hook for a while. Can't blame a guy for trying."

"Yeah? Well, forget it. It wouldn't be worth the hassle. Let's drop this now. I've got to make sure Bill's all right." Jack slapped Kurt on the shoulder and headed for the house. "A couple of pictures a week. But hold the camera still from now on, would ya?"

"Why don't you show me how?"

"You'll do fine. Just figure it out before the Fourth of July. I won't be able to put pictures like the ones I just saw in the paper then." Jack slung his arm around Bill's shoulder and led the other man through the kitchen door.

Kurt looked back at the barbecue grill and pushed the nearly burned burgers away from the coals. He obviously had to do something before Jack got used to thinking of him as a member of the staff. He ought to check out some of Abby's pictures— just to see their quality. If they looked good, he'd get her to show a few to Jack. And if Jack liked them, he'd probably ask Abby to work for him. He'd no doubt claim it'd been his idea in the first place.

Tossing the tongs down on a tray, Kurt picked up a plate heaped with burgers and hot dogs and headed into the crowd. The first chance he got to catch Abby alone, he'd approach her about the pictures.

ABBY STIFLED a sigh and let her gaze travel over the small crowd. Michael had gone inside with Brody and the other boys after dinner to play Nintendo, but Erin hadn't left her side all evening. Even when Amber Morgan, knee freshly wrapped, invited her to make root-beer floats, Erin hadn't budged. If anything, she'd stayed even closer to Abby.

Not for the first time, Abby wondered if Erin had suffered a different kind of abuse at Vic's hands than Michael had. And as always, she worried about her ability to handle Erin's special needs.

They'd spent time with Theresa and some of the other women on the patio, but a few minutes ago Abby had sensed Erin's need for quiet, so they'd wandered to the back of the deep lawn to sit under the tree.

Meeting the girl's eyes, Abby worked up a reassuring smile. "Are you having any fun at all?"

"Sure." Erin smiled back but didn't sound convincing.

Abby pursed her lips. "Sure."

Erin's mouth twitched and she ducked her head. But this was the first honest smile Abby had seen on Erin's face, and her heart soared.

"What do you want to do now?" she asked the girl.

Erin turned her head and watched Abby with one eye. "Stay here for a while?"

"Okay. That's easy enough." Abby stretched her legs out in front of her on the cool grass and leaned back on her hands.

From the house, raised voices caught her attention. It took a few minutes to realize they weren't friendly. At her side, Erin tensed and reached for her hand.

A second later Bill Franklin stumbled onto the patio, his face twisted with rage. "What I do is none of your damn business," he shouted to someone inside.

Jack came through the door, his hands raised in a placating gesture. "Now look, Bill—"

"No!" Bill turned away, stumbling a little over his own feet. "I came to this damned party for my boy. For my *boy!* I don't need you or anybody else telling me what to do."

Bill's son clutched the doorframe and watched his father warily. A second later Naomi appeared behind Jason, but instead of offering her son comfort, she brushed past him onto the patio.

Erin's eyes widened and a whimper escaped her throat. Abby wrapped an arm around her shoulders and pulled her close.

Shaking her finger in her husband's face, Naomi shouted, "This is what you always do, Bill. It's *always* somebody else's fault, isn't it?"

Jack stepped between them and said something to Naomi that Abby couldn't hear. Naomi folded her arms across her chest and backed away, but she didn't look pacified.

"Why don't we go around front and talk," Jack said, and took a step toward Bill.

Bill hesitated, then broke away again. "No, dammit. I'm not going around front to talk. I'm going over there to be with Jason. That's why we came, wasn't it?" He spat the last words at Naomi and tried to push past her to his son, but Jack caught his arm. Bill spun around. "What the hell are you trying to do, Jack? This isn't any of your business. It's between me and my wife."

He gestured angrily toward Naomi and she stepped forward, but Jack waved her back again. Jason said something Abby couldn't hear and lowered his head in what Abby thought was an attempt to hide his tears. Naomi answered, but her words obviously failed to provide the boy any comfort.

Erin clutched Abby's hand. "I don't want to listen to this."

"Then let's get out of here." Abby got to her feet and put her arm around Erin's shoulder again, wondering about the best means of escape.

From the side of the yard, a man moved in their direction, and Abby jerked backward before she recognized Kurt. He glanced toward the patio. "Sorry about this. It doesn't happen every time Bill's around, but it seems to be happening more often lately."

Erin looked up at them, her eyes bright with unshed tears. "Can we leave?"

"Of course, sweetheart." Abby took a step away.

"Is she all right?" Kurt asked softly.

"She'll be fine. Things like this upset her, that's all."

He'd want to know why. And what could she say? That Erin

was an extrasensitive child with tender feelings? He *might* believe it.

From the patio, Bill Franklin shouted an obscenity that made Erin cringe against Abby's side.

"I hate that word. My dad always says that word."

Abby cast a quick glance at Kurt. His eyes were riveted on the patio and his face looked as if it'd been carved from stone. She couldn't tell whether he'd heard Erin or not.

Willing the girl not to say another word, Abby studied the layout of the backyard. They might make it through the side gate, but it looked like Jack was trying to lead Bill in that direction. The only other choice was straight past Naomi and Jason through the kitchen door. Abby didn't like either alternative, but opted for the route farthest from Bill.

If Erin maintained her composure long enough, Abby could get her into the bathroom and calm her down without anyone asking questions. Whispering words of encouragement, she led Erin toward the house slowly, but she could feel Kurt shadowing them.

They still had at least twenty feet to go when Bill pulled away from Jack and ran back to the patio, taking Naomi by the shoulders and pulling her slightly off balance. Under no circumstances would Abby have called the action abusive, simply the uncontrolled movements of someone under the influence.

But when Jason ran toward his mother and Bill lurched in the boy's direction, Erin pulled away from her and cried, "No! Make him leave them alone!"

Abby jerked as if she'd been struck. This time she knew Kurt had heard. His eyes met hers and held, and when he didn't look away, she turned from him and grabbed Erin's hand. "Please, excuse us."

Kurt stared after Abby, speechless. Never in his wildest dreams had he imagined Abby in an abusive situation. Now he couldn't believe anything else. After all his experience with abused spouses, nothing should have surprised him. Abby did.

But Erin did not. How many abused children had he seen in his life? Too many to count. He should have recognized her withdrawal, her too-quiet shyness, her almost pathetic eagerness to please those around her.

He should have understood their situation sooner. If he had, he could have——

What? Approached Abby? Pumped Michael for information? And now that he did know, what would he do?

Nothing.

Was that why they were here? Was that why Abby was so secretive? Had she left her husband?

Although his heart might leap at the possibility that Abby was in the process of divorce, would she want to get involved with him immediately after? *Should* she? It'd taken him a full year—all the holidays, birthdays and anniversaries alone—to truly get over Laura. Even if Abby got a divorce, she wouldn't be ready to get involved anytime soon—if ever.

Some women ended one abusive relationship only to leap straight into another. Some healed, adjusted and then entered a healthy relationship. Some swore off men forever. Abby might be the type to rush into a relationship, but he couldn't allow himself to take advantage of that, no matter how badly he might be tempted.

He watched her flee from him. Even if he'd known how to react, he couldn't have made himself move. And while he stood frozen to the earth, Abby and Erin reached the patio, ducked into the crowd and disappeared.

WITH THE BATHROOM DOOR locked behind them, Abby finally felt secure. She knew they'd earned a few curious glances as they dashed through the kitchen, but she hoped people would pass off Erin's tears as those of some minor childhood woe.

She wiped the girl's tearstained face with a cool cloth. "Are you all right?"

Erin nodded and gripped Abby's hand. "I'm sorry. I know I'm not supposed to say anything, but he made me think about my mom. Do you think she's all right?"

"She has to be. We can't let ourselves believe anything else. Besides, she's not going to let Vic win."

Erin smiled tremulously and blew her nose. "Kurt's a nice man, isn't he?"

All the times Kurt had picked up on an inconsistency in their stories, Abby had waited for the other shoe to drop. Waiting for it had been like walking through a field of land mines. But now he *knew* something was wrong. He might not know what, but if he tried it wouldn't take him long to find out.

"Yes," she answered truthfully. "A very nice man. They're not all like Vic."

Erin made a face. "I wish *he* was my dad."

"Who? Kurt?"

Erin nodded and Abby stifled the groan that rose to her lips. The first really positive sign from Erin and it had been because of Kurt.

"Don't you like him?" Erin persisted.

"Yes, of course I do."

"He likes you, too. I can tell."

"I didn't mean I like him *that* way, Erin. We're friends, that's all."

"He's not married, you know."

"Erin—"

"And he likes you."

"But he thinks I *am* married."

"But you're *not*."

Their eyes met and held. Abby resisted the logic in Erin's statement and the frantic hope for a deeper relationship with Kurt that came with it.

A heartbeat later, a knock on the bathroom door broke the tension. Turning off the water, Abby smoothed her hair and checked Erin's face once more. Maybe nobody would notice she'd been crying.

"Ready?" she asked, and at Erin's nod Abby unlocked the door and ran straight into Kurt's chest. His eyes sought hers again, and she couldn't fight his look of genuine concern.

"Are you all right?" he asked softly.

"We're fine. Thank you."

But when she tried to pass, he touched her arm. "Do you want to talk about it?"

No. She didn't want to talk about it. She didn't want him to turn those incredible eyes in her direction. She didn't want that frown to crease his face or his mouth to tip down at the corners when he looked at her.

Taking her arm gently, he guided her and Erin down the hall and into an empty bedroom. She wanted to resist, to turn away, but even more she wanted to avoid a scene, especially in front of her niece. Kurt closed the door behind them and pointed to the bed. Abby sat on the end and Erin perched beside her.

Kurt faced them, his hands on his lean hips, his face solemn. "I think we need to talk."

"There's nothing to talk about." When he hesitated, Abby dared hope he'd change his mind.

Instead, he turned to Erin. "Would you let me talk to your mom alone?"

Knowing that Erin would refuse to leave her side brought Abby small comfort. But to her surprise, Erin nodded and ducked out of the room, closing the door quietly behind her.

Shocked, Abby jumped up. She wouldn't—*couldn't*—stay in this room alone with him. But when she took a step toward the door, he leaned against it and didn't look inclined to let her leave.

"I think you're in trouble, Abby. I want to help."

She tried to laugh, but the sound came out more like choking. "And I think you're imagining things. Now, please excuse me."

"Tell me about your husband. What kind of man is he?"

"That's none of your business."

Straightening, he took a step toward her, his eyes dark with some emotion. "What company does he work for? When was the last time you heard from him?"

"Stop it."

"You've been telling stories that don't add up since the day you got here. It may not be any of my business, but if you're in trouble, I'd like to help."

She flinched and took a step back.

"Come on, Abby. You can't do this alone."

She wanted to trust him. She longed to tell him the truth and take comfort from him, draw on his strength.

"What about the kids?" he demanded. "And don't tell me they haven't been going through something terrible. All anyone needs to do is take a close look at Erin. And do you know that Michael never mentions his dad? Why?"

Abby's mind reeled, but no words formed, no thoughts coalesced from the swirling mists. Why did he even care? Tears threatened to spill, but she blinked furiously, willing them away. The need to tell him the truth hit her full force. He was right, of course; she couldn't do this alone. She didn't have the skills to deal with Erin's needs—or Michael's. She didn't want to live with lies any longer. She didn't want to ask the kids to keep lying. And if she could trust *anyone,* it would be Kurt.

As if sensing her weakening resolve, Kurt stepped toward her. "What is it, Abby? Tell me."

He placed his hands on her shoulders and warmth spread through her. For the space of a heartbeat, he held her gaze. For the length of a sigh, he stayed too close for comfort. And for the measure of a breath, she thought he would kiss her.

She grasped desperately at her reasons for keeping the truth from him, but they skittered away, refusing to form a coherent thought.

"Tell me Abby." With his lips inches from hers, she could feel the warmth of his breath when he spoke, could almost feel his lips on hers.

Shivering, she closed her eyes and sought vainly to hold on to reason.

Uttering a low growl deep in his throat, Kurt pulled her to him and settled his lips on hers. Where his fingers had sent warmth spiraling through her, his lips ignited fire.

Softly at first, his mouth worked magic on hers, drawing a response from deep within her. She lifted her arms and let her fingers touch the back of his neck then trail to the lean bulk of his shoulders. As his kiss intensified, desire exploded within her. She met his kiss and returned it, losing herself in the feel of him against her.

He released her suddenly and stepped away. "I'm sorry. I shouldn't have done that."

Sorry? Abby struggled to regain her composure, to calm her rapid breathing, to hide her embarrassment at his apology.

She had to get out of this room and away from him. "I'll find Erin and Michael, then I'll ask Theresa to give us a ride home."

His head shot up and he stepped toward the door again, blocking her path. "Abby—"

Every instinct told her to melt into his arms, to seek strength from him, to tell him the truth. But logic forbade it.

She waited without speaking until he stepped away.

"If you need anything, call me" was all he said.

She didn't acknowledge him, but as she walked through the door, she wondered if he had any idea how hard this was for her. And she wondered what Rachel would say if she knew the price she was paying for keeping the children safe.

CHAPTER EIGHT

WHEN KURT ENTERED the kitchen a few minutes later, he found Theresa standing over the sink. He leaned against the counter and watched her dry a pan and slip it into the cupboard.

Untying her apron, she smoothed her clothes and turned toward him with a little laugh. "You caught me. Don't tell Merilee I was helping—she'd kick me out."

"Your secret's safe with me."

"It's just so much easier if you don't have to do everything yourself when you're the hostess." She found a tube of lotion by the window and applied some to her hands, nodding toward the bedroom he'd just vacated. "So what happened in there?"

Her question surprised him, but he couldn't tell her the truth. After all the stones he'd cast at Laura for her infidelities, how could he confess he'd just kissed a married woman?

When he didn't answer immediately, Theresa planted herself in front of him. "I saw you both go into the bedroom, and I saw her come out a minute ago looking upset. What happened between you two?"

He'd let desire get tangled up with compassion and he'd made a mistake. "Nothing."

Her face betrayed her disbelief.

Kurt had grown closer to Theresa since her marriage to Jack and he'd never been able to hide anything from her, but maybe half the truth would divert her. "I think she's hiding from an abusive husband."

"Abby? You're kidding!"

"I wish I was." He pushed away from the counter, pacing the length of the kitchen. "After that little scene with Bill, Erin got pretty upset. Something she said hit me like a ton of bricks.

I should have seen it before. I should have recognized the signs." He should have kept his attraction to Abby under control.

"So you followed Abby into the house and confronted her. And you told her what you suspected?"

Among other things. He nodded.

"And what did she say?"

"That it's none of my business."

"She's right."

"Not entirely."

Theresa blocked his path. "It *isn't* any of your business."

Though her advice about Laura had always been right on target, tonight she was missing the mark. "I don't believe that. That's what people say because they're afraid to get involved, afraid of rejection."

"So what do you intend to do?"

He jerked away and walked to the doorway. But he couldn't make himself go through it, and he couldn't answer. He'd come away wanting Abby desperately, but bitterly aware that kissing her had only magnified her problems.

Slumping against the doorjamb, he said, "I don't have any idea."

"But you're determined to step in."

"She's in trouble."

"I see. And that leaves you with no choice but to do something about it."

"I can't turn my back on her any more than you could walk away from me when I needed a friend."

"You're my brother-in-law, and I've known you since I was three. There's a difference. I don't understand why you feel compelled to help Abby."

"You're deliberately misunderstanding this. She needs help."

"From you? You'd better think this over carefully, Kurt. You're not the kind of man who could get involved with a married woman and still respect yourself. Don't do anything you'll regret."

This time he didn't answer. He'd already crossed the line.

Theresa touched his shoulder gently. "I've known you all my life, and I've been watching you since she came to town. You're not admitting to yourself how you feel about her, but I can see it."

He hadn't admitted it before and he couldn't deny it now, but he still tried to sound convincing. "I know what I'm doing."

She stepped in front of him and fixed him with the same look he'd seen her use on the kids when she suspected a lie. After a moment, she squeezed his hand. "Just do me one favor, okay? Figure out *why* you want to help before you get involved."

"She's a married woman," he insisted, more as a reminder to himself than to Theresa.

"Exactly. Don't compromise yourself. You'll never be able to live with it if you do."

Theresa gave him a quick hug and left him standing there, torn apart by her logic. Everything she said was true, and he hated it. Her argument made sense. His inner voice urged caution, but this time he wasn't able to listen to any advice.

Theresa was right. He couldn't live with himself if he followed his instincts and gave in to his desires knowing Abby had a husband—good or bad. On the other hand, he couldn't live with himself if he let her struggle through this alone. He wouldn't be able to face himself knowing he'd turned his back on her. But if he got involved, he'd be drawn farther into her orbit. And he already felt powerless to pull away.

ABBY FOUND ERIN in the living room, and after taking a few minutes to compose herself, they went in search of Michael. They found him attacking another plate of strawberry shortcake at one of the tables outside.

When he looked up and saw them, he called, "Mom! Come and have some of this. It's really good."

Brody looked up from his own plate and waved.

But Abby didn't want to stay here any longer. She wanted to collect the children, find Theresa and beg her for a ride home. She stood her ground at the edge of the patio and said, "I think it's time for us to go, Michael."

"But I just got this." Michael's whine floated across the air and several people at nearby tables looked up.

"Please, Michael. Let's go—now."

"But Brody's not finished, either, and I don't know where Kurt is. We're not ready to go."

She couldn't let Michael drag her into a debate, and she didn't want to offer any explanation about her desire to avoid Kurt. "Finish that quickly. I'm going to look for Theresa."

From behind her, Kurt's voice sounded low in her ear. "Sit down and join your son, Abby. I won't bite you."

She wheeled around to face him. His lips curved, but the smile went no farther.

With at least four sets of eyes watching her, Abby realized that to refuse would only invite trouble. Michael's protests would raise questions from others, and she didn't need that.

The set of Kurt's jaw told her he wasn't pleased, but he wouldn't ask any more questions tonight, she was sure. And he wouldn't kiss her again. Still hesitant, Abby sat beside Michael, and Erin took the space next to her.

"Do you want anything, Erin?" Kurt asked. "Strawberry shortcake? Watermelon?" When she nodded, he stood. "What do you want?"

Shyly Erin told him, smiling easily when he went off to do her bidding. Within minutes he returned with a plate and placed it on the table with a flourish, earning another timid smile from Erin. His eyes danced and he gave her one of his deep-dimpled grins in return.

But when he faced Abby across the picnic table again, his smile died and his eyes lost their luster. And when he looked away, a sense of loss invaded her and her heart fell.

She tried desperately to listen to Michael's chatter, to pay attention to Brody's enthusiastic responses, to think of something to say. Instead, she sat in painful silence. And Kurt did nothing to relieve it.

To anybody watching them, they probably looked normal enough. Kurt's face gave nothing away, and Abby knew she

could control her own facial expressions sufficiently to mask
her inner turmoil. But she knew she'd lost something during
those few minutes they'd spent in the back bedroom.

For one fierce moment, Abby resented Rachel for putting
her in this situation. In the next, remorse hit her like a lead
weight. This wasn't Rachel's fault.

Rachel hadn't made her come to Pine Cove. Rachel hadn't
placed Kurt in her path. And Rachel certainly hadn't made him
so attractive. If her proximity to Kurt for the rest of the summer
made Abby uncomfortable, she had no one to blame but herself. She was the one who'd let things get out of control. From
here on out, every time she came in contact with him, she
would have to be extra careful.

She dragged her thoughts back to the present. Brody and
Michael were chattering, and Erin was eating silently, responding to Kurt's occasional comments with little smiles. Both her
niece and nephew were taking their time about their food, but
Abby wished they'd hurry so she could leave. Though Kurt
ignored her, his presence unnerved her.

When Theresa wandered toward them, Abby finally felt relief. Straddling the picnic bench, Theresa sat next to Kurt and
rested her arms on his shoulder.

An unexpected surge of jealousy jolted Abby at the easy way
Theresa acted around him. In fact, everyone in Pine Cove
seemed to treat him that way. Abby had met plenty of men
whose charm, charisma, even good breeding, drew people to
them. But she'd never met anyone whose sincerity acted as a
magnet.

"What's going on over here?" Theresa reached across Kurt
to ruffle Brody's hair.

"The kids wanted to eat together," Kurt said.

Theresa nodded, but Abby sensed an undercurrent between
Kurt and Theresa that hadn't been there before. Dropping her
hands to her thighs, Theresa turned to Erin. "You haven't met
my daughters yet, have you?"

"I met one," Erin answered.

"Which one? Amber? The one with the gimp knee? She's
my sports addict. Sara's about your age and I think you two

would get along. After you eat, come find me and I'll introduce you."

Abby expected Erin to refuse. Instead, she sought Abby's permission silently and Abby nodded. To her surprise, Erin looked at Kurt next.

"Sara's the one who tackled me on the front porch when we went to get the barbecue things," he explained.

Erin smiled a little and nodded. "Okay."

"Great." Theresa turned to Abby. "One other thing. We have a Fourth of July pageant every year. All the kids in town are in it." She looked from Erin to Michael. "You kids want a part?"

"George Washington!" Michael hollered.

"Taken," Theresa said with regret. "But we've got an Erin-size hole in the chorus and there's one soldier's uniform we haven't filled yet."

An avalanche of excitement rocked the table. Michael and Brody both started talking at once, and Erin looked happier than Abby had ever seen her. If the kids were going to take part in the pageant, she'd have to, as well. And it might give them all something new to look forward to.

When she opened her mouth to speak, Kurt caught her eye as if he anticipated her reaction. He expected her to refuse.

"How about you, Abby?" Theresa asked. "Can you give me a hand with the costuming and makeup?" Theresa asked.

Before Abby could speak, Erin pressed her. "Say yes. Please?"

Abby had grown tired of picnics and exploring, and she'd been hoping to find something new for them to do. Maybe this would fit the bill. And if she volunteered, she'd be able to keep an eye on the kids. Plus, thinking about something new might prevent her from thinking about Kurt all the time.

She nodded. "All right."

"Great. I'll give you a call and tell you what I'll need you to do." Theresa patted Kurt's shoulder, smiled at the kids and left. In her wake, the uneasy silence between Kurt and Abby returned.

While Michael and Brody made enthusiastic plans and Erin

concentrated on her dessert, Abby smiled at the irony of her situation. Costuming and makeup for the Fourth of July pageant? She'd never done anything like that before, and she hadn't put a needle and thread through cloth since her seventh-grade home-economics class.

It was a measure of her desperation, she supposed. But if it helped, she'd do it willingly. With Kurt occupied at work and Little League, and with Abby involved in the pageant, they'd never run into each other.

But Kurt's frown deepened and his face looked even more solemn if possible. "Well. I guess that means we'll be seeing a lot of each other. Doug Pierce just drafted me to help with the props and scenery."

TWO HOURS LATER, Abby settled into the passenger seat of Theresa's station wagon as the kids belted themselves into the back seat. Not only did she not question Abby about not returning home with Kurt, Theresa seemed almost eager to give them a ride home. Jack and his daughters all insisted they wanted to walk.

"Thanks for agreeing to help with the pageant," Theresa said as she pulled onto the highway. "It's nothing fancy. The costumes won't be anything spectacular and the acting's—well, you know. But the kids love it. They look forward to it all year long. The Fourth is almost as big a deal around here as Christmas."

"It sounds very nice."

"Nice? It's a lot of fun, but getting ready for it is a pain in the neck! Half the town refuses to be on the committee and the other half can't imagine life without it. We start off with a sunrise breakfast and then we have a parade. There are games and booths all day long and enough food to make you sick for two days after. There's a huge barbecue in the evening and then the pageant and fireworks. It takes months to get everything ready. Some of the women have been baking and freezing since February."

Last Fourth of July, Abby had gone with a date to the symphony and heard a selection of John Philip Sousa's best works.

They'd had champagne and watched fireworks from the balcony of his condominium. This year, she'd be sewing costumes, putting makeup on little faces and eating hamburgers. If anybody had told her a year ago how she'd be spending this Fourth of July, she wouldn't have believed them.

Theresa glanced into the back seat. "How are you and the kids getting along?"

"We're fine. Everybody's been so friendly. Michael loves the team and Erin...likes it here," she finished lamely.

Theresa took a deep breath, as if steeling herself for an unpleasant task. "I saw you and Kurt talking earlier. Did he say something to upset you?"

Abby froze. "No."

"You looked upset when you came out of the bedroom."

"No, everything was fine."

"Good. He's been kind of—I don't know what you'd call it—persistent, I guess, about some things since his wife left. He's got the idea that it's his responsibility to make sure everyone around him is happy."

Abby didn't respond, and Theresa didn't seem to expect her to. They drove the rest of the way in silence. But when Theresa stopped the car, she put a hand on Abby's arm before she could climb out of the car. "Can we talk for just a minute without the kids?"

Abby hesitated, then handed her keys to Erin. With a silent nod, she faced Theresa, hoping her anxiety didn't show.

"It really broke Kurt up when his wife left. They met when he was at Willamette in law school and she was working in the placement office there. They were married before any of us ever met her. I tried to like her, but I'll be honest, I never did. She wasn't Kurt's type. He's always had this dream of helping people, but she wanted somebody who'd make a lot of money and buy her a big house and keep her in style. For a while, he tried to be what she wanted, but it didn't work. And when he finally came back here—which he had to do for his own peace of mind—she couldn't stand it."

Abby was puzzled by Theresa's sudden need to confide in her. Though part of her wanted to hear everything she could about Kurt and his marriage, an inner voice warned her that knowing the intimate details of his life would ensnare her further. "She didn't want to come here?"

"She wanted to move up in the world. Seattle was fine at first, but she had her heart set on L.A. or New York, where she could have really advanced. She wants to be one of the top headhunters in the country. But Kurt hated every minute of the time he spent away from here. He's a small-town guy, I guess."

"If he knew she didn't want to live here, why did he insist on coming back?"

"I think he'd given up trying to make her happy by that time. Some people are never satisfied, even when you do your best. Laura was one of those. Kurt's best was never good enough."

"So he just packed up and moved to Pine Cove and expected her to follow?" The same way Steven had accepted a position in Baltimore shortly after their wedding without even consulting her.

"It wasn't exactly like that. He gave her a choice to come with him or not, and she came. But until she saw him on his home ground and realized how happy he was here, I think she believed she could convince him to leave again. One day just before Kurt's birthday, she left and never looked back. Not even for Brody. I think Kurt could forgive her almost anything, but not what she's done to Brody. Kurt and Laura's breakup was inevitable. They didn't belong together, here or anywhere else."

"Why are you telling me all this?"

Theresa met her eyes for an instant and her look was frankly assessing. Then, as if she liked what she saw, she smiled and touched Abby's arm. "Because I suspect you and Kurt have feelings for each other. And because I don't want to see him get hurt again."

Abby wanted to deny that she would ever hurt him, but she knew she might. She wanted to protest that she felt nothing for Kurt but friendship, but that would be a lie, and she couldn't add another one to the list. More than anything, she wanted to tell Theresa the truth, but that was absolutely out of the question. So she said nothing at all.

"Please don't misunderstand me, Abby," Theresa continued. "I really do like you. And if you and Kurt were attracted to each other under *any* other circumstances, I'd be happy. I'd like to see him get married again, maybe have more children—that's what he needs. What he *doesn't* need is to get involved with someone who's already married. He thinks you're in trouble of some sort. If his suspicions are right, Abby, then please find help. But don't let it come from Kurt."

Tears blurred Abby's vision. Everything she'd done had been with the best of intentions. "I'm not trying to seduce him," she whispered. "And I never asked for his help. Believe me, Theresa, I have no intention of getting involved with Kurt or any other man at this point in my life." She opened the car door and started to climb out.

But again Theresa touched her arm. "I'm sorry, Abby. I didn't mean to hurt you, but I can see the writing on the wall, even if you and Kurt can't."

Abby slid from the seat and closed the door quietly behind her, then watched as Theresa reversed onto the highway and drove away. She needed a minute to collect her thoughts, to steel her emotions and ready herself to face the children. When Theresa had gone, Abby hurried into the house, seeking sanctuary.

Still battling her emotions, she tucked Michael into bed, pressing a kiss to his forehead. When she stepped into Erin's room, she felt the now familiar wrenching of her heart. Had Erin really thawed a little tonight? Had some of her barriers cracked? Abby knew they needed a father figure. Life with their own father had never been easy, but it hadn't been all bad. And both Erin and Michael seemed to gravitate to Kurt to fill the void.

She pulled the quilt up over Erin's shoulders and kissed her cheek. On top of everything else, Erin worried about her mother. So did Abby. Vic might not have always been homicidal, but he'd gone 'round the bend in the past few months, and Abby fully expected that he'd continue to assault Rachel and try to make good his threats to kidnap the children.

Closing the door behind her, Abby stepped out onto the landing. Within an hour, Michael might have his nightmare and she'd have to soothe and comfort both children. But for the moment, she was alone. And for these few minutes, she didn't have to keep up the pretense any longer. Lowering herself to the top step, Abby let the tears wash down her face.

KURT KICKED the covers off his feet and punched his pillow into shape. Brody had fallen asleep the minute he'd gone to bed after the potluck, but Kurt had been tossing for hours. The memory of Abby in his arms and her lips under his danced through his mind.

Rolling onto his side, he folded the pillow under his neck and thought about Theresa's warning. He should forget about Abby completely.

He flopped resolutely onto his back and tried to push her from his mind. Outside his window, the river surged onto the shore. Usually restful, tonight the sound frayed his already jangled nerves.

Finally, unable to find a comfortable position, he got up and crossed to his bedroom window. Moonlight streamed from the sky, dancing across the waves, reflecting off the rocks. He studied the shoreline and wondered whether Abby was asleep. Or did their kiss linger in her memory as it did in his?

Outside his room, he could hear Pride moving restlessly about. Pulling on his sweats and shoes, Kurt whistled softly to the dog and stepped through his French doors into the fresh night air. Maybe a little exercise would do him good.

The moon lighted the shoreline well enough for Kurt to walk without a flashlight. He set off aimlessly, but after several minutes he reached the shore across from Abby's house. He told himself he hadn't headed in this direction deliberately, but in his heart he knew he had. As the moon controlled the tide, something about Abby pulled him, and he felt just as helpless to resist.

Standing in the shadows, he watched the house for a moment. Every light was out except the one in the front bedroom. *Her* bedroom. Feeling like a voyeur, Kurt turned away. He shouldn't be doing this.

Was this how Laura's affair had started? Had her lover been attracted to her, unable to control himself? After ten years of marriage to her, Kurt couldn't imagine how anyone could feel that way about Laura.

He'd thought he was in love with her of course, or he wouldn't have married her. But his affection for her had diminished over the years until the pain he'd suffered when she'd left had been more for the loss of an ideal than for Laura herself. He'd stayed under the pretense of providing Brody with security, and for their last few years together he'd tried to convince himself that comfort had replaced passion in their lives. But what they had couldn't be called comfort, either.

Only Kurt's fear of the unknown had kept them together at the end. And his determination not to let the marriage fail.

He imagined life with Abby. How different that would be from the marriage he'd known. Abby had none of Laura's grim competitiveness or her reverence for status.

Shoving his hands in his pockets, he started home. He shouldn't have come here. He'd never do it again. Allowing himself one last glance at Abby's house, he turned. But this time the doors to the bedroom were open and Abby stood on the deck in a white robe, captured by the moonlight.

His heart hammered in his throat and he stepped back into the shadows. Had she seen him?

She stood unmoving, her gaze steady as she looked toward the shore, and the fear grew that she knew he was there, watching. The wind danced through her hair and lifted it, plucking at the hem of her robe and teasing it away from her ankles. He wanted to be there beside her, to feel her softness against him again, to taste her lips. She looked so beautiful he fought to catch his breath.

After a long minute, she turned and went inside, pulling the doors closed behind her. She hadn't seen him.

Relief buckled his knees. Feeling as stupid as a thirteen-year-old with his first crush, he vowed he would never, *ever* do this again.

But all the way home, he knew the image of her standing in the moonlight would haunt him for many nights to come.

"DAD, WAKE UP. Dad—" Brody shook his shoulder impatiently "—you're late. Naomi called and said she needs you at the office right away."

Grabbing the alarm clock, Kurt tried to force his eyes to focus. "What time is it?"

"After nine."

He shook his head, trying to clear it of sleep and memories. "Is there any coffee?"

Brody turned away. "I made some."

"Great. Pour me a cup while I grab a shower, would ya please?"

"I guess. Come on, Pride."

They'd had a great time last night, but obviously nothing had changed. Brody was still determined to resent every intrusion by Kurt's career.

Showering quickly, Kurt dug out a shirt that wasn't too badly wrinkled and a clean pair of pants, then gulped down a cup of coffee on his way out the door. Brody and Pride had moved to the edge of the deck, where they watched the flow of the river. Cindy must have arrived while Kurt dressed because she sat in one of the deck chairs near Brody.

"I'll call you later," Kurt called as he jogged to the driveway.

Brody lifted his hand in a wave, but he refused to look at Kurt. The boy dropped his hand to Pride's back and leaned against the railing. Kurt wished he could stay, but ignoring his practice wouldn't bring in a salary. He turned away, blocking the picture from his mind. Cleaning the house, doing the laundry and cooking the meals had been easy to master. The hardest part about being a single parent was juggling his son's needs with his career.

During the school year, Brody often brought his homework to Kurt's office and studied—or didn't—until Kurt was ready to leave. But with the increase in his client base, Kurt was spending less time with Brody, and his son obviously resented it. At least this summer, Brody could go to Abby's. And he did almost every day.

Kurt drove quickly, passing Abby's house with scarcely a sideways glance. No more schoolboy tricks for him. No more stolen kisses. It didn't matter how much he tried to deny it, Theresa was right. He'd lose all self-respect if he compromised himself further with Abby.

He reached the office in under ten minutes and left the Cherokee on the street. Inside, Naomi sat at her desk, her face flushed with impatience.

"You're late," she stated. "What happened?"

"Overslept. What's the emergency?"

"I need to talk to you."

Kurt stopped in his tracks. "You?"

She nodded. "Can we go into your office?"

He'd seen this look on her face before, and after Bill's outburst at the party last night, it could only mean one thing. He opened the door and closed it after Naomi followed him through.

She settled herself in one of the chairs by his desk and crossed her legs. "I want a divorce."

He knew it. "Have you said anything to Bill yet?"

"No."

"Isn't there some way you can fix things between you?"

"You saw the way he was last night. Do you know how embarrassing it is when he gets like that? Do you know what it does to Jason? Kurt, I can't live like this anymore."

"Didn't you talk about counseling once?"

Naomi flicked her hand at him dismissively and made a noise with her teeth. "He won't even consider it. He doesn't think he's doing anything wrong. According to him, this is all my fault."

"What does he want you to do differently?"

"What doesn't he want? He thinks I'm disloyal. He thinks I don't support him. He thinks I ought to follow his dreams with him and live off the clouds. Oh, hell. I've told you all this a dozen times.''

Kurt kept his voice level. "Let's take it one point at a time. He thinks he can find another job if you leave Pine Cove.''

Naomi waved his words away impatiently. "Doing what? That's what I want to know. All he knows is construction, but who's going to hire somebody who's drunk all the time to run heavy machinery? I'm the only one working, but he wants me to quit this job and run off with him when he doesn't even have anything lined up.''

"And you don't want to.''

"Dammit, Kurt. Everything's a fairy tale to him. He refuses to face reality.'' She leaned forward suddenly and placed her hands on his desk. "Look, I don't want to go over this again. I've made up my mind and I know what I want. I'm filing for divorce and I want you to represent me.''

He'd been expecting this. Naomi was his cousin, but he'd known Bill all his life. How could he choose between them? Most divorces happened this way. Two sides. Two stories. Two sets of right and wrong. "I wish you wouldn't ask me to do this.''

"Are you refusing?''

"No.'' He leaned toward her and took her hands. "I'm not refusing. I just wish it wasn't necessary.''

Naomi flashed him a wary look. "You'll do a good job, won't you? You're not going to sabotage me?''

"Of course not.'' He'd take the case and he'd give it his best. But he'd hate doing it. "Bill's going to despise me for this.''

"You and me both. I'll go get the forms.''

He watched as she crossed the room and opened the door. Seeing a marriage fall apart was never easy. As an attorney, he rarely came across a case where one person was entirely at fault and the other blameless. In his own divorce, he and Laura had each played a part.

He shuffled through the files in the center of his desk, pushing them aside when concentration evaded him. So what part had Abby played in the breakup of *her* marriage? What blame lay at her door? Was he right? Was she hiding in Pine Cove because her husband was abusive and she was frightened of him? Or was it something else?

He fingered the Rolodex on his desk. He'd asked Tony Graham to check on her, but he hadn't heard anything back yet. And now that he'd kissed her, keeping a private investigator on her trail seemed dishonest.

Pushing the Rolodex away, he pulled a file from the top of the stack and tried to concentrate. Hiding from an abusive spouse might explain the confusion over where Abby and the children lived. It certainly explained Michael's nightmare their first night in town. But it didn't explain why Abby didn't know about Michael and baseball. Or whether her children could make their own beds. Or who was or wasn't allergic to dogs.

He closed the file and shoved his fingers through his hair. If he called off the investigation, he might never know. But would that be so bad? Did he *have* to know what Abby was hiding?

He picked up the telephone.

She hadn't exactly been truthful with him. And he'd long ago outgrown the age where he'd trust a woman because of the way he felt when he kissed her. He replaced the receiver and stared at the file on his desk. He couldn't call off Tony Graham's investigation. Not yet.

CHAPTER NINE

"DON'T YOU EVER miss your mom?" Michael took aim with his slingshot and fired at a dead branch dangling from a tree.

Abby stopped just inside the house, her hand frozen on the screen door.

Brody tossed a rock at the side of the house and scowled. "No."

"Why not?"

"She didn't want me, so why should I miss her?"

Michael gave Brody's answer some thought, nodded and loaded a pebble into the sling. "Does she ever call you?"

"Are you kidding?" Brody sent a rock flying.

Michael took another shot at the tree and missed. "Why didn't she want you?"

Brody shrugged. "Dad says it's because she didn't really want to be a mom. Not because of me, you know, but because she wanted to live somewhere else for her work. You're lucky your mom lives with you."

"Yeah, I guess."

Abby released her grip on the door and leaned her head against the wall. Michael must really be missing Rachel. Or was it Vic he missed, even after everything they'd gone through? She knew there'd been good times mixed in with all the bad. Vic's abuse had finally driven Rachel to divorce, but his good qualities were what had kept her with him for so many years. The attacks that put Rachel in the hospital had come after the divorce. As terrifying as those attacks were, Michael still might miss his father, especially as the terror of them faded, and time gave him a false sense of security.

Instead of feeling more secure with the passage of time, each day without word from home increased Abby's anxiety. If Vic wanted Erin and Michael badly enough, he wouldn't hesitate to attack Rachel again. He'd already hospitalized her once. And he'd hurt anyone else who got in his path. Abby looked out at the boys once more.

Michael grinned suddenly and punched Brody on the shoulder. "Let's ask my mom if she'll make us some cookies."

"Chocolate-chip?"

"Yeah."

Abby envied their ability to switch gears so quickly. She knew the snatch of conversation she'd just overheard would haunt her for a while.

Brody's face lit up. "Do you think she'll say yes?"

"Sure. Why not?"

"My mom didn't like to do stuff like that."

"My mom's cool," Michael assured him.

Though Abby had no doubt about Rachel's culinary skills, she hoped she could measure up. She couldn't remember the last time she'd made cookies.

Abandoning her spot on the porch, she found Erin at the kitchen table, her nose buried in a book. "What are you reading?"

"Nancy Drew."

"Really? I *loved* Nancy Drew when I was a kid."

Interest sparked in Erin's eyes. Laying the book aside, she smiled shyly. "I've read almost all of them."

"Did you bring the rest with you?"

"No. They weren't mine. I had to borrow them from a friend." She smoothed the open pages of the book almost reverently. "I didn't have time to give this one back to her before we left."

"You can't spend the entire summer up here without something to read. What do you say we go book hunting tomorrow?"

"To the library?"

"I was thinking about finding a bookstore where we can buy you a few of your own. I hear there's a good one in Clam Beach."

Erin's face was a mix of emotions. Hope and doubt battled inside this child who'd suffered endless broken promises and shattered dreams. In the end, skepticism won. "Okay, I guess. If you want to."

Stuffing her hands into her pockets, Abby leaned against the table. "Do you want to help me with something?"

"Sure."

"Michael's out there telling Brody that I'll bake cookies tonight. Will you help me?"

Erin nodded.

"Or would you rather keep reading?"

"I'll help."

"You're sure? You don't have to, you know. If you want to, that's great, but I won't be upset if you don't."

"I want to."

"Okay. What do we need?"

"A recipe," Erin suggested softly, but a ghost of a smile tugged at the corners of her mouth.

"And boys," Abby said firmly. "If they want cookies, they can help, too."

To her surprise the boys seemed eager to help, and within minutes they'd formed an assembly line around the kitchen table. While Michael fetched ingredients, Erin measured and Brody added them to the bowl. But the boys' enthusiasm proved almost more detrimental than helpful, and by the time the batter was complete, the kitchen and all four participants wore a fine dusting of flour.

While Abby worked the wooden spoon through the dough, Michael raced down the hall toward the front of the house, and seconds later, rock music filled the air.

"It's too loud," Abby protested when Michael returned, but her words fell on deaf ears.

The boy hopped around the kitchen in time to the music, grinning at Abby. "Bet you can't do this."

"Bet I don't want to."

Brody laughed. "Come on, Abby. Do it."

"No." She dropped spoon-size globs of dough onto the cookie sheet.

"Come on," Michael pleaded. "Look, it's easy." Slowing his feet, he showed her an easy step.

Brody followed, embellishing the dance with wide arm movements.

Laughing, Abby shook her head. "Absolutely not. You don't know how silly you look."

"It's not silly. It's cool," Michael protested.

In the corner, a shy smile of pleasure lit Erin's face. More to keep the smile in place than for any other reason, Abby gave in with a show of reluctance. When her first few awkward moves actually brought a laugh from Erin, Abby increased her efforts.

She knew she looked frightful—wearing old sweats, covered with flour and chocolate smudges, her hair flopping wildly in a ponytail—but she didn't care. These three children were laughing and forgetting, and Abby couldn't remember when she'd felt better.

Kurt reached the back door and stopped, staring at the sight that greeted him. He'd promised to bring Brody's things by after work, and he needed to fix the broken screen door. Knowing that Abby would find an excuse to keep him away, he hadn't called ahead. Now he wondered if he'd been wise.

She danced around the kitchen with abandon, to the delight of the children. Michael had stopped dancing to watch, Erin's face shone with pleasure, and Brody looked happier than Kurt had seen him in a year.

Maybe Theresa was right. Maybe Brody needed a mother figure to help him get over Laura. Or maybe Abby had charmed his son as thoroughly as she had Kurt.

Unexpected emotion shook him, and Kurt backed into the shadows of the porch, unable to tear his eyes from Abby. She positively glowed. Finally, breathless, she stopped dancing and collapsed into a chair by the table.

Brody hitched himself onto her lap and smiled up at her. "That was great!"

She leaned back, exposing her glistening neck to the harsh light of the kitchen bulb. Kurt couldn't remember ever seeing a woman look more beautiful.

Having caught her breath, she smiled devilishly. "Okay, now you owe me one."

Brody nodded, but Michael groaned aloud. "You don't know what she wants. She's going to make you *waltz!*"

"That's right. Go put on that Strauss tape, Michael. It's time for my revenge."

Stepping out of the shadows, Kurt knocked on the door as Michael darted out of the room. He could either stand here watching Abby all night, or deliver Brody's things and fix the screen. And knowing how the past few minutes had made his pulse race, he couldn't afford to take chances.

Three faces turned at his knock and two smiles remained in place when he entered. Abby's slid from her face and wariness replaced it.

He held up his toolbox. "I thought I could fix this screen door for you since I had to bring Brody's things..."

Abby's face offered no encouragement, but Brody actually grinned and Erin looked almost welcoming. The strains of a waltz broke the silence, followed by Michael's running footsteps.

"There," Michael cried when he returned, "but don't make me dance with you this time. It's Brody's turn."

Looking confused, Abby shook her head. "I don't think now would be a good time."

Kurt regretted his decision to intrude. He'd put Abby on guard and ruined the spontaneous fun for the children, but he couldn't think of a skillful way to withdraw.

"Go ahead. It looks like you were having a great time." He handed Brody the small case he'd packed for his stay and hunkered down by the screen door.

Abby reluctantly allowed Brody to drag her to her feet, but the joy had vanished from her face and insecurity had taken its place. "Have you ever done this before?" she asked the boy.

He shook his head and Kurt nearly laughed aloud at the serious look on his face. Abby showed Brody where to place his hands and patiently taught him to count, waiting until he started to sway before stepping in time to the music.

Kurt watched them as they circled the room, slowly and clumsily, his eyes feasting on the curve of Abby's waist and the round swell of her bottom. Remembering the way she felt against him, longing to hold her, to kiss her once more, Kurt became aware of his reaction to her and tried to turn away. But the sight of her dancing to the recorded orchestra drew him back.

Concentration eluded him, fascination lured him, and he watched Abby hungrily, almost jealous of the way Brody's arm circled her waist and the way her hand rested on the boy's shoulder.

By the time he noticed the argument between Michael and Erin, it must have been going on for several minutes. It was hearing his own name that pulled his attention away from the dancers, and he realized the two children were staring at him, waiting for an answer.

"What?" he asked uncertainly.

"I said you'd teach Erin—won't you?" Michael repeated.

"Teach Erin...?"

"To dance like that. I'm not gonna."

"I don't think—"

"You know how, don't you?"

Kurt lowered the screwdriver to the floor. "Yes, I know how. But..." He intended to refuse, and then noticed Erin's expression. Her eyes were wide, her face full of fear—not that he'd touch her, but that he'd say no. That he'd reject her. She'd allowed herself to trust him on some level he couldn't begin to guess at, and he couldn't rebuff it.

"There's no one in the world I'd rather dance with," he said warmly.

Erin felt small and fragile. He held her at arm's length, unwilling to hurt her in any way. Her posture was rigid as she responded to his lead with wooden arms and legs, but a tiny smile graced her face when she looked up at him.

The music swelled, increasing in fervor and carrying them in the same magic countless other generations had known.

When the music ebbed and broke the spell, Abby forced a tiny laugh. "Well, enough of that foolishness."

"Not yet!" Erin protested. "Once more, please? I just got to try it for a minute."

"What about the cookies?" Abby asked.

"Please?"

Her enthusiasm surprised Kurt, and he met Abby's startled glance with a shrug. "I don't mind."

"Me, too, then," Brody insisted and assumed the position, leading Abby across the floor when the music began again.

Kurt and Erin began to move across the floor when, without warning, Erin stopped dancing. She frowned up at him. "I can't get it. I can't do it right."

"You're doing fine. It just takes a little practice."

"No," she insisted, twisting away. "Show me how it's supposed to look."

As Erin pulled away from Kurt, she maneuvered him directly in front of Abby. With a tug on Brody's shirt, Erin dislodged him, leaving Abby only a heartbeat away.

"Show me—please?"

The only consolation Kurt could find was that Abby looked as flustered as he felt. This wasn't wise. If he held her in his arms, even to dance, he might cross the invisible barrier again. And this time he might not be able to go back.

Telling himself to leave, Kurt closed his arm around Abby's waist. Cursing himself for a fool, he took her hand and swept her up in the rhythm of the waltz. Her scent enticed him, her softness enthralled him, her reluctance held him captive. Physical desire stronger than anything he'd ever felt exploded within him. Against his better judgment, he pulled her closer.

Only knowing that Abby was a married woman and that the children were watching kept him from sweeping her up the stairs and into the front bedroom where his imagination had taken him so many times these past few weeks. He fought to ignore her eyes, her mouth, the inviting spot just below her throat. He concentrated on the music for as long as he could, but eventually lost himself when she noticeably softened against him.

The music swelled, keeping pace with his own frenzied heartbeat. Abby swayed slightly and leaned against him, her

arm inching around his neck. Only Abby and the music were
real. The rest of the room faded away, blurred in Kurt's consciousness until he could have imagined himself anywhere—
with Abby.

When at last the music stopped, he slowed, unwilling to
release her. With her face just below his, Abby's eyes closed
and her lips parted slightly. It would take so little to kiss her
again, hardly any effort at all. Without even moving, he could
lower his mouth to hers. She wouldn't fight him. She wouldn't
refuse him. Every instinct told him she would welcome him if
he made the slightest move.

And they'd be as wrong as Laura and her lover had been.

He couldn't do it. Too many people could get hurt, and he
wasn't about to put Brody through more heartache. *He* couldn't
afford more heartache. Whether or not she returned to her husband, Abby would leave him at the end of the summer. Only
a fool would get involved when so much heartache awaited.
And he was no fool.

Abby's eyes opened lazily. He waited for her to regain her
naturally wary expression, but to his surprise, she didn't. With
a smile of apology Kurt released her and stepped away.

Spots of color flamed in her cheeks and she stammered, "I—
I'm sorry…"

"No. You didn't do anything. I'm the one who should apologize…" he began, but she turned on her heel and fled the
room before he could finish his thought.

As she disappeared through the door, Michael ran after her
and Brody followed his friend, sparing a small grin for his
father. But Erin didn't move.

With her eyes riveted on Kurt's face, Erin pressed her hands
to her side. "That was nice."

"Maybe I shouldn't have danced with your mother."

"It was okay."

"Maybe," he said doubtfully. Then, wanting to change the
subject, "I guess I ought to get that door fixed. What do you
say?"

Erin took a few tentative steps toward him, but when she
didn't speak again, Kurt got to work, trying not to let her scru-

tiny bother him. He checked the screws in the hinge, replaced the catch and cut another length of screen to replace the torn one.

Though he remained aware of Erin's presence, when she spoke again the sound of her voice startled him. "Do you want to get married again?"

"What?"

"Would you ever want to get married again?"

Lowering the pliers to the floor, he searched his mind for the right answer. With another kid he might make a joke, but knowing Erin's history of abuse, the wrong answer could easily have an adverse affect on her. Abby had her hands full enough without him unwittingly adding to her stress. He scratched his chin and looked thoughtful. "Well, now, I suppose I would if the right woman came along."

"Really?"

"Sure. Being married can be real nice if you pick someone who has the same values as you and if you find someone you can form a kind of partnership with."

A smile crept across her face and her eyes lit up. A second later, she turned and ran from the room. He must have said the right thing—she didn't look upset at all.

Whistling, he picked up the pliers and returned to his task.

THE NEXT MORNING, Abby had driven almost the fifty miles to Clam Beach before she felt better. For the second night in a row she hadn't slept well. But with the car radio turned up for Erin and Michael and the windows open so she could feel the wind on her face and in her hair, fatigue eventually began to recede.

The task of finding a bookstore couldn't have come at a better time. She wanted to help both kids pick out a couple of books, and she'd promised Michael they'd find a sporting-goods store. They'd pick someplace along the way to have lunch and do a little sight-seeing before they headed home. With luck, she'd be able to stay out of Pine Cove all day. She wouldn't, under any circumstances, put herself in Kurt Morgan's path.

After last night, she realized how close she was to losing control. She'd almost let him kiss her again. She'd wanted him to kiss her. She hadn't cared about the kids, Rachel, or the danger they all faced.

At the memory of her eager response, embarrassment flooded back. Since Steven had left, she'd taken pride in her ability to restrain her reactions to the men she dated, but she had to struggle to control herself every time Kurt came near.

Gripping the wheel, she tried to fix her attention on the road. She hated the way Kurt made her feel, the way her body took over and her resolve weakened whenever he was around.

She couldn't run from him—not without leaving Pine Cove. And she couldn't leave. She had to stay where the family could contact her. She only hoped the end of her stay would come soon and she could go back home. But her heart still ached whenever she thought of leaving Kurt behind.

Well, today, she would put him completely out of her mind. The clerk at the FoodWay had given her directions to the mall in Clam Beach where most of the Pine Cove folks did their shopping. And with the spectacular scenery along the Gorge, the drive had been refreshing. Erin and Michael seemed to be enjoying themselves, too.

When they reached the mall, Abby found a parking place with ease. "We'll find the bookstore first, okay, Michael?" Abby said as they walked toward the entrance. "Then the sporting-goods store."

Michael shrugged. "I don't care. As long as I get my new glove."

"You will. After we get the books. I promised, didn't I?"

Michael ran ahead, but Erin lingered and laced her fingers through Abby's. "I never had any books of my own before. Well, once I did, but my dad ripped it up, so I don't really count that one."

"He ripped up your book?"

"He didn't like me to read. He said I looked stupid with my nose in a book all the time."

"There's nothing stupid about reading, Erin. Most really smart people like to read."

"He didn't read."

Though that proved Abby's point, she refrained from saying so. She hated Vic Harrison with every ounce of her being, but she refused to criticize him in front of the children, no matter how great the temptation. She had no desire to protect his reputation in their eyes, but as they grew older and realized they'd inherited some of his traits, she didn't want them to remember things she'd said and begin to doubt themselves.

She squeezed Erin's hand. "If you like to read, you should do it. Don't worry about what anyone else says."

"I do like to."

"Of course you do. You're my niece, aren't you? All the Drakes like to read. Did you know that when your mom and I were young, we spent every Saturday at the library? We read all the time."

"My mom used to read?"

Abby faltered and nearly missed her next step. "She doesn't now?"

"I don't think so. My dad hates it. I don't remember ever seeing her have a book."

Abby couldn't imagine Rachel without a book in her hand. As young girls, they'd left books piled everywhere—under their beds, beside the bathtub, on the kitchen table. If anything, Rachel had been a more avid reader than Abby.

Gripping Erin's hand tighter, Abby increased her pace. The next time she saw Rachel, she'd give her an entire bag of books. And insist she read every last one of them.

No matter how often she heard about it, Abby couldn't get used to women giving up parts of themselves in the name of love. It happened every day and she'd seen it often, but she didn't like it.

Women did it because they thought they were protecting themselves, but the security never lasted. With an abusive partner, any behavior was grounds for brutality. Giving in gained nothing in the long run, but women imprisoned in those relationships could rarely understand that logic, and little by little they allowed themselves to be whittled down to nothing. Abby had always vowed to find a way to stop the abuse, but she never had.

Now she'd learned that her own sister had given up the thing she loved most, rather than suffer abuse because of it. And her daughter had done the same thing. Unless the cycle was broken with Erin, she'd wind up in a marriage like her mother's. She'd grow up believing she had to sacrifice herself for her husband, thinking she deserved nothing better than her mother had.

For the hundredth time that morning, Abby thought of Kurt. Would he demand such sacrifices of his wife? Had he demanded those things of Laura? Though Theresa had told Abby about Kurt's decision to move to Pine Cove against Laura's wishes, she had a hard time reconciling the image of a domineering Kurt with the one she'd formed on her own.

She remained silent until they reached the bookstore. Leaving Michael and Erin to browse the children's books but keeping an eye on them, Abby moved into the mystery section. She took her time selecting three new paperbacks and then returned to the kids. Michael was looking decidedly restless.

"Can we go now?" he asked, waving the two books he'd picked.

"In just a minute. Be patient a little longer." Abby moved to Erin's side. "Having trouble deciding?"

Erin had yet to make a choice. She nodded and lifted one finger to trace the spine of a book. "There are too many to choose from."

"You don't have to pick out just one."

Erin tried to smile, and the sadness in her eyes twisted Abby's heart. Hugging Erin to her, Abby fought to control her expression.

Erin snuggled closer, returning Abby's embrace. "Why doesn't my dad love me?"

How was Abby supposed to answer that? What could she say that wouldn't make Erin feel worse? As hard as she'd tried, Abby couldn't understand how Vic could treat his children the way he did. But before she was able to frame a response, Erin spoke again.

"Kurt wouldn't ever hurt Brody, would he?"

"No, of course not."

"Why don't you marry him, Abby?" Michael put in. "And have lots of babies so we can have some cousins. And Brody can be our cousin and we can stay here forever."

If only things were that simple. If only she could fulfill that dream. But though her heart ached for children of her own, she'd never have them, and though the thought of Kurt filled her mind all the time, too many obstacles stood in the way of a successful relationship.

Still, the memory of dancing in Kurt's arms made her tingle, and the memory of his kisses sent heat spiraling through her. Closing her eyes, she felt again his warmth, his strength, and his overwhelming masculinity.

And for just a few seconds, she let herself dream of a future she knew could never be.

"WE'VE ONLY GOT a week before the pageant," Doug Pierce announced to the crew of volunteers and recruits on the scenery committee, "and none of us can work on this full-time. I don't think we're going to make it, but quite frankly, I don't intend to tell my wife that."

Several of the men chuckled and Kurt let his gaze wander to Merilee Pierce, deep in conversation with Theresa across the room. At only five-three, she could fit neatly under Doug's arm when he extended it, but she gave him a run for his money. And he worshiped the ground she walked on. Everyone in Pine Cove knew it.

Doug held up one beefy hand to silence the group. "Jack and Bill have agreed to help us out. I want all the rest of you to get on the horn and line up a few more volunteers. I don't care what this scenery looks like, as long as there's something in back of the kids on the Fourth when they start marching around. Jack, you and Kurt start on the Old North Bridge. Bill, you still got that lantern they used last year?"

While Doug handed out the rest of the assignments, Kurt and Jack headed toward the pile of lumber that would eventually look and act like a bridge—at least long enough for ten enthusiastic soldiers to march over it countless times during the next seven days.

But before they reached the corner, Bill Franklin called after them. "Kurt? Got a second?"

A little uneasy, Kurt turned to face him and shrugged. "Sure."

Jack took a few steps away and Bill approached, head lowered, hands in his pockets. "I heard you're representing Naomi in the divorce."

Kurt tensed, but kept his tone light. "Yeah, I am."

Bill looked up. "This isn't what I want, you know."

"Look, Bill, I can't talk about it with you. As her attorney—"

Bill raised his hands and took a step back. "I understand. I just wanted you to know there's no hard feelings." He extended his hand and Kurt shook it.

"I'm glad to hear it."

"I'm only sorry she got to you first. I'd have liked to have you on my side."

Kurt met Bill's eyes, saw the haze of emotion there and felt his throat tighten in sympathy.

"I'm not going to let her take Jason without a fight," Bill said, and looked out over the room. "I don't want to lose her, but I won't lose my boy."

Kurt wondered how he would've felt if Laura had ever presented such a threat to him. He'd have reacted much the same way. But though he could understand, even share Bill's feelings, he couldn't help him. If Naomi wanted to fight for custody, he'd have to devote his energy to winning it for her.

Bill might have no hard feelings now, but Kurt doubted they'd come out of court with their friendship intact, and for a moment he hated the career he'd chosen.

"You guys going to spend the whole day yakking or are you going to build that bridge?" Doug shouted from the other side of the room.

With a halfhearted grin, Bill turned on his heel. "Keep your shirt on, Pierce."

Kurt watched his friend jog across the room to rejoin the

others. At least he'd put the bottle aside for today. If Bill stayed sober, the divorce would be much easier on all of them. Then again, if Bill stayed sober, there wouldn't have to be a divorce.

He started back toward Jack, half expecting some joke about Doug being afraid of Merilee or a comment about Bill and Naomi. He got neither. Instead, Jack walked beside him in silence, as if he had something on his mind.

Kurt battled a vague feeling of uneasiness. "So what do you think? Two-by-fours for the frame?" he asked, trying to lighten the mood.

Jack stopped and faced him. "Theresa told me what's going on with you and Abby."

"*Nothing's* going on with me and Abby." Nothing he'd admit to.

Waving Kurt's objection away, Jack propped his foot on the pile of boards. "I don't mean you've had sex with her or anything like that. But after thirty-four years, I know how your mind works. She's a beautiful woman, I'm not denying that. But are you sure you know what you're doing?"

Abandoning all pretense, Kurt let his shoulders sag. "No."

"Has anything happened?"

"Not really."

"Well, thank God for that. Look, Theresa and I only care about this because we know how you are. We saw what you went through with Laura." Jack kicked at the top board and shrugged. "If you let yourself do this—"

"I'm not letting myself do anything, Jack. That's the point. I'm going crazy. I can't seem to think of anything else. Every time I close my eyes, I see her face. Sometimes I think if I just let myself go to her and get it over with, I'd stop feeling so obsessed."

Jack's frown deepened. "It's serious, then?"

"Who knows?" Kurt laughed shortly. "I'm not even sure what I feel about her, much less how she feels about me."

"Have you talked to her?"

"About how I feel? How can I when I don't even know myself? Besides, she's got her own problems to deal with."

"Are you in love with her?"

"No!" The word exploded from Kurt's mouth before he'd even thought about his response. Of all the possible outcomes of this nightmare, he could not allow that one. To fall in love with a married woman? Never.

He'd never fallen in love easily. Looking back on his marriage now, he didn't think he'd ever really loved Laura. He'd wanted to be in love, Laura had seemed perfect, and the timing had been right. When several of his friends at Willamette had pushed them together, he'd fallen into the relationship. But he hadn't fallen in love.

He knew enough about himself now to realize that if he ever did fall in love, it would be forever. And it would not be with a married woman. He didn't want a clandestine affair he could never share, never talk about, never admit to. He wanted to tell everyone how he felt. And every time his feelings for Abby tried to assert themselves and every time he had to hide them away, he felt miserable. As if he was cheapening something precious.

Jack patted his shoulder and smiled. "So what can I do to help?"

"Decide whether you want to use the two-by-fours for the frame."

"I'm not talking about that."

Kurt hefted a plank to his shoulder and met his brother's gaze squarely. "It's the only damn thing you *can* do anything about."

CHAPTER TEN

ABBY PULLED into the FoodWay parking lot and glanced nervously at her watch. She'd easily avoided Kurt the past four days by making sure she'd finished with the costuming committee at the school and returned home before he left his office at five o'clock. But today she'd lost track of time and stayed at the school longer than she'd planned. She needed to get some groceries, and she knew he usually stopped at the FoodWay on his way home from work. Still, if she and the kids hurried, they could avoid him.

She slid out from behind the wheel and started toward the store, urging Erin and Michael to hurry. But they walked slowly, comparing notes about the day's practice, immune to her sense of urgency.

Keeping an eye on the door for Kurt, Abby shopped quickly. When she reached the meat counter, she studied the whole fryers as Michael tugged at the hem of her shirt.

"Can I have five dollars?" he asked.

"Why?"

"I want to play the video games. Please?"

"I don't think so."

"Please?"

"No, Michael. Not today."

"If I got an allowance, I'd use my own money. But since I don't..."

"Allowance?"

Michael sent his most winning smile up at her. "Kurt says that's the best way to teach kids how to take care of money."

"Is that right?"

Michael nodded and tried to look innocent, but it didn't

work. Abby recognized manipulation no matter what size package it came in.

"And just how much allowance does Kurt believe is fair?"

Michael beamed. "Five dollars."

"A month?"

"A week."

"Every other week."

"Mom—"

"Take it or leave it, kiddo. I'm through negotiating." Abby reached into her purse for her wallet.

When she couldn't find it immediately, she removed the bag from her shoulder. Placing it in the cart, she searched again. Slow panic began to grow outward from the pit of her stomach. Not only did the wallet contain more than a hundred dollars, but it held her identification—her true identification—and she couldn't risk that falling into someone's hands.

Erin looked up from a book she'd plucked off the rack as they came in. "What's wrong?"

"I can't find my wallet." Abby shook her purse and peered into its depths again as if it might suddenly appear.

If anyone found her driver's license in the name of Abby Drake, she'd have to field questions she couldn't afford to answer.

Erin looked at her feet and scuffed one toe along the floor. "Um…"

Abby stopped searching. Erin's hesitation was almost as good as a confession. "What?"

"Well, your purse fell on the floor in the back seat when we left the school. I tried to pick everything back up—"

"Then it must be in the car." Relieved, she handed the keys to Erin. "Will you run out and see if you can find it please?"

Erin nodded and headed toward the automatic doors. Relaxing slightly, Abby checked her watch and picked up the recipe she'd torn out of *Ladies Home Journal,* studying the list of ingredients. Even if Kurt came shopping today after work, she could still be out of here before he arrived.

KURT SWITCHED OFF the ignition and opened the door. With a silent groan, he surveyed the parking lot. He'd managed to get away from the office a few minutes early and he wanted to quickly pick up a few things for dinner, but the number of cars parked outside the FoodWay told him he was in for a long wait.

He fingered the message slip he'd tucked into his pocket on the way out the door. Tony Graham had called in to give a routine report, but Kurt wasn't ready to phone him back. He told himself he needed to call from the privacy of home, but in truth he didn't know whether he wanted to hear what Tony Graham had to say. In truth he didn't intend to phone Tony for a day or two—if ever.

As he hesitated, the automatic doors opened and Erin jogged into the parking lot. Seeing her and realizing Abby must be here somewhere, Kurt decided he needed the groceries desperately.

He tugged off the tie he'd had to wear for an afternoon court appearance and made his way through the crowded lot. He had no idea what he'd say to Abby, but the desire to see her again pulled him toward her. As he reached the car next to Abby's, he realized hers was empty, except for Erin who seemed to be looking for something in the back seat. When the automatic doors swished open again, Kurt looked up, half expecting to see Abby and Michael coming out of the store.

Instead, Naomi and Jason emerged. Scanning the parking lot, Naomi looked straight at Kurt, but when he raised his hand in greeting, she looked away. Two cars down, Bill was leaning against the trunk of his car, waiting for his wife and son and glowering in Kurt's direction.

Naomi slowed, obviously reluctant to reach her husband, and when Jason's footsteps halted, Kurt guessed Bill had been drinking again. Erin was closing her door, clutching a wallet, her face alight. But when she saw Naomi and Jason approaching and Bill waiting, her smile faded.

Bill let his eyes flick over Kurt. "What's up, Morgan? Want to talk my wife into something else?"

He'd obviously been drinking. "Of course not, Bill."

"Of course not." Bill snorted and pushed away from the

car. "She kicked me out, you know. My house. I worked hard for that house. Broke my butt for it, and she kicked me out."

"I don't think this is the time or the place to go into this." Kurt took a step toward him, but Bill was already past being rational.

Ignoring her husband, Naomi pushed her cart toward the old Chevy Bill had bought her a few years ago when times were better. Jason followed, but he stole a few covert glances at his father.

"Naomi?" Bill followed her. "I want to talk to you."

She kept walking.

"Dammit, Naomi!"

"Mom, please?" Jason tugged at her arm and tried to get her to stop.

"Naomi!"

Erin had been watching the exchange with wide eyes, but when Bill's voice changed, she cringed against the side of the car. Crossing to her, Kurt touched her shoulder tentatively, not wanting to frighten her. She flinched and her arms lifted instinctively to protect her face. If he'd still had any doubts about whether she'd been abused, they vanished instantly.

"It's all right, sweetheart."

With an embarrassed laugh, Erin lowered her arms. "I just…I don't like arguing."

"Neither do I."

Erin hesitated, shot a look toward Naomi and Bill, and let her gaze linger on Jason. "I'll bet he hates this."

"Probably."

Jason stood a little apart from his parents, watching them. Though they'd moved too far away for Kurt to hear every word, their agitation was still obvious.

Again he touched Erin's shoulder. "Go back inside, okay, sweetheart?"

She turned, obviously intending to comply, when Bill's voice rose to a shout.

"You can't do this to me. Dammit, Naomi!"

Erin stopped in her tracks.

"Just leave me alone, Bill," Naomi shouted back. "Stay

away from me and stay away from Jason or I'll get a restraining order. I swear I will."

"You're not going to keep me away from my own son." Bill looked around, locating Jason and crossing rapidly to him. "You want to leave, fine. I don't care what you do. But you're not taking my son."

Torn between concern for Erin and the need to do something for Jason, Kurt said to the girl, "Wait for me in your car, okay?"

When Erin nodded, he watched her start for the car, then ran through the lot to where Bill stood with one arm around Jason's shoulder.

As a member of the family, he owed it to Naomi to support her; as her attorney, he owed her complete loyalty. And as Bill's friend, he didn't want to antagonize him. But when he looked at Jason's tear-streaked face, all concern for Bill and Naomi evaporated.

He slowed and approached Bill cautiously, his hands in plain sight, his voice level. "Hey, Bill, what do you say we do this someplace else."

"Go to hell."

"I'm not trying to make any decisions here. I'm not taking sides. I just think it would be a good idea for all of you if you went someplace besides the parking lot of the supermarket."

"He's not taking Jason," Naomi shouted. "Let him go!"

Bill sidestepped her, but kept his arm around the boy. "He's my son."

Jason tried to hold back a fresh wave of tears, but he lost the battle and Kurt's heart went out to him.

"You're not thinking rationally, either one of you," Kurt continued. "Bill, why don't you let Jason go. He's not your prisoner. Naomi—" He snagged her arm as she tried to grab at Jason again. "Naomi, if you'll quit trying to attack him, Bill will let Jason go. Then we'll all calm down."

"Go to hell, Morgan." Bill pulled Jason toward his car.

Naomi tried to follow and screamed for Bill to stop.

Kurt rushed forward, trying to reach Bill's Mercury first. "Dammit, Bill. The boy's not a commodity. He's your son."

But Bill reached the car and pushed Jason inside before Kurt got close enough. "Damn right he's my son, and he's staying with me. If she wants to do something about it, let her take me to court." He climbed behind the wheel and gunned out of the parking lot to the squeal of tires and the smell of burning rubber.

"You let him take my baby!" Naomi screamed, racing toward her own car.

Kurt outran her easily, but he couldn't hold her without hurting her. She broke away and slipped into her car, following Bill's car by only seconds.

Kurt wheeled around, trying to orient himself and find the Cherokee so he could follow her and make sure she didn't get hurt.

But instead of the Cherokee, he saw Erin's tear-streaked face pressed against the window of Abby's car, her slender body shuddering with heartbreaking sobs. As he approached, she opened the door and flew into his arms.

"I hate him," she whimpered. "I hate him."

"I know, sweetheart. But it's over now."

"No, it's not. He stole him. And he's never ever going to give him back to his mother, is he?" Erin pulled away and wiped her cheek with the back of her hand.

"Do you know Jason?" Kurt asked.

Erin shook her head.

Kurt pulled her close to him again. "That man was his father. He's not going to hurt him."

"He *stole* him. And he's not ever going to give him back." Erin buried her face in his neck and her sobs increased. He'd intended to console her, but he'd obviously said the wrong thing and upset her more.

"I don't know what happened to you back home, Erin, but I know something did. You don't have to tell me about it, but remember, you're away from it now."

"I want my mom," she said softly.

"Okay. She's right inside the store."

"No." She shook her head, drawing away again.

"Yes, sweetheart. I'm sorry you had to see that, but you're safe here."

"But my mom—"

"—is fine. Let's go inside and you can see for yourself."

Erin pushed him away angrily. "She's *not* my mom. My mom could be dead for all I know, and Aunt Abby won't even let me call her to find out."

She turned and ran from him, leaving him staring after her in stunned disbelief.

Abby reached the front door just in time to see Erin break free of Kurt and race toward the store. Tears streamed down the girl's face and her fear transmitted itself to Abby.

Kurt stood beside her car and watched until Erin reached her, then walked slowly back to his Jeep.

Abby held Erin tightly. "What happened?"

Erin gulped back her tears and shook her head, but didn't answer.

"Did he hurt you?"

Again, the girl shook her head. Pressing her face to Abby's shoulder, she began to cry again.

Blind panic blotted out reason. Holding Erin so that she could see the girl's face, Abby demanded once more, "What happened?"

"Nothing!" Erin cried. "I'm all right."

Abby silently cursed herself for letting Erin out of her sight. She should never have sent her into the parking lot alone. This small town and the people here had lulled her into a false sense of security, but obviously she couldn't let down her guard for a moment.

"But why were you running from Kurt?" Abby insisted.

Erin wiped her eyes with the back of her palm. "I wasn't running from him. I just wanted to get back here before you started to worry."

Abby knew it wasn't true, but Erin had already closed the door between them. Pushing her now wouldn't produce the truth. "You're sure?"

"Yeah. I'm sure." Erin managed a tremulous smile.

It should have made Abby feel better, but it didn't. Something dangerous had happened out in this parking lot—she'd have bet her life on it.

She watched Kurt pull onto the street and glanced at the sky, wondering if the sun had gone behind a cloud, since she felt a chill. With a shudder, she hugged Erin again. "Come on. Let's find your brother and get out of here."

KURT WATCHED the group of women across the gymnasium anxiously. For two days he'd been waiting to speak with Erin again. And for two days he'd missed Abby and the kids at pageant rehearsals and Little League games. But today he'd left work early and come to the school when he knew they'd be here. Abby hadn't acknowledged him, but neither had she run away.

When Theresa and Abby led a group of children from the room, Kurt knew this might be his only chance. Unsure how long he'd have before Abby returned, he looked around for Erin. But she'd disappeared.

Dammit. How had he missed her leaving the room?

"Kurt?"

The soft voice behind him startled him. He whipped around, coming face-to-face with Erin.

"Can I talk to you for a minute?" she asked.

"Sure, sweetheart. I wanted to talk to you, too."

She looked wary. "What about?"

"Suppose you tell me what you wanted first. Then we'll see if I still have anything to say."

She appeared to consider that, nodding finally as if satisfied. "Can we go outside?"

"Sure." He followed her out the door into a darkened corridor that led to the playground behind the school.

With her shoulders back and her head high, Erin looked different, but when she faced him in the bright sunlight she lost her confidence. She didn't speak for several minutes, so Kurt took the initiative.

"What can I do for you, Erin?"

"You won't tell, will you?"

"Tell?"

"What I said to you the other day. You won't tell anybody, will you?" The words escaped her in a rush.

"I don't think so."

Panic twisted her features. "You have to promise."

Kurt hunkered down until his face was level with hers. "I don't think I'll need to tell anybody without your permission. But I can't judge that, sweetheart, because I don't know what's going on. Can you tell me?"

Erin shook her head. "Promise you won't tell Abby what I said."

"If you'll tell me what's going on with the three of you so I can be certain you're not in any danger, I'll promise you."

Tears puddled in Erin's eyes and she looked away. "I can't."

The sun beat down on Kurt's back, scorching his neck and arms. A mosquito droned near his ear before the sound was drowned out by the sudden shouts of a group of children nearby. He waited, drawing on his well of patience, hoping that Erin would reconsider her refusal to confide in him.

Tears slipped down her cheeks and her shoulders sagged as if under a great weight. "I'm not supposed to tell," she said weakly.

"Erin, look at me." He took her shoulders gently and waited until her eyes met his. "I'm not going to hurt you. I don't want you to break a promise you've made to Abby or anyone else. But I really think you ought to tell me what's going on. I think the three of you are in trouble and I'd like to help you."

"You can't help. *Nobody* can."

"Try me."

Erin didn't answer.

"Abby's not your mother, is that right?"

No answer.

"You called her Aunt Abby."

A small nod.

"Where's your mother?"

"At home. In Tempe."

"Why is Abby pretending to be your mother? To protect you from something?"

Again a timid nod was his only answer.

"From your father?"

Erin jerked away, her eyes wide. "How did you know?"

"It's all right." Kurt held up one hand in a soothing gesture. "It's all right. I don't know him. I'm not going to tell him where you are. But that's why you're here, isn't it?"

"Yes."

"Are your mother and father divorced?"

"Yes."

"And your father—"

"Don't keep calling him that. He's not my father anymore. The judge told him he couldn't even know anything about us. But he told my mom that if she took us away, he'd kill her and he'd get us back somehow."

Kurt's stomach clenched at her fear. "But he doesn't know where you are."

She shook her head slowly.

"Because Abby's been hiding you from him."

"But if he finds us, he'll probably kill her. And he'll kill my mom, too. And he'll take us away and nobody will ever know where to find us."

Kurt pulled her into his arms and rocked her gently until her sobs subsided. "First of all, Erin, you're not a baby. If he came and took you, you're big enough that you'd be able to contact somebody and let them know where you were, right? Do you know anybody's phone number? Your grandparents, maybe? Good. If nothing else, you could dial 911 and get help. So even if the worst happens, you're not helpless, and neither is Michael."

She looked up at him with new interest and gave him a tiny smile.

"But from what I've seen of Abby," Kurt continued, "she's not about to let him get you. Anybody who thinks they'd be able to take you away from her doesn't know what he's up against. And I'm here to help you, too. I want you to remember that."

"Okay."

"Are you still worried about your mother?"

"Yes. I don't even know if she's all right."

"Does she have anybody with her?"

"My grandpa and grandma live there. They're supposed to call somebody and let us know if anything goes wrong, but maybe they're not all right, either."

"My guess is that everybody's fine, especially if you haven't heard from them. Whose idea was it to bring you up here?"

"Abby's. She came back to Arizona just after my mom got out of the hospital."

"From Baltimore."

Erin looked surprised. "Yeah. She's lived there forever."

"So she came back to take care of you?"

"No. She didn't even know what was going on until she got there. Mom never told anybody until *he* broke three of her ribs and she had to go to the hospital. Abby just came to stay with Grandpa and Grandma for a little while. She said she needed to think about whether or not to quit her job. Anyway, she was supposed to be on vacation until all this happened." Erin paused and took a deep breath, looking around for the first time. "We've been out here a long time, haven't we?"

"A few minutes, I guess."

"I've got to get back in there. Promise me you won't tell Abby that I've told you?"

"I promise I won't tell unless I need to. In case you're in danger or something, okay? If something goes wrong, I may need to tell Abby what I know. She'll never tell me the truth."

Erin shrugged, but looked unconvinced. "I guess that's all right."

"It will be. I promise that. Now you go back inside. I'll come in through the front door in a few minutes."

"Okay." Erin sprinted for the door, looking back over her shoulder as she pulled it open. "By the way," she said, "she's not married." Slipping through the open doorway, she disappeared into the building.

CHAPTER ELEVEN

WHEN THE TELEPHONE rang, Abby folded the morning edition of the *Patriot* and placed it carefully on the counter. As she reached for the receiver, she smiled at the blurry headline photo. A local paper certainly didn't demand the same level of professionalism as those in larger cities.

"Hello?" She half expected to hear Kurt's voice on the line. After the scene at the FoodWay the other day and the way he'd watched them at rehearsal yesterday, she'd been waiting for him to contact her.

Instead, Zelda's voice warbled across the line. "Abby, how are you dear? Is everything all right at the house?"

Abby looked at her watch and suppressed a sigh. Ten minutes before she needed to be at the school for dress rehearsal.

"...I had thought I'd see a little more of you than I have. Now, I don't mean anything by that. I know how it is. You get busy with one thing and another, and you can't be bothered with an old lady..."

Did the obligations of renting this house include visiting the landlady? If she lived to be a hundred, Abby would never get used to small-town protocol. "I'm sorry—"

"Now don't you apologize, dear. If anyone should apologize, it's me. I really could have checked with you sooner about the house, even though your coming was spur-of-the-moment. Kurt mentioned a broken screen door and a leaky sink when I saw him a few days ago. Did he ever get over there?"

"Yes, he fixed them both."

"I'm so glad. I wouldn't want your stay in Pine Cove to be unpleasant. But I really called to ask you about the Fourth of

July celebration tomorrow. You are coming, aren't you? Breakfast in the square. A parade down Front Street. Dinner at the school yard and fireworks after dark. There's absolutely no excuse for not coming."

"Yes, of course. The children both have parts in the pageant—"

"Wonderful. I'm so glad they're involved. I wonder whether you and your family might like to spend the day with our family. We always have a big group, and I know how close your boy and Brody are. And I would like to spend a little time with you—get to know you better. In fact, if you don't mind..."

Abby held back a sigh. "What is it?"

"No, never mind. It would be too much to ask."

"Don't be silly, Zelda. What can I do for you?" Abby felt a headache coming on.

"Well, I was going to ask if you'd mind helping me get over to the square, but I'm sure it would be an imposition."

"I'd be glad to help, and we'd love to spend the day with you."

"Oh, thank you, dear. You ought to come by early and park in the drive, or you'll never find a place. You're just as sweet as you can be. I know you're busy, so I'll let you go and I'll see you at seven in the morning." With a click, Zelda severed the connection.

Abby leaned her forehead against the wall and moaned. She'd been manipulated, and not even very cleverly. Zelda reminded Abby of her own grandmother—a master at the art of not-so-gentle persuasion.

She'd planned on going, of course; she wouldn't let Erin and Michael down by not attending. But she had no desire to spend the entire day in Zelda's company. Experience had taught her that elderly women with extra time on their hands asked questions. And time spent with Zelda might prove more dangerous than annoying. She'd have to be on guard every minute.

Before she could get out the door, the telephone rang again. This time she jerked the receiver to her ear. "Hello?"

"Abby?"

"Yes." She hesitated a second before demanding, "Who is it?"

"Ted."

Abby's heart leapt into her throat. With shaking knees, she lowered herself onto one of the kitchen chairs, trying not to anticipate disaster. "What's wrong? Has something happened to Rachel?"

"No, everything's all right," Ted hastened to reassure her. "I'm not calling about that. I debated for a week whether to call you at all, but we got word that the governor's going to need a photographer for his new securities-fraud task force. Considering the state you were in when you left here, I thought you might be interested in the spot."

Her mind whirled as she fought to comprehend his words. "So Rachel's okay?"

"I haven't heard a thing from her or your parents. Look, I'm sorry if I frightened you—"

"No, don't worry. It's all right." And it would be, just as soon as she got her breath back.

"So do you want me to let them know you're interested? Is there a copy of your résumé around here anywhere?"

"In my bottom-right desk drawer. I updated it about three months ago, so it's current."

"Should I submit it for you? The deadline's next Friday."

This could be the answer she'd been looking for. A new position without all the violence and ugliness she'd been forced to witness lately. There wasn't one good reason to pass up this opportunity. So why did she feel hesitant?

"Abby?"

"How would I interview if they're interested in me?"

"That's no problem. Richard Schurtz is heading up the task force. He knows you well enough not to bother with the formalities. Besides, I already talked to him about you. So what do you think?"

"Sure, I guess."

"Great. It's as good as yours. Look, I gotta run. I'll keep you posted. You won't regret this, I promise."

Abby replaced the receiver slowly. It was probably the answer to her dilemma. After all, she had to have something to go to after she gave the kids back to Rachel and left Kurt behind. But though the decision to apply for the job made wonderful logical sense, she couldn't help feeling she was making a mistake.

KURT WET HIS FINGER and tested the iron before pressing it to the shirt he'd found in the back of his closet. He'd forgotten he owned this shirt until he'd started searching for something to wear to the Fourth of July celebration today—something that would make a good impression on Abby.

Whistling softly, he worked the iron around the row of buttons. He'd had a day and a half to think about Erin's story— thirty-six hours to digest her parting words. And long enough to reach some decisions.

He admired the way Abby had gone to such lengths to protect Erin and Michael. Putting her own life aside, she'd traveled across the country and taken in her sister's children. With no thought to the risks she was taking, she'd put herself in the middle of a dangerous situation to help her family.

Running the iron down a sleeve, he thought of the times he'd tried to pry information out of her. She'd protected those kids against everyone and everything, including him.

He wanted to keep Erin's confidence, and though his respect for Abby had grown with his new knowledge, he saw no reason to upset her by admitting what he knew.

Giving the sleeves a final inspection, he slipped the shirt onto its hanger, unplugged the iron and glanced at his watch. Almost seven o'clock; time to head into town for breakfast in the square.

Abby would be there. Abby, with her hair like ripe grain and her eyes like the summer sky. Abby—without a husband.

He heard a noise behind him and turned to find Brody in the doorway. "Come on, Dad. Aren't you ready yet?"

One look at his son's face forced Kurt to pull himself back sharply. Since last summer he'd promised himself to make this Fourth of July special for Brody. Before his mother left, Brody had loved the holiday. But last year Brody had been sullen and unresponsive through it all, and Kurt had no intention of letting history repeat itself.

"Just about. Have you seen my keys?"

Brody held up a hand, dangling the keys from one finger. Leaning against the doorframe, he met Kurt's gaze with a challenge. "Come on. We're going to be late."

"I'll be ready in a minute." Kurt slipped into the warm shirt and buttoned it quickly, trying to shelve his thoughts of Abby. He'd diverted too much attention from Brody lately, and no matter how much Abby played on his mind, he needed to concentrate on his son today. He put a hand on Brody's shoulder as they walked out the door. "This is our day, sport. Nothing's going to interfere."

Brody looked away. "Sure."

Forcing a smile, Kurt snagged the keys from Brody's hand and jogged toward the driveway.

Brody pushed past him, and by the time Kurt got behind the wheel, Brody had already fastened his seat belt. "We're going to be late," the boy repeated.

"We've got plenty of time." Despite his assurances, Kurt pulled onto the highway and sped past Abby's house. He forced himself not to look to see if her car was gone.

Once they reached town, traffic slowed. Every car in the county must have been pulling into Pine Cove. If Zelda hadn't lived just across from the square, he wouldn't have found a place to park within two miles.

Working the car through the traffic, Kurt breathed a sigh of relief when Zelda's big board house loomed into view—until he saw Abby's car in the driveway and Zelda coming down the front walk on Abby's arm.

How could he hide his feelings from Abby if she spent the day as part of the family, which, given her appearance now with his aunt, seemed highly likely? How could he even hope to devote his attention to Brody when Abby's mere presence commanded more than her share of it?

And how could he keep Erin's secret if every time he saw Abby he longed to pull her into his arms and kiss her? Especially since he now had no good reason not to.

292

As he watched, the front door opened again and Theresa emerged. She carried Zelda's huge wicker picnic basket filled with the homemade rolls and candy she brought every year to snack on.

Pulling into the drive, Kurt tried to look casual, waving to the women while Brody leapt from the car and raced toward Michael and Erin. "Can we go over now—please?" he begged him. "I'll show Michael and Erin where everything is."

But Kurt wanted Brody to spend the day with him. He wanted to spend some quality time with him and strengthen their relationship. And more than anything, he wanted Brody to *want* to spend the day with him. But one look at the boy's face convinced him Brody had other ideas. "If it's all right with Abby."

"Please?" Brody turned hopeful eyes toward her.

With a throaty laugh that sent a pleasurable shiver up Kurt's spine, Abby nodded. "Go on. But just let me know where you're going to be, okay?"

"Sure thing." Darting away, Brody led Michael and Erin through the nearly stalled traffic.

Shaking her head, Theresa held out the hamper to Kurt. "Jack's over there somewhere trying to tell everybody how to make hotcakes. Why don't you divert him?" She took Zelda's other arm and smiled at Abby. "Jack's so obnoxious whenever there's a party. He's absolutely convinced he's the only one in the world who can cook outdoors."

When Abby laughed and her eyes sparkled, Kurt felt a stab of desire. Now that he knew she was free, he wondered how long he'd be able to keep himself from acting on his impulses. Every instinct had sharpened his attraction for her, even as reason had told him to ignore her.

Her smile was as bright as the sun, her eyes matched the sky, and her hair hung down her back in a thick plait that made his fingers itch to pull it from its restraints and spread it across her shoulders. He wanted to bury his face in her hair and breathe in her scent. He longed to hold her in his arms and melt into her softness.

But instead, he took the basket and crossed the street in

search of Jack. He'd see Abby again throughout the day, and he'd be far wiser to walk away now, before he let his imagination run any farther.

Already the square was abuzz with activity. Long tables filled one end, with a profusion of camping stoves set up nearby. As he'd known he would, Kurt found Jack coaching Doug Pierce, whose face betrayed his annoyance.

Looking up from his task, Doug spotted Kurt and grinned in relief. "It's about time you showed up. Get this guy out of here, would ya? He's driving me up the wall."

Jack made a face at Doug's back. "Wouldn't know a decent hotcake if one bit him on the nose. Look at these—they're all too small. Might as well feed them to the dogs." He slapped Doug on the back and chortled as he came out around the table to join Kurt. "Where's the camera?"

Kurt groaned. "In the Cherokee."

"It's not going to do any good in there. We need shots of the breakfast and the parade—"

"I can't take a decent picture. You know that, and so does everybody else in town. And personally, I'm sick of hearing about it. Why don't you get Abby Harris to do your dirty work—at least for today?"

"I'm sure she'd love it."

Kurt pretended not to hear the note of sarcasm in Jack's voice. "She might not mind."

"Yeah? Well, I'll think about it. In the meantime, get the camera." Jack waved at someone he knew and moved a few steps away. Pausing, he turned and called back to Kurt, "If you honestly think she wouldn't mind, go ahead and ask her. Otherwise, just take them—all right? I'm doing my best to work something else out."

Resigned, Kurt started back across the street.

"Take Jack with you!" Doug shouted.

Kurt waved, but didn't break his stride. He felt ridiculous with the camera around his neck. Everyone in Pine Cove already knew how poorly his pictures turned out, and they didn't hesitate to let him know.

By the time he made it back to the square, the family had

gathered at the far end of one long table. And Abby stood squarely in the middle of them.

"Kurt." Michael waved his arms. "Over here."

Joining the group, Kurt ruffled Brody's hair, patted Erin's shoulder and fielded an enthusiastic embrace from his niece Sara. Meeting Abby's eyes, he gave her a smile, and as she returned it, his heart lurched in his chest.

"I didn't know you were a photographer," she said.

"I'm not. Jack's torturing me."

"Torture?"

"He lost his photographer at the beginning of the summer and he thinks that my being his brother automatically makes me part of the newspaper staff whenever he needs help."

"He works for the paper?"

"He's the editor—and his own most highly prized columnist. But he's even worse at photography than I am."

"So you're the one who's been taking the pictures for the *Patriot*? I've seen your work."

"Don't say it. I know I'm bad. Believe me, it's not my idea."

"Maybe you ought to look through some photography magazines or take a class."

He laughed. "Not a chance. I don't intend to be at it long enough for that. Jack's going to have to work something else out."

Theresa stepped between them. "Easier said than done, I'm afraid. Come on, Kurt. Brody's saving a place for you." Her words sounded light, but displeasure glinted in her eyes. Still believing Abby was married, she obviously intended to keep the two of them apart.

And since he couldn't set her straight, Kurt allowed Theresa to lead him away. Better not to make waves. Besides, this was what he wanted—to be with his son.

Brody heaped hotcakes on his plate, covering them with syrup. "Can we show Michael the dunking booth after breakfast?"

"Jack wants me to get some pictures of the mayor before the parade starts. We can join Michael later."

Brody's face fell. "I don't want to take pictures of the mayor."

"It'll only take a few minutes."

"Can Michael come with us?"

"If Abby says it's okay."

Brody abandoned his breakfast and raced to the other end of the table, but when he returned his face gave Kurt the answer. "She wants Michael to stay with her. But she said I could go with them."

And Kurt had no doubt what Brody wanted to do. He nodded. "Go ahead. I'll catch up with you later."

Damn Jack. He should be able to spend the day with his son instead of taking pictures for Jack's newspaper. Jack should be the one who had to leave his children while he chased news stories.

Kurt had started out this summer with every intention of helping Brody complete the adjustment of his mother's absence. But so far, he hadn't done much. He'd wanted to make today different, but it looked like it'd be another day like all the rest. Brody would make adjustments, but without Kurt's help.

KURT HUNKERED DOWN at the edge of the street, took aim at the trombone section of the marching band and pressed the shutter. *Twelve.* A dozen shots of the celebration so far, and most likely not one would be worth printing. Cursing Jack's stubborn refusal to approach Abby, he focused on the Elks Lodge's contribution to the parade and caught Erin in the frame.

Lowering the camera, he watched her move into the front row of spectators. A little behind her, Brody and Michael peered into a paper sack. Abby had to be somewhere close. Just a few more pictures, he promised himself, and he'd rejoin his son—and Abby.

The float rolled past and another came up behind it. Lifting the camera again, Kurt stepped backward as he tried to catch the entire float in the shot. Too big. Cursing, he took a second step back and bumped into someone.

He whirled around to apologize and came face-to-face with Abby. His heart jumped and his hands immediately grew clammy.

Abby's lips curved into a smile. "Can I help?"

"What?"

"The pictures. Can I help?"

"Please." He pulled the camera over his head and held it toward her.

"What kind of film are you using?"

"Thirty-five millimeter."

"I meant, what's your film speed?"

"Am I supposed to know?"

Abby lowered the camera and met his gaze. "It helps."

"I told you I don't know what I'm doing."

She grinned. "I know. I've seen your work." She lifted the camera again and scanned the street. She took a shot of the crowd and advanced the film, turning to catch the next parade float.

"Where did you learn how to do that?" Kurt asked her.

"It's a hobby."

"Some hobby. Have you ever thought of doing something with it?"

Abby lowered the camera and replaced the lens cover. "Once or twice."

"If Jack likes your work, maybe you could get your foot in the door by taking some pictures for him while you're here."

She didn't respond to that and pushed the camera back into his hands. "That ought to give you one or two shots you can use. Just don't shoot into the sun without a filter, and pay attention to your settings before you start shooting."

She stood so close he could've reached out and touched her. He could have pulled her into his arms the way he'd imagined and felt her softness against him. But until he was free to tell her what he knew, he had to maintain his control.

Before he could say anything, someone tugged at his shirt-tail. Turning, he saw Michael holding out an envelope. "They want you to pass this to Mrs. Hobbs."

As Kurt reached for the envelope and turned to look down

the line of people for Mrs. Hobbs, an image flashed through his mind. Michael on the deck, handing him an envelope addressed to Rachel Harrison in Tempe, Arizona. And Abby saying, *Erin looks just like my sister, Rachel.* Like her sister—Rachel.

Faintly aware of his actions through the buzzing in his ears, Kurt took the envelope and passed it to Mrs. Hobbs. But his mind churned and the sick feeling grew as his mind kept repeating, *my sister Rachel.*

He hadn't known. He *couldn't* have known what he was doing by mailing that letter. But there was no question in his mind now that he'd inadvertently put Abby and the kids at risk. Nausea welled in his throat as he remembered Erin's very real, very tangible fear of her father.

Thinking quickly, he tried to calculate the number of days since he'd mailed the letter. It'd been the night of the potluck dinner: not quite two weeks. He tried to convince himself that enough time had passed to mean that nothing bad would happen. But in his heart, he didn't believe it.

And he knew he'd have to tell Abby what he'd done and what he knew.

He looked at her, at her face lighted with delight as she watched the parade, at her lips curved in a gentle smile. He looked at the children with their eyes bright and faces relaxed. Not today. Let them enjoy today. Tomorrow, he promised himself. Tomorrow would be soon enough to bring up the terror.

ABBY HELD Zelda's arm and guided her across the uneven surface toward the edge of the school yard. Behind her, Theresa carried a lawn chair for the older woman and three large blankets for the rest of the group to sit on while they watched the fireworks.

The last remnants of the summer sun clung to the edges of the horizon as darkness muted the sky. Excitement mounted in the crowd. Even Abby felt it, and her anticipation surprised her.

Though they walked slowly, Zelda paused often to rest or to share a bit of gossip with Theresa about a neighbor. By the time they reached everyone on the lawn, the first of the fireworks exploded overhead, followed by a loud cheer from the crowd.

After she settled Zelda in her chair, Abby found Erin on one of the blankets with Brody and Michael, but she couldn't see Kurt anywhere. She dropped down beside Brody. "Where's your dad?"

Brody shrugged casually, but Abby sensed disappointment in the gesture. And she hated to see Brody so discouraged.

She'd seen Kurt only briefly after the parade, and then only at a distance. At the pageant, he'd neatly avoided her by staying behind the scenes. Afterward, he'd disappeared, and she hadn't seen him since.

Avoiding her was one thing, but ignoring his son's needs was another. Brody needed his father, and every day Brody seemed to grow closer to her and farther from Kurt. At first, she'd been convinced of Kurt's love and concern for the boy. Now she didn't know what she thought. She only knew Kurt ought to be here, sharing this experience with his son.

If she'd had a child like Brody, she wouldn't have put anything before his needs. *If* she'd had a child. Tears burned her eyes and stung the back of her throat. Fighting back the empty feeling that always accompanied thoughts of what might have been, Abby struggled to focus on the present.

She couldn't remember the last time she'd watched fireworks on the Fourth of July—at least not from a blanket on the ground. She'd forgotten how wonderful the cool night air felt against skin warmed by a full day in the sun. And the earthy smell of freshly mowed grass. And the taste of ice-cream cones. And the thrill of lying beneath the sky as it came alive.

Beside her, Erin sought her hand and held it. "I've never seen fireworks this close before."

"It's been a long time since I have, too."

"Can we do it again next year?"

"I hope so." Abby squeezed the girl's hand.

"Can we come back here next year?"

The thought made Abby's heart skip a beat. She'd like to

come back next summer, to see the town and the people. Especially the people. Especially one person. "Maybe."

"He's awfully nice," Erin said, as if reading her mind. "And I think he likes you. I wish you could be his girlfriend."

"Erin—"

"But why can't you? He wouldn't tell anybody."

"You know we can't take any chances. And I don't think we should discuss it here."

Erin looked away and watched the fireworks without speaking, but a small sigh escaped her lips. At last she said wistfully, "I hope we can come back here next year. I'm never going to forget this night."

At the other end of the blanket, Michael and Brody whispered and laughed and cheered aloud when a particularly bright explosion lit the sky. Abby wanted the evening to go on forever. With all her heart, she wished she could promise the children the permanent security they craved. But she had only this moment to give, and it wasn't enough.

Zelda interrupted her reverie. "Brody," she said, "I wonder, dear, if you would do me a favor. I'm a little chilly and I wonder if you'd run over to the house and get my sweater."

Brody sat up reluctantly, but Abby motioned him to stay and stood up herself. She wanted the children to at least have this night. "I'll go, Zelda. Where is it?"

Zelda shook her head. "No, my dear. You don't need to go. Let one of the children—"

But she wanted the children to stay. "I don't mind. Really. Where is it?"

"Well...if you're sure... It's the blue one and it's probably on my rocking chair in the living room."

In less than fifteen minutes she'd made it to Zelda's house, located the sweater and started back. She walked slowly, watching the fireworks explode overhead. If anything, leaving the crowded lawn heightened her awareness of the display. In the silence of the deserted street, the explosions and noises of the crowd seemed remote.

Following the broken sidewalk back to the school, she reveled in the momentary solitude, pulling the tangy river breeze into her lungs and seeking the rhythm of the current. Who would've thought she'd grow to enjoy this little town so much?

Without warning, a shadow stepped onto the sidewalk in front of her and a scream tore from her throat. Vic had found them.

The shadow shifted and moved closer. "Abby, it's me," Kurt said softly. "I'm sorry. I didn't mean to frighten you. I thought you saw me standing there."

Fighting to control the trembling of her limbs and the tears of relief that stung her eyes, Abby let anger take over. Stepping away, she said sharply, "What in hell were you doing there?"

"Trying to stay away from you."

His answer stopped her in her tracks and brought her back around to face him. Another explosion of red and gold lit the sky, reflecting the fire in his eyes.

"What?"

In answer, he closed the gap between them and took her face in his hands. "Oh, Abby, I *can't* stay away from you." His voice, low and thick, sent delicious shivers of anticipation through her.

She knew she should turn away, but she wanted to stay. Her arms tingled with the thought of his touch, her breasts ached to feel him against her, her lips burned for his kiss. She wanted him with a passion stronger than anything she'd ever known. Her throat constricted, preventing her from speaking. And her heart hammered in her chest, almost choking off her breath.

He caressed her mouth with his thumb, searching her eyes for the answer to his unspoken question, and she knew what answer she gave. With a low moan, he lowered his head and gently touched his lips to hers. She longed for him to kiss her harder, to demand a response from her. Instead, his mouth lingered over hers until she pressed upward, her lips urging his.

In reply, he pulled her into his arms, holding her tightly against his chest. His kiss deepened, demanded, sought her on a level she'd never known before. And she replied, melting into him, meeting him, giving and then taking. When she thought she could stand no more, he ended the kiss, but continued to hold her against him, kissing her hair, her eyes, her brow.

Rational thought returned slowly, through a haze of smoke and fire. Yearning swelled within her, keeping pace with the rhythm of the grand finale above their heads, fading only after the last flare paled, silence returned, and Abby remembered who—and what—she claimed to be.

Summoning her courage and resolve, she forced herself to break away. She walked quickly, afraid that if she hesitated, she'd never leave.

CHAPTER TWELVE

OVER HIS MORNING COFFEE, Kurt decided he was an idiot. He shouldn't have let Abby run away from him last night. He shouldn't have been so afraid of losing his chance with her that he hadn't told her about the letter while they were alone. He hadn't wanted to spoil their day yesterday, and he'd believed his decision to be the right one. But this morning he realized that keeping the truth from Abby an extra day increased the risk of danger. And she'd be angry with him for doing it.

He drained his cup and slammed it down on the table. "Brody?"

Pride sidled around the corner and raised his big eyes, but Brody didn't answer.

Yesterday's pleasant weather had disappeared with the night. Today had dawned gray and gloomy. Now rain fell in heavy sheets, darkening Kurt's mood even further.

"Brody!"

"What?" Rubbing the sleep from his eyes, Brody padded into the kitchen.

"Get dressed. We're going to Michael's."

"Why?"

"I need to talk to Abby. What's wrong? Don't you want to go to Michael's now?"

"Yeah. I want to, but you sound mad."

Fighting his frustration, Kurt tried to soften his tone. "Not mad, son. But there's something important I have to talk with Abby about, and I thought you'd like to come with me."

Brody shrugged and turned away. "Sure. I guess."

Kurt poured another cup of coffee, settling back to wait. But in spite of his apparent lack of interest, Brody dressed and returned to the kitchen before Kurt had a chance to finish it.

Driving the rain-slick highway, Kurt practiced what he wanted to say to Abby, changing his words over and over. Finally, realizing that nothing he said would make up for the damage he'd done, he gave up.

He refused to allow himself to imagine her potential responses to his confession, but he feared the worst. She'd be angry about his deception and frightened at the possibility of discovery. She'd probably never speak to him again.

Slowing in front of her house, he pulled into the gravel drive. Empty. Abby was out. Hell.

"Let me just make sure they're not home," he said to Brody as he shifted into neutral and set the brake. But even as he dashed up the walk, he knew the house was empty.

Still, he rang the bell three times, just to be certain, before heading back to the Jeep through the rain. He didn't know where she'd gone or for how long, but he couldn't wait. He had to find her and tell her before he lost his nerve.

Though he'd turned the defrost on high, the windows were steamed over. Using his sleeve, he wiped the windshield and the driver's-side window, trying to improve visibility. "Any idea where they might have gone?"

Brody used his own sleeve on his window. "Nope. Unless they're at the store."

Determined not to act as desperate as he felt, Kurt shrugged. "Want to check?"

Brody frowned up at him uncertainly, then nodded. "Okay, if you want to."

"We might as well, I guess. Nothing else to do today, right?"

"Right." But the boy's voice reflected skepticism, and his face betrayed doubts about his father's mental condition.

And maybe Brody was right. What Kurt hoped to accomplish by chasing Abby into town he couldn't begin to explain. He had no idea how he'd get her alone or what he'd say to her when he did.

The windshield wipers zinged back and forth, barely clearing the window enough to allow Kurt to see the center line.

Beside him, Brody peered through the glass. "Dad, look."

Trying hard to concentrate, Kurt kept his eyes focused ahead. "I can't—"

"I think it's Abby's car."

Tearing his attention from the road, Kurt saw the small dark car on the side of the highway as they passed. Easing his foot off the accelerator, he came to a stop several yards in front of the Toyota. When he stepped from the Cherokee into the rain, he could see Abby and the kids inside.

"Stay here," he told Brody. Hunching his shoulders as if that would keep him drier, he ran back toward them.

As he approached, Abby rolled down her window. With her bedraggled hair and wet clothes, she looked as bad as she had the night he met her. Only this time, he wanted to pull her into his arms and warm her.

"I've never been so glad to see anyone in my life," she said.

"What's wrong?"

"I don't know. The car just died. I wiggled every wire I could find under the hood, but nothing worked."

"Maybe it's the distributor cap. Pull the hood release."

Kurt knew a few basics about cars, but within minutes he'd eliminated every possibility he could diagnose. "We're going to have to get it towed into the garage. Lock it up and I'll give you a ride."

While Abby gathered her things, he ran back to the Cherokee, turned it around and pulled in front of the Toyota.

The three kids climbed into the back, and Abby took the front passenger seat. When she smiled up at Kurt from under her wet hair, an electric shock raced through him. Her face was fresh-scrubbed and her hair smelled of rain and she looked beautiful.

As he studied her, Kurt's shivering slowed and a welcome warmth enveloped him. "Where to?"

"Home."

"I don't mind taking you wherever you were headed."

"No, that's all right. It's probably better if I don't go grocery shopping right now." Her eyes sparkled and her lips twitched. She acted as if she knew the effect she had on him, and he liked her this way: a little flirtatious, slightly provocative—all right, terribly provocative. But, hell, she'd tempt him if she wore flannel pajamas with feet.

And he hated to destroy the mood. He wanted to prolong her smiles, to hear her laugh again. But he also knew he had to tell her about the letter and he might not get another chance.

Pulling into the driveway, he laid his hand on her arm. "I'd like you to let the kids go into the house alone for a minute. I need to talk to you."

Her smile faded. "I—"

"It's important, Abby."

She pulled her keys from her purse and handed them to Erin, but her eyes never left Kurt's face, and the question in them didn't fade. "You guys go on in," she said. "We'll be right there."

Kurt watched the children run through the rain and up the stairs. He watched until they disappeared inside and, because he dreaded telling Abby what he had to say, he stared mutely at the empty porch after they'd vanished.

"What's wrong?"

He shifted in his seat so he could face her and gauge her reaction. "I think I've made a mistake."

Her face fell and she looked away. "It was a mistake, but it doesn't have to happen again."

Her reaction baffled him. Had Erin told her already?

"I was as much to blame as you," she went on. "I guess the fireworks got to me. I don't know what it was—"

As enlightenment dawned, he held up a hand to stop her. "I'm not talking about kissing you. That wasn't a mistake."

"Then what...?"

His throat constricted. Maybe he didn't *have* to tell her. Maybe she didn't need to find out.

"Kurt?"

"I wish I knew a better way to say this. Or that I didn't have to tell you at all. After Erin saw Naomi and Bill Franklin arguing in the parking lot the other day, she said some things. She was upset and worried and she slipped. I promised her I wouldn't tell you unless I had to, but yesterday I remembered something I think you need to know.''

Abby's face paled and she touched the fingertips of one trembling hand to her lips. "What did she tell you?"

"That you're her aunt. That her mother is still in Arizona and she's worried about her. And that you're protecting them from their father."

"No."

"She couldn't help it, Abby. Don't be angry with her. That's a horrible burden for an eleven-year-old to carry. I wouldn't be telling you about it now except yesterday I remembered that Michael gave me a letter to mail the night he slept over. To Rachel Harrison in Tempe, Arizona. I thought you ought to know."

"He *what?*"

"If I'd had any idea what you were doing here I never would have mailed it."

"You mailed it?" She covered her mouth with both hands and closed her eyes. Kurt reached for her, touching her arm softly.

She pushed the door open, moving away from his reach. "I'm glad you told me." She jumped from the Cherokee and ran toward the house, away from him.

As Abby pounded up the front steps, her heart hammered crazily. *This couldn't be happening.* Not now. Not when everything had started to feel right.

She slammed the door and leaned against it for a second or two until the trembling in her legs forced her to move. How could she tell Erin and Michael? What should she do? Where could they go?

Panic drove her the length of the hall and back. Terror refused to let her mind function clearly. What had Michael been thinking when he wrote that letter? Why had Kurt mailed it?

In an attempt to calm down, Abby tried to count the days since Michael had given Kurt the letter, but she had to start over twice in her confusion.

It'd been a week and a half—more than enough time for Rachel to receive the letter and get word to Abby that security had been breached. But Rachel hadn't sent word. Why? Because she hadn't received it. Because Vic had it. And now he knew where they were.

Kurt's footsteps echoed up the walk and Abby tried to stem the tears that burned her eyes. She swallowed thickly, but her heart beat so rapidly she couldn't draw a breath. When he knocked on the door, she stepped aside and let him in, but she couldn't see him clearly through her tears.

"I'm sorry," he whispered. And before she knew it, he'd gathered her into his arms and hugged her tightly. Even through her wet clothes she felt his heat.

She melted against him, wanting to believe the soothing words he whispered, wanting to trust his assurances. But in her heart, she faced the inevitable: they couldn't stay in Pine Cove.

Kurt held Abby until she refused to let him comfort her any longer. He felt the moment her resolve strengthened and released her reluctantly when she pushed him away. She paced the length of the front hall. Obviously frightened, she plowed her fingers through her wet hair repeatedly.

"Let me help, Abby—please. I feel responsible."

The look on his face twisted her insides. "You aren't responsible," she said softly. But in the next breath, her voice hardened. "She must not have received the letter or she would have called."

"You can't be certain. Before you panic, you should call her and make sure where things stand."

Immediately she turned on her heel and walked rapidly toward the kitchen. Though he knew she didn't want him here, Kurt followed and watched as she punched out a long-distance number on the telephone.

She waited, shivering in the chill of the kitchen, for what must have been several rings before someone came on the other end. "Ted?...I'm afraid so."

Ted?

"Something's wrong. Michael wrote a letter to Rachel over a week ago. No, I just found out about it. She hasn't called and I'm afraid..." She paused for a moment, listening. When she spoke again, her voice sounded calmer. "You will? Oh, Ted..."

Kurt's heart plummeted. Just because she wasn't married, he'd assumed she was free. He should've known there was a man in the picture.

"Thank you," she said, her voice softer still and almost husky. "I don't know what I'd do without you."

Replacing the receiver, she stood with her back to him. Kurt wanted to go to her, to take her into his arms and comfort her, but he couldn't. The sound of her voice when she talked to Ted held him at bay. He wanted to ask her who Ted was and what he meant to her, but he couldn't waste breath on something as trivial as his own insecurity when her and the children's lives might be in jeopardy.

"He's going to call Rachel and see what he can find out," she said softly, still not looking at him.

But despite his resolve, Kurt felt like a fool. Here he stood, ready and willing to help, and Ted was the one she called in a crisis.

She turned then and held his gaze. "You don't need to wait. We'll be fine."

Though she said she didn't blame him for putting them in danger, she'd closed herself off from him and pulled away. But he wasn't ready to let her go. "I'll stay."

Without responding, she busied herself with the coffeepot, and soon the earthy aroma of the fresh brew filled the kitchen. Compared to the terror of the moment, the soothing sound of the coffeemaker seemed strangely out of place.

Kurt wasn't sure how to help, but he knew he couldn't leave. Abby didn't speak as she placed a steaming mug in front of him. When she took the chair across from his and didn't meet his eyes, Kurt's heart dropped. But he still refused to let her drive him away.

He wrapped his hands around the mug, letting its warmth combat the bone-deep chill from his wet clothes. It didn't warm him completely, but he wouldn't move until he knew she was safe.

Abby had just filled her mug for the third time when the telephone rang at last. It sounded so loud in the silent kitchen that she cried out. Grabbing for the receiver, she gulped a deep breath, hoping to steady her heartbeat.

"Abby? Bad news, kid. Your sister never got that letter."

Though she thought she'd prepared herself, hearing Ted say it made Abby's knees weak. Reaching blindly for a chair, she forced herself to sit, vaguely aware that Kurt had risen from his place at the table and was standing behind her. She wanted him to touch her, to provide comfort. But he stood rigid and unmoving.

"And there's something else," Ted warned. "I couldn't reach Rachel right away, so I called the number you gave me for your parents. Apparently your brother-in-law came after Rachel and put her in the hospital again. The police arrested him, so nobody saw any need to frighten you."

"Is she all right?"

"She's okay. But your parents don't think the kids should be told."

She knew he was right—this would destroy them. But how could she hide it? Tears of anger blurred her vision while her hatred for Vic grew. "At least he's locked up."

After Vic hurt Rachel badly enough to require hospitalization the first time, he'd spent some time in jail. But the laws governing spousal abuse were inadequate, and the punishment even more so. Before long, Vic had been out on the streets again, still angry and violent.

"That's the trouble—he's not. He made bail a few days later. Your parents say they've checked Rachel's mail, but they never saw Michael's letter. The police have a few reports that Vic's been hanging around your sister's house the past few days, but nothing they can do anything about. Still, I'd say chances are pretty good he's got the letter and knows where the kids are."

"No!" Though she'd feared the worst since Kurt told her about the letter, hearing this somehow set a seal on it. Abby cradled the receiver and fought to control her mounting terror.

"If you're lucky, he won't have enough money to get up there," Ted continued. "But you'd better be careful just in case." He paused and then said softly, "You going to be okay, kid?"

Abby forced a response from her burning throat. "I hope so. And, Ted? Thanks."

"It was nothing. Keep in touch. Have you got the name of the sheriff up there? Maybe I ought to have a talk with him."

"I only know Doug Pierce—he's one of the deputies."

"I'll keep you posted. Watch your back."

After he rang off, Abby held the receiver against her ear, listening to the dial tone while she fought to calm herself. When at last she could move, she hung up and met Kurt's eyes. "We'll have to leave here—immediately."

Wanting to help her, to take away some of the pain, Kurt reached for her. "If he hasn't shown up here by now, he probably won't."

"You're willing to gamble our lives on that?" She jerked her arm out of his grasp.

"Of course not. But you don't need to leave town."

"We can't stay. I can't put these kids in jeopardy. I promised Rachel I'd keep them safe. Now—"

"Then let me help. Let me do something."

"There's nothing you can do."

Lightning flashed and illuminated the gray sky, darkening the shadows of the forest outside. After a few seconds thunder rumbled heavily, and a sense of foreboding filled him.

Maybe she was right. Maybe they should leave Pine Cove and find someplace safer.

When the second flash of lightning whitened the sky, Kurt met Abby's gaze. After everything she'd been through to protect Erin and Michael, it wasn't fair she had to run again. He admired her courage. He respected the way she'd put her own life on hold to protect the children. And in the face of this disaster, she intended to handle the situation herself. No running for help, no looking to the nearest man for a solution to her problem.

Rain splattered against the windows. Abby stood before him, strong and fierce as lightning lit the room, thunder shook the earth, and Kurt realized how much he loved her.

He couldn't let her disappear from his life. Somehow he had to do something for her—and the kids. She wouldn't want to accept his help, but he couldn't let her fight alone.

"Let me call Gary over at the garage and get him to tow your car in this afternoon. At least then you'll have an idea of how long it'll be before you have transportation."

"The car! You don't think it's anything serious, do you? He *has* to be able to fix it today."

Kurt reached for the telephone and dialed. "I'm no mechanic, Abby. I exhausted my limited knowledge out there on the road."

Gary answered after six rings, and with only a little prodding Kurt elicited a promise from him to tow the car in and check it over immediately. "Call me back here at Mrs. Harris's," he said, and gave the number. "And, Gary—thanks. I owe you one, buddy."

Replacing the receiver, Kurt glanced at Abby.

If anything, she'd grown paler in the last few minutes. "How long do you think it'll take?" she asked.

Kurt ached to hold her and ease her terror, if only temporarily. "If it's something simple, you might be on the road within a couple of hours. If not—"

"He has to be able to fix it *today*. We can't stay here any longer." Rising panic edged her voice.

Giving in to impulse, Kurt pulled her into his arms. After a slight hesitation, she relaxed against his chest. His arms tightened around her and he wanted to stay like this forever, but holding her wouldn't solve anything. "I wish I could tell you that it's something minor, but I can't. I *can* promise to help you in whatever way I can. Why don't you and the kids get your things together. I'll stay down here and wait for Gary's call. If I haven't heard anything in an hour, I'll call him."

Turning quickly, she ran from the room. He listened to her footsteps retreating down the corridor, then running up the stairs. A few minutes later, he could hear another set of feet on the staircase and Brody joined Kurt in the kitchen.

"What's wrong, Dad?"

"Why? What happened upstairs?"

"Abby came in and said she had to talk with Michael and Erin alone. She told me you were here and asked me to come down and stay with you."

Without going into detail, Kurt filled Brody in on the situation. Expecting the boy to react with surprise, shock, fear or even anger, Brody's response stunned him.

"So his mom never got the letter? Wow. And now his dad's on his way here?"

"Maybe. But it's too dangerous for them to wait here to find out."

The telephone jangled and Kurt grabbed it before it could ring again.

"Bad news, buddy," Gary drawled. "Her timing chain's slipped. She's out of commission for a while."

"How long?"

"At least a week, maybe longer. Depends on how soon I can get the part ordered in."

"Damn. Can't you put a rush on it?"

"That *is* a rush, Kurt. We're talking about a major repair job here. No way I can do it faster than a week."

Kurt swore again. "All right," he said grudgingly. "Thanks, Gary. I'll let you know what she decides to do."

"The sooner the better," Gary said, and broke the connection.

Why did this have to happen now? Abby and the children had to leave Pine Cove, but they had no transportation and nowhere to go. Even if they could decide on a safe place, there'd be no way to escape if the kids' father found them again.

Kurt slammed the receiver down on its hook and turned, startled to see Brody standing right behind him.

"Dad? Why don't we take them to the cabin?"

Kurt felt a slow smile creep across his face. Though Jack and Theresa spent summer weekends there, he hadn't been to his parents' old cabin in so long that it hadn't even come to mind. But it would be the perfect place for Abby and the kids to wait out the danger. Together, Kurt and Abby could protect Michael and Erin if the need arose.

"That's brilliant. What would I do without you?"

Brody cocked his head to one side as if measuring Kurt's words. "You think it's a good idea?"

"Absolutely." Kurt reached an arm around Brody's shoulder, expecting him to stiffen or pull away, but this time he didn't. Kurt's spirits leapt. Working together to keep Abby and the kids safe might help close the gap between them.

Assuming, of course, he could convince Abby to go.

"A CABIN?" Abby asked, her voice thick with skepticism. "That's just what we need, Kurt—a remote spot where nobody can see what Vic has planned when he finds us." Abby zipped the duffel bag and tossed it onto the floor.

"He won't find you. The place is hours from here, and nobody but Jack and Theresa will know that's where you've gone."

"It won't work."

"Why not?"

Struggling to maintain her feeble hold on her patience, Abby turned to face him. "Because if Vic does come here, I want to have Erin and Michael as far away as I can."

"Look, I don't want to be the voice of doom, but just exactly how to you propose to do that? You don't have a car, and though I'd be glad to take you to the airport, if Vic's even halfway clever he'd have little trouble tracing you. You won't be able to leave Seattle without leaving a paper trail—credit-card receipts, car-rental forms..."

"And he wouldn't be able to trace us to your cabin?"

"He might find you here in Pine Cove—I can't guarantee he won't. But you can slip away from here without telling anyone where you're going. We'll get Jack and Theresa to plant a believable story around town, and we'll alert Doug Pierce to keep his eyes open. Nobody else would ever think of the cabin. I haven't been there since before Dad died."

She shook her head, but this time she couldn't find any words of protest. She could feel herself weakening, but she still didn't want to give in. She'd never admired women who expected a man to save them when the going got rough, but here she was contemplating that very thing.

Snapping her suitcase shut, she shouldered past him into the hall.

"Where are you going?" Kurt followed her and his tone suggested he was nearing the end of *his* patience. "Come on, Abby. Don't be so stubborn that you end up doing something foolish."

"If I don't do what you want, I'll be doing something foolish?"

"You're putting words in my mouth. I just don't understand why you won't let me help."

"Because it's not your problem."

"You're wrong."

"I don't want you and Brody involved."

"We're already involved, dammit. We have been since the day you got here." He stood at the top of the stairs, blocking her exit. His face darkened and his eyes blazed. "Isn't the aim to get Michael and Erin to safety—"

"Of course, but—"

"Nobody's going to question if Brody and I both leave. Jack and Theresa can make up a dozen stories to cover. But if I disappear and leave Brody here, it's going to raise all sorts of eyebrows."

"This doesn't make any sense. You'll put Brody in jeopardy to protect Michael and Erin?"

"I'm not putting Brody in jeopardy. If we do this right, we'll be perfectly safe up there. But we're all going to have to go together or it won't work. Heading off somewhere without transportation and money is no solution. Digging in right here where you're safe, and fighting if necessary, is your only option if you don't want this to go on."

"We're *not* safe here."

"You're safer here than you would be in a lot of other places. You've got people who know you and care about you. What happens if you take those kids someplace else? Who's going to notice if a strange man drives off with them in some big city? Who's going to care?"

She hesitated. Maybe he was right.

"Michael and Erin aren't the only ones in danger, Abby. I'm thinking about protecting *your* neck, too. I spent a number of years working with this kind of situation in Seattle. Vic might want his children back, but I'd bet money that he won't be happy until he's dealt with you. You can't run from him forever."

Abby lowered her suitcases to the floor and met his eyes. Maybe they *would* be safer with Kurt in some remote mountain cabin than they'd be anywhere else. "I hope you're right."

"I'll do anything I can to help you. I won't let you face this alone."

He took a step toward her, never letting his eyes leave hers, and pulled her into his arms again. Abby wanted him to hold her there forever where she could listen to the steady beat of his heart and know everything was all right. She didn't want to do this alone anymore. And for the first time in her life, she felt stronger with someone than by herself.

She leaned into Kurt, absorbing his heat, his lean strength. She'd never felt like this with any man. Steven's arms had never seemed as if they belonged around her the way Kurt's did. Steven's kisses had never demanded the depth of response Kurt's did. She wanted this feeling to last.

But though she enjoyed the fantasy of it, reality would intrude again soon enough. Fear had driven her into his arms. Concern had prompted him to take her in. But she couldn't let herself imagine that there existed something deeper between them.

Watching Kurt with Brody and seeing the way he responded to his nieces told her how important children were to him. And listening to him talk about his childhood and his plans for the future convinced her she had no place in it. She'd suffered humiliation once before when she'd allowed herself to believe in love conquering all. She wouldn't do it again.

She'd enjoy this moment and accept help, since he seemed so intent on giving it. But she couldn't delude herself: she could never be what he wanted.

CHAPTER THIRTEEN

THE ROAD WOUND steeply through the dense forest, cutting a path in land that seemed to close around them as they passed. For the hundredth time since they'd left Pine Cove, Abby checked on the children in the back of the Cherokee.

Trying to find a comfortable position, she strained against the seat belt. They'd been driving for hours, and the muddy roads and pouring rain hadn't made for an easy trip.

"There's some beautiful country up here," Kurt said, breaking the silence.

Abby nodded, but she didn't totally agree. The country *was* beautiful, but it also made her uneasy. All around them the forest hugged the narrow road, occasionally reaching tendrils of green across the mud as if trying to reclaim its own. No wonder Kurt hadn't been to the cabin in years. Who would willingly spend time in a place so remote?

As if sensing her uneasiness, Kurt spoke again. "It'll seem more inviting when the rain stops."

"I hope so." She didn't turn from the window, but she could feel Kurt casting glances at her. "Is there a telephone up here? A way for us to let someone know if—" She broke off, unable to voice the fear aloud.

"I'm afraid not. The cabin's pretty rustic. My mom used to ask Dad to fix it up, but he never got around to it. And after he died and Mom moved to Florida, Jack and I never bothered. So we'll have to use camping equipment for almost everything. Have you ever roughed it before?"

"No." She wanted to sound lighthearted, but the word came out more like a sob.

"I'll teach you how to use the stove, then we can take turns

cooking. Michael and Brody can help me gather some firewood
as soon as we get there, while you and Erin set up your gear
in the loft. You'll be warmer up above—and safer. The boys
and I can sleep on the floor in the big room.''

"That sounds fine.''

"The best way for us to get through this is to treat it like
an adventure. We'll keep the kids busy—maybe take them on
a few hikes. It just might help you, too.''

She couldn't make herself answer.

"It's going to be okay, Abby,'' Kurt said.

She studied his profile. "I hope you're right.''

The Cherokee hit a bump in the road. Mud sprayed across
Abby's window and she tried not to feel frustrated and out of
her element. But again she wondered whether she'd been wise
to agree to an indefinite stay in the mountains.

"It's not much farther now.''

"Thank heaven,'' she muttered. Surely once she got out of
the Jeep, out of the rain and into someplace warm, she'd feel
more like herself. But half an hour later they were still on the
road, and she realized Kurt's definition of "not much farther''
didn't match hers.

Why had he turned his own life upside down to bring them
here? He'd put his law practice on hold and closed up his
house; he'd made all the arrangements and paid for most of
the food and supplies.

She gave up the thinly veiled pretense of looking at the scenery and, instead, watched Kurt—the way his fingers gripped
the steering wheel, the way the muscles in his neck strained
against his collar.

She also watched Michael and Erin with him and thought
back to how they'd been five weeks ago. Now, even with the
threat of Vic looming on the horizon, they were both healthier
and more relaxed than she'd ever seen them. She'd worried
that telling them about Vic would throw them both into a tailspin. But she couldn't keep the truth from them. That would
have left Michael and Erin defenseless if Vic *did* find them.

Michael said something funny, and Erin giggled. Kurt
grinned as he responded to the boy, and the dimples Abby had

begun to watch for dipped into his cheeks. Her heart jumped, and suddenly she knew why she lost control and couldn't concentrate whenever he was near. Why the thought of him never left her mind.

She loved him. She loved every good and honorable thing about him. She loved the way he looked and the way he smiled and the way he cared about her and the kids. She loved the way he walked and the way he drove and the way he watched her when she spoke.

Tears filled her eyes and she averted her face quickly, overwhelmed by the intensity of her emotions. She'd never meant for this to happen. He knew she wasn't married, and there was nothing standing between them now. Except her inability to give him the family he wanted—and the fact that he'd never asked her to try. And with her heart on the line, she couldn't let herself get caught up in a physical relationship with him. She'd lose too much when the time came to leave.

Just sitting here beside him, she'd relived the warmth of his kisses a hundred times. How would she survive living in the same cabin as him, seeing him before she went to bed at night and when she awoke in the morning?

At long last, he slowed the Cherokee and gestured to a narrow trail cutting into the woods. "The Warners' place is just up there. They're the closest neighbors and they usually spend most of their weekends up here. We might see them, so don't let it throw you. Our cabin's about a mile up the next fork in the road."

A few minutes later he turned off the main road and followed a muddy track through a valley. When he finally stopped in a small clearing before an old cabin, the sun had disappeared behind the mountain peaks, but twilight lingered. Abby glanced at her watch. It was just after eight, but between the storm and the mountains, darkness had come earlier than in Pine Cove.

Kurt pushed open his door and stepped down. "Wait here. I'll make sure none of the local wildlife has moved in."

When he came around to her side and reached for the flashlight in the glove compartment, his hand brushed her knee. Even the slightest contact with him sent a bolt of electricity

through her. As if he could read her thoughts, he flashed her a
broad grin before closing the door between them.

Unable to tear her eyes from him, Abby watched as he
crossed the muddy parking area, searched above the door for
the key and slipped off his shoes before entering. The cabin
looked too small to offer much privacy. On one hand, she'd
love being stranded up here with Kurt. But on the other, fear
of getting him involved in a potentially dangerous situation
would make her hate every minute of it.

He reappeared in the doorway and beckoned them inside.
Michael and Brody climbed out first, almost slipping in the
mud as they eagerly scrambled toward the cabin. Abby followed with Erin.

"Take your shoes off," she called after the boys as they
jumped onto the porch.

Removing her own shoes, she stepped through the front
door. Kurt had lit a kerosene lantern, and an eerie glow flickered across surprisingly comfortable-looking furniture: an old
couch and two chairs stood before a wide fireplace, a big table
surrounded by eight chairs occupied space before a large shuttered window, and a bookcase full of reading material and
games climbed the wall next to the steep ladder that led to the
loft. It wasn't as bad as she'd feared.

Though the cabin wasn't large, its vaulted ceiling and the
placement of the loft more than ten feet above the floor of the
main room kept the space from feeling cramped. The air inside
smelled musty, but the room looked clean and dry. Just getting
out of the damp night helped Abby feel a little better.

While the kids climbed the ladder to the loft, Kurt pulled
kindling from a box near the fireplace and smiled at her over
his shoulder. "I'll have to thank Jack for getting the place
stocked up before he left last time. We won't have to gather
any firewood until morning."

He opened the flue and cleared away old ashes from the
grate, and within minutes the fire had taken hold.

"If you want to change clothes, you might do so in the loft,"
Kurt suggested. "Let me light another lantern for you. And

here, leave this up there in case you need to go out in the
night.'' He pushed a flashlight into her hand.

Abby clasped it, but it took a few seconds for his meaning
to hit her. She felt her face grow hot with embarrassment.
"You mean…''

"The outhouse is around back. Come on, I'll show you.''
He crossed to the rear window and used the flashlight to illu-
minate a rough plank structure.

An outhouse? Her anticipation faded and grim reality returned. This was *much* worse than she'd feared.

She opened her mouth to protest, but Erin popped up behind
her, eyes bright with excitement. "This is going to be fun!''

Hiding from a maniac in a remote mountain cabin with no
running water and no decent bathroom—fun? Abby clutched
her jacket and surveyed the room once more. She really had
no alternatives at the moment, and obviously both Erin and
Michael were thrilled with everything.

She suppressed a sigh. The kids needed to keep their spirits
up, and luckily they seemed happy right now. She just had to
make the best of things. But Abby had no idea how she was
going to keep her own spirits up, her thoughts away from Kurt
and her fears under control.

WHEN MORNING DAWNED to the sound of a running brook and
the cries of birds outside the cabin, Abby stretched and forced
herself to open her eyes. She felt as if she'd been dragged
through a wringer. Though she'd slept on a small cot, her back
ached and her head pounded from listening for Vic most of the
night.

For the first time, she got a good look at the loft she and
Erin shared. It ran the length of the cabin, but was no more
than six feet in width. They'd made their beds on the end above
the kitchen, where the wooden railing had been completed. At
the other end, near the ladder, only a skeleton of the railing
had been built. The rest of the boards leaned against the wall.

Dragging herself from her sleeping bag, Abby surveyed the
floor below. Morning sunlight filtered through the trees, and
Kurt had opened the windows to let in light and air. He and

the three kids halted their conversation and turned to look at her when she reached the railing. They all glowed with health and vitality. She felt like death.

"Good morning," Kurt called. In a fresh shirt and well-worn jeans, he looked incredible. If she'd entertained any hope that she wouldn't love him in the cold light of day, she just lost it.

Abby pushed her hair out of her eyes and tried to smile. "Good morning."

"Come on down and join us. Breakfast is almost ready."

"I thought it was my turn to cook."

"You can do lunch." Though his words were innocent, his eyes burned into hers and warmth curled through her.

She stumbled backward on the uneven plank floor and threw on her clothes, shivering in the frigid air. When she climbed down the ladder, she could still feel Kurt's eyes on her.

But when she turned at the bottom, he looked away and focused on breakfast. He spooned scrambled eggs and sausage onto a plate and held it out to her. "How do you feel this morning?"

"Like dirt."

He laughed. "Eat. It'll make you feel better."

She doubted anything could work that miracle, but she accepted the plate, anyway. Kurt poured two cups of coffee and helped himself to the rest of the eggs and sausage. Abby took the cup he offered and followed him to the table near the front window where the kids had nearly finished eating.

Though Kurt's appetite seemed to have been affected positively by the mountain setting, Abby had no taste for food. She pushed her breakfast around on the plate and tried not to stare at him too blatantly. She couldn't trust herself to discuss the weather as if this were just an ordinary outing, and she certainly couldn't tell Kurt what, despite everything, was uppermost on her mind. So she said nothing.

But when she stood to help herself to a second cup of coffee, Kurt broke the silence.

"What do you say we hike up to Angel Falls this afternoon when the trail's dry?"

"A waterfall?" Erin cried, nearly jumping out of her seat.

Kurt turned an expectant face toward Abby, but she couldn't echo the girl's enthusiasm. Though she had to admit she felt less threatened by the environment now that daylight had brightened the dark corners of the forest, trekking through the mountains sounded not only exhausting, but unsafe.

She shook her head. "I don't think it's a good idea."

"Just what the doctor ordered," Kurt insisted. "Lots of fresh air and exercise. Besides, you'll love it."

"Yeah, you'll love it," Brody repeated. "We haven't been up there since you made Mom go with us."

At the mention of Laura, Kurt scowled and turned away.

But Brody didn't seem to notice. "It's so cool. All of a sudden the waterfall is *right there*. And you can get pretty close to it. Remember, Dad? Remember how scared Mom was that I'd fall in?"

"I remember." But Kurt's voice sounded flat, and Abby suspected his memory of that day didn't match Brody's.

"You can't really fall in," Brody assured Erin and Michael, "because there's a fence down by the river and you're pretty far away—far enough to be safe, anyway. But she sure was worried."

This time Abby definitely heard the wistful note in the boy's voice, a longing for a mother who cared about him. And from the look on Kurt's face, she knew that woman hadn't really existed. For the first time, she realized that Kurt and Brody would be fighting their own demons on this mountain.

Though her concerns hadn't lessened, her resolve weakened. Maybe taking a hike to Angel Falls wouldn't be too dangerous—as long as she didn't let the kids out of her sight and it wasn't too far.

"All right, you win. Rinse your plates and silverware. You can explore around the cabin this morning—but no farther. We'll go to Angel Falls after lunch."

With a shout, Michael raced toward his sleeping bag and dug into his suitcase while Brody chattered excitedly and Erin scrambled up the ladder to get her things. A few minutes later, the kids scampered outside and Abby could see them playing like puppies on the fringe of wild grass that rimmed the clearing.

Kurt wiped his mouth with his napkin and gathered his dishes as he rose, but Abby reached across the table and held his wrist. "I'll agree to take this hike with you and the kids, but I don't think it's a good idea to wander very far from the cabin."

"It's only a few miles up the road. There's an easy path—"

"That's not what I mean."

Lowering his dishes to the table, Kurt met her gaze. "Cowering inside and waiting for disaster isn't going to help. We won't go far, but if we don't keep the kids active and interested in things, they'll go crazy. And so will we."

"I agree with you—in principle. I just don't think it's very safe."

"Believe me, I know how serious the situation is or I wouldn't be here with you. I'm not going to suggest that we do anything foolish." He turned away, as if the argument was settled.

"It's not that I don't—"

He turned back, his face taut. "Don't fight me every step of the way, Abby. I have my son up here, too, and I'm not going to do anything that would put him in danger. The kids are already excited about going. Don't ruin it for them."

"I'm not trying to ruin anything. I just want to keep them safe."

"As a parent, you learn that you can't keep your children safe by hiding them. The best thing you can do for Erin and Michael is to make them aware of the danger and equip them to deal with it if it comes."

Stung, Abby looked away from him. No, she wasn't a parent. She didn't know all the correct methods for dealing with children, but she'd been with Erin and Michael for the past five weeks and she knew better than Kurt how volatile their situation really was. And though she wasn't their mother, *she* should be the one to decide what was best for them, not Kurt.

She knew he wouldn't jeopardize his son's safety, but she

hoped he wouldn't unwittingly jeopardize Michael and Erin for Brody's sake.

Pushing away from the table, Abby rose. "If I feel that our safety is being compromised, I'll bring the kids back here immediately. I might not be their mother, but I *am* capable of seeing to their well-being."

Kurt's jaw clenched and his face reddened. "Fair enough."

Immediately Abby regretted her words. What was wrong with her? Why did she challenge him when he only wanted to help? He'd hurt her with his comment about parenthood, but she knew it hadn't been intentional. She wanted to apologize for sounding so sharp with him, but any explanation would require the truth about her inability to have children. Was she ready to share that with him? She honestly didn't know.

Abby crossed the room and climbed back into the loft to retrieve her jacket. She couldn't tell him. She wasn't ready to see his interest in her die.

Not yet.

KURT WATCHED as Michael scrambled over a large boulder on the side of the path. When Brody started over it and Erin looked about to follow, he shouted, "Be careful, you guys. Stay where we can see you."

Beside him, Abby walked in silence. Though she'd hardly said a word since they'd left the cabin, she did seem a little less tightly wound. He knew how serious their situation was, but he also knew that if Abby didn't lose some of her edge, she wouldn't be able to deal with danger if it came. For now, they had a respite from the terror and he wanted to help her relax a little.

"So what do you think of our mountains?" he asked.

"They're beautiful."

"Peaceful, too. That's probably the thing I like best about being here."

"Peaceful? It's silent. Different from what I'm used to."

"That's why I had to come back. I lived in Seattle for a while, but I sure missed this country." He clambered over the boulder and turned to offer his hand to Abby, but she made the climb easily, without his help.

"So you packed up and came back to Pine Cove." Was he imagining it, or did her voice hold a challenge?

"It wasn't that simple. I met my wife while I was in law school. She wanted me to join a large firm and work my way to the top. She wanted—well, that's not important. I tried, but I never did fit in there."

Abby stared at him and fire leapt in her eyes. "Why is it that men always believe their wishes and their careers should come first? It's none of my business, I know, but why did you insist on coming back if Laura didn't want to? Couldn't you have reached some sort of compromise?"

Obviously he hadn't imagined the challenge. Battling anger and a sense of injustice, he struggled to keep his voice level. "I didn't make any snap decisions, and they certainly weren't based only on what *I* wanted. In fact, I didn't decide to come back to Pine Cove until after—" He stopped, annoyed at himself for rising to the bait and allowing her to draw him into an argument.

Abby stopped. "After what?" Shaking her head, she took a few steps away. "Forget it. It's none of my business, anyway."

Suddenly Kurt *wanted* to tell her what had happened between him and Laura, if only to vindicate himself in her eyes. "The marriage was over long before I decided to leave. I knew almost as soon as we got married that I'd made a mistake, but I kept trying to make it work. For her I stayed in a job I hated and pursued a career and a way of life I detested. I thought a compromise on my part would hold the marriage together. Until I came home early one day and found out she'd returned from a business trip ahead of schedule. I caught her in bed with a friend of ours." He stopped and looked away, taking a deep breath to blot out the memory of his pain and humiliation. "That's when I left Seattle and came back to Pine Cove. To me, it was over. But Laura insisted on following me. She still thought I was the key to her financial success and she wanted to convince me to go back with her. She thought I should be big enough to put her little infidelities behind us and concentrate on the more important things in life—like money. When I wouldn't, she finally left us.''

"She had an affair?''

"Make that plural. The one I caught her in and the one she left me for.''

"I didn't know.''

"Yeah. Well, that's all water under the bridge, isn't it? She's happy where she is, and I'm doing fine. The only thing that still makes me angry is the way she hurt Brody. He's had a terrible time coming to grips with his mother walking out on him.''

"I'm so sorry.'' She blinked rapidly, and her tears tugged at Kurt's heart.

"No need to be sorry.'' Trying to shrug off her concern, he started on the path again. "I won't make the same mistake again. I know myself better now. I know what I want to do and where I'm happy.''

"You're lucky. Most people struggle all their lives to figure that out.''

"The most important thing to me right now is what's best for Brody. He needs love and stability—the kind of life Jack's managed to give his kids. Sometimes when we're over there I see something in Brody's face that tears me apart.'' Frustrated, he stopped himself. He sounded so maudlin. He didn't want her sympathy, he wanted her love.

He was supposed to be concentrating on Abby and the kids, buoying up her spirits, not causing them to crash around her. Forcing a smile, he looked at her again. "Someday things will be different, I guess. And when Brody's got a houseful of brothers and sisters bothering him, he may wish for the good old days.''

He took Abby's hand, wanting to touch her, to strengthen the bond between them. But her hand felt limp in his. "What about you? Have you ever been married?''

"Once. A long time ago.''

He waited, wanting her to share her past with him, wanting her to trust him with it. But after a long moment, he realized she didn't intend to confide in him.

"Tell me about him," he urged.

"About Steven? He was a pharmaceutical rep. Bright. Ambitious. Handsome. Exciting, too, I guess. He swept me off my feet."

He tried to ignore the stab of jealousy. "How long were you married?"

"Three years."

She was so unresponsive. He shouldn't push—she obviously didn't want to talk about it—but now that he'd started, he had to know the rest. "What happened?"

Her eyes flew to his face, and the pain he saw there startled him.

"It just didn't work out."

He squeezed her hand, knowing how little comfort he could offer. "I'm sorry. You didn't any children?"

Abby hesitated and watched Erin and Michael round a curve in the path. "No."

Her answer surprised him. Not the word itself, but the way she snapped it out.

She remained silent for a minute, then looked up at him again. "I can't have children, and Steven wanted them—at least a son to carry on the family name. So he left and found someone who could give him what he wanted." Her voice sounded brittle.

Obviously her inability to have children had upset her husband's plans. A reaction like that, divorcing a woman simply because she couldn't give him a child, was inconceivable to Kurt. But saying so would only make her feel worse.

"And then what? After the divorce?"

"I kept working. I was a crime photographer. Homicide, then domestic violence. But I can't do it anymore. I'm too burned out. I guess I've lost my faith in human nature. I just can't witness any more violence."

"So what will you do…?" He couldn't finish the question. He couldn't make himself say, *when this is over.*

"My friend Ted called last week and told me the governor has initiated a new securities-fraud task force. He's looking for a photographer to work the stakeouts with the members of the force. Ted put in my application for a spot on it and I think my chances are pretty good. I guess the governor will decide within the next few days, and then, as long as he can wait until I've cleared up everything here, I'll go back to Baltimore and start work. I think white-collar crime is something I could work on without too much trouble.''

Kurt's stomach clenched as if Abby had punched him. From three thousand miles away Ted held the carrot that would lure Abby back to his world and leave Kurt spinning out of orbit.

"Ted." He heard the way he said the name and tried to soften it with a smile. "So this Ted—is he someone special?" He'd wanted to sound casual, but the look on her face told him he'd failed.

"Very special. But not in the way you think. After Steven left, Ted saw me through the rough times. I spent Saturday afternoons with him and his wife and kids. I went to church with them a couple of times. Thanksgiving, Christmas.''

"Sounds like the same kind of thing Jack and Theresa did for me. You were lucky to have good friends around.''

Abby sighed. "He's still looking out for me. That's why he's trying so hard to get me this job.''

The job again. Well, what had he expected? Since the day Abby had come into his life, he'd known she would leave. But hearing her actually voice her intention, he realized he'd imagined her staying. Now he had to face reality. She intended to go back to her life in Baltimore.

Trying to keep his face impassive, Kurt looked away. "It sounds interesting." He hoped his voice didn't betray his pain.

"Does it? I hope it turns out to be.''

Before he could say anything else, someone cried out from a few feet ahead, dragging his attention back to the kids. At the top of the path, Brody waved his arms excitedly and pointed. "Dad? Dad, look!"

They'd arrived at the waterfall. At least he still had Brody. Things were a little better between them today; getting away from home and the office seemed to be doing his relationship with his son some good. He shouldn't have let himself get so caught up in Abby's spell, though. He should have known not to pin his hopes on something as fragile as his fantasy of a future with her. From here on out, he'd concentrate on Brody and forget his silly romantic dreams.

But he couldn't make himself release Abby's hand. Instead, he guided her up the path toward the kids. "Can you see it?" he called out to Brody.

Brody nodded and pointed again. As they neared the place where the children stood, the water changed its voice. No longer sliding lightly across the polished stones in the riverbed, it began to churn, then to roar. And by the time they reached Brody's side, Angel Falls appeared like an apparition out of the mist.

As always, the sight took Kurt's breath away. White water thundered down the rock face, boiling over the rocks below before running away downstream. It seemed to echo his own unsettled feelings.

He sensed, rather than heard, Abby's indrawn breath, and he saw the look of wonder in her eyes. Rationally he knew he should distance himself, but he wanted to share this with her. He wanted her to love it as he did. He pulled her close, and when she smiled up at him, he knew she belonged beside him and he *couldn't* let her go.

No matter what it took, no matter what sacrifices he had to make, she was his future. And he was hers. Now he just had to find a way to convince her.

Abby knew that as she surrendered her hand to Kurt, the gesture had far more meaning to her than he could possibly imagine. When he touched her, a tingling warmth started low inside her. When he smiled, her pulse raced.

Hearing him talk about the end of his marriage had made her heart ache, and sharing a part of her past with him had opened a piece of herself she'd closed off long ago.

She loved him. And she didn't want to leave him. But the life he envisioned, a house full of brothers and sisters for Brody, was something she could never give him. And the pain of knowing she had to go made her feel as if she'd been torn in two.

In silence she watched the falls thunder over the side of the

mountain and felt the churning water at the base of the river
in her soul. In fairy tales, the heroine always ended up with
her heart's desire. In life, it rarely happened.

As much as she wanted this scene to continue forever, common sense told her it couldn't. Still, she kept her hand in the
warmth and security of Kurt's larger one. She allowed herself
this moment to stand beside him and feel the heat emanating
from him, to drink in his utterly masculine scent, to burn where
he brushed against her. This would be a memory she could
take home with her, something bittersweet she could draw on
during the lonely nights that lay ahead.

Closing her eyes, she let herself remember his kiss under the
fiery sky on the Fourth of July. She felt again her breasts
pressed against him and his arms around her....

"Abby? Dad? Hurry up." Brody's shout brought Abby back
out of her dream with a jolt. Reluctantly she opened her eyes
and drew her hand from Kurt's.

The children scrambled down the rocky hillside toward the
riverbank. The boys nearly fell over each other in their excitement, and even Erin got caught up in it. Halfway down the
hill, the girl sprinted ahead of the boys and was the first to
reach a clearing some distance from the base of the falls. Turning, she waved her arms, beckoning to Abby and Kurt.

Kurt started down the path, his back to Abby, but she could
tell by the tilt of his head he was still very much aware of her.

If she didn't follow, he'd return for her. And he'd want to
know what was bothering her. Pushing aside her doubts and
sadness, Abby concentrated on getting herself down the side
of the hill.

CHAPTER FOURTEEN

THAT NIGHT Abby listened to the crackling fire, waiting for a
clue that Kurt had gone to sleep. Stuck in this loft high above
the cabin floor, she felt confined—claustrophobic. And she
couldn't stop her mind from churning. While half of her wanted
Kurt to sweep her into his arms and beg her to stay with him,
the more practical side realized it would never work. Kurt
wanted more than Abby could ever give him, and though she
might convince herself she could love him enough to make
him forget his dreams of more children, realistically she knew
it wasn't possible.

When several minutes passed and she hadn't heard anything
to indicate that anyone else was still awake, she inched out of
her sleeping bag and strained to look through the narrow slats
of wood into the room below. Firelight leapt and painted the
walls orange and yellow, leaving the corners black where shadows played.

She needed to escape for a few minutes, to gather her
thoughts and come to terms with all her conflicting emotions.
Tiptoeing toward the ladder, she descended quietly and crept
across the room. Pulling open the front door, she slipped into
the darkness and waited for her eyes to adjust.

In contrast to the heated cabin, the frigid air outside bit into
her. Shivering, she rubbed her arms and walked to the edge of
the small porch, scanning the darkened landscape.

In just twenty-four hours she'd actually started to enjoy it
here. She breathed in the aroma of pine and relived the delighted shrieks of the kids at the falls earlier.

She reminded herself sternly that she belonged in Baltimore,
not in the mountains of Washington. She needed the satisfac-

tion she derived from doing a job well, the fulfillment that came from the professional recognition of her abilities. But when had she started hating the idea of going back? And when had she allowed herself to fall in love with Kurt and dream of staying?

Sitting down on the step, she listened to the peculiar silence of the forest. She didn't feel frightened tonight, even though the isolation of this spot still bothered her a little. It helped to have Kurt close.

She wasn't sure how long she sat staring at the tops of the trees, listening to them sway in the slight breeze, before a twig snapped near the corner of the cabin. Stiffening, she turned toward the sound.

Kurt came into view. Her pulse raced and she pushed herself to her feet. He stopped when he caught sight of her, hesitating only a moment. "What are you doing out here?"

"I couldn't sleep."

"Anything I can do?"

She could think of a lot of things, but nothing she could ask for, especially with the kids a few feet away. "Find me a shower."

He laughed and tossed a towel, gleaming white in the moonlight, over one shoulder. "You could always go down to the creek, but the water's freezing."

"I might do it, anyway."

He narrowed the distance between them, coming close enough for her to smell the faint aroma of his soap. When the cry of a night creature split the silence, a chill ran through her. Shuddering, she hugged her arms around herself and saw Kurt staring at her.

"You're cold. Are you sure you don't want to go back inside?"

"I'd rather stay out here for a few minutes." She wanted to turn away, but his gaze held her.

When she didn't move, he stepped closer. Even in the dim moonlight, the look in his eyes made her tingle. "The kids enjoyed themselves today," he said softly.

"Yes, they did."

"And did you?" He took another step.

Her heart hammered in her chest and she knew he must be able to sense her confusion. "I—"

He took her hands in his. "*I* had a wonderful time."

There was so much she wanted to say, but his touch left her tongue-tied. When she couldn't answer, he pulled her into his arms, touching his lips to her temple.

He nuzzled her as he brushed his lips down her cheek until he found her mouth. His scent surrounded her and she felt as if she were drowning.

When his lips settled on hers, fire leapt inside her. Her lips parted, welcoming him. With a low groan in the back of his throat, he shifted and held her tighter. Where they touched, even beneath her clothing, her skin burned.

Abby lost her power to pull away. Love surged within her and with it the desire to make her future with Kurt.

His tongue brushed her lips and she held her breath, as if breathing might break the spell and lessen the sensation. Gently he lifted her arms to his shoulders and she indulged herself, running her hands across the steel band of muscles beneath her fingers. Lowering his own hands, he touched her lightly on the sides, moving his hands inward until he nearly touched her breasts. But there he stopped, and Abby felt herself straining toward him, longing for more.

His kiss deepened and his tongue moved between her lips. Abby opened herself to him, accepting the warmth of his mouth, the almost sinful pleasure of his tongue touching hers.

Every nerve in her body screamed for him, cried for his hands to caress her, for his desire to equal her own. She wanted him to say something, to tell her he needed her and beg her to stay. She wanted him to love her and want her as much as she loved and wanted him. But even after the kiss ended, he didn't speak, and his silence left her suspended between desire and fulfillment.

Slowly Abby realized that he was holding back. His touch might rob her of reason, but she apparently did not affect him the same way. "I—I really should go in." she said softly.

Kurt held her hand and tried to keep her from leaving, but she pulled away and turned, forcing her legs to hold her up and her eyes to stop burning with tears of humiliation. Though she would have given herself to him here and now, he didn't want her. And rather than resolving her hurt and confusion, she was more confused than ever.

Shaking, she shut the door behind her, leaning her back against it for a second or two until she could trust her knees to carry her across the room.

Kurt watched the door close, unable to say anything to make Abby stay beside him. Despite the demands of his body, he'd forced himself to release her and step away. He'd wanted to lift her and carry her away, to lose himself in her. But simply making love to her wouldn't be enough.

No matter how badly he wanted her to stay, stacking the deck with sex wasn't how he wanted to win her. He needed her to stay because she loved him.

He watched her shadow cross between the flickering fire and the window, and his heart burned with the urge to follow her and make her his. No woman had ever felt so right in his arms. No one had ever captured his heart so completely. Desire had never torn him apart the way it did tonight.

Could he let her go back to Baltimore? No. Whether or not she knew it, they were meant for each other.

He stood for a while in the moonlight, giving her plenty of time to climb back to the loft and into bed. She hadn't said a lot about her marriage, but he knew she'd been hurt badly by her husband. Erin and Michael weren't the only ones with wounds to heal, and Kurt could be a patient man when he had to be.

Especially when the stakes were high enough.

ABBY RELUCTANTLY abandoned her hold on sleep and gave in to the enticing aroma of frying bacon, Kurt's deep baritone voice and the happy shouts of the children. Stretching in the clear morning sunlight that streamed through the tiny window, she awoke slowly. She marveled that after just four nights in this loft, she'd almost gotten used to it.

Yesterday Kurt had lugged an old washtub out of a shed on

the edge of the property and she'd actually been able to take a warm bath and wash some of their clothing. Heaven.

In the past three days, Kurt hadn't referred to the embarrassing topic of their kiss, and Abby was almost able to forget it had ever happened. And it nearly worked—except when she closed her eyes, smelled his soap, heard his voice or accidentally brushed against him.

She crawled out of her sleeping bag and pulled on clean jeans and her Hard Rock Café sweatshirt. Last night Kurt had promised the kids he'd take them back to Angel Falls this morning, and Abby surprised herself by feeling almost eager to go along.

After four days without any sign of Vic, some of her fears were already starting to evaporate. While her apprehension hadn't completely disappeared, she felt safer than she had in months.

As each day dawned to the sound of birds staking their territory and other woodland creatures chattering in the heavy stillness, her jangled nerves quieted more and more. Kurt had been right. Here in the woods they'd immediately notice the movement of any unexpected visitor. If they'd gone to a large city, Vic could have found them and watched them for days without her knowing it.

To further calm her fears, Kurt made a circuit of the property three times a day looking for signs that someone else had been here. So far, he'd found nothing.

Brushing her hair quickly into a ponytail, she descended to the main room for breakfast. Erin stood at Kurt's side, as usual, her face intent as he counted bacon strips onto five plates. Becoming aware of Abby's presence first, Erin grinned broadly. "Are you going to Angel Falls with us?"

"I suppose I will." Abby stopped by the fireplace and picked up a log, adding it to the blaze. "We're running low on wood. Maybe I ought to bring some in."

Kurt looked up and smiled, and when the now familiar lines appeared around his eyes, Abby's heart skipped a beat.

"I'll bring it in after we get back," he said, and turned to

Erin. "What do you say we make scrambled eggs, instead, so
we can get out of here fast?"

Erin nodded and rummaged through the cooler. After several
minutes, she held out an egg carton. "I think these are the last
ones and somebody drank all the milk."

"Then I'm going to have to head into town for some more
food and ice this afternoon." Kurt cracked two eggs at once
and dropped them into a bowl.

Kurt leave? Abby had known they didn't have enough food
to last long, but the thought of giving away their location made
her weak with fear.

"Then we should all go." She tried to keep her voice level
so she didn't startle Erin.

Kurt shook his head. "I think you and the kids should stay
here. I'll go after lunch and be back before dark. Do you think
you can wait for the firewood until I get back?"

Though she realized he was right, panic knotted her stomach
and a lump formed in her throat. If Vic managed to follow
them as far as the town, he wouldn't necessarily recognize
Kurt. But if they all went together, they might give themselves
away. Still, she didn't like the idea of Kurt's leaving them
alone.

"Where do you have to go?"

"Milford. It's about fifty miles away."

She turned so he wouldn't see the fear in her eyes. Fifty
miles! On these rutted roads? If he didn't leave until after
lunch, he'd be lucky to return before dark. It would be much
better to have him gone for hours during the daylight and back
before the sun set. "Maybe you ought to start now."

"What about our trip to Angel Falls?"

"We can do it tomorrow."

"Okay," Kurt said uncertainly. "I'll tell the boys."

Erin groaned in protest. "Why can't we go ourselves?"

Under any other circumstances, Abby would've agreed. But
a vague sense of uneasiness warned her not to give in. Pushing
the thought away, she told herself she was just feeling nervous
at the idea of being here without Kurt.

Nothing had happened to them yet. Angel Falls wasn't far

and the path was fairly easy. She and the kids could make the trip without trouble, and it would keep all their minds off Kurt's absence.

"Fine," she said with a forced smile. "We'll go today. Call the boys in and let's eat."

Erin dashed toward the door and Abby reached for the stack of plates, but Kurt's hand arrested hers. "Maybe you shouldn't—"

"We'll be fine."

"I don't know, Abby. I—"

Withdrawing her hand, Abby forced herself to meet his eyes. "We'll be fine, Kurt. You were the one who told me we shouldn't hide here waiting for disaster. Well, you were right. You go after the supplies and I'll keep the kids occupied."

When he didn't look away, Abby made herself move. She placed the plates and cutlery on the table before turning back to him. "We'll be fine. Really. Would you stop worrying?"

She meant her words to sound light, to maybe bring a smile to his lips.

His face lightened a little. "Promise you'll be careful?"

"Of course."

"I guess I'm worrying about nothing."

"You are."

He smiled. "Anything special you want from town?"

"From Milford? Do you think they have any decent caviar?"

This time he laughed. "Absolutely. I'll bring you a case."

"And champagne."

"And candles?"

His eyes glinted and Abby shivered at the warmth in them. Ducking his head, he brushed her lips lightly. The brief kiss took her breath away, and even after he'd climbed into the Cherokee and driven off, Abby couldn't stop the thudding of her heart.

KURT LOOKED OUT the window of the small general store and watched the pouring rain. The sky had darkened ominously and the rain had started before he'd reached Milford. A storm could last forever in this country, and every minute he waited in town lessened his chances of making it back up the mountain. But gut instinct warned him not to start the return trip without getting through to Doug Pierce.

Over the past hour he'd tried four times, and so far he'd been unsuccessful. He'd wait another fifteen minutes and try again.

Rain, propelled by a sudden gust of wind, battered the window. Behind him, the clerk shifted something heavy and dropped it to the floor with a thud. "Better figure on settling in for a while," the man warned. "You ain't going nowhere on these roads."

Under normal circumstances, Kurt would agree. He'd grab some coffee and a book and watch the storm from inside. But not today. It might not be wise, but he'd have to start back soon. He could only hope the Cherokee's four-wheel drive would be enough to pull him back up the mountain.

"That wind's whipping up pretty bad. Maybe you ought to try your call again before the lines go down."

He hadn't thought of that. He *had* to get through to someone in Pine Cove. Abandoning his plan to wait, Kurt left his vantage point by the window and crossed the rough plank floor to the back of the store. With an urgency he didn't entirely understand, he punched the numbers from his calling card, then the number of the sheriff's station.

Wind rattled the window again and the lights flickered. Willing Doug—or anyone—to pick up, Kurt counted the rings. After eight, he broke the connection and repeated the procedure using Jack's home number.

This time he was rewarded with an answer almost immediately as Sara's voice floated to him through the storm. "Uncle Kurt! Are you back? Why didn't you let me go with you? I *love* the cabin."

"I couldn't bring you this time, sweetheart. Maybe next time, okay? Is your dad there?"

"No, but you'll never guess what. I still can't believe it. Guess where my dad is...."

"Where?"

"At Abby Harris's house. You'll never believe what happened."

All the misgivings he'd battled throughout the day returned, magnified by Sara's excitement. He clutched the receiver, trying to keep his voice steady. "What?"

"Dad went over there this morning and found one of the back windows broken."

"From the storm?"

"No. Somebody broke in. Can you *believe* it?"

A sick terror filled Kurt. "Are you sure?"

"Positive. Dad found something inside that made him think somebody had been in there."

"What was it?"

"I don't know. I'm not even supposed to know that much. You won't tell, will you? Dad told us to go upstairs and clean our rooms, but I wanted to read my book so I came back down...."

Fighting to steady himself, Kurt pressed one palm against the wall and closed his eyes. "Maybe I ought to call your dad over there."

"You can't. I heard him say the telephone had been ripped out of the wall. Isn't that weird? I mean, who would do something like that *here?* It's like we're living in L.A. or something, don't you think?"

Pictures of Abby and the kids, hurt or held hostage, whirled through Kurt's mind. With the realization of how narrowly they'd escaped, nausea rose in his throat. "Is Doug Pierce over there with your dad?"

"I don't know. Maybe."

"Listen, Sara," he began shakily, then stopped and forced his voice to a steadier pitch. "Can you find Doug and give him a message for me?"

"I can't go anywhere. I'm supposed to stay here and watch the little monsters."

"Okay. Where's your mom?"

"With Aunt Zelda, I think."

Damn. Of all places. Sweat dripped from his brow into his eyes and he blinked. Wiping his shirtsleeve across his forehead, he thought quickly. He had to get a message to Doug and find out the details of the break-in. Worst of all, he'd have to carry this news back to Abby.

Praying that the phone lines would stay up long enough for one more call, he dialed Zelda's number. On the third ring, Theresa answered.

"Kurt! I'm so glad to hear your voice." The line crackled and Theresa's voice faded out and back in.

"What's going on down there?" he shouted over the static.

"Somebody's been in Abby's house. Doug's over there now and they've called everybody in, but whoever it was got away. Are you all okay?"

"We're fine. Are there any leads?"

The line crackled again and he had trouble hearing Theresa's answer.

"I can't hear you," he said.

"It's got to be the kids' father. Zelda told me somebody claiming to be Abby's husband came by here this morning looking for her." Theresa's voice rose as she shouted to be heard over the interference.

Sick dread formed a tight knot in Kurt's stomach. "What did she tell him?"

The line buzzed and for one dreadful moment he thought he'd lost her, but the connection cleared and Theresa shouted, "...get out of there now. Sara told her you'd taken Abby and the kids to the cabin..."

"What? Theresa?"

No answer. The line had gone dead.

He pounded the telephone with the palm of his hand, as if sheer force could restore the connection.

Nothing.

Zelda must have directed Vic to the cabin, thinking she was reuniting Abby with her husband and the kids with their father. Slamming the receiver into its cradle, Kurt raced through the store and out into the rain.

Fumbling with the ignition, he wasted precious seconds trying to get the Cherokee started. He'd known Abby and the kids faced potential danger, but he hadn't believed Vic would find them here.

His mind raced with questions as he sped through town and started back up the mountain. How long ago had Vic left Pine Cove? What was he driving? Had he stopped anywhere along the way? Was he armed?

Had Kurt been wise to insist they go to the cabin? Maybe he should've let Abby leave the area as she'd wanted. Would he be able to protect them? And if not—if anything happened to either of those kids—would Abby ever forgive him for bringing them up here? Would he ever forgive himself?

"DON'T GO any farther away than that," Abby called as Brody rounded a curve in the path ahead of her. Though she knew they weren't taking any unnecessary chances, she still felt a little uneasy.

Michael turned and waved his arms. "Hurry, Abby. We want to go faster."

Stepping up her pace a little, she met Michael as he jogged down the path and joined her, his eyes bright, his smile wide. "This is great. I love this place. When I grow up, I'm gonna move back and live here forever."

"And I'll come visit you every summer."

"Will you really? I want to build my mom a cabin right next door to mine. Right up by the falls."

"She'll like that." Abby put an arm around Michael's shoulders and hugged him to her.

She'd been right to take the kids on this hike. If they'd waited all day back at the cabin for Kurt to return, they'd have gone stir-crazy. And Abby would've done nothing but think about him—and worry—all day.

She drew in a deep breath of the forest's earthy scent and reluctantly admitted that, given a few millennia, she might come to like the outdoors. Ferns and greenery of every kind grew out to the path, even over it in some spots. This time, she'd brought her camera along and she intended to get a few close-ups of some of the incredible undergrowth.

Not far from here they'd seen a small field of wildflowers

she wanted to shoot. Attaching her teleconverter lens, she set
the F-stop and adjusted the shutter speed. She wouldn't make
the kids wait long—just a few shots as an experiment. Maybe
when all this was over, she'd take up photographing nature as
a hobby.

Strangely the shutter speed felt wrong. Too short. She
glanced up, wondering whether the sun had gone behind a
cloud. What she saw sent a chill down her spine. Instead of
the harmless cumulus clouds she'd expected, dark thunder
clouds covered the sky. In the distance came a foreboding rumble.

She removed the lens and put it in her case. "We'd better
go back. It sounds like rain."

"Can we go just a little farther?" Brody begged.

"I don't think we should."

Erin shielded her eyes and looked into the sky. "The clouds
are so faraway."

"They don't look all that far to me." Abby returned her
camera to the case as a gust of wind lifted her hair and rustled
the leaves on the trees overhead. If it started to rain the way it
had the night they'd arrived, they could be in serious trouble.
"No. This is it, we can't go any farther."

Abby didn't think they'd gone more than a mile or so from
the cabin, but it was already dark as twilight, even though a
quick glance at her watch confirmed it was still early afternoon.

Before long, rain slashed at them with the fury of a winter
storm; needle-sharp raindrops chilled by the wind assaulted
them. Abby dragged her jacket around her camera and tugged
the zipper up to her chin. But the cold rain burned her hands
and numbed her fingers. She dug her fists into her pocket, only
to nearly lose her balance without the steadying use of her arms
on the uneven path.

Within minutes the path turned to mud, slippery beneath
their feet and making walking difficult. She felt as if she'd been
fighting the storm for an hour. By the time they reached the
steepest incline on the path, frustration filled her when she realized what a short distance they'd actually come.

A gust of wind tore out of the mouth of the canyon, and

Abby nearly lost her balance. She had to get the kids inside where they could dry off and change into warm clothing.

Gesturing for Brody and Michael to go in front, Abby stayed at Erin's side on the narrow path as they worked their way down the mountain. The sky teemed with rolling gray clouds and wind slashed their faces with pellets of rain. Abby's hands, exposed to the elements as she hugged Erin to bolster the girl's flagging courage, had long ago lost their feeling.

Erin trembled under Abby's arm, from cold or fear—or both—and Michael's face, reddened by the wind and rain, had taken on a grim expression.

Brody radiated anxiety, but he turned and looked at Abby and squeezed her arm, as if sensing her unhappiness. "We're almost there, don't worry."

"I'm fine."

Giving her a quick once-over, he managed a smile. "Yeah, I can see that."

In spite of her near-frozen state, Abby smiled back. "I look that good, do I?"

With a shrug Brody turned away and lunged up another short incline. "The cabin's just over this hill."

"It is!" Michael shouted, "I know it."

Knowing they neared the end of their journey gave them all fresh energy, and within just a few minutes they reached the cabin. But when she remembered how low their supply of firewood was, Abby's heart sank. "We'd better bring in some dry wood from the shed before we go inside."

"Okay." Obviously not as worn-out as Abby, Brody raced off, and Michael followed him across the clearing.

Erin started after them. "I'm coming, too."

With shelter only a few feet away, the cold seemed even more intense as Abby forced herself to follow them. Inside the shed, she quickly stacked firewood into Brody's outstretched arms and piled a similar bundle into Michael's. Though she didn't want to overload them, she didn't want to have to come back out into this storm in the middle of the night for more wood, either.

Ducking back outside, the boys started toward the cabin as

Abby settled Erin's load and gathered several large logs to carry back herself.

Even under the weight of the logs, she managed to catch up with the boys a few feet from the cabin. "Come on, guys. Let's get inside quickly. I'm freezing."

Abby lowered the logs to the porch and drew the key from her pocket. But when she fit the key in the lock, the door creaked open on its own. All this talk about being careful and she hadn't even made sure they'd pulled the door fully closed when they left this morning.

She pushed the door open the rest of the way and tried to make out the kerosene lantern on the table. But even in the dim light, she could see that the lantern wasn't where she'd left it. A cold chill crept up her back. Something was wrong.

As she turned to the kids, a shadow near the fireplace caught her attention. An alarm screamed its warning in the back of her mind. Something—or someone—was in there. Scarcely daring to breathe, Abby searched the shadows for signs of movement.

Fear dried her throat and pulsed blood through her veins with a thunderous rush. Panic rose like bile in her throat. "Run!" she shouted, shoving Erin toward the door. "Get out of here!"

With a crash, the shadow moved and a man lunged toward her. Even in the half-light of the storm, Abby could see his wild eyes as he swung a gun in her direction. Like a cannon, the barrel of the .357 Magnum loomed into her vision, blocking everything else for a moment. Beside her, the kids froze in place.

"It's about time you came back."

Anger robbed his face of softness and left him looking ugly. He'd changed since she'd last seen him. Thin almost to the point of emaciation, he still had thick black hair, but now a swatch of graying whiskers cupped his chin. Her heart pounded high in her throat as Abby met his black eyes, and she shuddered at the emptiness there.

"So you thought you could steal my kids from me." Crossing the small room in three heavy strides, he pointed the barrel into Abby's face, then nuzzled it against her temple.

"Tell me, what did you think you were going to do? How did you think you'd get away with it?"

With a clarity of mind that surprised her, Abby watched the gun out of the corner of her eye. So this was it, the moment she'd feared for so long. Funny that she didn't feel as terrified as she'd imagined. As if time stood still, she waited for Vic's next move.

She stood little chance of protecting the children from this maniac without a weapon. She wanted to tell him to go to hell or refuse to answer him. But with a certainty she couldn't explain, she knew he would kill her if she did.

Though she felt no immediate fear at the thought she might die, the idea of Erin and Michael being at this man's mercy horrified her. Like a silent film, pictures of them flashed before her and she saw them living empty desolate lives full of despair.

Vic studied her with his soulless black eyes and prodded her with the gun. Without her, the children had no hope of escape. If she died trying to protect them, Vic would end up with them, anyway. Knowing others might condemn her for giving in, Abby met Vic's gaze. She'd do whatever it took. She had to remain alive for the children.

THE WHEELS CHURNED helplessly as Kurt stepped again on the gas pedal, spraying the back window with chunks of black mud. Swearing aloud, he shifted gears and pressed the accelerator, but the Cherokee refused to budge. If anything, it settled further into the bog.

Damn! Kurt shoved the door open and jumped out onto the hillside, nearly losing his balance. Gripping the handle, he barely managed to keep himself upright. He struggled up the short incline to the road and searched the landscape. The turnoff to the Warners' cabin was just ahead, which meant he was less than a mile from home.

He began to run, praying that Vic hadn't beat him up the mountain. Rain poured from the sky, and the afternoon light faded steadily as Kurt followed the track through the woods.

He'd passed the turnoff to the Warner place before he noticed a deep rut in the mud, slowly filling in with rain.

Someone else had passed this way not long ago.

Sweating in spite of the cold, he raced along the tracks left by the other vehicle and wound his way into the heart of the mountains. Driving himself harder than he would've believed possible, he ran to the rhythm of his frantic heartbeat.

He longed for the warmth of the cabin, for the sweet smell of Abby's shampoo when she passed him, and the comforting feeling of home he'd felt the past few days. He ached for the reassurance that he'd have it all again, and that he'd be in time to get Abby and the kids away before Vic found them.

The rain fell more heavily and he pulled the hood of his jacket over his head. Just ahead the road split, and he knew he'd be home in less than ten minutes.

On a level path now, he increased his pace. Lightning lit the sky and thunder crashed. He followed the road across the valley, running parallel to the deeply rutted track for several feet before he realized the other vehicle had also come this way.

This fork of the road ended just past the cabin. Nobody else had any reason to turn up here.

Sick with dread, Kurt tried to reassure himself that the tracks belonged to Howard Warner's four-wheel drive. But when he reached the cutoff to the cabin and the tracks followed it, his heart plummeted.

Nearly blind with panic, Kurt pushed himself up the trail. Heavy with moisture, branches hung low over the drive, obscuring his already limited vision. When lightning flashed again, he saw a dark-bodied truck in a narrow clearing out of sight of the cabin.

Kurt crept off the path and into the trees. He tried to tell himself the truck belonged to someone who just wanted to wait out the storm. But he couldn't convince himself. An innocent visitor would've parked in the clearing; this truck was purposefully hidden from view.

Kurt crept closer to the cabin, skirting the clearing and staying in the shadows of the trees. Though lantern light shone through the chinks in the shutters, something felt wrong. He watched the cabin closely, but when several minutes passed and he still hadn't seen any sign of normal activity inside, his worry grew.

Rain whipped at him with heightened fury as the wind rose again. What now? If Vic had found them, Kurt had to assume he carried a weapon. Without one of his own, he was no match for the other man.

The Warner place was too far for him to reach in time to save Abby and the kids. Why hadn't they put in a telephone line up here? Why had they insisted on keeping the place so rustic?

Sick to his stomach, Kurt didn't dare cross the open clearing. Refusing to give thought to the fear that something had happened to Abby or the kids, he crept closer still, taking care to stay in the shadows.

If his worst suspicions were correct, one error in judgment could cost at least one of the lives of the people he loved most.

CHAPTER FIFTEEN

"WHO ARE YOU?"

"Brody."

"Brody? *Brody?* What kind of punk name is that?"

"Dad…" Michael sidled closer to his friend.

Vic ignored him and kept his eyes riveted on Brody. "What are you doing here with my kids?"

"Nothing."

With a powerful backhand, Vic sent Brody stumbling toward the fireplace where he nearly hit his head on the rock hearth. "What are you doing here?" he demanded again.

Erin screamed and would have run to Brody, but Vic stopped her and pushed her onto the couch beside Abby.

"Sit down and shut up." He wiped the back of his mouth with his sleeve and chuckled. "Girls, huh, Mike? Worthless." He whirled back around to Erin and jabbed one finger at her. "Just like your damned mother, aren't you? Always sticking your nose in where it doesn't belong. And you—" he pointed at Abby "—you just don't know when to keep out of things that don't concern you, do you?"

As a member of the police force, Abby had attended a number of seminars on domestic violence over the years, and she'd heard the officers give advice to women. Standard counsel included the warning that each incident was different and only the woman involved could weigh the situation to determine her appropriate line of defense, if any. And it had always sounded so easy—until now.

But nothing she'd read, nothing she'd seen before, prepared her for the absolute terror of such incoherent rage being directed at her. Frightened almost beyond rational thought, she still had to protect the children.

Anything she said might antagonize Vic enough to use the gun. So might her silence. No wonder many women stayed with abusive partners. After just a few minutes, Abby already felt her options closing off.

But she wouldn't give up. There must be *something* she could say or do to strike a spark of decency in him. But if there was, it eluded her.

With one last hate-filled glance in her direction, Vic turned back to Brody.

"Don't hurt him," Abby whispered.

"Shut up!" Vic whipped his gun around and shoved the barrel in her face again. "Just shut up before I kill you right here and now."

Beside her, Erin whimpered. But when Vic tore his eyes away from Abby and sent his daughter a venomous look, Erin withered and began to sob quietly.

Vic's hand trembled and the gun shook in Abby's face.

"Don't do this," she pleaded. "Not in front of the children."

"What's the matter? You scared? Why shouldn't I kill you? Why shouldn't I make you suffer like I suffered when you stole my children?"

"Not in front of the children, Vic. They've been through too much already."

"And whose fault is that? Huh? Whose damned fault is that? *You* stole my kids and hid them from me. *You're* the one who's put them through all this." Vic dug a pint-size bourbon bottle from his pocket and downed a shot. "Well, guess who's got the upper hand this time. Not you. This time you're playing *my* game."

Shoving the gun under her chin, he forced her to look up at him. He leaned closer, breathing heavily and sizing her up. The smell of his breath sickened Abby, but she fought to keep her face expressionless.

"What are you going to do now?" Vic grabbed her chin with his hand, squeezed painfully, and shoved her backward.

Erin cried out as though she'd been struck.

"Can't you see what you're doing to these kids?" Abby tried again. "You say you want them back because you love them. How can you give so little thought to what you're putting them through?"

"They're *my* damn children. Don't you tell me what I can and can't do. They *belong* to me. You stole them from me." He took another belt from the bottle and wiped his mouth with the back of his hand, staring around the room with hate-glazed eyes.

"They're not your children any longer. The courts—"

"To hell with the courts. To hell with the judges. And to hell with *you*."

"I just want what's best for Erin and Michael. Look at them. They're scared half to death."

"Scared like little babies." Vic glanced at Erin cowering into the couch. With a shout of fury, he turned to Michael. "What are you scared of?"

"N-nothing."

"Are you scared, boy?"

"No."

Abby could see Michael trembling and could hear his voice falter, but the answer seemed to satisfy Vic.

A second later, he became aware of Brody again. Abby's heart thumped sickly in her chest as she willed Vic to look away from the innocent boy.

"Vic—"

He ignored her and gestured toward Brody with the gun. "Who'd you say the little bastard over there is?"

"A friend of Michael's," Abby answered quickly.

"Is that so? Is that your friend, Mike?"

Michael nodded, but fear played across his features.

Even if Vic only got like this when he drank, how had these children survived all those years under his roof? How had Rachel?

"So what's he doing up here?" Vic lifted the bottle again.

Michael's eyes widened. "N-nothing. I mean he's up here with—"

"I brought him up here with us," Abby interrupted. "Michael wanted him to come." She didn't think Vic knew about Kurt, and she wanted to keep it that way as long as she could.

"You wanted your little friend up here with you?"

Michael nodded.

"What's the matter, boy? Didn't I teach you to be a man? You don't need some stupid friend to hold your hand, do you?"

Trembling with fear, Michael met Vic's gaze squarely and shook his head.

"Little mama's boy now, are you?" Vic gestured at Abby with the hand that held the gun. "*She's* the one who's taught you to be weak, isn't she? Turning you into a wimp who needs his little friend to sit with. Well, we'll fix that, boy. When we get out of here—"

"No." Without warning, Michael jumped to his feet. His eyes brimmed with tears, but his face had darkened in anger.

Vic lowered the bottle and glared at the boy. "What the hell did you say?"

"I'm not leaving here with you. I don't want to go anywhere with you." Michael turned and tried to run for the door.

Lunging, Vic grabbed Michael's collar, and as if the boy were no more than a rag doll, Vic dragged him back and shook him in Abby's face. "This is *your* fault. You turned my boy against me. You brought him up here and made him into a little priss and now just *look* what I've got for a son. He's no damned good."

"Vic, please. Leave him alone." Abby shot to her feet. She had to do something, but what?

"He's no damned good to me now." Shoving Michael away, Vic struck Abby across the face with the back of his hand. She collapsed onto the cushions. Her cheek stung and her lip throbbed and the salty-sweet taste of blood in her mouth nauseated her.

In a blur of motion, Michael leapt at Vic, striking his back and shoulders. As Michael landed one blow after another, Abby vaulted to her feet. Michael couldn't possibly hit Vic hard enough to hurt him, but the man could easily kill the child.

Hoping Michael could keep up the distraction long enough for her to get between them, Abby charged Vic, but he twisted away before she reached him.

Vic caught Michael's arm, twisting viciously as he peeled the boy from his back. For one sickening moment, Abby thought Vic would throw Michael across the room, but before he could, Erin launched herself from her seat.

"Leave him alone!" she screamed, and ran at Vic as if she intended to attack him.

Obviously unprepared for the assault from his children, Vic let loose a barrage of obscenities. Abby searched desperately for something she could do to protect them all. She needed a weapon, something she could throw or use to hit him with.

She scanned the cabin quickly and saw the heavy cast-iron skillet across the room on the table. She might be able to reach it before he shot her.

But after only two steps Vic grabbed her by the arm and dragged her toward him, shoving the barrel of the gun into her face again. "Don't even think about it."

"Vic, please. Can't you see what you're doing to the kids? They're scared to death. Please—"

His fist descended before she could turn her face, and a scream tore from her throat, sounding strangely faraway as she slid out of his grip and slipped to the floor.

CROUCHED BENEATH the window, Kurt strained to hear the sounds from the cabin over the increasing gale of the storm. He wanted to believe that the kids and Abby were safe, but instinct told him otherwise. If he moved too fast, he might jeopardize them. But if he waited too long...

He just needed a look inside; at least then he'd know what he was up against. But with the shutters closed, he could only rely on what little he could hear over the storm.

Had they pulled the kitchen curtains closed, also? Maybe if he went around to the back of the cabin he'd be able to see inside from there.

As he turned, the sound of raised voices reached him clearly over the wind, followed by a scream. He couldn't wait any longer. He had to get inside—now.

He took the front steps two at a time and grabbed up a piece of firewood as he hit the door with his shoulder and turned the knob. Surprisingly it opened easily, and suddenly he was inside.

In a split second he took in the scene before him. Brody, pale and shocked, cowered near the fireplace. Michael and Erin clung to each other near the window. Abby lay on the floor, her face swollen and bloody, and a man with a gun stood over her.

Vic.

Kurt launched himself at the other man. He wanted the son of a bitch dead, and *he* wanted to be the one to kill him. He swung the log, but at the last moment, Vic reeled away and Kurt brought the wood down harmlessly on the side of the table.

Behind him, Kurt heard Abby frantically urging the kids outside to safety. He swung the wood again and again, longing to connect with flesh and bone, needing to keep Vic distracted while the kids got out.

"Keep the hell away from me." Vic rushed at Kurt, hitting his arm with a shoulder, dislodging the wood and sending it skittering across the floor.

Kurt charged again. This time, he caught Vic under the chin with his fist, and satisfaction ripped through him as he felt Vic's head snap back.

Vic staggered, nearly falling over a chair before he caught his balance. Kurt lunged, but Vic managed to deflect the blow with his arm.

Needing to feel his fist smashing into Vic's face again, Kurt shot forward once more. He wanted to bring down this man who thought he could make the world go his way by force.

Before Kurt could land another blow, Vic turned and aimed the gun at a target over Kurt's shoulder. "Where the hell are my kids?"

Throwing himself between the gun and Abby, Kurt tried to

hit Vic's arm and deflect the shot. Instead, he heard a blast and felt a searing burn in his shoulder.

The force of the bullet knocked him backward. He fought to stay on his feet, but his knees buckled and his legs refused to hold him. His vision blurred. He tried to shout at Abby to get out, to save herself and the kids, but he couldn't get any sound from his lips.

Abby reeled backward as if she'd been shot herself. *Dear God, don't let him be dead!*

Vic loomed over him, weaving slightly, but holding the gun steady on Kurt's forehead. Grabbing up the skillet, Abby swung at Vic's gun hand. She brought the skillet down on his arm with more force than she'd ever imagined she possessed.

With a roar of pain, Vic dropped the gun and dived toward her, murder raging in his black eyes. He stumbled over something in his path, missing her by just inches, but he succeeded in knocking the skillet to the floor.

Jumping aside, Abby fought her mounting horror. Knowing she had to think clearly if she hoped to survive, she tried to ignore her rising panic. The door. She could get outside, find the kids and hide with them in the woods. But she couldn't leave Kurt unconscious and alone inside.

When fear rose in her throat and threatened to escape as a whimper, she bit it back and scanned the floor for Vic's gun. If she could only find it—

Vic staggered to his feet and grabbed at her again. Twisting away, she ran to the window, putting the heavy oak table between them as she searched frantically for a weapon.

Across the room, Kurt moaned and lifted his head. Thank God he was still alive, she thought. But she had to keep Vic away from him, at least until he could get to his feet. She had no idea how badly he'd been hurt, or whether he could do anything to defend himself.

Shouting vile obscenities, Vic lifted one side of the table and shoved it out of his way, blocking Abby's only escape route. With a vicious backhand, he struck her across the face and wound his fist into her hair, dragging her closer until they were face-to-face.

"You're dead." He twisted her hair and pulled backward until her neck felt as if it would snap.

At least the kids had gotten away, she thought. She wouldn't die in vain.

Vic's other hand settled over her throat, choking off her breath. She fought him, trying to tear his hands from her neck, but she gradually lost strength. Then, strangely, her breath seemed to come easier and she wondered if it was some trick of death. Her ears roared so loudly she almost didn't realize Vic's grip had loosened. Until he screamed the second time, she didn't know she could move.

"Abby, run—"

Kurt's voice reached her through the haze of fear and pain, and she ran blindly toward the ladder that led to the loft.

"You dirty son of a bitch!" Vic shouted.

Halfway up the ladder, Abby turned back in time to see Vic kick Kurt in the stomach twice. As Kurt doubled over, Vic landed a third kick to his kidneys and then turned toward her.

Abby scrambled for the next rung, pulling herself up. Never had the ladder seemed so steep or the loft so impossible to reach. Panic overwhelmed her. The only weapon left to her was the pile of lumber in the corner of the loft.

Two rungs from the top, just as she thought she'd made it, Vic's hand curled around her ankle. With a mighty tug, he tried to pull her from the ladder, but she clung to it with both arms. She couldn't let go. If she fell from this height, she'd be hurt too badly to fight.

Frantically she kicked out with her free foot, but she met only empty space, and the force of her kick nearly sent her flying off the ladder. Vic leered at her from below—too far down for her to hit. Straining upward, Abby managed to haul herself up another rung just before Vic jerked on her leg again. This time, her grip on the ladder loosened slightly.

No! She wouldn't let him kill her. She would not die and leave the kids without protection. Drawing on every ounce of strength she had, she strained once more and managed to drag herself onto the floor of the loft.

Vic jerked her ankle and she lost precious inches. Wrapping

one arm around a slat of the wood railing, Abby used the other hand to grope in the darkness for the pile of old boards. If only she could protect herself somehow, she might be able to slow Vic down enough for them to escape.

Beneath her, the ladder shuddered under Vic's weight as he rushed after her. She had no time to find the wood now. Rolling to her back, she raised her free leg and brought it down with all her force into Vic's shoulder. But it wasn't enough.

She kicked him again and again, frantic to escape his grip. When Vic finally released her ankle, he lunged at her, reaching for her neck with his hands. Using both legs now, she kicked with every ounce of fury and fear inside her.

Vic lashed at her with his fists, striking her several times and filling the air with profanity.

Abby tried to drag herself farther into the loft, but Vic caught her waist and pulled her toward him. She fought, twisted and kicked with all her strength. If she didn't get away from him now, she would die. Digging her fingers into the floor, she hoped to find something she could hold on to that would keep her anchored. But she encountered only bare boards and a sleeping bag.

Death loomed before her, and Abby kicked one last time, almost ready to give up hope. But this time her right foot landed squarely on his chest. Feeling a solid connection at last, she shoved with all her strength.

Vic grabbed for the wooden railing, but missed it by less than an inch. For one long moment, he seemed poised in the air. Then he disappeared from sight, his scream echoing in her ears. An eerie silence fell over the cabin.

Scarcely daring to move, Abby dragged herself up with bruised arms and looked down over the railing to the floor below. Vic lay near the fireplace, motionless.

Fighting to shake off a gray mist, Kurt drew himself to his feet using one of the chairs for leverage. His shoulder burned and every inch of his body ached. Holding up his good arm, he gestured for Abby to stay where she was and approached Vic cautiously.

Lying on his back with one leg twisted beneath his body,

Vic didn't look as if he'd rise again, but Kurt didn't want to take any chances.

"Are you all right?" Abby cried as she scrambled down the ladder.

"I'm fine. Let's find the kids and get out of here. I don't want them coming back inside."

"I don't know where they went."

"Let's check the woodshed first." He looked back over his shoulder at Vic's inert body. "Thank God they weren't in here to see him fall."

Abby wrapped her arms around his waist and held him tightly. She turned to look at Vic again, as if reassuring herself that he wasn't coming after them.

Wincing at the pain that seemed to grow steadily worse, Kurt held her against him as he led her out the door and across the clearing. "We'd better let them know it's us, or we might be attacked when we open the door."

"The kids were wonderful. You should've seen them. I couldn't believe how they fought Vic. They've always been so afraid of him."

"They're fighters, Abby. That's how they've survived this long." He pressed a gentle kiss to her lips and drew away reluctantly. "Hey, kids," he called to them, "drop your weapons and come on out here. We're getting out of this place."

The door of the woodshed creaked open slowly before Brody stepped out. The boy's eyes widened and a look of horror spread across his face. "Dad? Are you all right?"

"It's nothing serious. I'll be fine."

"I thought he was going to kill us."

"I'd have killed him first or died trying." Kurt pulled Brody to him and held him tightly. "Do you know how much I love you?"

As he raised tear-filled eyes to look at his father, Brody's lip trembled. "I love you, too, Dad."

Erin and Michael emerged from the woodshed, their faces pale and frightened. "Abby? Kurt? What happened?"

"We'll tell you the whole story later. Right now, we're getting out of here." They'd have to walk to the Warners's, but if they hurried, they'd beat Vic even if he did regain consciousness. Hopefully, Warner would be there, but if not, Kurt wouldn't hesitate to break into the cabin and deal with the damage later.

"You've got to let me at least bandage that before we go anywhere. We need to stop the bleeding." Abby pulled back the fabric of his shirt to reveal the wound.

"We'll stop when we're just a little farther away from the cabin. I really don't think he's coming after you ever again, but let's not take any chances." He spoke quietly and hoped the children couldn't hear him. No matter how crazed he'd been at the end, Vic Harrison was Erin and Michael's father. They'd suffer enough from the horror of this evening once the shock wore off. Kurt didn't want to make it worse for them now.

Motioning the kids to go ahead, he grabbed Abby's hand and kept her at his side as they started toward the road. When they reached the grove of trees where Vic had hidden his truck, Kurt stopped. If they took the truck, he could get Abby and the kids safely to town and let the sheriff know what had happened up here.

He scarcely dared hope the keys would be inside, but miraculously they were. Glinting in the moonlight, they dangled from the ignition, issuing an invitation.

"Everybody in. You'll have to sit on laps and squeeze together. Abby, you're going to have to drive. Let's move!"

Galvanized by the urgency in his voice, the kids climbed into the cab of the truck and Abby got into the driver's seat. In the crowded space, Kurt pressed against the door and bit back a moan. With concern evident in his eyes, Brody clutched Kurt's good hand and watched the road as Abby drove.

Each time they hit a rut, Abby flinched but didn't tear her eyes away from the road. Kurt wanted to smile at her concern, but even smiling hurt too much. Closing his eyes, he tried to keep the pain at bay as the truck jolted over the rutted drive. And he focused his thoughts on the future he wanted when this was all behind them.

ABBY GRIPPED the dashboard as the sheriff's Blazer bounced over a series of bumps in the road. Back on the road less than an hour after they'd arrived in Milford, she'd had to leave the kids with the sheriff's wife and Kurt in the doctor's care. She wanted to be back in Milford with them, safe and warm, not jolting over this washboard road on the way to the scene of her worst nightmare.

"Shame about your friend getting hurt like that." Sheriff Travis leaned back in his seat and sent Abby a gap-toothed smile. "I wouldn't drag you all the way up here if I was absolutely sure about where to go, but when you get up in these mountains some of the cabins are pretty remote. Don't want to spin my wheels looking for the place in case that old boy's heading back down the mountain. We'll make sure you're safe, though. Don't you worry about that." He lit a cigarette with the Blazer's lighter and exhaled noisily. "Kind of a strange thing, wasn't it—him finding you all the way up here?"

After all the precautions she'd taken, she still couldn't believe it. She'd thought that by keeping their situation a secret she could protect the kids. Instead, it was the secrecy that led to their discovery: Zelda would never have told Vic where to find them if she'd known the truth.

"Well, the important thing is that you and the kids are safe." Sheriff Travis flicked ash off his cigarette and studied the rearview mirror. "And Dr. Lowe says your fella's going to be fine. Bullet chewed him up a little on the way through. He'll be sore for a while, but he'll be all right."

"Thank God for that." Watching Vic shoot Kurt had been worse than anything Abby had ever experienced. She couldn't imagine what she would've done if he'd been more seriously injured.

Sheriff Travis dragged on his cigarette and pointed at the road ahead. "Is that the turnoff I want?"

Abby studied the landscape, surprised when she recognized where they were. "On your left."

The sheriff slowed and checked his mirror again for the vehicle carrying his two deputies. Apparently satisfied, he turned onto the rutted lane that led to the cabin. "Brinkman'll wait

out here with you while Chavez and I check the cabin. I hope
you're right and our man's still inside. But in case he's not, I
don't want you out here alone, and Brinkman's one of our best.
He'll see nothing happens to you."

Bringing the Blazer to a stop, the sheriff rolled down his
window and motioned the deputies to pull up beside him.
Though she'd seen Vic lying on the floor and knew that *if* he
was still alive he'd be too badly hurt to harm her, Abby tensed,
half expecting Vic to charge out of the cabin. Her heart beat
rapidly and her throat constricted again. *Why* did they need her
up here?

"Let me just parley with the boys for a minute." Sheriff
Travis pushed open the door and disappeared into the night,
leaving her cold and alone and frightened.

Minutes dragged by like hours before the tallest of the two
deputies opened the car door and folded himself onto the front
seat beside her. "You all right, ma'am?"

Abby nodded, but kept her eyes on the sheriff and the other
deputy as they approached the cabin. Both men had drawn their
weapons and they skirted the clearing, staying in the deep cover
of the trees.

Brinkman leaned forward, his eyes alert and trained on the
surrounding landscape. "It shouldn't be too much longer
now."

She hoped not. After their narrow escape earlier, she didn't
know how much more of this she could stand.

Sheriff Travis climbed the steps and took a stance on one
side of the door while Chavez pushed it open with his hand.
When nothing happened, Chavez disappeared inside, and a few
seconds later Sheriff Travis followed.

What would they do if Vic had survived the fall? If he'd
gotten away? It would mean more running, more hiding and
greater fear, since he'd be angrier and more violent than ever.
Rachel and the kids may have simply traded one hell for another.

For the first time, Abby realized how much courage Rachel
had shown to break away. And at the same time, she thought
of Kurt and realized how lucky she'd been to find him.

A light flickered inside the cabin. Brinkman tensed and lowered his hand to the holster on his hip. Abby tried to will her heart to beat more slowly. Tears stung her eyes at the thought of dying here in the dark, miles from Kurt and the kids.

Memories of other nights spent in patrol cars flooded over her. Visions of a future working stakeouts for the governor's task force taunted her. She couldn't do this—not now, not next week, not ever again.

Something had happened to her during the past few weeks. She could never go back to her old way of life. She wanted to be with Kurt and Brody, with Erin and Michael. She wanted to tell Kurt how much she loved him, how deeply the thought that he might die had cut her, and how she didn't want to live without him.

Brinkman cleared his throat softly and scanned the clearing. "Come on, Travis, you slow son of a…gun," he whispered. "Get your…get out here and tell us what the…heck's going on."

Abby could feel his tension, almost equal to her own. She'd begun to wonder if she was the only one who thought the sheriff and Chavez were taking too long.

Somewhere in the distance, thunder rumbled. A breeze picked up for a minute, rustling leaves and brushing through the undergrowth. Abby's senses pricked. What *was* happening inside?

Far away, lightning flashed and thunder rumbled again as a shadowy figure appeared in the doorway. "Brinkman," someone shouted. "Come on in here."

Relief washed through Abby as she recognized Sheriff Travis's voice.

Brinkman stuck his head out the window and shouted back, "What about Ms. Drake?"

"Tell her to stay there."

"What the…" Brinkman shot a puzzled glance at Abby. "I'm going to have to go see what he wants." He opened the door partway, but instead of getting out, he shouted, "Hadn't I better stay here and keep an eye on her?"

"She'll be all right now. Looks like the guy in here's dead. Broken neck. We'll get an ID from her in a minute."

Dead. The picture of Vic lying on the floor of the cabin flashed before her eyes, and with it came a strange peace and the realization that Rachel and the kids were finally safe.

Brinkman slid out of the car and smiled down at her. "You going to be all right out here, or do you want me to stay with you?"

She shook her head. "I'll be fine."

But as she watched Brinkman cross the clearing, she began to tremble, and by the time he reached the cabin, she felt sick to her stomach. She'd played a part in a man's death. And no matter how sick and evil he'd become, he'd been her brother-in-law.

She closed her eyes and took in great gulps of fresh mountain air. She saw Vic again—Vic as he'd been fifteen years ago. Young and handsome in his tuxedo as he waited for Rachel at the altar, holding Erin the day they'd brought her home from the hospital, teaching Michael to play pat-a-cake. Tears slipped down her cheeks and she buried her face in her hands, letting her grief take hold.

She wouldn't have changed her actions tonight—Vic had left her with no alternative. He'd died trying to kill her. But she couldn't help wishing it hadn't been necessary.

It could easily have been her life lost. Or Kurt's. If the shot hadn't been deflected, he might have died from the gunshot wound.

Maybe she wasn't able to give him the life he wanted, and he might not want to make a life with her, but she loved him. With her heart and her soul, she loved him.

She didn't expect him to love her back. And she didn't want him to *try* to love her just because he thought he should. A relationship built under those conditions would inevitably fail, and too many people would get hurt when it did. Leaving Kurt and Brody now would hurt worse than anything she'd ever done. But if she stayed, she'd fall even more deeply in love with Kurt—and with his son. And when the time came to leave them, her pain would be unbearable.

CHAPTER SIXTEEN

"IF YOU'LL TAKE these, Mr. Morgan, you'll be ready to sleep through the night after your visitor leaves." The nurse shoved the small paper cup holding pain pills under Kurt's nose.

He felt like a child again. "Let me see Abby first."

"Mr. Morgan—"

"I'm not taking that stuff until I know what's going on." Kurt leaned back against his pillow and shifted his weight, trying not to flinch when pain tore through his shoulder.

The nurse smiled knowingly. "Let me know when you're ready for them."

"You'll be the first to know."

"I'm *sure* I will." Opening the door, the nurse stepped back to admit Abby and pulled it closed behind her.

Kurt watched Abby pass under the light on the wall opposite his bed. Even in the dimness of the hospital room her hair looked like spun gold, and he ached to hold her. It amazed him that he'd never felt like this about any woman before.

Abby. How could he live without her? He'd treated her cautiously since the day she'd walked into his life. But discretion had gotten him nowhere. After all this time he was no closer to winning her than he'd been the night they met.

If he kept worrying about moving too fast, he'd lose his chance with her for certain. Well, he wouldn't be cautious any longer.

When she reached his bedside, he stretched out his good arm. "You look tired."

"I'm fine. But how are you? Did the doctor get the bullet out? What did he say?"

"I'm all right. Nothing to worry about." Her hand felt so

good in his he never wanted to let her go. "I've been waiting for you. What happened?"

"Vic's dead, Kurt. His neck broke when he fell..."

"Dear God. Have you told the kids?"

"Not yet."

"I want to be there with you when you do." The death of their father, no matter how vicious he'd been, would be devastating to Erin and Michael.

But Abby shook her head. "I'm going to tell them as soon as I leave here, and you're obviously not going anywhere for a few days."

"I don't want you to have to do this alone. You've been through too much already. At least let me give you moral support when you tell them."

Again she shook her head. She obviously didn't intend to let him assume even a minor role in her life any longer, when what he wanted was a whole future with her.

Kurt caressed her hand with his thumb. "We've got a lot to talk about, Abby."

"I don't think—"

Straining upward, he kissed her lightly. "I hated your being back up there while I was stuck here, not able to help."

"I was fine, Kurt. I worried about you."

He held her gaze with his own and kissed her again. If he didn't say it now, he never would. "Abby, I love you. Please stay. Don't go back to Baltimore."

When she twisted her hand away from his, a sick feeling crept over him.

"I can't stay."

"What?"

"I've got to take the kids back to Rachel—"

"I'll go with you."

"—and there's the new job."

"Turn it down."

She hesitated for a second before she shook her head. "I can't. It's not that simple."

"It's *exactly* that simple. I love you and I want you to stay.

I want you to be my wife. And Brody would love to have you for a mom.''

"I can't."

"Why?" He reached for her again, but she escaped to the foot of his bed and faced him across it.

"Kurt, I care about you deeply. You're a wonderful man and my life is going to feel empty without you—"

"It doesn't have to. Why *can't* you stay?"

"Kurt, please—"

"I'm telling you that I love you, Abby. With all my heart. And you're telling me you *care* for me? That I'm *wonderful*? Is that all?"

"What you want—what you *need* from a wife—I can't give you. I can't have children, Kurt. I've told you that before."

"Is that what this is all about? Children? I don't care."

"You think that now, but it does matter. Ever since I met you, you've talked about giving Brody brothers and sisters— about wanting a life like Jack and Theresa's. And I know how much Brody wants that."

"Abby—"

"No. Don't say anything else. I've been through this once already with Steven. I'm not going to go through it again. Not with you."

Abby watched Kurt's eyes lose their spark, and she thought her heart would break. "I see. You expect me to be exactly like Steven, to react the way he did, to reject you eventually because you can't give me children?"

"I know—"

"No, you don't know. What I want, Abby—"

A movement near the door caught their attention. Kurt broke off just as Jack poked his head into the room. "Hey, you two, are you okay?"

Abby couldn't make herself speak and Kurt answered only with cold silence, but Jack seemed not to notice. "Theresa's talking to the doctor. She'll be here in a minute." He crossed the room and pulled a chair up to Kurt's bedside.

Abby turned away, hoping Jack wouldn't see her face. She had to get out of here. If she stayed in this room another second, she'd lose control completely. Besides, they'd already said everything they had to say.

While Jack badgered Kurt with questions, Abby slipped out. Walking quickly, she almost made it to the front door before tears blurred her vision and the lump in her throat threatened to choke her. With a sob, she burst through the door and hurried into the night.

She'd done what she had to do, but nothing in her life had ever hurt this much.

ABBY ZIPPED CLOSED the last bag and lifted it from the bed, then ticked items from her list of things to do before she and the kids left Pine Cove. She'd reserved a motel room for tonight in Seattle and called the airline. She'd cleaned the house thoroughly, washed the bedding and arranged to leave the key on the kitchen table for Zelda.

She'd sold her car to the garage and talked with Richard Schurtz on the governor's task force. Though her heart wasn't in it, she'd accepted the position and agreed to start work on Monday. Now she had nothing left to do but wait.

But waiting meant thinking of Kurt, as she had every spare moment of the past few hours. And thinking of Kurt only brought fresh pain.

For probably the millionth time, she assured herself she'd done the right thing. Sooner or later, he'd have begun to resent her—just as Steven had. He'd look in greener pastures for the kind of wife he really wanted. And he'd leave her.

It'd been painful enough to live through losing Steven, but she hadn't loved Steven as she did Kurt. Steven had hurt her, but if Kurt stopped loving her, it would destroy her. By leaving now she would save herself from watching his love die.

She smoothed the cover on the bed and crossed to the open French doors, intending to close them before she went downstairs to check everything for the third time. But on the highway, a car slowed and turned into the drive. For one heartstopping second, she thought it was Kurt, but in the next moment she recognized Theresa's car. She descended the stairs quickly and pulled open the door just as Theresa reached the porch.

Rushing up the steps, Theresa threw her arms around Abby. "I can't believe this whole thing. I'm still in shock. Are you going to be all right?"

"We're fine."

"How are the kids taking it?"

"Hard, as you can imagine. No matter what he did, he was their father. I'm just grateful they didn't actually see him die." She shuddered at the memory of Vic's death and pulled out of Theresa's embrace. "I talked to Rachel this morning and she's already checking into some counseling for them."

"I still can't believe you're not their mother. Why didn't you tell me the truth?"

"I couldn't tell anyone. But if I could've confided in anyone, it would've been you." Or Kurt.

"You could at least have told me you weren't married. To think how much I worried about you and Kurt getting involved and all the time— Well, I must've sounded ridiculous that night in your driveway when I said those things."

"You were just worried."

"I didn't want to see him get hurt again. I still don't."

"How is he?"

"He's getting out of the hospital this morning. He's planning on coming straight over here to see you."

Abby couldn't see him again. It would hurt too much. "I won't be here."

"Abby—"

"No, Theresa. You don't understand."

"He told me. But I don't understand why you're running away from him now. You're going to have to make me understand how you can do this to the man you love."

"I don't want to talk about it."

"*Do* you love him?"

Abby turned and walked into the parlor, but Theresa followed.

"*Do* you?"

"Yes."

"Then stay and talk to him. He was so upset when he found out you'd left the hospital I thought he'd leave in the middle of the night, but we finally convinced him to wait until this morning. He wants to work this out with you."

"Don't you think I want that? Don't you think I wouldn't rather stay here with Kurt than go back to Baltimore? But I can't, Theresa. I've watched Kurt with Brody and your kids since the day I met him. I can't give him the kind of life he wants."

"Abby, don't be a fool. That doesn't matter to Kurt."

"Maybe he thinks he loves me now, but in a few years, after he's had a chance to think it over, he'll realize how empty his life is and he'll leave. I can't go through that again."

"Look, Jack's on his way to pick Kurt up now. Promise me you'll still be here when he gets back."

She couldn't stay. If she stayed and gave in, she'd only be setting herself up for heartache. "I have a flight out of Seattle at seven-thirty, and my parents are picking us up in Phoenix. The taxi's already on the way here."

"Don't leave yet. Stay one more day."

"I have to be back in Baltimore by Sunday."

Theresa settled her hands on her hips and demanded, "Why?"

"I start my new job on Monday morning."

"But you two have so much to talk about—"

"There's nothing to say." Abby's throat burned and her eyes stung, and she knew that in a matter of seconds, she'd be crying again.

"Dammit, Abby—"

"Please don't, Theresa. I know you mean well, but you really don't understand."

"You're right. I don't understand how you can walk out on Kurt if you love him."

"I'm doing this *because* I love him. I know what he wants and I can't give it to him."

"Why don't you ask *him* what he wants?"

Abby waved her words away. "I've been through this before, Theresa. I know what he'll say, and I know what he really means. Look, I can't talk about this anymore. The taxi will be here any minute, and I really need to help the kids get ready.''

Without waiting for a response, Abby squared her shoulders and walked down the darkened hallway into the kitchen. She waited there until she heard the front door close and the engine of Theresa's car roar to life in the driveway.

She listened to Erin and Michael's voices drifting to her faintly through the screen door, and her heart shattered. Lowering herself to a chair by the table, she tried to steady her trembling hands, to stem the flow of tears. By tomorrow morning, she'd have lost the kids, Kurt—everything. In two days, she'd return to her old way of life and go on.

In this short time with the kids, she'd grown to love them so completely the pain of losing them nearly tore her apart. Could she love them any more if they were her own children?

She didn't want to go back to her sterile empty life, to her lonely apartment. She would never have chosen that life for herself, but fate had limited her options.

But Kurt had choices. He *could* have more children—without her. And because she wanted that life so much herself, she would never deny him the chance to have it. She only hoped this pain would dull sometime soon.

KURT STRAINED against the seat belt, ignoring the soreness in his shoulder. "Can't you drive faster?"

"I'm already going ten miles over the speed limit. Any faster and I'll get us killed. Try to relax, would you?" Jack twisted the wheel and brought the car around a sharp curve in the road.

"Tell me how relaxed you'd be if you knew Theresa was leaving."

"Abby will still be there when we get back to Pine Cove. Theresa's with her and, besides, the woman loves you."

"I'm not so sure."

Jack's eyes left the road for a second and flicked over Kurt. "It's obvious to me even if *you* can't see it."

Kurt had thought he could see it once—before she turned down his proposal. How could he have been so wrong? Had he simply seen what he wanted to see? Had he invented Abby's reactions to him because he wanted so badly for her to love him?

He honestly didn't know anymore. He *did* know he couldn't let her leave without talking to her again and clarifying their relationship in his own mind. She'd run out of his hospital room so quickly the other day that he hadn't been able to stop her.

He needed to see her again, to look into her eyes and read her emotions. If she honestly didn't love him, at least he'd know for sure. It would tear him apart, but he'd have to let her go if that's what would really make her happy.

"Can you please go a little faster?"

"I'm doing the best I can. We'll get there in plenty of time."

"Plenty of time for the next Fourth of July picnic. Hell, Jack—"

But Jack wouldn't be pushed. "Can we talk about Brody for a minute? I know you're worried about how he's going to handle all this, but he actually seemed all right last night. We let the kids make popcorn and watch a movie. He acted pretty normal."

"It might hit him later." The ordeal at the cabin and losing Abby, Erin and Michael would throw Brody for a loop. But they'd come a long way this summer, and now Kurt knew how to help his son over the rough spots.

These weeks with Abby and the kids had been good for Brody. Abby had given him unqualified acceptance, Michael had given him friendship, and Erin had given him trust. And he'd slowly realized that Laura hadn't left because of him. He was starting to believe that her refusal to accept her role as his mother said nothing about him.

Kurt didn't doubt Brody's recovery. He *did* doubt the future he'd seen so clearly that day at Angel Falls—his future with Abby.

Jack adjusted his rearview mirror and let his foot off the gas as they approached another curve. "Between you and me, having Abby around has done Brody a world of good. He needs a mother—"

"I'm not trying to convince Abby to stay so she can be a mother to Brody."

"I know why you're trying to convince her to stay." Jack grinned.

"Then get me back to Pine Cove, would you?"

Jack increased his speed slightly. "I saw Naomi yesterday."

But Kurt couldn't think about Naomi now. He couldn't concentrate on anything but Abby and the life she was throwing away.

"She had Jason with her," Jack persisted. "Sounds like she and Bill have cooled off a little. I wonder if they'll really get divorced."

"I hate to see it, but maybe it's the best thing for them. Whatever they decide to do, I hope they'll quit using Jason as a pawn." He craned his neck toward the control panel. "How fast are you going?"

Jack laughed, but he increased the speed a little more. Kurt settled back against his seat and watched the road steadily, as if his concentration would somehow get him to Abby sooner.

The road had never seemed so long, so narrow or so full of curves. He checked his watch again.

Maybe he shouldn't worry about it. Maybe he should realize that if Abby left Pine Cove without seeing him again, she really didn't love him. But he *couldn't* have been so wrong, could he? He'd felt her response when he kissed her and he'd seen the look in her eyes when they were together. And after everything they'd been through together, he knew she felt the same way he did.

When they reached Pine Cove at last, the car crawled through the center of town. Cursing Jack silently for obeying the speed limit, Kurt strained to see every passing vehicle. He couldn't miss her now that he'd come this far.

Just past the post office, Jack picked up speed again and at long last, Abby's house loomed into view. But when Jack slowed to turn into the driveway, Kurt's heart sank. The windows stared out at them blankly, shuttered and curtained. The house had obviously been abandoned.

Clinging to one last hope, Kurt climbed the steps and rang

the bell. Nothing. He rang again, but got no response. Almost desperate, he pounded on the front door. Shock waves tore through his shoulder, but he welcomed the pain. It nearly matched the agony in his heart.

"LADIES AND GENTLEMEN, we'd like to thank you for flying Delta Airlines from Atlanta and welcome you to Baltimore. If you are continuing on with us this afternoon, please remain in your seats. If you are staying in Baltimore, we hope you've had a pleasant flight."

Abby tried not to watch as the airport grew larger. She wanted to ignore the increasing dread with which she faced the life ahead of her and dredge up some feeling that she'd come home. But she felt only emptiness.

She'd spent less than a day in Phoenix. It hurt too much to stay with Erin and Michael and prolong the pain of leaving them. It was better to cut all the strings quickly and get on with her life. In a while, the pain would dull.

By Christmas, she'd probably even be able to visit Rachel and her kids without too much unhappiness. Unless Michael and Erin were successful in convincing Rachel to move to Pine Cove.

Even with Vic gone, Rachel didn't want to stay in Arizona. She'd told Abby that she needed a clean break, a chance to start over. The kids had liked Pine Cove so much that Abby feared Rachel would actually move up there, which would mean she could never visit them without running into Kurt. Which meant she could never visit them.

Abby pulled her carry-on bag from the overhead compartment and joined the slow-moving line of passengers as it crept toward the front of the airplane. When movement stopped, Abby looked up to see who had halted their progress.

A man in a suit had turned to retrieve his bag, and for a second, Abby thought he was Kurt. But more than once during the past two days she'd imagined seeing him. And more than once she'd had to stop and catch her breath when she realized it was just another man with brown hair and a similar build.

Looking away, she wondered whether Ted would be on time

to meet her flight. She'd called from Phoenix and given him the flight information, but Ted ran on some personal clock that was usually twenty minutes slow. And today probably wouldn't be any different.

She hoped once she saw Ted again she'd feel more normal, that once she got back to her apartment she'd feel better. And that eventually she'd readjust and put the summer behind her and stop imagining she saw Kurt everywhere.

She reached the front of the airplane and started up the ramp to the terminal. Ahead of her, a woman began to move quickly, running into the waiting arms of a man who kissed her deeply. Abby's heart twisted and she looked away.

All around her, people greeted friends and relatives with wide smiles, and irrational jealousy filled her. She scanned the crowd. Just as she'd expected, Ted was late again.

Lowering her bag to the floor, she looked for a pay phone. At least Ted's wife could tell her whether he'd even left home yet. If not, she'd take a taxi.

At the edge of the crowd, a man with brown hair and wide shoulders in a plaid shirt stood with his back to her. Once more, her heart leapt to her throat. How long would it take her to stop this painful habit of seeing him everywhere she went?

As she dragged her eyes away the man turned, and his face made her heart thud furiously. She bent to pick up her bag again as he shouldered his way toward her through the crowd. But when they were separated by only a few feet, she let her bag slip from her fingers.

"Abby?"

She couldn't speak, could hardly see him through her sudden tears.

"We've got to talk, and this time you're not leaving until I'm through." He picked up her bag and wrapped one arm around her waist.

"Your shoulder—" she protested.

"It's fine. It's the least of my worries." Kurt propelled her through the terminal toward a dimly lit restaurant.

Settling her in a corner booth, he sat beside her. His thigh and shoulder brushed hers, and her skin tingled where they touched. She wanted to bury herself in his embrace and never emerge. She wanted to feel his arms around her, feel his lips on hers...

"Abby, listen and don't interrupt."

She touched his sleeve and felt the comforting warmth of his skin through the fabric. He really was there. He'd come after her.

"Sweetheart, if you think I'm not going to want you because you can't have children, you're wrong. Yes, I love Brody. He's the only good thing that came out of my marriage to Laura. But I don't care if I ever have more children as long as I have you. The *only* thing I want is your love."

"You say that now—"

"And I'll say it in thirty years. I don't want to marry you so I can have more children. I want to marry you because I love you. Abby, listen to me. I got married the first time for all the wrong reasons, and no matter how hard I tried, I could never make it work. This time, I'm not going to make the same mistake."

She wanted to believe him. She *needed* to believe him.

"You don't marry someone because you want something from them. You do it because you can't live without them. And Abby, I can't live without you."

"But—"

"There are no buts. The only thing that matters to me is you. I could find a hundred women who could give me more children if that's what I wanted. But children grow up and move away, and a marriage has to last longer than that. I want *you*. Only you."

"I can't believe you're here," she breathed.

His eyes burned into hers and willed her to accept. "Is there anything else? You don't like Pine Cove? If you aren't happy there, I'll move to Baltimore."

Her tears flowed faster now, but the pain in her heart melted away. "I can't let you do that."

"Abby, I'll do whatever I have to. I love you."

"You know how miserable you were when you tried to live in Seattle."

"I was with the wrong woman."

"And with me you think you'd love the city?"

"I'd love anywhere you agreed to be with me." He leaned toward her and touched his lips to hers.

Fire leapt inside her and she lifted her arms to his shoulders, opening her mouth to him and welcoming his kiss. His arms came around her, molding her against him.

He broke away and trailed his lips to her neck, pressing his heat into her skin. "Don't leave me again."

She tried to catch her breath, but the fire grew each time his lips touched her. "I won't."

"You'll marry me?"

She could only nod.

"Let's get out of here."

He kissed her again and when heat exploded inside her she knew he was right—they couldn't stay here any longer.

Standing, Kurt held out his hand to her. "Where do you want to go?"

"Home." For one long moment, their eyes held before she smiled. "If you think we can wait that long."

"How far is it?"

She reached for her bag and slipped her hand into his. "About three thousand miles."

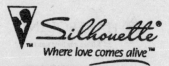

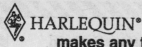

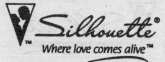

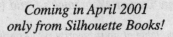